Praise for the Cat Star Chronicles

"This phenomenal series just gets better and better. Awe inspiring… It's sexy space travel at its finest."
—*Night Owl Romance*

"You will laugh, fall in love with an alien or two, and be truly agog at the richness Ms. Brooks brings to her worlds."
—*Long and Short Reviews*

"Sexy and fascinating… leaves the reader eager for the next story featuring these captivating aliens."
—*RT Book Reviews*, 4 stars

"A steamy, action-filled ride. Ms. Brooks's world-building is impressive as well as creative."
—*Anna's Book Blog*

"Cat Star Chronicles has become one of my favorite futuristic series… There's plenty of kick-butt action as well as laugh-out-loud moments."
—*Romance Junkies*

"Interesting, full of humor and love… Almost too hot to hold."
—*BookLoons*

"High caliber entertainment from beginning to end… I couldn't put it down."
—*Whipped Cream Erotic Reviews*

**Other books in
The Cat Star Chronicles series:**

THE CAT STAR CHRONICLES

WILDCAT

CHERYL BROOKS

sourcebooks
casablanca

Published by Sourcebooks Casablanca, an imprint of Sourcebooks, Inc.
P.O. Box 4410, Naperville, Illinois 60567-4410
(630) 961-3900
FAX: (630) 961-2168
www.sourcebooks.com

Printed and bound in the United States of America
VP 10 9 8 7 6 5 4 3 2 1

For my friends, my family, and my readers.
You give me joy each and every day.

Chapter 1

Every woman in the galaxy wants to tame him.
Except one…

———∿∿∿———

SARA COULDN'T SAY SHE HADN'T BEEN WARNED. After all, Jerden *was* Zetithian, and though she'd expected his waist-length hair and stunning physique, when he came cantering up on her missing stallion—no bridle, no saddle, no *clothes*—with a black leopard bounding alongside, her breath caught in her throat. Ordinarily his good looks wouldn't have mattered to a woman like Sara, but the picture they presented was nothing short of spectacular. Even so, skuzzy Cylopean or Zetithian hunk, Jerden had her horse, and Sara wanted him back.

She'd heard the rumors that Jerden was dangerous, insane, and lived like a hermit in the wilderness. But although her good friend and neighbor Bonnie Dackelov had assured her those rumors were completely unfounded, he *did* look the part, especially with that huge cat shadowing his every move.

Closing her eyes, she gave herself a mental kick for going to his place alone. Bonnie was cute and kind, and Jerden already knew her. She could've easily convinced him to part with Danuban, simply by being her pretty little self. Sara was out of her league.

Still, she did have the law on her side and documentation to prove she was the stallion's owner, giving her a bona fide excuse to finally meet her newest and nearest neighbor without being introduced as a potential love interest. She was there to get a horse that, as part of the carefully overseen equine importation program on the recently colonized planet of Terra Minor, was a very valuable animal.

Black as night, standing sixteen hands high with a long, flowing mane and tail and a high, arched neck, Danuban had a bloodline that could be traced back over a thousand years, and the Andalusian breed itself dated back to Earth's fourteenth-century Spain. Moving with an elegance few other breeds could match, he looked like something straight out of a romantic fairy tale.

Unfortunately, horses were the only things about those old tales that interested Sara. She had no use for romance and had stopped trying to be charming long ago. It never worked for her. Even as a teen, any time she made the attempt, the boy in question stared at her almost as though another guy had displayed interest—and the only time a male classmate *had* shown interest had backfired on her in a way she still didn't care to think about, nor had she ever shared that experience with anyone.

She'd heard all about this Jerden—how he used to sell himself in a brothel on Rhylos for a thousand credits per session—and had avoided Bonnie's attempts to introduce her to him. She had no desire to meet yet another man who wouldn't give a damn if he ever saw her again.

A thousand credits. A man would have to be awfully

good at what he did to charge that much for an hour's…
work. Sara didn't even want think about how much she
would have to pay him to look at her twice. She knew
there was nothing feminine about her—with the possible
exception of an affectionate heart. Unfortunately, only
animals seemed to appreciate that quality.

Though Andalusians were characteristically doc-
ile and gentle, the long voyage from Earth had left
Danuban wild and unmanageable, and he'd broken
away from his handlers in Nimbaza before his tracking implant could be placed. Impossible to track, where
he'd run off to was a mystery until Bonnie, whose farm
lay to the north of Sara's land, reported that Jerden had
acquired another stray.

Which was apparently something else he was good at.
She'd heard about the leopard that followed him everywhere, as well as the pack of dogs and domestic cats
he'd managed to accumulate in the short time he'd been
living on Terra Minor. According to Bonnie, the murder
of a woman on Rhylos had affected him so strongly that
he'd become a recluse. But though he might have been
avoiding people, animals seemed to be welcome, which
might explain why Danuban had wound up on his land.

At least he hadn't ended up on Nathan Wolmack's
ranch. Nate had a decent herd of horses and was one
of only two men who'd ever sought her company, but,
like the first one, he gave Sara the creeps. Thankfully,
his land was even farther north than Bonnie's, or Sara
would have had more visits from him, though she did
have to pass by his place on the way to Nimbaza. Rumor
had it that he was trying to buy the spread to the east of
hers, and Sara prayed that the deal would fall through.

The last thing she needed was Nate showing up whenever the spirit moved him.

She'd had no such problems with Jerden, though there were plenty of women in the district who would've loved to have a problem like that, and for that matter, quite a few who wouldn't mind if Nate came sniffing around. Sara would've preferred to avoid dealing with either man, but in this instance, she had no choice.

Having parked her dusty speeder in front of Jerden's rustic lakeshore home, she stood waiting by the porch, taking in the scenery. A picturesque lake stretched out behind the house, mirroring the snowcapped mountains that loomed above it. Open grassland lay to the north, ending where Sara's fences began. Surrounded by a grove of tall conifers, the ranch-style house was built of logs, with two steps up to a wide veranda where at least six dogs and as many cats lay sleeping, both on and under the chairs that were scattered about. All appeared to be healthy and well-fed, in addition to being surprisingly well-groomed. Two of the dogs got up to greet her with panting smiles and wagging tails, but the rest didn't bother. The cats didn't even wake up.

Sara had been confident that her experience with horses would make a difference in Danuban's unruly behavior, but she couldn't help envying the way Jerden rode without benefit of bridle or whip. The stallion seemed to do his bidding without question, and he sat on the Andalusian's broad back as if he'd been born there. With horse whisperers scattered throughout human history, it should have come as no surprise that members of some alien species—such as the Mordrials, some of whom could communicate with animals through telepathic means—might possess the same abilities. Nevertheless, a tingle tightened the back of Sara's neck as she watched him ride.

But Jerden Morokovitz was a Zetithian, not a Mordrial. The only things his kind were noted for were the occasional prescient vision, their attractive feline characteristics, and, if the reports were correct, sexual abilities that were second to none.

Not that Sara would have been a good judge of anyone's sexual prowess. Bonnie, on the other hand, was married to Lynx, who was not only Zetithian, but a former harem slave. She could have enlightened Sara, but the fact that Zetith and nearly all of its people had been destroyed at the instigation of one insanely jealous and very powerful man was proof enough. Zetithian males were irresistible, particularly to human women, which was what Sara feared far more than the leopard by Jerden's side. She had no desire to develop an interest in another man only to be ridiculed or ignored—or even abused.

Determined to keep this meeting friendly, Sara waved at Jerden as he approached. When he dismounted with a catlike grace that many a rider would envy, she saw that her eyes hadn't been deceiving her. He wasn't wearing *anything*. Not even a ring or a watch. She reminded herself that her visit was unannounced and that this was *his* land. She couldn't fault him for his nudity, but his total lack of modesty surprised her. He made no attempt to cover himself, though Sara was at a loss to explain how he would have accomplished this. She doubted he could have done it successfully even if he'd used both hands.

Danuban trotted off, his black coat gleaming in the sun, but the leopard never left Jerden's side. Jerden didn't say

a word, walking steadily forward until he stood directly
in front of her. Close, but not *too* close—though Sara did
have to look up to meet his eyes, which was unusual for
a woman of her height. The gaze from his dark, feline
orbs was so intense Sara felt her resolve crumbling. She
stiffened her spine, refusing to be intimidated.

"Hello, Mr. Morokovitz. I'm Sara Shield, one of your
neighbors. I own the land bordering yours to the north."
Forcing herself to smile, she held out a hand in greeting.
"Thought it was time we met."

He remained impassive for a long moment, giving her
time to study him. Beneath eyebrows that swept upward
at the outer tip, rather than down, his vertical pupils emanated a golden glow that was clearly visible even in broad
daylight. A firm jaw, straight nose, and cleft chin marked
him as a very handsome man, but his feline fangs added
a touch of the exotic, perhaps even a whisper of danger.
In typical Zetithian fashion, his ears curved upward to a
point, and shining hair hung to his waist in ebony spirals.
Deeply tanned skin covered a lean, muscular frame, and
his genitals rivaled Danuban's.

Sara had seen other Zetithians, but this one, like her
stallion, was the epitome of his breed. He was flawless,
charismatic, and alive with vibrant health. Suddenly, that
thousand-credit stud fee didn't seem quite so exorbitant.

Ignoring her outstretched hand, he nodded toward
Danuban, who was grazing nearby. "That's your horse,
isn't it?"

Apparently he wasn't one to beat around the bush.
Neither was she. "Yes, he is. And I want him back."

"Take him." Without another word, he turned and
stepped up onto the porch. The leopard followed close

behind, giving her a sidelong glance that seemed almost smug.

Sara stood gaping as the front door closed behind them. Somehow she hadn't thought it would be quite that easy.

It wasn't.

Danuban wouldn't let her near him. And he didn't dance sideways or act coy, either. No, he threw up his magnificent head and took off at a gallop, aiming for the foothills of the mountains on the far side of the lake. Shaking her head, she climbed back into her speeder and headed for home.

Well… at least I know where he is.

———

Once inside the house, Jerden breathed a sigh of relief. Before he'd realized why she was there, he'd come very close to ordering her off his land, which wasn't the best way to treat a neighbor, and a close one at that.

Plopping down in his favorite chair, he leaned back, staring up at the ceiling while his eyes burned with unshed tears. As he rode up to the house, for the one brief moment when he realized that a woman had come calling, his old habits had attempted to surface. His old *seductive* habits. But then the vision of Audrey's crumpled body and lifeless eyes slammed the door shut as firmly as ever.

He focused on the horse instead. He would miss him, but since horses weren't native to Terra Minor, it was apparent that the stallion *had* to belong to someone, and sooner or later, the owner would come in search of him. The question was, how had she known he was there?

She could have been visiting all of the neighboring homesteads in the hope that she might spot him, but it was more likely that one of Bonnie and Lynx's children had seen him out riding. After their parents' first visit, the kids had been sneaking over to his place fairly often. They'd never spoken with him openly, but he heard their laughter.

The eldest girl, Shaulla—Bonnie's daughter by a previous liaison with a Vessonian—was also part Treslanti and could blend in with her surroundings, disappearing at will. She could easily have seen the horse and then told her parents about it. After that, it would only be a matter of time before this Sara Shield paid him a visit.

Still, he wished he could have kept the stallion a little longer. Riding him through the foothills of the mountains had forced Jerden to look outside himself, allowing him to view the world through new eyes. Now, even that respite would be taken from him.

Jerden had found the beautiful stallion drinking from the lake when he'd come down from the mountains several weeks before. Exhaustion was one of the few ways Jerden had found to help him cope with his loss, and he'd taken to hiking up the mountainsides, often running until his muscles screamed in protest. Nothing kept his despair at bay for long, though, and being around other people made it worse. He saw Audrey's face on nearly every woman he met, no matter what planet she hailed from. And in other women's faces, he saw her murderer's eyes, the insane electric blue eyes of the Davordian woman who had killed Audrey in order to take her job as "fluffer" at the Zetithian Palace.

After Audrey's death, Jerden had sold his share of

the Palace to Onca, who was now the sole owner—
their other partner, Tarq, having married not long before. Onca hadn't found any new partners, so he was
going it alone, but hinted that he might be retiring soon.
Looking back, Jerden had to wonder what the hell they
were thinking to prostitute themselves in that manner.
Jealousy had already destroyed their world. Whatever
made them think it couldn't happen again?

Cria must've sensed his despair, for she leaned
against his leg, purring as she nudged his hand with her
broad head. The leopard seemed to enjoy when Jerden
purred back, but for him to purr required some degree of
contentment, and, at the moment, he felt none. The other
requirement for purring was sexual desire, something
that had eluded him ever since Audrey's death.

Sara apparently hadn't felt it, either. He'd have
scented her desire if she had. A neutral female scent was
rare, though he *had* picked up something faintly floral.
Roses, perhaps… She'd even met his gaze directly, not
allowing her eyes to roam over his naked body, which
was also odd. Women normally couldn't keep from staring at him, whether he was dressed or not. She hadn't
even seemed embarrassed by his nudity. Bonnie had
mentioned that Sara had never married. However, now
that he'd finally met Sara, he wondered why Bonnie had
seen fit to tell him that.

It didn't matter. Sara would take the horse back to
her farm, and he'd probably never see her or the stallion
again. Jerden couldn't explain why this thought made
him feel suddenly bereft. Was it the loss of the horse, or
did it have something to do with *her*?

Closing his eyes, Jerden emptied his mind of

conscious thought but found it difficult to keep Sara's image at bay. Tall and slim, she'd stood ramrod straight, her sleek arm muscles clearly defined as she held out her hand. Her coppery hair was cut short, and though her green eyes were friendly, they didn't beckon. Lips that should have been curved into a sensuous smile were pressed into a firm line. She was all business. No allure. No desire. Nothing seductive.

This posed no real problem, for the last thing Jerden wanted was for a woman to feel anything for him. He'd put all that behind him when he'd left Rhylos to settle on Terra Minor, fully intending to live out the rest of his life in relative seclusion. He didn't need a woman and he didn't want one. His mind was clear on that.

But if that was true, then why did it bother him so much that she didn't seem to want *him*?

Rather than going straight home, Sara decided to drop in on Bonnie, whom she found out by the henhouse, feeding the chickens. After hearing the tale of Sara's meeting with Jerden, Bonnie was sorry Danuban had proven uncatchable, but for the rest, she was unrepentant.

"Gorgeous, isn't he?"

Sara rolled her eyes, not bothering to ask to whom Bonnie was referring. "I suppose so—though you might have warned me about the lack of clothing."

"Why spoil the effect? Ulla told me she'd seen him out riding. She's fascinated by the way animals follow him around. Actually, I've thought of sneaking over there to watch him ride, myself."

Though married to another Zetithian, apparently even

Bonnie could appreciate Jerden's own brand of animal magnetism, whether it pertained to his ability to attract animals or women. "I wasn't sneaking and I got the full treatment. Though I must say, I've never seen a naked man riding bareback before. Seems like it would be… uncomfortable."

"Maybe for a *human* male," Bonnie said with a wicked grin. "But you've got to remember, Jerden isn't human."

"True," Sara conceded. "Not very talkative, is he?"

Bonnie's expression sobered. "He wasn't always like that. He's been through hell and hasn't quite recovered. In fact, he may never recover completely."

"The woman who was murdered on Rhylos—she meant a lot to him?"

"Evidently," Bonnie replied. "Aside from the fact that she was killed by a crazy woman who only wanted her job at the brothel. You see, Zetithian men have to smell the scent of a woman's desire in order to function sexually, and not every woman has the right scent. Audrey's scent enabled the men to service their clients, but once a Zetithian man becomes imprinted with a particular woman's scent, he can't do it with anyone else. That seems to be what happened with Jerden and Audrey."

Yet another difference between them and human males. "And that imprint remains even after she dies?"

"So it would seem." Having finished scattering the feed, Bonnie checked the nests for eggs, putting straw in the bottom of her bucket to keep them from breaking.

"Does that mean he won't *ever* get over her?"

"It's hard to say. Working in a brothel isn't exactly normal behavior for a Zetithian. They're usually quite monogamous. No telling what will happen in his case."

Sara stood there, absently watching the chickens

pecking at their feed. He was grieving over the death of a woman to whom he'd become strongly attached, perhaps more so than he'd realized at the time. "How sad."

Bonnie nodded. "We hoped he would improve after coming here to live, but so far, he hasn't."

"Maybe he needs to get out more."

"I agree, but so far, he's been unwilling. He doesn't have a speeder—by choice—and I doubt if he ever leaves his land. Lynx delivers food to him once in a while. I'm not sure that's a good idea, but Lynx refuses to let anyone go hungry, and I can't say I blame him for that."

Sara had heard how Lynx was captured and sold as a sex slave for a harem of fifty slave women, used and starved until he was no longer of any use to them. Bonnie had healed his spirit, but to hear her tell it, bringing him back had been an uphill battle. Sara had long ago decided that Bonnie's deep blue eyes, golden hair, and petite figure might've had something to do with why she'd been so successful, as much as the fact that she was kindness itself. If the task had fallen to her, Sara was fairly certain she would've failed.

Bonnie glanced down at the clutch of eggs in her bucket. "I should probably encourage the kids to pester him more. Maybe send them over with eggs and fresh vegetables every week." She paused, smiling. "Everyone has pretty much left him alone, except for Salan. She's still holding out hope that she'll snag a Zetithian."

Salan was the dairyman's daughter. A human/ Davordian cross, her blonde hair and luminous blue eyes were the envy of many local women, but so far, they hadn't done her any good when it came to finding a husband. Sara didn't think much of Salan, or any woman who threw herself at men. It seemed so... shallow. On the other hand, sitting around waiting for Prince Charming to come calling hadn't worked for Sara, and if her limited experience with men was anything to go by, she'd just as soon they didn't.

Not that she hadn't done anything in the meantime. She'd gone ahead with her life and, for all practical purposes, had shut down her sexual nature as a waste of time and energy, and a source of heartache and pain. By her thirtieth year, she'd emigrated to Terra Minor and been at the forefront of the project to introduce horses to that world. She'd already been settled on her ranch for a year or more when the ship bearing one hundred Zetithian refugees arrived, and there were plenty of women who jumped at the chance to relocate to Nimbaza just for the chance of seeing one.

Sara didn't bother to look. She already knew Lynx, and yes, he was a very attractive man, but if human men ignored her, there was little chance that the greatest lovers in the galaxy would treat her any differently. "I don't suppose he's been very chatty with Salan, has he?"

Bonnie giggled. "She took him some milk and cheese, but he told her it wasn't necessary, that Lynx could bring it to him."

"Somehow I can't see that stopping her."

"It didn't. She went there again, and that time he told her he didn't even *like* milk or cheese—though I know for a fact he feeds gallons of milk to those cats. He's got about a dozen of them."

Sara nodded. "He's got lots of dogs, too." Shaking her head, she added, "Poor Salan. Maybe she should just give up." *Like I have.*

"Or lower her sights. I thought she and Wilisan would end up together, but they didn't last a full season." Bonnie frowned. "Not sure what happened there. I never heard the whole story."

Sara found this hard to believe. Even without knowing Salan very well, it was apparent that she'd never been one to keep anything to herself, though in this case she might have been too embarrassed to share the details — something Sara understood all too well. Wilisan didn't have a lot of respect for women, plus he had a bit of a temper. Sara didn't consider his exotic good looks worth putting up with either of those traits. Perhaps Salan had decided she didn't either.

No longer interested in pursuing what to her was a touchy topic, Sara merely shrugged. "I could still use some help getting Danuban home. Maybe you or Lynx could go with me next time."

Bonnie appeared to consider this. "Why don't I have Lynx ask Jerden to ride the horse over to your place? That way you won't have to go traipsing through the mountains to catch him."

The vision of Jerden riding up on Danuban resurfaced in Sara's mind. No, once was quite enough. She didn't need to see it again. "Actually, I was hoping Jerden would catch him and then I could lead him home."

"Then why would you need one of us to go with you?" Bonnie smiled smugly. "You don't want to go back there alone, do you?"

"Not really. Would *you*?"

Bonnie snorted a laugh. "To see Jerden ride a horse naked? You bet I would. I may be happily married to another Zetithian, but that doesn't mean

I couldn't appreciate an awesome sight like that. I mean… *wow*."

Sara didn't know how to respond to that. But she did know that Bonnie was lucky to be able to acknowledge the beauty without feeling the embarrassment. She was a married woman, and she'd been with other men before Lynx, had seen them unclothed and made love with them—Ulla wasn't even Lynx's child. Sara had never been that intimate with anyone. At least, not by choice.

Sighing, Bonnie gave in. "Okay, I'll ask Lynx to talk to him. We'll figure out something. But it wouldn't kill you to go see him again, would it?"

Sara shook her head. "No, it wouldn't kill me, but it did make me… uncomfortable."

Her smirk led Sara to suspect that Bonnie thought being uncomfortable would be of some benefit to Sara. If so, Sara disagreed. She saw nothing beneficial in being reminded of what she could never have.

Chapter 2

THE SKY WAS STILL DARK WHEN A LOUD NEIGH WOKE Jerden from his nightmare. The horse had been doing that more and more, almost as though he sensed Jerden's disturbing dream and refused to allow it to continue. Jerden had fallen asleep in his chair. *Again.* He had a perfectly good bed, but without Audrey's soft, warm body to share it with him, it wasn't a haven of respite or slumber, but a place to be reminded of what he'd done and what he'd lost.

Rising from his chair, he went out on the porch, Cria's soft tread following close behind. The horse stood near the steps, his ebony coat gleaming in the moonlight. "I was having another bad dream." He ran a hand down the animal's elegant yet powerful neck. "But you knew that, didn't you?"

The horse snorted, nudging Jerden's chest with his nose.

"You should've gone with her. You belong to her, and she needs you—for different reasons than mine, perhaps—but she *does* need you."

The stallion tossed his head, seeming to disagree. With a soft nicker, he turned sideways, inviting Jerden to mount, just as he always did.

One last ride.

Grasping the thick, flowing mane, he swung onto the stallion's back. The horse pivoted on his hindquarters and launched into a gentle, rocking canter—a gait that lengthened into a thundering gallop as they left the house and its stand of pines behind. Jerden's night vision was excellent, but he trusted the horse to find a clear path and let him run, knowing that the rush of wind in his hair would dispel the dregs of sleep as well as the lingering shadows of the dream.

The dream was always the same; one moment Audrey was walking beside him, the next, she lay crumpled and lifeless in the middle of the street while a crowd gathered. The murderer was quickly apprehended, her blue Davordian eyes wild with insane excitement. She didn't seem to understand that committing murder was a crime that made her ineligible for Audrey's job or any other. In her twisted mind, she had only to eliminate Audrey and the job was hers.

But as the powerful horse carried him onward and the moonlit landscape rushed past, those visions were thrust aside. His mind focused only on what his body needed to do to remain astride the stallion. The rest was pure sensory input—the scent of the horse's sweat, the echo of his pounding hooves, the flow of the night air over his bare skin, the surge of speed when the terrain allowed it. A quick, downward glance revealed Cria keeping pace alongside, never slacking, running effortlessly through the night.

Before moving to Terra Minor, Jerden had never been alone like this, with only the land and the animals surrounding him. On board the refugee ship, he had been crowded together with other boys, and later, when he worked with Onca and Tarq, he seldom spent nights alone, only sleeping when his work was done.

If it could be called work. Later, when they'd hired Audrey, she'd often shared his bed, eventually sleeping with him exclusively. Jerden hadn't realized what was happening then. It was simply the progression of events that occurred over time.

And now, he couldn't have carried on with his work even if he'd wanted to. No, this seclusion was best. Nature might heal him eventually, but until then, solitude was the cure—no matter what others might think. He'd been urged to turn his land into a working ranch—to raise livestock, hire hands to help with the chores, build quarters for them, hire a cook—but Jerden wasn't ready for that. For now, he enjoyed the peace that came with not having to discuss anything with anyone, often going for days without hearing another voice or having to answer a question.

He'd been rude to Sara Shield, but he'd only been able to see her as an intruder who would take from him his greatest source of solace. He harbored no illusions that she might not return. She would be back with whatever and whomever she needed to capture the horse and take him home. Jerden knew he should have offered to deliver him to her ranch—and in his other life, he would have done that and more; anything to make her smile. After all, pleasing women was what he did—what he'd *always* done—and he'd done it very well. But not anymore.

The horse slowed to a walk as they reached the foothills. The mountain range was public land, but Jerden had never seen anyone there, and he could enjoy his solitude on those rocky slopes as well as in his own home, perhaps even better. There he found freedom, fresh air to breathe, and space to roam—things he hadn't had since his early childhood on Zetith. With the war already raging all around him, there wasn't much of that even then.

There had been plenty of freedom on Rhylos, though of a different kind. A man could walk the streets of Damenk wearing nothing but a smile, but Terra Minor was a more family-oriented world. There were no brothels or casinos here. No laws against them; they simply didn't exist. It was out of character for that world, if a world could be said to have a character. His nudity may have embarrassed Sara Shield, but he'd spent the last several years of his life wearing clothing only on rare occasions. He liked being naked. It was comfortable and natural for him.

Living in his own house on his own land with no outsiders was also comfortable and natural. The walk out onto his porch in the middle of the night to step over sleeping dogs and cats didn't draw the censure of anyone. Not even the dogs and cats, none of which Jerden had purchased or adopted. They'd simply arrived on his doorstep, seeming to expect very little other than a place to sleep. Jerden had discovered a certain solace in brushing them, and they would take turns lying on the porch while he tended to them, removing parasites and treating them for fleas with herbs that Bonnie had given him. Feeding them wasn't a problem; in fact, they ate most of the food Lynx supplied. These days, Jerden ate only to sustain himself, sometimes forgetting to eat at all.

Cria reminded him, though. If the horse renewed his spirit, Cria improved his health, growling at him if he didn't clean his plate and lulling him to sleep with her purring. Like the others in his growing menagerie, the leopard had simply arrived one day. Following a particularly desperate run, he'd returned to the house, his legs cramping with fatigue, and had collapsed in a chair on the porch. Later that evening, he'd awakened to find her head resting on his thigh. She hadn't left his side since, and he'd named her Cria because of the sound she made when she yawned.

He hadn't named the horse, though. Perhaps because he'd known their relationship would be short-lived. Still, whether he had a name or not, all Jerden had to do was think about where he wanted to go, and the horse took him there. Having never ridden before, he didn't know for certain but suspected that wasn't always the case. Ultimately, however, it made no difference. Dawn would break and this interlude would end.

Unless he could make a deal with Sara Shield.

Sara was trying hard not to lose her temper, but it had been simmering near the surface ever since her meeting with Jerden Morokovitz, and what Lynx had to say wasn't helping. Her eyes narrowed as she studied his image in the viewscreen. "Let me get this straight. He wants to *buy* my horse?"

"That's right," Lynx replied. "And, believe me, he's got more than enough money to make it worth your while."

"I doubt it," Sara said bluntly. No amount of money could compensate her for the time she'd already spent, and there was no guarantee she could find another stallion of Danuban's caliber anytime soon—another *available* stallion, that is—and then there was the eleven-month equine gestation period. She had mares that would be in season soon and paying stud fees wasn't part of her plan, not to mention having to deal with Jerden. "I don't suppose he'd settle for one of the foals, would he?"

"I got the impression it was *this* horse he wants. Not a replacement."

"Well, that makes two of us," Sara retorted. "Danuban is mine and he's not for sale. If I'd wanted to deal with another stallion owner, I'd be breeding my mares to Nate Wolmack's stud."

Lynx snickered. "I don't know much about horses, but I've seen his stallion, and there's no comparison."

"No kidding. Why else would I go to this much trouble? I've waited a long time for this horse, and believe me, going horse hunting on another planet isn't easy." To be perfectly correct, Sara had been waiting for Danuban all her life. He was the culmination of a lifetime of hard work, dedication, and planning. "I'm sorry, but the answer is no."

I sound like a real hard-ass. She closed her eyes for a moment, schooling her voice to sound less harsh. "Look, if he wants to ride him once in a while, I'm fine with that, but Danuban isn't just another horse. I need him."

"I know you do, but Jerden needs him too. He's... well, he's improved some, but you never knew him before. He was *nothing* like this."

"And if the horse helps him, I ought to be shot for not letting him keep him? Is that what you're saying?"

"No, but nothing I've done to help him has worked. All he wants to do is hole up on his land and never see or speak to anyone. At least the horse gets him out of the house." Lynx smiled. Not as tall as Jerden, with yellow eyes and curly, light brown hair, Lynx had been in even worse shape than Jerden when Bonnie hired him. Having come a long way himself, he obviously knew how difficult the journey was. Bonnie loved him enough to see him through it.

Sara had no such tie to Jerden and didn't want one. She could see it now. She would sell him Danuban, enabling him to get back to his seductive playboy self—which is what Sara imagined him to have been before—and then he'd run off and marry Salan or some other sweet young thing. She'd be out a horse and a man in one fell swoop.

Sara stopped that thought cold. It shouldn't matter who Jerden wound up with or what he did. And she wasn't heartless. Far from it. If Danuban could help a grieving man return to normal, she ought to be more flexible and understanding.

But what about me? What about my *life?* Sara suspected that a man like Jerden could bring out her quashed romantic inclinations without even trying. She didn't want to dig up those old feelings. She was better off without them.

"Of course, if Jerden had to come over to your place to ride him," Lynx went on, "that might be even better. That way, he'd have to leave his place for a while."

"That's a pretty long walk," Sara said drily. "I'd probably have to go and get him."

"Might help," Lynx said with a nod.

Sara started to voice her own approval when it hit her that if she did that, she'd be riding in a speeder with him. Sitting side by side. In an enclosed space. *Too close.* Being in close proximity with a man still made her heart pound and her throat tighten. She'd never been able to get past the fear and had discovered that the best strategy was to deny her feelings and avoid men as much as possible. She'd hoped that using Lynx as a go-between would eliminate the need for any further contact with Jerden. This didn't sound like she'd be avoiding him, especially if he didn't bother to dress for the occasion. "I… I'll think about it."

"Then again, if he really wants to ride that horse, it might convince him to get his own speeder if we made him walk."

"It'd be good for him," Sara agreed. "Downright therapeutic, in fact." Though Jerden didn't appear to need any form of therapy—at least, not the physical type. Overall, he was the fittest-looking man she'd ever seen. *And I've seen every square centimeter of him.* A flash of visual memory shook her to the core. *No. Not going there.*

Lynx nodded. "It'll take some time to bring him around—that, and a little love. You'll see. Since he came here he's gotten a reputation as a wild man, but he's really nothing like this."

Love? It was an echo of her earlier thoughts, prompting Sara to wonder whose love he might need, but she bit back her question only to have it replaced by another. "Why would it matter to me what he's like?"

"Well, he *is* your nearest neighbor," Lynx reminded her. "It would be nice if you two at least got along with one another."

"I suppose so." Considering he'd already lived there for several months without the two of them ever meeting, Sara couldn't see the relevance. It wasn't as though she'd ever needed to borrow a cup of sugar from him. Then again, disputes between neighbors were to be avoided whenever possible, and the situation with Danuban had all the makings of a feud waiting to happen.

"I'll run the idea past him," Lynx said. "But I'll also make it clear that you aren't interested in selling." He paused, smiling in that bone-melting way that all the Zetithians she'd ever met seemed to have, with the possible exception of Jerden. "Thanks for not being… nasty about it. He really doesn't need that right now."

"If it had been any other horse…"

"I know. This one is special."

Sara nodded. "*Very* special."

She'd already established herself as a breeder of fine Arabians, but she only had four Andalusian mares, and she hated to dilute their bloodlines by crossing them with one of the Arab stallions. Though they would have been high-quality foals, they wouldn't hold a candle to Danuban's offspring.

If only she could catch the sonofabitch.

After the call from Lynx, Sara went out to tend her roses, needing their graceful beauty to settle her frayed nerves. As she pruned the spent blossoms and pulled a few stray weeds, she found the sense of balance these tasks always gave her. Peace restored, she went out to the main barn where Reutal, her Norludian stable hand, was leading a bay Arabian back to her stall, closely followed by the mare's young filly.

Nodding toward the Andalusians stabled at the far end of the barn, he waved his sucker-tipped fingers and licked his fishlike lips in a lascivious manner. "That Katy mare is so ready, one touch made my tongue hard."

Sara rolled her eyes. She'd long since learned to ignore Reutal's sexual remarks—and because a Norludian male's tongue did double duty as his sex organ, this comment was *definitely* sexual. "Thanks, Reutal, but a simple 'she's in season' would've done."

In the three years he'd worked for Sara, the horses had stepped on Reutal's flipper-like feet so many times, it was a wonder he could still walk. However, he had the uncanny knack of being able to simply touch a finger to a mare's lip and know when she was in estrus, which made him a very handy fellow to have on a breeding farm. He could also predict almost to the minute when a mare would foal. Unfortunately, he also liked to sample the "essence" of other females, and the fact that Norludians rarely wore clothing was disturbing to most people.

"Still true," Reutal insisted with a cheeky grin. "Can't lie to the boss."

"Thanks, I appreciate that."

Drania popped her head up over a stall door, her piglike ears pricked forward through the snowy fleece of her curly hair. "Did you find the stallion?"

A Rutaran native, Drania's body was similar to that of a chimpanzee—though not nearly as hairy—which made her an absolute wizard when it came to starting the young horses under saddle. She could leap onto the back of an unruly colt, clinging like a burr until it finally settled down. Sara had yet to see one throw her.

Sara sighed. "Yeah, I found him. He's on Jerden Morokovitz's place. Trouble is, Jerden wants to keep him, and Danuban doesn't seem to care that I've got four mares over here that are dying to meet him."

Reutal snickered but somehow managed to keep his mouth shut—for once. Sara knew it was simply a matter of time before the comments about Jerden began but was thankful for the respite. "Where's Zatlen?"

"Over at the stud barn," Drania replied. "He was going to check on the yearlings and feed the stallions."

Sara nodded. "I need to go over there myself. After meeting Danuban, something tells me that paddock isn't going to be enough to keep him in."

Reutal waggled his eyebrows. "A real wild man, is he?"

"Yeah. *I* certainly couldn't catch him. Dunno how well he can jump, but we may have to add another rail to the fence."

"And Jerden wants to *keep* him?" Drania asked. "How?"

"Beats the shit out of me," Sara replied. "He was riding him without so much as a halter, but I couldn't get near him."

A chill ran down her spine as a booted footstep behind her heralded more bad news, and she suppressed a groan.

"I know the feeling," Nate said. "You're a hard woman to get close to, Sara."

Mentally counting to three before she turned around to face him, Sara did her best to maintain a neutral expression. Nate always rubbed her the wrong way, and she didn't appreciate him sneaking up behind her. At least she wasn't alone.

Reutal was well aware that Sara didn't particularly care for Nate and seldom missed the opportunity to make a quip at his expense. This time, Nate had left himself wide open. "Must be your aura keeping her away, Nate. But then, I've noticed that flies don't like you, either."

Nate shot a disdainful glance at the Norludian before directing his gaze at Sara. "You need to teach your hired help to watch his mouth."

It was quick, but Sara saw Reutal's tongue dart out in the silent, Norludian version of *fuck you*.

Sara faked a cough, covering her smile with her hand. "Haven't met anyone yet who could control a Norludian's mouth. I gave up a long time ago." It wasn't true, of course, but Nate didn't have to know that. She'd made it very clear at the outset that while Reutal could talk all he liked, she was the boss, and therefore off-limits in terms of romantic liaisons.

"Any luck finding your stallion?" Nate asked. "Damn shame, him running off like that."

Sara wasn't fooled. She knew Nate was fishing for her to use his stud, Kraken, though why she would want to breed her mares to an unapproved stallion when Danuban was around defied explanation.

"Oh, haven't you heard?" she said blithely. "He wound up on Jerden Morokovitz's place. He'll be bringing him over soon." Or so she hoped.

Nate's steely blue eyes narrowed with suspicion. "Is that so?"

Sara nodded. "Yes, and you should see that man ride," she said, not bothering to hide her admiration. "He doesn't even need a bridle."

Nate's brow rose, albeit very slightly. "Never knew Zetithians were any good with horses. Best I can tell, all they do is steal women from other men."

Sara was surprised at just how much this comment

galled her. "Hadn't noticed that." Her shrug was carefully indifferent. "But then, I don't get out much."

"Had one stolen from you, Nate?" Reutal's tone was all innocence, but his bulbous eyes were aglow with mischief.

Sara doubted it. Tall, blond, and ruggedly handsome, Nate was one of the region's more eligible bachelors. What Sara couldn't understand was why he kept dogging her—if this was romance, she wanted no part of it. His attentions were too... calculated, and like most men, he made her feel uneasy. Since she'd never been pursued for herself alone, she could only conclude that he wanted something from her.

Other than a trace of irritation marring his chiseled features, Nate gave no indication that he'd even heard Reutal, addressing Sara instead. "I've noticed that about you, Sara. Nimbaza isn't exactly the playground of the galaxy, but there are some nice restaurants and clubs. Places a man can take a woman that are a little more"— his eyes swept the interior of the barn, ending with a sidelong glance at Reutal—"private."

Oh, God. Is he asking me for a date? "I'm sure there are, but I don't have the time for it. Too much work to do."

He took a step closer. "You know what they say about all work and no play, don't you?"

Though a tremor of fear ran up her spine, Sara lifted her chin slightly. "I don't put much stock in that crap."

Nate's retort was cut off by the sound of approaching hoofbeats.

Sara glanced up as Jerden entered the barn astride Danuban, the pair of them seeming more like a centaur than two separate beings. The black leopard stalked alongside them like a warlock's familiar. As they came to a halt a few paces away, tingles raced over Sara's skin and a hush fell over the barn. Even the birds nesting in the rafters ceased their incessant chirping.

Jerden's eyes met hers with an impact Sara could almost feel.

"I brought your horse back."

Chapter 3

SARA HAD THE SATISFACTION OF SEEING NATE'S JAW drop, though she didn't know whether it was due to the perfection of the horse or the entire picture they presented. At least Jerden wasn't naked this time—if a loincloth qualified as clothing.

For a long moment, no one moved or said a word. Drania was the first to spring into action, snatching up a halter and lead rope from a nearby hook. Danuban's head was so high she had to climb up his neck to buckle it in place. The surprising thing was that the stallion actually stood still for it.

Sara passed by Nate without a glance and took the lead from Drania. Jerden dismounted, landing on his feet as easily as a cat, his glowing eyes still fixed on Sara. "Lynx said you would allow me to ride him."

"That's right," Sara said.

Jerden nodded. "I'll be back tomorrow."

"I'll be waiting," Drania whispered breathlessly, an expression of adoration on her pixieish face.

Barely acknowledging Nate or anyone else, Jerden turned and started toward the entrance, the huge cat padding along behind him. Noting Jerden's bare feet, Sara was about to offer him a ride home in her speeder when Nate broke the silence with a snort.

"You see?" He nodded toward Drania, who was still gazing after Jerden with speechless admiration. "Even

Rutarans fall all over them." Nate's glare followed
Jerden out of sight. "Fuckin' man-whore."

Sara didn't have the opportunity to comment, for
just then, Danuban tossed his head and let out a ringing neigh, nearly yanking the rope out of her hands.
For a moment, Sara thought he would go charging after
Jerden, but then Katy put her head over her stall door
and nickered. The stallion surged forward, dragging
Sara along with him.

"Sorry, Nate," she shouted over her shoulder.
"Duty calls."

—∿∿∿—

Jerden couldn't blame Sara for not wanting to sell her
horse. And he couldn't blame the horse for wanting to
stay with the mares. But that man standing there in the
barn with Sara irritated the hell out of him.

He'd arrived right in the middle of… something. An
argument, perhaps? He had an idea that tempers had
been about to flare. It was none of Jerden's business
whom Sara Shield argued with, but nevertheless he
caught himself listening for the sound of voices as he
headed for home. Stopping as he reached a small stand
of trees, Jerden waited until he saw the man storm out of
the barn and climb into his speeder, his anger clearly evident in every move he made. As the speeder screamed
off toward the road leading north, Jerden wondered who
he was. Perhaps Lynx could tell him—or he could ask
Sara when he returned the next day.

All the walking back and forth would take up a fair
amount of the day, since Jerden had three hundred acres
of land himself, and Sara's farm was probably of a

similar size. It wasn't quite as tiring as running up and down the mountain slopes and wasn't anywhere near as rocky, but for once he didn't feel the need to exhaust himself. He could easily walk back and forth between their farms without shoes, for smooth turf covered the gently rolling landscape, the occasional grove of trees dotting the hills.

The line between Sara's land and Jerden's was quite evident, for his wasn't nearly as well kept. Her tractor droid worked the hay fields and pastures on a regular basis—seeding, fertilizing, mowing, raking, and baling hay. Farther out toward the surrounding mountains were fields of oats, which provided her horses with grain and bedding. The horse barns and pastures were nearer to the house, each section of the farm ringed by the regulation firebreak—something Jerden wasn't required to have due to the location of his house, which was situated beside a lake at the foothills of the mountains.

The open grasslands were prone to wildfires started by the fierce storms that swept through the region during the rainy season, but Jerden hadn't seen any yet. The greatest danger of fire came at the end of the dry season, when the lightning from the early storms set the parched grass aflame and spread across the open plain. According to Lynx, those fires only posed a danger to buildings and unharvested grain. Afterward, the grass grew up from the ashes, turning the blackened land to green in a matter of days.

Since they were currently in the latter part of the rainy season, the weather was warming up, but the rains were still frequent enough to keep the fields green and the grass cool between Jerden's toes. Later on, the heat would drive him indoors, which was something he wasn't looking forward to. Out here in the open, he could forget his previous life and nearly everything about it. Terra Minor wasn't exactly like Zetith, with its shady forests and rushing rivers and streams, but it was closer to home than Rhylos or the refugee ship had been.

Like many others on that ship, Jerden had felt cramped and stifled. He'd spent several months on Terra Minor before he, Onca, and Tarq had come up with their plan for a brothel on Rhylos, a planet where pleasures of all kinds were available to anyone. The playground of the galaxy, Rhylos hadn't had much in the way of open fields, and the city of Damenk never slept. Nights here were quiet, with only the sound of night birds and the wind breaking the silence. Sometimes that silence had seemed like a curse, but other times, when his sleep was untroubled, he slept the night through, awakening with a feeling that better days lay ahead.

Jerden wasn't sure this was one of those better days. After all, he'd just relinquished a horse that he would miss very much, and even though he hadn't given it up completely, he knew he would be losing something else. Solitude. He could regain it while he walked or rode, but in between times, he would have to interact with Sara and her staff—the greatest advantage being that they were so alien he wouldn't see Audrey or her murderer in their eyes.

Jerden slowed to a halt as the realization struck. He hadn't seen either one in Sara Shield's eyes. And he'd been staring right at them.

He had no idea how long he'd stood there, his mind a total blank while the world kept spinning and the sun shone down on his shoulders. At last, Cria grew impatient, stropping herself against his leg, recalling him to his surroundings. Standing at the crest of a low rise, he was gazing out across his land, the lake in the distance mirroring the sky and the mountains beyond. But it wasn't *his* land he was seeing—at least, not the way he knew it to be. It was smooth and green, dotted with flowers, shady trees, and grazing horses.

Blinking against the brilliance of the shining vision, he glanced down and saw that his feet were planted on the dividing line between the two properties. When he raised his head, he saw that his land was as rough and wild as it had ever been. Turning to compare what he'd envisioned with Sara's farm, he saw that it was very similar—prosperous, pastoral, and peaceful, but without the lake and mountains.

Cria nudged him again.

"You're right," he said. "It's time we went home."

The dogs spotted him as he rounded the lake and the whole pack ran out to meet him—the six he recognized, plus one more. At least, he *thought* it was a dog. It looked more like a little rat, but it *was* barking. Jerden wondered when all the dog owners in the region would come round to collect their missing pets, though none had appeared to be well cared for when they arrived.

They were certainly cleaner now and had each picked up weight. What amazed him most was that Cria hadn't eaten any of them. Although he fed her regularly, he'd seen her catch the occasional field rat, so he knew she went hunting, but she had never bothered his other pets.

The house had been uninhabited for a year or more when Jerden moved in, and though there had been plenty of evidence that rodents had taken shelter there, he hadn't seen any mice in a long time, thanks to the smaller cats, despite the fact that his door normally stood open. He'd only closed it when Sara was there because he didn't want to talk to her anymore.

He now realized that may have been a mistake, particularly in light of what had happened since. He'd been rude and inhospitable, something that went against his nature, as well as his upbringing. But he'd also been hurt. He wouldn't have admitted it at the time, not even to himself, but it was true. And it wasn't because she wanted her horse back. No, he was hurt because she hadn't wanted him—as a man or anything else.

It wasn't as though hundreds of others hadn't wanted him, and he'd made love with most of them, fathering children on a large percentage. Why it should bother him that this one particular female wasn't interested in him was a mystery. He still hadn't reached the point where the scent of a woman's desire could affect him. The little Rutaran had smelled as cute as she looked, but his own arousal was as elusive now as it had been at the moment of Audrey's death.

For a man whose life had been based on his sexuality, this left him feeling rather lost. He'd spent his time focusing on the sexual needs of women but very little on the other aspects of their lives, Audrey included. She'd had her basic needs, of course, but he'd never talked with her about her life before she came to live at the Palace. He now realized that he knew next to nothing about her. To be sure, he knew her body better than anyone; however, her mind was something he'd never even attempted to penetrate.

Although it was Onca's opinion that there *were* no depths to Audrey's mind, Jerden had always felt that this was unfair. He'd always assumed Audrey would eventually grow tired of her life at the Palace and go on to do something else.

She might have done just that if she hadn't been murdered, and Jerden *still* wasn't sure how his attachment to her had occurred. Perhaps it was due to the fact that he not only needed her scent but also enjoyed being able to see her while he was servicing his clients—so much so that he began taking her along with him for every session. Unlike Jerden, Tarq and Onca hadn't been affected by Audrey's death—at least, no more than they would have been affected by the death of anyone close to them. At the time of her murder, Tarq had already left the Palace to go off on his own, traveling from planet to planet, leaving pregnant women in his wake like a farmer sowing seeds. If he hadn't fallen in love with Lucy and married her, he might have been doing it still.

Jerden sat down on the porch step, letting the dogs fuss over him as much as they liked, pawing him and licking his face. There was no question about a dog's feelings. They wore them on the surface for anyone to see. In contrast, the depths of the female mind were murky and obscure. Even when they told the truth, they might not be telling all of it.

These were the sort of ruminations that the horse had put a stop to. The horse had been his salvation. It was clear now. He wouldn't have been thinking any of this if he'd been riding.

The question was, would any horse do, or was Sara Shield's stallion the only one who could save him from himself? There were other horses on this world. Granted, there weren't many, and they were expensive, but money was something Jerden had in abundance. If he were to buy a different horse, he wouldn't have to associate with Sara Shield and be reminded of what he had once been. Unfortunately, never having dealt with horses before, he couldn't be sure. He had a sneaking suspicion that there was something about that stallion in particular.

Still, it couldn't hurt to try. Jerden had enough sense left to know that he didn't want to slip back into the mental torment that had been his constant companion since Audrey's death, and if a horse was the solution, he would find a way to get one. When he went back the next day to ride, he would ask Sara if she had other horses for sale or knew of any. If not, well, she'd said he could ride that one, and he would. It was better than nothing.

Gazing out over the lake to the rolling fields beyond, he tried to envision his land as Sara's well-tended pastures, but though the image was firmly planted in his mind, it was no longer visible. Tough prairie grasses covered the ground, rather than the tender green shoots that horses preferred, and there were no barns, fences, or hay fields. It would take a lot of work to bring about the change, but he would do it. His life had lost purpose. It was up to him to find it again.

———∾∾∾———

Danuban was as bullheaded as he was big, black, and beautiful. He'd given Sara trouble every step of the way from the breeding shed to the stud barn. Once in his stall, he'd nearly kicked the walls down, forcing her to turn him out in his paddock. Thus far, he hadn't jumped the fence, but Sara knew it was only a matter of time before he made the attempt. How Jerden had managed to ride him the way he did was nothing short of amazing—either that or the stallion just plain didn't like Sara.

He'd liked Katy very well, though. According to Reutal's sensitive fingertips, the mare had not only ovulated, she had conceived.

In the beginning, Sara had been leery of hiring the Norludian, but he'd saved her a small fortune in vet bills, not to mention the trouble involved in palpating the mares—which was a rather antiquated practice anyway—or the price of a portable scanner. She'd also been afraid that he would bother Drania with his constant sexual remarks, but the two of them got along reasonably well. Drania had a room in the yearling barn, while Reutal slept with the broodmares.

Zatlen was in charge of the stud barn and had a room out there. A genderless Tryosian, he *seemed* male, but not quite, and could have passed for a human of either gender; the aggressive nature of a human male tempered with some of the more feminine traits. He/she was good with the stallions—not that there had ever been any real trouble with them, until Danuban arrived.

Sara was already awake, half expecting trouble when Zatlen pounded on her door in the middle of the night to report that Danuban was missing.

Pulling on her boots and throwing a jacket on over her nightgown, she grabbed a flashlight and followed Zatlen to the stud barn. "You don't think Jerden took him, do you?"

Zatlen shook his head. "No, he jumped the fence. I

heard him galloping around the paddock and then heard him land. He hit the ground running." He ran a hand through his shoulder-length brown hair. "Do you want me to go after him?"

"No, go on back to bed. Whether Jerden had anything to do with it or not, I'd still bet a million credits Danuban went back to him." Surveying the paddock with her flashlight, she could see the deep hoofprints outside the fence. The ground was soft enough that he'd left clear tracks leading off to the south—straight toward Jerden's house. "I've been around horses a long time, but I've never seen one get so attached to anyone before. It's kinda spooky."

Zatlen didn't argue. "Think he'll bring him back?"

Sara sighed. "He did it once. I guess he'll do it again." She nodded toward the fence. "I suppose we'll have to put another rail up all the way around."

"Wouldn't it be easier to just leave him there and have Jerden bring him over when we need him? I mean, there are only three mares left to cover. After that, we won't need him again for another year."

"Unless someone else wants to breed their mares to him." Sara heaved a weary sigh. "It may come to that eventually, but for now, let's at least *try* to keep him here. I didn't have him imported all the way from Earth for him to live with Jerden." She snorted a laugh. "It's like getting a mail-order bride delivered only to have her marry someone else."

Zatlen quirked an eyebrow. "A mail-order bride? That sounds pretty barbaric."

"Yeah. Tell me about it."

There had been plenty of men Sara could have

married if she'd wanted a man in her life. There were many immigrants to Terra Minor who advertised for wives or husbands in lieu of a job. She realized that some had simply been unable to find work and were trying to avoid deportation any way they could, for the laws on Terra Minor were very specific. Immigrants had to have money to buy land or start a business, or they had to find gainful employment within a specified length of time. Otherwise, they were deported. The tracking implants inserted in the base of the skull of every immigrant ensured that the Trackers could find them. Second-generation residents and Zetithians were exempt from these laws, but there still weren't many bums around. Marriage to a current citizen, however, was a free ticket to remain on the planet.

"Well, good night, then," Zatlen said. "I'll get to work on the fence in the morning."

Sara nodded and headed back to the house. The crescent moon didn't offer much in the way of light, but her eyes had adjusted enough to see. She switched off her flashlight as she crossed the stable yard. As she walked, her gaze drifted southward, toward Jerden's place. Though the house wasn't visible from where she stood, she could see the mountains rearing up in the distance and knew that at the base of the foothills were a lake and his home. Two days ago, she'd never given him a thought. Now their paths seemed destined to cross on a regular basis.

"This will work out somehow," she muttered as she went inside. "Everything always does."

Sara tried to focus on what Bonnie had said about Jerden—how he'd been through hell. She didn't want to be rude or hateful to him, but how far did she have to go to be nice? He hadn't seemed very friendly either time she'd seen him. And he'd said, what—two sentences to her? Unlike many men she'd known, Jerden wasn't one to complicate matters with a lot of chatter, something she had to admit she found refreshing.

Too bad it wasn't his normal behavior. Given his previous occupation, Jerden was bound to have been the smooth-talking Don Juan type, and if there was one thing Sara couldn't stand, it was a man feeding her a line of bull.

Nate was a prime example. They'd met for the first time at a meeting of the Nimbaza Horse Breeders Association, and the sound of his voice was like fingernails on slate even then. Though she'd done her best to avoid him ever since, he seemed oblivious to her attitude toward him.

Jerden, on the other hand, hadn't elicited that immediate, negative response, despite the fact that he had possession of a horse whose arrival she'd been anticipating for nearly a year. After all, it wasn't as though he'd stolen him. The stallion had *chosen* Jerden. Admittedly, she might be a little jealous, but she wasn't annoyed—at least, not yet.

She was still thanking her lucky stars that she'd found the horse at all. There were plenty of predators on Terra Minor, and though there were few that could outrun a horse, Danuban could have easily been injured to the point that he might have fallen prey to a flock of enocks. The carnivorous ostrichlike birds were a danger to the unwary, though, thankfully, they tended to hunt much smaller prey. Still, they'd been known to attack a full-grown human when cornered. Bonnie and Lynx had captured a large flock, and though they'd made a tidy sum on the eggs they sold, as dangerous as the big birds were, most of the region's settlers avoided them.

Sighing, Sara kicked off her boots, stripped off her jacket, and crawled back into bed. No, she wasn't annoyed with Jerden yet. However, if past history was any indication, she probably would be tomorrow.

Chapter 4

JUST AS HE HAD DONE ON SO MANY OTHER NIGHTS, THE stallion woke Jerden from his nightmare with a ringing neigh at the window. Jerden had actually gone to bed this time, something he hadn't even attempted in weeks. Whether he'd been feeling better that evening or not, he should have known it wouldn't work. Sleep never did. The best he could say was that he hadn't resorted to drugs or alcohol. No one could accuse him of losing himself in the scents of other women, either. He didn't overeat, nor did he starve. Vigorous, relentless exercise was the only thing that helped stave off the dreams. That and the stallion.

Getting up from his bed, he crossed to the window. "Go home. Sara needs you more than I do. I can run the hills until my muscles scream. Then I can sleep. You don't need to monitor my dreams."

Which was what the horse seemed to do. *The horse.* I've got to ask her what your name is. I'm sick of thinking of you in such an impersonal way. I need to connect, need to feel, need to know. I'm so tired of not knowing anything."

As before, the nightmare had sent him sinking back into the abyss, splitting his mind apart. Despite the fact that he was awake, his nerves were still on edge. "Leave me alone and don't come here again!" he shouted. "I can't *do* this! I need something else! I need

to be able to fuck again so I can go back to the Palace
and live out my life as a fuckin' man-whore. It's all
I'm good for."

No, that isn't true. He could do plenty of things. Raise
horses. Hell, he could raise dogs and cats. He seemed to
be well on the way to doing that already. There were
tons of them around, just waiting for a bit of animal
husbandry. Even this thought didn't stop the howls of
anguish rising from his chest. Cria stood with her back
arched and her hair standing on end. The dogs outside
were restless and whining.

"I can't do this anymore!" he bellowed. "For God's
sake, someone help me!"

His plea went unheard by anyone who could answer
him. In desperation, he stormed out of the house. The
stallion was standing by the porch as always, and Jerden
swung up onto his back without a thought, his salvation
as elusive as ever. Turning his head toward the mountains, he thought to ride up them, but the stallion ignored
him this time. The great beast spun on his haunches and
leaped forward, racing around the lake and up the hillside in the direction of Sara's house.

Jerden made a few feeble attempts to turn him using
his seat and legs, but the horse plunged onward through
the night. Finally, weaving his fingers through the long
mane and melting into the stallion's back until they became one being, Jerden simply let him run, sweeping
across the open field like a wildfire.

Skirting the fences, they came clattering into Sara's
stable yard and rode right up to the house. His limbs
no longer obeying his mind, Jerden slithered from the
horse's back, falling in a nerveless heap on the back

porch. Shouts rang out from the barns. He'd managed to awaken just about everyone, including Sara. The door flung open and she stepped out into the darkness.

Moments later, her hands touched him, and he felt life and fire and purpose flood his being. "Are you all right?"

Jerden couldn't answer. He was beyond knowing. Beyond thinking or speaking. Her eyes gleamed brightly in the moonlight and her face was softer than he remembered, as though the moon had washed over her skin, leaving her unearthly and ethereal.

Reaching up, he touched her cheek. *Help me*.

The others gathered around. The Norludian was the first to speak. "What should we do with him?"

"I'll take care of him," the Rutaran volunteered. "He can stay in my room."

Sara spoke again, seeming not to have heard the Rutaran's offer. "Zatlen, you and Drania put Danuban back in his paddock. Reutal, help me get this man inside. I don't know what his problem is, but I can't leave him lying on the porch."

The sound of Cria's purring filled his ears as she nuzzled his neck. As always, she had followed him. *Cria*... Jerden knew he'd said the leopard's name aloud, or tried to, but the attempt failed, just as it had done when he'd begged for help. No sound, barely a breath issued from his lips. He was dying. *Finally. Thank all the gods above*. Despair and misery filled him again and he was lost, bereft of hope and of joy.

When her hand gripped his, he felt lighter. She lifted him so easily, the Norludian must've taken hold of his feet to assist her. She wasn't that strong. Or perhaps she was. He knew nothing about her, except that her touch was feeding his spirit with strength while it sapped his ability to move.

What an odd contradiction. He couldn't say it aloud, and even though he felt like laughing, once again, no sound passed his lips. *Is this insanity?*

His body swung to and fro as he was carried across the threshold. Light hovered above, seeping past his eyelids to pierce his brain like a blade. It hurt. He needed darkness; something to shroud him from the light.

Shroud. That was the right word. He was already dying, or insane, needing either restraints or a shroud. Sara probably had all kinds of leather. She could tie him down before he hurt anyone.

Pain. Great waves of it deluged him with its horror. He hadn't been injured, but every muscle and joint was on fire with it. *Why is there so much pain?*

"Here, on the bed," Sara said. She wasn't panting with the effort, nor was she groaning under his weight. *She must be very strong.* Jerden sank into the cool sheets, feeling partial relief, yet he was still unable to move or open his eyes. A cool hand rested briefly on his forehead. "He's burning up. I'd better call Vladen and hope he isn't on the far side of the territory."

Another finger touched his arm, igniting a new focus for the agony. "Think he's got the flu or something?"

"No idea," Sara replied. "Vladen will know if there's anything going around."

Vladen. Jerden remembered the name. He was the regional physician who had pronounced Jerden fit and healthy upon his arrival to Terra Minor. He was an odd sort of fellow, but then, Levitians usually were, and his peculiar sense of humor was something Jerden was in no mood for. Besides, he didn't need a doctor. He needed a priest or a holy woman to help his spirit cross over to the great beyond.

Smooth fur brushed against his hand, accompanied by vibrations that penetrated clear to his bones as the contact grew stronger. *Cria.* She hadn't left him. Who would care for his animals when he died? That was one concern he didn't need. *Bonnie, perhaps?* She was very kind and had all sorts of animals on her farm. He wouldn't have to tell anyone to do it. She would do it whether he asked her to or not.

As Jerden's mind registered that this was no longer a problem, Reutal spoke again. "Do you need me for anything else?"

"No, go on back to bed for what's left of the night." Sara's sigh conveyed some sort of emotion. *Irritation? Resignation?* Jerden couldn't decide which. "Looks like tomorrow is gonna be a *very* long day."

The Norludian's flipper-like feet made slapping sounds on the smooth floor as he left the house. A door closed. Now, only Cria's purring was audible. Until she started growling.

"I'm only going to call the doctor. You can keep an eye on him until I come back."

Sara's tone was much more soothing than it had been a moment ago, but who else was there with her in the house? Then as Cria licked his hand, his fevered brain registered that she had been talking to the big cat. She probably talked to animals as much as he did. *We have so much in common.* The irony almost made him laugh, except that, as before, his body wouldn't respond. Helplessly paralyzed, he had no idea why he couldn't move. He only knew that he must be lying naked on Sara Shield's bed.

And the possibility of making love with her was about as likely as a hailstorm in space.

With the sound of Sara's retreating footsteps, Cria's touch became lighter—or was it simply that he couldn't feel it anymore? For one brief instant before darkness engulfed him, he knew he was correct.

——~~~——

Sara was still shaking. She'd done her best to remain calm—something she normally had no problem doing in a crisis—but the beseeching look in Jerden's eyes had struck a chord with her unlike anything she'd ever felt before. It was almost as though their souls had touched.

She shook her head, banishing the thought. Souls didn't touch or connect or any of the mumbo jumbo mystical nonsense that people wrote sonnets about. It simply didn't happen. It was a trick of the moonlight, or a feeling of compassion, no more.

That's what Ebenezer Scrooge thought.

Sara stomped her foot in protest. "I am *not* being visited by ghosts. And I am *not* like Scrooge. Besides, that was fiction."

If there was one thing Sara prided herself upon, it was being firmly grounded in reality. There was a simple, rational, logical explanation for everything. Granted, there were aliens with strange powers, but those abilities were natural for them. In Sara's opinion, humans who claimed to have supernatural talents were just plain lying. The feeling she'd had was probably brought on by the lack of sleep, for which the man now resting on her bed was largely responsible.

That sounded odd. Men were not normally anywhere near her bed, for any reason whatsoever, and she liked it that way. Giving herself a mental shake, she went into the living room and tapped the comlink pad to call Vladen.

A few moments later, the Levitian's image popped up on the screen. He appeared to be fully awake, but his bright blue eyes looked tired and his short blond hair, which normally stood straight out like the bristles on a hairbrush, was lying flat on one side. "And here I thought I was going to get to sleep the night through for the first time in weeks." Sighing, he ran a hand over the bony ridges along his jaw. "What's up, Sara?"

"I'm not sure," she replied. "Jerden Morokovitz just rode up on a horse and then collapsed on my porch. I don't know the normal body temperature for a Zetithian, but he feels hot to me."

Vladen snickered. "They're *all* hot, Sara. I'm surprised you had to touch him to realize that."

Sara rolled her eyes but didn't laugh. She'd never felt less like laughing in her life. "Would you mind telling me what their normal temperature is, or would you rather come and see him for yourself?"

"Don't need to. Zetithians are better at healing themselves than anything a mere doctor can do. Just put him to bed and let him sleep for a day or two. He'll wake up good as new."

"A day or two?" She was beginning to wish she'd left him on the porch. "I'd like to get a little sleep myself."

Vladen wasn't stupid. He knew precisely what she'd

done with him. "You just snuggle up beside him. He won't bite if he's asleep, and you'll keep each other nice and warm."

"Maybe I could sleep on the couch." She'd have slept in a second bedroom if she'd had one, but her house was a simple one-story cottage with only a small attic and a basement for storage.

"No need for that," Vladen said briskly. "Just cover him up and leave him there. He won't bother you. His heart rate and respirations will slow way down, but that's normal. And don't worry about him wetting the bed. They never do."

This was a problem Sara hadn't even considered yet, but, since most of the galaxy's remaining Zetithians lived in his territory, Vladen obviously knew what he was talking about. "But what about that big cat of his? She followed him into the house and is sitting right there beside him, licking his hand and growling at me."

Vladen appeared to consider this for a moment. "Well... you *could* treat her for fleas, if that's what you're worried about."

She snorted a laugh. "I'm *worried* about getting eaten alive—and *not* by fleas!"

Vladen was patient but firm. "Now, Sara. You know a lot about animals. If she's protective of him, then don't act like you're trying to hurt him and you'll get along fine."

Sara took a deep breath. Part of Vladen's ability to tend to the medical needs of an entire region was in knowing when to act and when to take a wait-and-see approach. In his eyes, this was clearly not an emergency. "Okay. 'Nuff said. I'll keep him warm and his leopard fed."

"You do that." Vladen yawned, revealing double rows of sharply pointed teeth. "Meanwhile, I'm going back to bed."

"Good night, and thank you."

"No problem. Feel free to call me again if you get worried."

After terminating the link, Sara returned to her bedroom to find the leopard lying on the floor beside the bed, purring contentedly, the tip of her tail twitching in a lazy rhythm. Jerden lay right where she'd left him, flat on his back, the contours of his perfect body accentuated by the pale moonlight. Both he and the cat seemed harmless enough at the moment, but one glimpse of him made her heart start pounding again. Vladen may have been reassuring, but he hadn't known anything about *that* part of the problem.

Having grown up with two younger brothers, Sara had never shared a bed with anyone—let alone a man who was essentially a stranger. Fortunately, snoring wasn't an issue; Jerden's respirations were so shallow, the difficulty would lie in determining whether or not he was breathing at all. He could die during the night and she'd never know it. Lying down next to a strange man was one thing. Waking up beside a dead man was quite another.

Oh, just crawl in beside him. It's no big deal…

Reutal would have a field day with it, though. That he hadn't made any suggestive remarks when they'd hoisted Jerden onto the bed was nothing short of a miracle. Then again, he was probably saving up a whole slew of comments for tomorrow.

If only they hadn't put him on her side of the bed!

Granted, it was nearer to the door, but his head rested on her favorite pillow, and she wasn't about to risk waking him up by switching them. Sighing with resignation, she went around to the far side, pulled back the sheets, and got in bed with a man for the first time in her life.

As she flipped the sheet up over him, his body heat flowed back toward her in waves, his scent carried along with the warmth. Tempered with the fragrance of horse—a smell Sara had always found pleasing—Jerden's own unique aroma was nothing short of delightful. Simply breathing it in calmed her nerves and allowed her heartbeat to return to a normal rate. Hair as black and shining as the stallion's mane lay on the pillow and she reached out to touch it without a second thought. Softer by far than the mane of any horse, the texture of his tresses drew her to him like forbidden fruit.

With her next breath, her heart filled with pain, for that was what he was. *Forbidden*. And if not technically forbidden, he was certainly not something she was entitled to, or ever would be. The thought of what might happen when he *did* wake up sent chills running down between her shoulder blades. It was wrong of her to touch him in such a manner when he lay sick and helpless. He'd asked for her assistance, nothing more.

Tears dampened her pillow, frustrating her further. She *never* cried. What was it about him, simply lying there asleep, that dragged so many different emotions from her? This was foolish, pointless behavior. She needed to be monitoring his condition, not weeping over him. Taking his wrist, she felt for a pulse. It was faint and slow, just as Vladen said it would be, and he drew in one shallow breath for every four she took herself. She reminded herself that he'd only come to her because he was riding her horse and she was his nearest neighbor. *Proximity*. That was the only reason he was there. His presence in her house didn't mean anything else.

She couldn't explain why she thought it *should* mean anything more. Perhaps this was why Zetithians had nearly been exterminated; they made you covet things you had no business wanting in the first place. After all, a woman had been killed to enable another to get closer to this man. He was a dangerous brew—intoxicating, deadly, and probably addicting. Sara was a fool to keep him there in her bed and decided to send him away as soon as possible. Bonnie could look after him far better than she could, and if she couldn't do it, Salan would take him in a heartbeat.

Poor Salan. She'd been bitten by the Zetithian bug long before Lynx had come to work for Bonnie. She'd fallen for Leo Banadänsk, the golden-haired husband of the Mordrial/Terran witch, Tisana, who traveled together with Cat and Jack Tshevnoe and their families aboard the starship *Jolly Roger*. Now, with more Zetithians to choose from than ever, Salan had renewed hope, but her blatant attempts at seduction had made her something of a joke within the Zetithian community. Not that they would ever openly laugh at her. They were too polite and kind, just as Jerden would be if he weren't drowning in grief.

Sara could imagine his smile, could almost hear him purring. No, she knew better than to think he would ever be interested in her. Men seldom were, and she was okay with that now. A lifetime of being the maiden aunt wasn't so bad. She had her own life. In another place and time, she would have been looked down upon, even ridiculed for being a spinster. But this was not that time, nor was this society one in which she would be good for nothing except as a governess to someone else's children. She would leave Jerden for another woman to heal with her love, and she would stick with her horses. She had all but lost a horse to him already. She wasn't about to hand over her heart.

The big cat let out a loud purr and then fell silent, apparently trusting Sara enough to sleep. *Wish I felt that way*. Closing her eyes, she tried to forget about Jerden and his leopard, but with every cell in her body screaming at her to get closer to him, he was impossible to ignore. And what difference would it make? She could snuggle up next to him and he would never know. Vladen had even told her to do it.

Jerden had lain with a thousand different women. What was one more? Lifting his arm out of the way, she crawled up beside him and laid her head on his shoulder, her own arm draped across his chest. She held her breath, waiting for him to stir, but he never moved. At last, she inhaled deeply, filling her lungs with his scent as her arms absorbed his warmth. The heartache she felt was fleeting this time, rapidly giving way to a deep, overriding sense of contentment and belonging.

None of these feelings made any sense to Sara, but as she drifted off to sleep, she knew one thing for certain. It wouldn't last, and when Jerden awoke from his healing slumber, he wouldn't remember any of it, nor would he wish to. He wanted nothing from her except Danuban, and if she were to sell the horse to him, he might never darken her door again.

In any event, she wouldn't agree to the sale without the stipulation that she could still breed her mares to Danuban. Perhaps when he recovered from this illness of his, Jerden might even be more... friendly.

Yeah, right. And pigs might fly.

Chapter 5

SARA DIDN'T HAVE TIME TO APPRECIATE THE FINER points of waking up next to a handsome man because she awoke to find the big black cat staring back at her with its huge yellow eyes. "I suppose you're hungry. Guess I'd better feed you something before you decide to eat me, huh?"

She had no idea what Jerden had been feeding the leopard, but it must've been enough because, despite the fact that some of the local cattle breeders had reported calves being killed, Sara had never lost a single foal. It must not have bothered his collection of cats and dogs, either. Unfortunately, Sara didn't have enough raw meat in the house to keep a cat that size happy for long.

Lynx had been delivering supplies to Jerden for some time now, so he would probably know what Jerden fed the big cat—that is, if she could get to her comlink to call him. After assuring herself that Jerden still had a pulse, she inched her way out from under the covers on the opposite side of the bed. Unfortunately, the cat was between her and the door. She reminded herself that the leopard hadn't tried to attack her the night before, though it *had* growled at her.

Don't act like a prey animal, Sara. The cat's gaze never wavered as she drew herself up and walked purposefully around the end of the bed. "Just sit still. I'll be right back."

The leopard replied with a yawn, which Sara took as a good sign. She made it to the comlink unscathed, but it was Bonnie's daughter, Ulla, who answered the call. "Mom and Dad are out working," she reported. "I'm fixing breakfast for the little ones."

Which was quite a job, seeing as how Bonnie and Lynx had seven children. At eleven, Shaulla was the eldest, with two younger sets of triplets, aged four and nine. "I've got a similar problem. Any idea what Jerden has been feeding his leopard?"

"Cat food," Ulla replied promptly.

"Really? How many tons does it eat in a week?"

Ulla shrugged. "I don't know, but he gives her a big bowl full of it at least once a day. I've seen him do it."

"Wait a minute. You've *seen* him?"

"Yeah. He gives her fresh meat sometimes too."

Sara scratched her head. Apparently Ulla had been over to Jerden's place more than she would've thought. "Do you mean to say you've been *visiting* him? He doesn't strike me as the type to want company."

Ulla grinned, her Vessonian forehead ridges crinkling as she brushed back a lock of long, blond hair from her face. "I never said he knew I was there."

"Ah. Sneaky little woman, aren't you?"

"Yes, I am," Ulla said, laughing. "Can't help it. It's the Treslanti in me." Her expression sobered. "I know I should've told Mom about the horse sooner, but I liked watching him ride it too much."

"Well, I certainly can't blame you for that. It's pretty amazing."

"Wish I could ride like he does," Ulla said wistfully.

"You're improving," Sara said. "Speaking of which,

I still haven't gotten word on the Welsh ponies. Guess you'll just have to keep taking your riding lessons on Akira. The way things are going, by the time those ponies get here, you'll have outgrown them."

Ulla nodded. "The older trips can still ride them, though. Brie and Jean are dying to have their own ponies. Trent's more into speeders."

"Typical boy," Sara agreed.

"Who is that?" One of the younger girls climbed up beside Ulla and stuck her face right up against the viewscreen. A huge smile revealed her fangs as she waved excitedly. "Hi, Sara!"

"Hello, Karsyn," Sara said, waving back. "Are you being a good girl?"

Karsyn made a face as Ulla tugged her ponytail. With her white-blond hair and Zetithian features, Karsyn looked like a cross between an elf and a Persian kitten. Folding her arms, she gave Sara a firm nod. "Yes, I'm good."

"Oh, she's good, all right." Ulla snickered. "You should have seen her dance recital last night. She was the star of the show. Danced all over the stage. Of course, she wasn't *supposed* to do that."

"See my shoes?" Karsyn asked, holding up a ballet-slippered foot.

"Yes, and they're quite lovely," Sara replied.

"I'm a great dancer," Karsyn confided. "Daddy says I'm the best Zetithian ballerina in the whole world!"

Ulla rolled her eyes. "More like the *only* Zetithian ballerina in the world."

"Doesn't matter," Karsyn insisted. "I'm still the best."

Ulla lifted Karsyn from the table and shooed

her away. "You never did say why you're feeding Jerden's leopard."

"No, I didn't." Sara gave Ulla a brief rundown of the events of the previous night. "Vladen says he'll be okay, but I'm not convinced. Anyway, the leopard was with him, and now it's sitting there next to the bed looking really hungry. I've never had to feed a carnivore of that size before, and I'll admit I'm a little unnerved by it." The leopard wasn't the only reason she felt nervous, but Sara didn't think it was a good idea to mention the part about having slept next to a naked Zetithian man, no matter how mature for her age Ulla might be.

"She's very tame," Ulla said. "I've never seen her chase his other pets, and she's never come after me, either. Jerden calls her Cria."

"Thanks. That helps a lot, though I may have to make a run over to his place to get more food. I doubt if I have enough here for more than a snack. I probably ought to feed the rest of his menagerie while I'm there."

"I can do it," Ulla offered. "I'll go over there before my riding lesson. They, um, sort of know me."

Sara chuckled. "Even when you aren't invisible?"

"Even then," Ulla replied. "Before he had the horse, Jerden went out running a lot. I'd watch him leave and then play with the dogs for a while. I don't think he realizes it, but I also clean his house sometimes."

"Does your mother know you're doing that? She didn't say a word to me about it. In fact, she said she should encourage you kids to pester him more."

Ulla's gaze faltered slightly. "Well... not exactly. I mean, she knows I've been over there *some*. She was kinda worried about him at first and said someone ought to check on him every day. Since I can disappear, I knew I could do it without him knowing. He's always seemed okay to me, and I probably don't need to go there anymore, but—well, maybe I do. You say he's sick?"

Sara blew out a pent-up breath. "I don't know *what's* wrong with him, but he was definitely feverish and now he's unconscious. Of course, you probably know all about how sick Zetithians behave."

"Yeah. They just conk out for a while. It's usually only for a couple of hours, but sometimes it's a couple of days. You get used to it eventually."

Sara wasn't so sure about that. Going into a coma whenever you caught the flu seemed a bit excessive. Still, it had suffering through chills and fever while you were awake beaten hands down.

After thanking Ulla for her help, she terminated the link and went back to the bedroom with a mixing bowl full of the dry food she normally fed to her own cats. Jerden still hadn't moved and neither had the leopard. She shook the bowl enticingly. "Here you go, Cria. Want to eat this outside?"

The big cat ignored her. Sara was about to call her again, but somehow saying "Here, kitty, kitty, kitty" seemed a little ridiculous. Stepping closer, she set down the bowl. Cria gave it a brief sniff and looked away.

"I sure hope you're housebroken," Sara muttered. "I do *not* want to have to clean up after you."

Cria got up suddenly, but instead of eating anything, she simply stalked around to the other side of the bed and leaped onto it. Settling down next to Jerden, she began licking his arm.

"Oh, *great*." Sara had her cats conditioned to stop

what they were doing whenever she snapped her fingers. She doubted Cria would respond the same way, but figured it was worth a try.

Cria ignored that, too.

The use of force was out of the question, but how did *anyone* get a leopard off their bed that clearly wanted to stay put?

"You don't," she muttered, answering her own question. "Well, the food's here if you want it, Cria. Guess I'll have to leave a door open so you can get out if you want. Something tells me the litter box in the bathroom would be woefully inadequate."

Not wanting the cat to think she was on the run, she left the room with careful nonchalance and went out to the kitchen. When she opened the back door, Jerden's other pets—at least a dozen cats and dogs—marched inside.

"What the hell?" Her next thought was that Ulla would be wasting her time going over to Jerden's place to feed them. "Guess I'd better call her back," she said as the entire menagerie trotted by, a tiny Yorkshire terrier leading the way.

When the last cat—a long-haired, bobtailed calico—had entered, Sara followed them to the bedroom, only to stop at the threshold in stunned silence.

Vladen might have called each of the animals and told them the same thing he'd told her. The cats were already settling themselves on top of Jerden and the dogs were curled up all around him, except where Cria lay stretched out next to his left side. Sara was about to protest this invasion when she heard a soft nicker outside the window.

Stepping carefully around the bed, she rolled up the

shade to find Danuban staring back at her. "Oh, you have *got* to be kidding me!"

The stallion snorted and tossed his head.

"You are *not* coming in my house!"

Danuban nudged the glass. Rolling her eyes, Sara unlatched the casement and allowed it to swing open. The big horse was tall enough that his head fit perfectly through the window and his subsequent neigh could've awakened the dead. Jerden didn't move a muscle.

"Okay, I give up." Shaking her head, she gave Danuban a pat on the nose and then went out to the kitchen to fix breakfast for the crew. "Just hope he doesn't start drawing enocks." Bonnie and Lynx might've made a lot of money raising the large, flightless birds, but though their eggs were delicious, the birds themselves were extremely vicious. Having a horse in the house was infinitely preferable.

She was whipping up a batch of pancake batter when Drania came in. "So how's Jerden this morning?"

Sara nodded toward the bedroom. "See for yourself."

Drania followed Sara's nod, moving with her odd, chimp-like gait. Sara gave it a few moments and followed, still stirring the batter. If she'd thought the animals draped all over Jerden would have freaked the Rutaran out, she'd have been wrong. Drania was standing next to the bed, combing her long fingers through his hair.

She glanced up as Sara entered. "Even zoned out, he is one fine hunk of a man."

Cria let out a loud purr, almost as though voicing her agreement while Drania resumed gazing at him, tracing the line of his brow with her fingertips.

"Yes, I suppose he is."

Drania sighed and turned away from him. "It's not fair. Here you've got something like *that* in your bed, and that's the best you can say about him?"

Sara shrugged. "I can't help it. I mean, I can *see* that he's a perfect specimen, but…" She stopped there, shaking her head. "He does *smell* nice, and his hair is beautiful, but I—"

"Don't like men, do you?"

The pang near her heart almost made her gasp, but she managed to control her reaction. "It's not that, I just—"

"Prefer women?"

"No." Sara didn't know what to say, or even how to explain it. Throwing the mixing bowl across the room seemed a more viable option. She controlled that impulse, too. "I—never mind. It doesn't matter anyway." She turned and went back to the kitchen.

No, it didn't matter.

So, why am I feeling like this?

Sara couldn't explain that, either. Her vision clouded with tears as she poured the batter onto the griddle. Thankfully, this was an action she could perform in her sleep. Her stable hands *always* wanted pancakes—never eggs or bacon or toast or cereal—and with enough syrup to drown a rat. *At least they all like the same things.*

Zatlen and Reutal came in just as she was setting the last plate on the table.

Reutal took a seat and inhaled deeply. "Ah! Smells wonderful." He glanced toward the bedroom. "Is the cat coming to breakfast?"

Sara rolled her eyes. "Which one? There must be at least six of them."

"Eight if you include Jerden," Drania said as she climbed onto a chair.

"He's the one I meant," Reutal said with a snicker. "Have a nice time with him last night, Sara?"

"He's still asleep," Drania said. Her tone was neutral, but her expression was wickedly suggestive.

The Norludian licked his lips lasciviously. "Ah, wore him out, did you?"

"He's *asleep*," Sara said firmly. "As in comatose—or whatever you call it when a Zetithian conks out like that."

Reutal grinned. "*Sure* he is. That's what they *all* say."

"It must've taken you all night to come up with that one." Sara had never given Reutal many opportunities to needle her on sexual matters before. If that was the best he could do, he was clearly out of practice. "Just because he's in my bed doesn't mean I did anything with him besides sleep."

Reutal shrugged and picked up the syrup bottle. "Your loss."

Sara stared at the syrup cascading over his stack of pancakes as she tried to sort out exactly what he'd meant by that remark. Was he actually encouraging her to… *consort* with Jerden?

After dabbing a suckered fingertip in the sticky sweetness, he licked his finger. "Just one taste of *his* syrup will give you the best orgasm of your life."

If Jerden gave her any kind of orgasm at all, it would be the best, by virtue of the fact that it would be the first. She couldn't very well admit that to Reutal, however. He'd never let *that* subject drop. "So I've heard." She was about to move on to the plans for the day when

Reutal opened his mouth to speak. It was time to set him straight. "I've also heard that he's still mourning that Audrey woman's death. He's not going to respond to anyone—at least, not for a while."

Reutal picked up a bowl of blueberries and sprinkled them on top of the syrupy mess on his plate. "Looks like you've got your work cut out for you, then, doesn't it?"

"I believe I'll leave that job for someone else."

Reutal nodded at Drania. "She'd probably be happy to help, except I'm not sure she's his type."

"I'm not his type, either," Sara said bluntly. "Can we talk about something else?"

"Yeah," Zatlen said, "like who's going to help me build up the fence around Danuban's paddock?"

Reutal snorted a laugh. "Can't keep him away from the cat, can you?"

The conversation had come right back to Jerden. *That didn't take long…* "I'm thinking it might be easier to leave him loose. With Jerden here, it's not like he's going to run off." She paused, grimacing. "He's probably already trampled my roses. I'm almost afraid to look."

The main rose bed wasn't directly beneath her window, but it was relatively close, and some of her oldest varieties were planted near the foundation. Destroying her roses was the one transgression that would be difficult to forgive. Horses may have been her livelihood and her passion, but roses kept her sane. Something about their scent and the way they responded to her care by producing such beauty affected her in a way that nothing else ever had. Gazing into the depths of a bloom while inhaling the intoxicating fragrance seemed to empty her mind, quieting the background noise of continuous thinking.

"I doubt it," said Zatlen. "Too many thorns. He'd avoid them." His words were dismissive, yet they contained a note of compassion.

Sara had seen the Tryosian sniffing the blossoms more than once, though whether they appealed to his masculine side or to his more feminine nature, she couldn't have said. Maybe it didn't matter. Either way, roses were good for the soul. "I sure hope you're right. I've got some varieties that would be tough to replace."

"I'd be more worried about what all of *his* animals are doing to your bed," Reutal said. "You'll have fleas all over the place."

"I know." Sara wasn't sure she ever wanted to sleep in that bed again. The couch was sounding better all the time. If she slept there, at least Reutal couldn't accuse her of messing around with Jerden while he was unconscious. "Vladen said something about treating the leopard for fleas. I'm just not sure I want to be the one to do it. Ulla seems to know Jerden's pets pretty well. Maybe she can do it. Speaking of which, I need to call her back."

The call proved unnecessary, however, for Ulla arrived just as Sara was finishing the after-breakfast cleanup and the others were heading out the door.

"Thought I'd come here first," she said. "How is he?"

"Still out," Sara replied.

"Still *gorgeous*," Drania added with a sigh. "I hope he never leaves."

Ulla snickered. "Don't you have a boyfriend in Nimbaza?"

Drania's ears twitched. "So what if I do? I'm not

blind and I'm not dead. If you'd seen him come riding into the barn…"

"Ulla has seen him ride," Sara admonished. "Though she probably *shouldn't* have." She paused, wiping her wet hands on a towel. "I was about to call you, Ulla. Jerden's pets followed him here, and even that dratted stallion has his head stuck in the window. Don't suppose you'd care to check the leopard for fleas, would you?"

"I could," Ulla replied. "But I bet I won't find any. Jerden takes really good care of his animals. I've seen him brushing them. Sometimes he's at it for hours."

Sara couldn't help but feel relieved. "That's one less thing to worry about."

Reutal's eyes danced with mischief. "Yes, and you can climb right in with him tonight without a care in the world."

"Ha! Not with that leopard in there. It was bad enough with her sleeping on the floor last night. There won't be room for me. We should probably turn him, though. Want to give me a hand, Ulla?"

"Sure."

"The rest of you can head on out to the barn. I'll be there in a little bit."

Ulla followed Sara into the bedroom. Danuban no longer had his head in the window, but was grazing in the yard nearby. Cria had shifted slightly, almost as though making room for them to turn Jerden. "If we can get these cats off him, it shouldn't be too hard. He's like a wet rag."

"Funny how they do that, isn't it?" Ulla asked. "It's really scary when they're babies. You think they're dead, but they aren't."

Sara nodded. "Yeah, that *would* be scary. They're completely helpless, too. It's a very odd trait—but useful, I suppose."

Though Sara probably could've done it alone, she was glad Ulla was with her. The animals seemed to know her, except for the little terrier that barked in protest the moment they began.

"I've never seen that little yappy dog before," Ulla said. "What is it, anyway? It looks like a rat."

"She's a Yorkie," Sara replied with a chuckle. "You sound just like my father. He never *could* stand those little lap dogs."

"Doesn't seem like Jerden's type, either. Somehow I can't see her running up the mountainside with him."

"Probably not." Sara gathered up Jerden's hair and spread it out on the pillow. "How do they *ever* keep this long, curly hair from getting all matted up?"

Ulla smiled. "Mom loves combing Dad's hair. She likes the way it makes him purr."

Sara let that remark pass. It seemed too... intimate, aside from the fact that it didn't answer her question. "At least he isn't tossing and turning all the time. With him lying so still, it should stay fairly neat."

"If it doesn't, you just have to start at the ends and work your way up."

"Like combing a horse's tail?"

Ulla nodded.

"Speaking of horses, you need to go get Akira saddled for your lesson."

"Sure thing," Ulla said brightly. "Let me know if you need any help with this lot." She gave the Yorkie a pat on the head and left, closing the door behind her.

Shaking her head, Sara glanced around what had once been her bedroom—a room that had become a zoo overnight. Every one of the cats and dogs was gazing at her, their eyes steady and calm, almost as if they had a message to convey.

This, too, shall pass…

Sara didn't doubt that for a moment. As she smoothed the covers over Jerden's shoulder, the warmth of his body crept into her psyche, creating waves of contentment. The leopard seemed to sense something similar, yawning as she lounged onto her back, licking her paw in a languid manner. The Yorkie curled up in the bend of Jerden's knee, and the calico cat sat perched like a sentinel on his hip. Her own bobtailed cats, Kate and Allie, were nestled between Jerden and Cria. "You traitors," she muttered. The rest of the menagerie surrounded him, pinning him beneath the blankets. He couldn't have fallen out of bed if he tried.

With a reluctant sigh, Sara propped the back door open when she left for the stable. Allowing animals and probably a lot of insects—to come and go from her house at will went against her better judgment, but she couldn't see that she had much choice. Nevertheless, she had a sneaking suspicion that a house full of fleas would turn out to be the least of her worries.

Chapter 6

FEARING THE WORST, SARA PULLED ON HER LEATHER gloves and rounded the house with her pruners and hoe in hand. Fortunately, though she found hoofprints between the climbing Don Juan and the Joseph's Coat, the stallion's legs showed no evidence of scratches, and the plants were undamaged. If he'd trampled the Burgundian or the cabbage roses—varieties which were every bit as ancient as the Andalusian breed itself—she and the stallion would've had words. She sighed with relief, grateful for whatever whim had dictated that she not plant any roses directly beneath her window and also for Danuban's relatively dainty feet. "You are one lucky fellow, Danny boy."

Without even raising his head, the stallion glanced at her and continued grazing on the strip of short turf between the rose beds.

"Going to do double duty as a lawn mower?"

Danuban shook his head and snorted.

Sara snipped the dead blooms off the nearest bush. "It *is* rather beneath you. By the way, Vladen assures me that Jerden will recover. Just wish I knew what was wrong with him." Cocking her head, she fixed a quizzical gaze on the horse. "You probably know exactly what's ailing him, don't you? Too bad you couldn't have taken him somewhere else—though if you had, you wouldn't be here, either. Would you?"

Danuban apparently thought the answer was obvious because he ignored her question and kept right on nibbling at the grass.

"Yeah, right," she muttered. "Shut up and get on with your chores, Sara." Truth be told, she didn't consider tending the roses to be a chore. Roses were therapy.

After she'd finished the pruning, she picked up her hoe. Cultivating around the bushes was a relatively simple task, which was fortunate because she could scarcely keep her eyes off the stallion.

She had nearly finished weeding the last bed when a gray leaf caught her eye. Picking it up, she turned it over in her hand, noting with relief that the edges were smooth, rather than serrated. She'd been fooled by that one before. "Not juluva weed, thank God. You don't need to be eating any of *that* stuff."

Danuban edged closer, and as she bent to pull another weed, he nudged her in the butt, driving her onto her knees. "Thanks a lot, buddy." Ignoring her attempt to push him away, he nudged her again. "Oh, so now you want to be friendly, do you? Okay, fine, but you are *not* coming in the house."

Still kneeling, she turned to face him. His dark, intelligent eyes gazed at her through a forelock so long and thick it nearly reached the tip of his nose. His ears pricked toward her as she trailed her fingers through his hair, unable to avoid comparing it to Jerden's. "Your hair is very pretty, but his is softer and curlier." Raising his head, Danuban nipped at her cropped locks. "And, yes, both of you have more hair than I do."

There was a reason for that. Throughout her childhood, Sara's hair had been practically orange and completely unmanageable, and though braids might've controlled the frizziness, she had never been able to endure the ridicule of her classmates long enough to make it past the "clown" stage. As an adult, her unruly hair had darkened to a coppery tint, but since shorter hair suited her lifestyle, she saw no point straightening it or letting it grow. She left the long, romantic locks to her horses.

And to Jerden.

There was no denying that his hair was romantic, whether he behaved in a romantic manner or not. He could've easily passed for a swashbuckling pirate, a poet, or an ancient warrior. Like Danuban, Jerden was beautiful without even trying.

Sara, on the other hand, saw herself as a tall, plain woman with fiery hair and not even the volatile personality to go along with it. Everything around her was beautiful—the horses, the roses, and the lush, green landscape—but she was simply their unlovely caretaker. She told herself it didn't matter, but the twinge of regret near her heart said otherwise.

Giving Danuban a quick pat on the nose, she got to her feet. Once her task was complete, she went to the arena for Ulla's lesson.

Ulla was already in the arena, warming up. A dappled gray Arab gelding with a silvery mane and tail, Akira was one of the first horses Sara had bred, and he'd won ribbons for her in many a show. Though past his prime, he made an excellent lesson horse—responsive, willing, and tolerant of novice riders.

Sara leaned over the rail. "How's he going for you today?"

"Fine," Ulla replied as they trotted by. "I think he likes me."

"He's always been a sweetie. I couldn't bring myself to leave him behind when I came here from Earth. He's almost like a son."

The only kind of son I'll ever have. Sara had never had a child of her own and probably never would. Bonnie, on the other hand, had seven. The disparity would've rankled if Bonnie's road to happiness had been an easy one. She'd been used to the point that she'd sworn off men completely before she had no choice but to hire Lynx to help her on the farm. Pregnant and alone with a pen full of nasty enocks, Lynx had come to her rescue, albeit reluctantly. *Maybe that's what I'll have to do to get a man… swear I wouldn't take one if he was offered to me on a silver platter.*

But do I really want one? She glanced toward the house. Jerden was right there in her bed—the closest thing to a platter she could imagine—though he *was* unconscious. Perhaps comatose men were the best kind. They were certainly less trouble.

Horses were better. Horses and roses. They gave back what you put into them. Men had a tendency to take what was offered and never give anything in return.

Not all of them, surely…

Returning her attention to Ulla, she saw that Akira had taken the opportunity to get a little lazy and had his nose up in the air. "See if you can get him to round up a little. Wiggle the bit and give him more leg."

She thought it odd to be giving such simple, basic instructions when Danuban was trained in classical dressage—even the airs above the ground. She'd waited all her life to have a horse capable of the spectacular leaps that the war horses of old had been trained to do. She still recalled the colors and movements as she'd watched the Lipizzaner stallions performing at the Spanish Riding School in Vienna—a tradition that dated back at least fifteen hundred years. Even as a child, their precision and power had given her chills.

Now she was here on a new world, working to establish similar traditions on a planet halfway across the galaxy, populated with alien beings and life forms not nearly as beautiful as horses. Horses were Earth's gift to the galaxy. Nowhere else had such a creature evolved that evoked the same sense of romance and beauty. There were horses on Statzeel, but even they had their origins on Earth. She marveled at how easily they adapted to new planets, adjusting to riders and handlers who weren't even human—though she was at a loss to explain why she thought it would matter to them.

She glanced toward the house where Danuban still grazed, never straying far from her bedroom window, occasionally sticking his head inside as though checking up on the Zetithian. The way he had bonded with Jerden was uncanny, though Andalusians were known to be selective. She would have been fascinated by the phenomenon if only it hadn't irked her that the horse she'd waited a lifetime for had chosen someone else.

Studying Akira's movements, she called out more instructions to Ulla. Reminding herself that Danuban had seemed friendlier helped to soothe her, though the slight hurt remained. She ought to sell the stallion to Jerden and start over. Or pay him stud fees. It was a workable situation, except for that feeling of being

denied, left out—no, *ruled* out—because she was somehow undeserving or inferior. Judged and found lacking, like the first-round elimination in a horse show, as
though her best was simply not good enough. Men had
always made her feel that way, and now a horse was
doing it.

Blanking out these thoughts, she went on with the
lesson, fine-tuning Ulla's seat, hand position, and sub-
sequently Akira's performance.

Afterward, she went on with her day—fixing lunch,
riding the young horses, making dinner—all the while
listening to the chatter of those around her and trying
not to think about what would happen that night. She sat
out on the porch until darkness began to fall and a storm
rolled in from the east, forcing her indoors. Danuban
should be safe in his stall, not standing out in the rain,
but he refused to budge. Sara could catch him now—the
fact that he wore a halter helped—but he wasn't leaving
Jerden without a fight, and fighting was the last thing
she felt like doing.

Exhaustion had crept up on her, gradually sending
her thoughts toward sleep—and her bed, which was
now filled with animals—and Jerden. A shower and a
change into a nightgown must've given his pets a clue,
for Cria raised her head as Sara entered the room. The
big cat rose to her feet, jumping as lightly from the bed
to the floor as any house cat. The dogs followed suit
and were soon joined by the remaining cats. A moment
later, she heard them crunching on the food she'd put
out for them—food which they'd previously ignored.
A quiver ran up her spine, the bizarre nature of their
behavior overridden by the notion that they seemed to

be changing shifts—she would sleep with him at night while the animals stood watch over him by day.

Turning him onto his back, as the light from the bedside lamp illuminated the planes of his face, Sara could see no change in him, no lifting of the stupor into which he had fallen. That he truly was a beautiful man was easy to see, yet she knew that beauty wasn't everything. Pulling back the covers, she checked for fleas at the foot of the bed and didn't find a single one. When she climbed in beside him, she turned away from him, refusing to succumb to the temptation of the previous night. Turning out the light, she settled in to sleep, doing her best to shake the notion that she had simply been biding the hours of the day until she could lie with him that night.

"Don't be silly," she admonished herself. "Just go to sleep." Perhaps he would wake up in the morning and go home, taking his menagerie with him. Life would return to normal. What were the odds that Danuban would let him go home and not follow him? As she closed her eyes, she knew it wouldn't help for Jerden to leave. What was normal before had already changed, perhaps irrevocably.

———————

As always, with the increase in his respiratory drive, Jerden's sense of smell was the first to return. Though his brain took longer than usual to process the scent, even before he could feel her warmth, he knew she was there. *Sara Shield*. Her own unique essence mingled with a floral fragrance that was still hers and hers alone. Unmistakable, yet given her attitude toward him—or lack thereof—he thought it strange that she should be so close, the merest breath away.

Muscular control reawakened slowly, and his keen hearing detected her breathing and that of something else. A purring sigh confirmed his suspicions. Cria was still with him. One other thing hadn't changed. Sara's scent held no trace of desire, and even though sleep would have kept it at low ebb, he should have been able to detect it.

Opening his eyes, the light from the crescent moon was more than enough to reveal that he was in her bed. Thinking back, he recalled being put there after that last wild ride. He'd been ill—or insane—but whatever had incapacitated him was gone now. He was able to move, to breathe, to feel. Sara lay facing away from him on the far side of the mattress, their bodies in no contact whatsoever. Clearly, she was only there in case he required care or assistance, not to take advantage of the fact that there was a man in her bed. She probably felt safe, thinking he wouldn't awaken until morning. Turning carefully in the direction of Cria's purr so as not to disturb Sara, he saw the leopard lying on the floor nearby. She looked up at him, her yellow eyes glowing in the darkness as he reached down to stroke her broad head.

"We should go now," he whispered.

The big cat yawned and eased her head back down on her front paws as if to say, *No, not now... I'm resting—and you should too*.

"I've rested enough." He didn't want to be there when Sara woke up. Her lack of desire should have been comforting, but it wasn't. It hurt.

A stray thought made him cock his head, searching

his mind for traces of the nightmares that had plagued him. They weren't there.

Had he been healed? But if so, of what? Madness? Frowning, he inhaled deeply and rolled onto his back, his eyes open wide as he gazed at the dark ceiling above him. A breeze wafted in through the open window, and he heard a sound he knew well. *Danuban*. He knew the name now; he'd heard Sara say it the night she'd found him on her porch. It fit him—regal, proud, distinctive. Glancing toward the sound, he saw the stallion's head, silhouetted against the pale moonlight. If he went out and mounted the horse now, would Danuban take him home? Was that why he was there, waiting?

Then Jerden realized that it hadn't been a nightmare that had awakened him. Nor had it been the earsplitting neigh that had so often snatched him from the hell of his dreams. It was something else entirely.

The scent of despair.

Animals didn't feel that emotion, at least, he'd never associated it with them. Sara was the only possible source. *She feels despair in her dreams?* He hadn't picked it up when she'd been awake. Perhaps it only visited her at night. *Like my nightmares.* He didn't envy her. His own dreams were filled with guilt, regret, and impotent anger... but not the depths of pain that now emanated from Sara.

Audrey's death had affected him in ways he could have expected under the circumstances. She had been murdered because of her relationship with him. Knowing that his own greed and arrogance had played a part in the tragedy made matters even worse. If he'd remained on Terra Minor and not gone to Rhylos—never sold himself in a brothel—he would never have met Audrey, and perhaps she would still be alive. He had these demons to plague him night and day, and he knew their source.

But what had happened to Sara?

If she'd been born as asexual as her scent, would she feel sadness about it? Would she understand the difference or even care?

Having always been a highly sexual being, Jerden couldn't relate to that, but he did know the sense of loss when those feelings were gone. He missed the heady aroma of a woman who wanted him, the rush of blood through his groin, the stiffening of his cock, and the flow of slick fluid from the crown.

No, she couldn't have always been like this. She had once been as much a woman as any other. Something must have occurred to make her this way—some event or trauma, or even a slow erosion of feelings. It had to have been something that was done to her. No one would do such a thing to herself, not when love and passion were such glorious things. He would never have voluntarily chosen to give up his sexuality and couldn't imagine what would make her do it. But then, he wasn't a woman and had no more insight into the workings of their minds than any man. Having spent most of his adult life in the company of females and learned everything he could about how to give them the ultimate pleasure, he still didn't know everything, and anytime he thought he did, another would come along to prove him wrong.

He glanced at Danuban. He was quiet, not screaming at Sara to interrupt her dreams. Perhaps he didn't have the same connection with her that he had with Jerden.

Still, the pain emanating from her was excruciating. Moving closer to her, Jerden did something he hadn't done in months. He began to purr.

Laying a hand on her shoulder so gently she might not have been aware of his touch even if she'd been awake, he leaned in to whisper softly in her ear. "Whatever it is, Sara, it isn't worth the pain. Let it go."

He almost laughed aloud at his words. She probably wouldn't heed them any more than he had when his friends had given him similar advice. How to let go was something she would have to learn for herself, and the gods only knew he hadn't learned the way of it yet—not completely. His nightmares might have ceased for the moment, but the guilt was still with him.

Even so, he noted a subtle change in her scent. Her misery was diminishing—at least, the misery in her dreams. What she would feel when she awoke was anyone's guess. He knew he shouldn't be there when that time came. She would be uncomfortable with him in her bed when he was no longer unconscious, perhaps even fearful.

He rose carefully and found the bathroom nearby. Closing the door, he turned on the light and stared at his reflection in the mirror. He looked like hell, which wasn't surprising, since that was where he'd lived for some time now. Had he truly turned the corner and moved on? He wasn't sure yet, but he did feel different—more like the self he'd been before Audrey's murder, though not *quite* the same.

A pawing at the door made him open it a crack, and a cat he didn't recognize sauntered in, eyeing him curiously. *So, she has cats in her house too*. The bobtailed tabby glanced up at him and stalked over to the litter box in the corner. After giving it a sniff to reassure herself that it hadn't been disturbed, the cat sat down to observe him. Jerden washed his face and hands and then took a good, long drink. *I should leave now.* As he shut off the light and turned to go, something drew him back to Sara's room and into her bed. He knew that leaving was the best option, but he wasn't quite ready for that yet. If he was careful, she wouldn't have to know he'd already awakened.

As though she'd known he would return, Cria hadn't moved at all. She knew him too well—perhaps better than he knew himself. The odd thing was, when he'd purred for Sara, it was intended as a means of comfort, rather than seduction. He'd rarely done that before— had seldom felt the need—but Sara was unlike any other woman with whom he'd shared a bed. She needed him; she simply didn't know it yet.

Somehow, without even meaning to, she had gotten Jerden through the darkest hours of his life. She wouldn't see it that way, of course. She'd simply provided Danuban, who had been the catalyst for change. His thoughts touched lightly on the notion that the horse alone hadn't been enough to cause the break. There was something about Sara that intrigued him, like the elusive solution to a puzzle, an enigma that made him want to delve further into her thoughts, her life, her *being*.

As he slipped between the sheets, she stirred briefly, not waking enough to question or even notice the movement. She was undoubtedly inured to her cats jumping up on the bed from time to time, and Jerden could be very stealthy when he chose. He would lie just as he'd been when he first awoke. She wouldn't know he'd moved, and he would be there to help if her dreams should turn sour again. He owed her that much.

———⁓⁓⁓———

Sara's eyes flew open as she felt the vibration and the heat. Her first thought was that the leopard was behind her until she realized that a hand rested on her arm, not a paw. So, Zetithians really *could* purr. She'd known of this trait—it was impossible to live in the Nimbaza region and not hear the talk—but she'd never experienced it firsthand. Unfortunately, she would have been more comfortable if it *had* been Cria snuggled up against her. The fact that it was Jerden sent a chill through her body. The first night she'd lain in a similar position, but having him draped over her in slumber made her nervous, apprehensive, even slightly afraid…

Her fear wasn't so much due to his position in her bed as it was to what he would surely do and say when he woke up and realized where he was and just whose bed he was lying in—the kind of reaction she'd done her best to avoid for almost as long as she could remember. Given that he was still grieving for another woman ruled out the other cause for her apprehension—that and the fact that if what Bonnie had told her was true, Zetithians never needed to resort to force—and probably *couldn't* if the scent of a woman's desire was necessary. Quashing these fears, she consoled herself with the fact that this meant he had recovered—if not fully, at least to the point that she no longer needed to remain close by. He might even be ready to go home.

What a relief! Now she could get back to normal.

Jerden would hole up in his house again, and Danuban's presence would keep Nate from coming around to offer his stallion's services to her mares. And if Nate wanted to think that with Jerden around, he didn't stand a chance of becoming Sara's suitor, so much the better.

The niggling suspicion that Jerden could change her attitude toward men was a thought she put firmly aside. She didn't need an attitude adjustment. She only needed the freedom to live her life the way she wanted. Catering to a man's whims held no appeal for her, and she enjoyed her own company as much as she enjoyed making her own decisions.

Except when it came to what to have for breakfast. She'd been letting the hired help dictate what she ate for so long, she'd forgotten her own preference. She was so sick of pancakes, she could scream. The time had come to assert her independence in that respect, if nothing else. She was skipping the damn pancakes and having two eggs over easy with toast. No syrup. No jam. Nothing sweet at all. Just butter.

She wasn't going to pussyfoot around with Jerden, either. Not caring whether she woke him up or not, she threw back the covers and sat up. His arm slid off her shoulder, landing on the bed to rest against her hip. If he'd been awake, he wouldn't have let it touch her.

Or would he? She gave him a nudge. "Hey, are you awake?"

Jerden exhaled with a loud purr and cleared his throat. "I think so."

"Feel well enough to go home?"

"Maybe."

"What the hell was wrong with you, anyway?"

"I'm not sure."

Sara felt him moving behind her and got up, hoping he would do the same. As she turned to face him, she remembered. *He's naked.*

She doubted that any of her pants would fit him. Zatlen's jeans would cut off his circulation, and Drania's tiny coveralls were completely out of the question. Maybe if she handed him a towel, he'd take the hint. On the other hand, Reutal never wore clothing, so perhaps ignoring his nudity was the best approach. It had worked before.

"Vladen said you'd wake up eventually, but I was beginning to have my doubts." She blew out a pent-up breath. "I'm getting ready to fix breakfast for the gang. Are you hungry?"

Yawning, he nodded and scratched his head, drawing her attention to his hair. That was one thing she would miss when he left. It was absolutely beautiful. "Starving."

"What would you like?"

He slid out from under the covers and sat up. "What do you have?"

Sara shrugged, averting her eyes from his groin. "The usual stuff. Eggs, pancakes, toast… that sort of thing." *Please, anything but pancakes…*

Tossing her a grin that was obviously intended to be disarming, he stood up.

His smile was disarming, all right—and breathtaking. It was a moment before Sara could speak. "I think that's the first time I've seen you smile. You really must be feeling better."

"I am." He yawned again, displaying his fangs. "How about a couple of eggs and maybe some toast? Not sure I'm up to eating a stack of pancakes."

Sara was almost afraid to ask. "How do you like your eggs? Scrambled, fried, boiled?"

"Over easy."

She could hardly believe her ears. "Butter on the toast?"

"Yeah."

"Tea?"

He nodded. "But no sugar."

"You got it."

If he kept that up, she might even let him stay for lunch.

Chapter 7

Drania peered down the hallway toward Sara's bedroom. "So, is he awake yet?"

Sara nodded. "Yeah. He's taking a shower."

The little Rutaran's ears wiggled with excitement as she took the stack of plates from the counter and set them on the table. "D'you suppose he needs someone to wash his back?"

"I dunno," said Sara, trying not to think about doing it herself. "You could ask him."

Drania paused, giving her a quizzical look. "Sure you wouldn't mind?"

Sara gaped at her. "Why would I mind?"

"Well, he *has* been in your bed for the past two nights. I would've thought…"

"And that gives me some claim to him? I don't think so. It was more like being his nurse—not that I did a whole lot besides turn him over once in a while."

If Drania's expression had been quizzical before, it was downright skeptical now. "*Sure*, you did. If he'd been in my bed, I'd have—"

"Done what?" Reutal said as he popped in through the back door, followed closely by Zatlen. "Sucked his dick? Licked his balls?"

"Wouldn't have done much good while he was unconscious, now would it?" Drania said with a wry grin. "Though it might have been just the thing to bring him around." She ran her tongue over her lips as though about to devour something truly delicious.

Sara refrained from comment, deciding that this was one conversation she ought to sit out. There was no point in egging Reutal on, aside from the fact that she couldn't begin to understand why anyone would want to do such a thing to a man, whether he was conscious or not.

"What's stopping you?" Reutal asked.

"He's awake."

Reutal's eyes lit up. "Ah! There'll be some interesting stuff happening now."

Frowning, Sara forgot all about her decision to keep quiet. "I doubt it. He'll probably go home right after breakfast."

The Norludian shook his head, pursing his fishlike lips. "Bet he doesn't."

He was right. There was the whole Danuban issue to be dealt with first. Sara had a feeling that if Jerden were to ride the stallion home and then turn him loose, the chances of Danuban coming back to her barn were slim to none. It seemed that the only way to keep the horse was to keep Jerden.

Her anxiety level went up a notch at the mere thought. Far better to put up a force field around the paddock. Or drug the stud into docility. Or just give up and let Jerden have him. "That's up to him."

Drania's ears pricked forward. "What, you mean you'd let him stay here?"

"Well, not *forever*," Sara said. Though if it meant she didn't have to eat pancakes ever again, she might consider it. Which was stupid; she could have her choice whether he was there or not. The question was, why hadn't she? She shook her head as she cracked the eggs into the skillet, trying to figure out why the breakfast menu had anything to do with anything. *Stupid.*

"Hey, what are you doing?" Zatlen was clearly horrified. "No pancakes?"

"Yes, I'll fix pancakes," Sara snapped. "Jerden didn't want any, and he put his order in first." Just why all of this should irritate her, she had no idea. Raking a hand through her hair, she nodded toward the table. "Just sit down and be patient."

As she returned to her task, Sara glimpsed the quick upward flick of Zatlen's eyebrows. Taking a deep breath, she exhaled slowly. "Sorry if I sound a little testy this morning. I didn't sleep very well."

"Bad dreams?" If the lilt in his tone was any indication, Reutal was baiting her, but, again, he was probably right.

"Maybe." Whatever the cause, she was still feeling the dregs of it. Not only was she irritated, but her heart beat faster than normal and her hands were like ice. She began mixing the pancakes and dropped the whisk, splattering little bits of batter all over the floor. "Shit."

"*Definitely* testy."

She threw a quelling glance at Reutal just as Jerden walked into the kitchen with the leopard at his heels.

His bronzed skin caught the early morning light, outlining thick veins that ran up his muscular arms. His hair hung to his waist in gleaming ebony spirals. As his glowing, catlike eyes swept over her, her trembling hands faltered, nearly causing her to drop the bowl.

He's still naked.

Sara's heart slammed against her sternum with the force of a horse's kick. *What is* wrong *with me? I've seen him naked before. Just now, in fact.* Swallowing with more effort than usual, she tried to smile, failing miserably. "It's good to see you." Heat flooded her face. *That didn't sound right.* "Up and about, I mean." She cleared her throat with an effort. "Not sure you've met the gang yet, Jerden—at least not officially. This is Drania, Zatlen, and Reutal." She pointed to each of them in turn. "H-have a seat."

Drania pulled out a chair. "Here, you can have my place."

Jerden's lips curled into an oddly secretive smile as he shook his head. "No need. I can stand." Returning his gaze to Sara, once again, he gave her a swift, downward glance. "Let me get that for you."

Completely bewildered, Sara stared at him as he came toward her and then bent down to retrieve the whisk with one swift, fluid movement. Crossing to the sink, he rinsed it off before handing it back to her. Cria was already licking the batter off the floor when a pop from the skillet startled her and she nearly dropped the whisk again. Jerden promptly turned and gave the eggs a quick, practiced flip as though he'd helped her in the kitchen a million times.

Then the reason for her nervousness hit her. *I slept with that man, and now I'm fixing his breakfast. I didn't have sex with him, but everyone assumes I did.* If it weren't so outrageous, it would have been funny. Sex? With *him*? *Not likely.* Sara wasn't the sort of woman men like Jerden lusted after, nor was she willing to pay a thousand credits for his services. Her one and only

sexual experience had been so degrading she had no
desire to repeat it. Ever.

~~~

Reutal gave Jerden the once-over with his strange, protuberant eyes. "Well, now… you look to be completely
cured. Feeling better?"

"*Much* better." But not cured. The fact that his cock
remained flaccid when Drania was pumping out sex
pheromones like crazy proved that. At the moment,
it was just as well that he *hadn't* recovered. Sara had
looked like she'd seen a ghost when he approached her.
If he'd had an erection, she probably would've screamed.

Standing right next to her, the only scent he could
identify was her anxiety. No desire whatsoever. He
should do her a favor and get lost as soon as possible.
He owed her that much.

He dished up the eggs just as the toast popped up. As
she buttered the toast, Sara nodded toward the glazed
teapot sitting on the table. "The tea's there by your cup."
Apparently Drania didn't need to give up her place. Sara
had already given up hers. "Help yourself."

"Thanks." In the past, he could have repaid her for her
trouble with joy if she'd been willing. Human pheromones
were so much more appealing to Zetithian noses than those
of Rutarans. Anytime he'd done a Rutaran, which was unusual, he'd always needed Audrey to enhance the effect.

Audrey. The nightmare was gone, but the guilt remained. No, he wouldn't be fucking a Rutaran or anyone
else anytime soon.

He glanced at Sara, who was still busy making pancakes. If he hurried, he could wolf down his meal and be

out of there before she even *needed* a place to sit. He sat in the chair she'd indicated and Cria took up her usual position beside him.

Although eating quickly was the best course of action, he hadn't reckoned on the change his long sleep had wrought. After months of eating food that tasted like so much dust, this simple fare was a sumptuous feast. The eggs drew a moan from him and the buttered toast was practically orgasmic. Chewing slowly, he savored each mouthful until a sip of tea nearly sent him over the edge.

"You must have really been hungry," Reutal commented. "But if you think that's good, you should try the pancakes." Licking his lips, he rubbed his flat belly. "They're *fabulous*."

Jerden hadn't wanted any before, but their delectable aroma was making him rethink that decision. He stole a peek at Sara. "Maybe just a couple."

She rolled her eyes. "And I had such high hopes for you."

"Meaning?"

"That it was nice to make something besides pancakes for a change. I'm sick of them!"

Reutal groaned. "Oh, Sara, say it isn't so!"

"No problem, Reutal." She let out a resigned sigh. "I was just enjoying the variety."

Reutal nodded toward Jerden. "Trust me, you want him to keep up his strength, Sara. Pancakes will help."

The Norludian's remark caught Sara in the act of handing a plate stacked high to Drania. She glared at Reutal. "And just what is *that* supposed to mean?"

Reutal gave her a saucy grin. "Men fuck better if you feed them. Didn't you know that?"

Without a moment's hesitation, Drania passed the plate on to Jerden. "Here you go, big guy. Eat up."

An odd feeling bubbled up inside him and Jerden heard something he hadn't heard in a very long time. His own laughter.

Reutal howled with glee and even Zatlen was chuckling as Drania wiggled her ears suggestively. "And be sure to use lots of butter and syrup."

With a knowing wink at Drania, he stabbed three of the pancakes and plopped them on his plate. Laughing felt so good, Jerden didn't stop to consider Sara's feelings, but one glimpse of her standing stiffly in front of the stove with her back to the others proved that he should have. Working diligently and displaying no hint of mirth— suppressed, or otherwise—she was clearly *not* amused.

He was about to tell her to lighten up when he remembered the waves of despair that had emanated from her during the night. No, getting Sara to lighten up with regard to him, or sex, or anything else, wouldn't be easy, and the mere suggestion would probably have the opposite effect, something Jerden knew from his own experience. He'd been the recipient of loads of good advice in the weeks following Audrey's murder, and he hadn't heeded a single bit of it. How could he possibly tell her to relax when he could barely do it himself?

That was changing, however. Putting a dollop of butter on top, he poured syrup all over the stack of pancakes. The first bite was a flavor explosion. So sweet, but not as sweet as the essence of a lady who desired him.

"Good?" Drania asked, her round eyes gazing at him through thick lashes.

"Very." The second bite wasn't nearly as intoxicating,

but it was still quite tasty. Women, on the other hand, tasted better as their arousal escalated, and the flavor of a woman in the throes of orgasm was the ultimate taste sensation—nearly orgasmic in and of itself. Drania was definitely cute. She would be fun to fuck. He could hold her in his lap and drill his cock into her creamy pussy—his preferred method of intercourse with a Rutaran—fucking her until her ears lay flat with bliss. Too bad he couldn't do it. She was probably hurt that her scent hadn't aroused him. It should have. Perhaps not to the degree that a Terran's could, but he should have been able to do *something* with her.

Then he remembered that his habit of fucking any woman who expressed an interest was what had gotten Audrey killed and his own sexuality essentially destroyed. Perhaps Sara had the right idea after all; deny it until it died from neglect. Channel that energy into something else. He glanced around the room. It was a simple, country kitchen, but with touches in design and decor that were distinctly feminine—not the plain functional manner in which his own home was furnished. Lacy curtains framed the windows, baskets of flowering plants hung suspended from the ceiling, and painted landscapes adorned the creamy yellow walls. Then there were the horses she bred and trained. Romantic, elegant... Indeed, there was romance in her soul; it simply wasn't directed toward men in general—or him in particular.

But all that could be changed. He could show her, teach her...

No, he couldn't. *Forget it. It's gone, and she doesn't want it anyway.*

Suddenly, the food lost its flavor and once again became just so much matter to stuff into his body to keep it alive. And for what? To sit around thinking about the old days when his life was one seemingly endless orgasm? Or to reminisce about the way in which every woman he touched sighed with pleasure as she sank into the peaceful serenity of *laetralant* delight?

His life had been occupied with women's desire for so long he was lost without it. What he needed now was a goal, a direction, a reason for living. Simply existing without purpose held no appeal for him whatsoever. He could make it his life's work to show Sara what she'd been missing, but without a functioning cock, that task would be difficult, if not impossible.

Jerden pushed his plate away, more than half of the food uneaten. He needed to be alone again. The chatter of conversation needled him sharply, reminding him that he didn't belong there, wasn't part of the group, and probably never would be.

"That's all you want?" Drania asked.

Jerden nodded. "Guess I wasn't as hungry as I thought."

"No problem. The dogs will eat it." She took his plate and set it on the floor. As if on cue, a pack of dogs trotted into the kitchen. *His* dogs. *So, they haven't left me.* The little rat-dog was crowded out and took up a position at Sara's feet, apparently recognizing her as the source of the goodies. He'd forgotten that one was also part of his menagerie. The newest member, perhaps, but certainly one of his—unless she'd been Sara's dog to begin with.

"That tiny one only showed up a few days ago. It isn't your dog, is it?"

He was speaking to Sara, but Drania answered him. "No. The black lab is the only one that lives here. The rest of them are yours."

"Sorry if they've caused any trouble. I guess they followed me."

Drania giggled. "Followed you? That's putting it mildly. They've been camped out in Sara's bedroom ever since you got here."

Jerden frowned. Only Cria had been at the bedside when he awoke. "They must've gone out during the night." He felt like a worm. *All the more reason for me to leave*.

Sara handed another stack of pancakes to Reutal, who passed them around the table. "They all left when I got ready for bed." She shivered slightly. "It was a little spooky. Do you have some kind of power over them?"

"I don't know about that," Jerden replied. "I'd never been around animals until I came here. They just started showing up. Guess word got out that I would feed them."

Sara shook her head. "It's got to be more than just the food. I feed every stray that comes around, but there haven't been many of them lately. They must like you better."

Her tone was neutral, but her tight-lipped smile conveyed a different message. The implication that Danuban also liked him better was quite clear—along with the fact that she didn't care for the idea. Not that he blamed her for feeling resentful. In her place, he probably would have felt the same way. Maybe that was why she didn't like him.

And he was pretty sure she *didn't* like him, which irked him more than he cared to admit. Even without a working cock, he could make her scream in ecstasy, but she probably wouldn't give him the opportunity to try. He nearly growled in frustration.

Perhaps sensing his annoyance, Cria gave him a nudge and looked up at him with knowing eyes. *Get over it*, she seemed to say. Either that or she was advising patience.

He cocked an eyebrow at the big cat. *Which is it?*

Cria turned and fixed her gaze on Sara, then blinked slowly. *Patience.*

Patience? Most of his clients had waited a year or more for the appointment. He was used to women practically drooling with anticipation. None had ever required patience or encouragement. What could he possibly say that wouldn't alienate her more?

"Maybe it's my pointed ears—or the fact that I can purr," Jerden suggested.

Drania giggled. "If they like you better because they believe you're one of them, they've obviously never bothered to check out your fabulous ass."

Sara's ripple of laughter surprised him. Had he ever heard her laugh? He didn't think so, but he liked the sound of it—musical, and so infectious he couldn't help but join in.

A moment later, Sara turned and their eyes met with an impact that shook Jerden's entire body. Suddenly, she was beautiful. Before he'd have said she was passably pretty, but in that brief instant when her eyes sparkled with mirth, he caught a glimpse of the Sara that might have existed if life had treated her differently, the Sara she could still be if only…

If what? She'd let him help her? He doubted she would. She was clearly as stubborn as he was when it came to accepting help from anyone.

"Looks like this is your lucky day, Drania!" Reutal

said. "Hot pancakes, hot ass… And speaking of hot, my tongue's getting a little warm."

As long as her reach was, Drania had no difficulty smacking the Norludian from where she sat. "You keep that nasty tongue to yourself, Reutal. I'd much rather have some of Jerden."

Sara clucked her tongue. *"Boyfriend?"*

"Oh, yeah. Boyfriend." Drania gave Jerden an apologetic smile. "Sorry. I keep forgetting I've already got one."

Jerden grinned back at her. "No problem." Noting that Sara was standing there with her plate in her hand, he got up and held the chair for her, motioning for her to sit.

"You Norludians put way too much emphasis on sex," Zatlen said, shaking his head.

Reutal rolled his eyes. "And you Tryosians don't put enough. No gender? I couldn't live that way."

Zatlen snickered. "You obviously haven't thought it through. We aren't genderless, we're hermaphroditic. We can mate with *any* member of our species, not just the opposite sex."

"I know that," Reutal said patiently. "And it sounds perfectly boring. I much prefer the difference between males and females."

"Me too," Jerden said. As Sara sat down at the table, her scent rose around her, curling through his head. Men shouldn't smell like that. Only women. No desire, perhaps, but nice. *Very* nice. "But I'm sure Tryosians think we're crazy."

Zatlen shrugged. "Not crazy, just different. We have trouble seeing the whole male-female thing. To us, it would be like mating with an entirely different species."

Gazing down at Sara, Jerden realized for the first

time that she *was* an entirely different species. Never mind that Zetithians and Terrans could crossbreed; some people simply couldn't get past that idea, and perhaps she was one of them. His clients certainly hadn't considered it to be a deterrent. The idea of sex with an exotic alien appealed to them. The problem had been more on his side of the equation, hence the need for Audrey. With her along for the ride, he'd even fucked a few Darconians, and though he'd never considered lizards to be even remotely sexy, he'd done it.

For money. Sara probably saw him as nothing but an alien prostitute—a man-whore who was beneath her notice. She might even believe he deserved what had happened to him, and perhaps even to Audrey for taking on what some would consider to be an immoral occupation—particularly when neither of them had been forced into doing it out of necessity. They'd both done it by choice.

It occurred to him that even the times he'd been with Audrey, it was considered part of her wages, so essentially *that* was done for money too. Not because he loved her.

Looking back, he couldn't recall ever having done it for love. He'd done it for pleasure—his own and that of whatever lady he happened to be with.

Love. How would it feel to hold a woman in his arms and make love to her, not merely engage in recreational intercourse? To gaze into her eyes and see love there, rather than simple lust?

Then it struck him that he might never know.

Chapter 8

IF THE FACT THAT HE WAS ZETITHIAN, AS OPPOSED TO human, was the only reason for Sara's apparent disinterest, Jerden could've lived with that. But he had a sneaking suspicion there was more to it. He was humanoid enough to feel an attraction to Terran women—Audrey was a perfect example—so why was it that Sara paid him no more notice than she did Reutal?

It was none of his business what she did or how she felt, but the need to know more hounded him. Revising his intent to leave her alone, he decided to stick around a while longer to see if he could come up with any clues as to the reason for her peculiar reaction—or lack thereof.

While Cria sat in the corner grooming herself, Jerden did everything he could think of to help Sara clean up after the others left for the stables, even to the point of mopping the kitchen floor. Unfortunately, she wasn't very talkative. Aside from a couple of mystified glances in his direction, she seemed determined to ignore his presence. It wasn't until he offered to change the sheets on her bed that he finally got a rise out of her.

"You don't need to do that," she said quickly. "I'll do it later."

Since almost the first thing she'd asked him was if he was well enough to go home, she clearly wanted him to get lost, but he simply didn't want to go. Not yet. "I feel like I should do something for you, Sara. I haven't thanked you properly for taking me in. I must've put you to a lot of trouble."

"No trouble at all." A touch of anxiety colored her voice. "Really. It was nothing."

"Well, thank you anyway—and thanks for breakfast. It was delicious."

Her shrug was almost a shudder. "Nothing special. As you can see, I'm used to feeding a crowd."

"They're an interesting bunch." Jerden leaned back against the counter while she rinsed the last of the dishes. "It's nice to see you don't have anything against hiring an assortment of different species."

She paused, eyeing him curiously. "The way the nonhumans outnumber Terrans on this world, nobody can afford to be choosy, or to have any prejudices. Granted, there aren't many Norludians or Rutarans around, but variety is the sort of thing immigrants have to expect." Her eyes narrowed sharply. "Are you suggesting that I *am* prejudiced against them, or that I *should* be?"

"No. I'm just trying to understand why you left Earth to begin with. Seems an odd thing for a single woman to do—leaving home and family to live here among so many different aliens. Makes finding a mate difficult, doesn't it?"

He thought she hesitated. "I liked the idea of being among the first to bring horses to Terra Minor."

"That's it?" He wasn't sure he believed her explanation. It seemed inadequate somehow, not completely answering his question.

"Isn't that enough?"

Jerden shook his head. "My homeworld was a

beautiful place. If it still existed, I would never have left it to come here." He was well aware that many planets fell far short of paradise, but he'd never heard that Earth was one of them. He'd been raised on the idea that it was as near perfect as a world could be. "And there are plenty of horses on Earth. Didn't you like it there?"

She put the last of the plates in the rack to dry. "I liked it just fine, but land like this is hard to come by anymore—at least in my price range. As an established horse breeder and trainer, I got an incredibly good deal on the land here—part of the push for cultural improvements that started up a few years back. There are incentives for artists, craftsmen, and musicians, too."

"Yes, but space travel isn't cheap. Nor is importing horses from halfway across the galaxy."

"True."

When she didn't elaborate, Jerden knew he should shut up and go home, but the need to understand her was overwhelming—baffling, perhaps, but undeniable. He tried to imagine all the reasons a woman would do what she'd done and couldn't come up with any that made sense. "Sure you weren't trying to escape from something? Or, perhaps… some*one*?"

A flicker of emotion crossed her features. "Escape? To Terra Minor?" Her short, mirthless laugh was heavy with sarcasm. "With the immigration regulations as tough as they are, I'm pretty sure I'd never have made it this far if I was on the run from the law."

Frowning, he shook his head. "I didn't mean to imply that you'd broken a law. In fact, you strike me as being law-abiding in the extreme. You didn't come here to be with family, did you?"

"No. Nor was I trying to get away from them." She took a step back, the tight line of her lips displaying her annoyance. "I don't understand why any of this matters to you. Look, I said you could come over and ride Danuban whenever you liked. If I'd known you were going to—" she paused as though searching for the right word, "*interrogate* me about my lifestyle choices, I wouldn't have made the offer."

"You could have sold me that horse and chances are I'd have never darkened your door again. Instead, you refused to sell, preferring to keep him." Jerden didn't have to look in the mirror to know he was the sort of man most women found attractive. Drania's reaction was fairly typical. How Sara could be so… *uncaring* that such a man was standing in her kitchen, completely naked, was driving him nuts. "Did you want to keep me, too?"

Her eyes flashed with anger. "No, I didn't. In fact, I'd appreciate it if you'd get the hell out of my house and leave me alone!"

He took a step toward her. "Are you *sure* that's what you want me to do?"

The color drained from her face. Jerden couldn't tell if it was because of what he'd said or his nearness. One thing he knew for certain, she was feeling no desire whatsoever.

"If you think you can frighten me into selling you my stallion, you've got another think coming. I will *not* be intimidated by you or anyone else."

"I'm not trying to scare you, Sara," Jerden said gently. "I'm just trying to understand you."

"You don't *need* to understand me. It's not important."

"It is to me. Don't ask me why, but it is."

"There's nothing to understand," she insisted. "I raise horses and roses. That's all you need to know."

"I find that hard to believe. There's more to you than that. I can feel it."

Her brow rose in a skeptical arch. "What about you? Why don't you tell me more about yourself? Until today, you've probably only said ten words to me. Now that you've mysteriously collapsed on my porch, spent two nights in my bed, and had breakfast in my house, you want me to tell you my deepest secrets? It hardly seems fair."

"Maybe so, but I'm still curious. Tell me your secrets, Sara. I'd be willing to bet I'll understand exactly how you feel."

She stood gaping at him for a moment. She obviously didn't believe him, but for a second there, he thought she might actually break down and confide in him. Instead, she picked up a dish towel and dried her hands. "I haven't *got* any secrets. You want to know why I'm living out here all alone? Because I *like* it. I like not having anyone trying to run my life, bullying me into doing stuff I don't want to do, and questioning every decision I make." She stopped and took a deep breath. "You know something else? I liked you a whole lot better when you weren't quite so nosy. You're starting to remind me of Nate."

Assuming that Nate was the man he'd seen when he'd ridden into her barn, he couldn't help but grin. "Oh, I hope not. You probably won't believe it, but if I'm nosy, it's because I'm in a lot better shape now than I was just a few days ago. Still kinda fucked up, but better."

"I'm glad to hear it," she said bluntly. "Now, do me a favor and go home."

He put up a hand. "Really, Sara. I didn't mean to upset you. I'm just... intrigued."

"Why? Because I'm not drooling all over you the way Drania does? Because I'm not begging you to stay?"

"Partly. And partly because you smell so... neutral."

"Neutral? What the devil does that mean?"

"I mean, you *don't* want me. And you should. It's... bizarre. I've never encountered a neutral female scent before. There should be an underlying scent of desire, even if you don't particularly like *me*. I smell it on every human female I've ever met—and not all of them were my clients. I don't mean to sound cocky or conceited; I'm just trying to understand."

"Well, don't bother. It is what it is. Get over it."

"What if I don't want to?"

"That's your choice. Just leave me out of it." She was still looking at him but carefully avoiding his eyes.

"Someone really got to you, didn't they?"

Her chin went up. "I don't know what you're talking about."

He edged closer. She stepped back. "You see? You can deny it, but it's so ingrained, so automatic, you don't even notice it." He shook his head sadly. "I bet I could kiss you, and your scent *still* wouldn't change."

Jerden was wrong about that, but he didn't need her scent to gauge her emotions, nor did he need to kiss her. The look in her eyes was quite enough. She was absolutely terrified.

"You have no need to fear me, Sara. I won't hurt you. I can promise you that." Cocking his head to one side, he attempted to recapture her gaze. He was only able to hold it for an instant before she glanced away again. "But someone else did."

Her voice came out as a rough whisper. "Please go away."

He studied her face for a long moment, then nodded. "I will. But I won't go far. You gave me help when I needed it. I'll do the same for you. Anytime. Remember that."

Without another word, Jerden turned and walked out the back door, the leopard following silently in his wake. Sara grappled with her emotions, desperately fighting to regain the control she'd lost. Stumbling to the table, she sat down, reaching for her cup. She was thankful that the tea was still hot, because she was freezing. Cold chills permeated her body; her hands and feet were like ice, and shivers racked her limbs.

How had he broken through her defenses so easily? If only she'd been able to ignore his nearness and the fact that he read her so clearly. Then she wouldn't feel as though he'd seen her more than just naked, wouldn't feel as though he'd examined her *soul*.

The clatter of hoofbeats sounded from the stable yard. So, he'd opted to ride home, rather than walk. She couldn't fault him for that and only wondered if the horse would come back without him.

That thought hung suspended in space—not quite a wish, but not quite a hope, either. Did she *want* the stud to come back alone? Or did she want to see him come galloping across the field with the Zetithian astride him? If she sold Danuban to Jerden, would he truly never darken her door again? Would it be worth it? Would she regret the loss of one? Or both?

No, she decided. She was not giving up the one simply to rid herself of the other. She'd worked long and hard for that horse. Giving up was not an option. Considering Danuban's affinity for Jerden, sharing the stallion was the only practical solution. The trick would be spending time in Jerden's company without losing control again. Perhaps she'd get better with it in time.

Or perhaps I'd find I don't need that control. Jerden had promised she had nothing to fear from him and that he would never hurt her. Trust was the issue. If she trusted him, she needn't fear him.

He trusted me. When he was sick, he'd come to her, landing on her doorstep, undoubtedly knowing he would be unconscious for days. He'd been completely helpless, yet had surrendered himself to her care. She would've had a very hard time doing that herself. Fortunately, she hadn't needed anyone's help very often, and certainly not to that extent. Rarely ill, she had seldom been injured—not that working with horses didn't carry with it an inherent risk.

As she sipped her tea, her nerves began to settle. It seemed that Jerden would've liked to be a calming influence on her, yet he was the one thing that disturbed her the most. Nate was simply annoying. She could brush him off and ignore him without too much trouble. Jerden was a different story.

It was difficult to admit, even to herself, but she liked him. He'd fit in well with the others; their conversation had even made her laugh. He'd laughed too. She liked the sound of it—even liked the way he looked when he smiled. *Funny, when he's not here, I like him just fine.*

"You're being silly, Sara." Her voice was stronger

now, and her heartbeat had returned to a normal pace. For a moment or two, it had hammered so hard and fast she'd felt almost faint. He'd been too close. When their eyes met in laughter, she'd felt the kind of camaraderie she'd never experienced with a man whom she actually saw as a man. As a rule, she got along well with Reutal and could laugh along with him, even though he was a male and always ready with a suggestive remark. He was easily tolerated. She wasn't sure what the difference was.

No, the difference was quite simple: Norludians were unattractive. Zettunans were gorgeous. Period. The one she took seriously; the other, she didn't.

Had he actually offered to kiss her? Mentally reviewing what he'd said, she couldn't say for certain, but the idea was exciting, if somewhat disturbing. "Better get a grip, Sara. He sure as hell won't kiss you now."

Swallowing the last of her tea, she got up and headed out to the barn. It was going to be a very long day. Best to get started and get it over with.

—◦◦◦—

Drania was turning the yearlings out in the south pasture when Sara stepped out onto the porch. She felt a thrill, just as she would watching any herd of horses, as they galloped up the hill. Danuban and Jerden were nowhere in sight.

"I am *not* looking for him," she muttered. If she told herself that enough, she might actually start believing it. Bonnie was right. Jerden on a horse was *definitely* a sight worth seeing, if only for the novelty. If nothing else, she'd like to know his secret for riding as well as he did without the benefit of clothing or tack.

Arriving at the barn, she took Yusuf out of his stall and cross-tied him in the aisle. After a quick grooming session, she saddled him up and headed out to the arena. The dark gray Arab was nearly four years old and had shown promise from birth. Unfortunately, he'd been a bit of a behavior problem, or she would never have gelded him. She had to remind herself from time to time that not every horse of hers had significant breeding potential, but it bugged her to rule out the possibility.

Still, most buyers of riding horses wanted geldings. They had the power of the male without the aggressiveness of a stud or the moodiness of a mare. But they weren't without personality. Some were more willing than others. Some, like Yusuf, were simply a little crazy.

With all the exuberance of youth, he fidgeted with the bit, wanting to run. Sara had worked hard trying to get him to relax and had finally managed to get him to canter from the walk—*and* on the correct lead—when the day really turned sour. She glanced up to see Nate Wolmack at the far end of the arena, his muscular arms draped over the top rail.

Squinting against the sun while the breeze ruffled his blond locks, he nodded when he caught her eye. "That's some pretty fancy riding, Sara."

Yeah, right. "Thanks."

"Heard that Zetithian was here again. Conked out in your bed too."

Sara gritted her teeth in annoyance. "He was sick, but he's better now. He went home this morning."

"Sick, huh?" Nate snorted his skepticism. "I wouldn't have thought that bastard would have to use such a weak ploy to get into a woman's bed."

Sara had been riding toward Nate, but after his irritating comment, she asked Yusuf for a quick turn on the haunches and headed back in the other direction. *He wants fancy riding, he'll get fancy riding.*

Unfortunately, that was the extent of Yusuf's cooperation for the day. He flat-out refused to canter on the opposite lead and gave a little kick to prove it. Sara tried again. One more kick. Settling for a shoulder-out at the trot, she nudged him into a leg yield, which he actually performed correctly, moving sideways as well as forward across the arena. Reaching the corner, she asked for a collected trot on the short end and then an extended trot as they turned down the long side. Yusuf, for once, gave it his all. *Guess I just have to be pissed at Nate to get him to behave.*

She collected the trot again as she approached Nate, opting for a shoulder-in so she didn't have to look at him, but switched to a shoulder-out as another thought occurred to her. "How did you know he was here?"

Nate shrugged as she and Yusuf swept past. "I dunno. You know how it is. Word gets around."

Sara couldn't imagine any of those people she'd actually told about Jerden's "visit" spreading the word— much less telling Nate. Had he been spying on her? Her annoyance level tripled, spiced with a healthy measure of fear. The mere thought of Nate watching her made her nape prickle and her stomach twist into knots. *Don't draw undue attention to it, Sara. Just let it drop.* Good advice if only she could follow it.

She found herself wishing Jerden had stayed. A naked man coming out her door right about now should have been enough to convince Nate that he'd been outgunned.

Sara pressed her lips together, suppressing a giggle. She'd never seen Nate's dick, but she was willing to bet that Jerden's would put it to shame.

Oh, God. Now I'm thinking like a Norludian! She glanced at her watch. Yusuf's workout had gone on long enough. She had other horses that needed riding. Dropping the reins, she let him stretch his neck and walk to cool down a bit. "Well, like I said. He went home this morning. No biggie."

Nate grimaced. "You start letting him hang around all the time and people will talk."

Why this could possibly matter to anyone was beyond Sara's comprehension. "What, you think having Jerden drop by now and then will keep anyone from buying horses from me?"

"Maybe not, but you know how it is. People like to gossip."

At the moment, the only one guilty of gossiping was Nate himself, but Sara chose not to point that out to him. "So?"

"So, some men might get the idea that they can spend the night with you anytime they want."

She burst out laughing. "I doubt it. And just in case you're wondering—though it's really none of your business—he might have been in my bed, but he was unconscious the whole time. He only woke up this morning. Then he had breakfast and went home." She thought it best not to mention that he'd mopped the floor. "Don't make such a big deal out of it."

"I'm only thinking of your reputation. I wouldn't want to see it ruined."

"My *reputation*? You sound like something straight

out of the Dark Ages. What about you? Won't people talk because *you've* been hanging around?"

"That's different. You and I share a common interest. We're both horse breeders."

"And Jerden is my closest neighbor." At the moment, she wished he was more than that. Perhaps she *should* claim to be Jerden's lover. At least it might get Nate off her back—might even get Bonnie to stop trying to play matchmaker. Bonnie had been subtle about it, but this wasn't the first time someone had tried to fix Sara up with a man. She knew the signs all too well.

Then it occurred to her that if she and Jerden *pretended* to be romantically involved, it might satisfy all of those who wanted them to get together and also eliminate the pestering attentions of those who were trying to nab Jerden as a husband. Sara only had Nate to avoid, but Jerden had captured the fancy of quite a few ladies in the region, not the least of whom was Salan. Just because he didn't get out much didn't mean the local women didn't know there was an unattached Zetithian living in the neighborhood. The gossip grapevine being what it was, they were bound to get wind of his recovery, too. Ulla probably wasn't the only female visitor he'd had—especially since he rarely seemed to bother getting dressed.

As she dismounted and headed toward the gate, Nate walked toward her, setting off the usual cold tightness in her chest, the worst she'd ever experienced. Suddenly, she wanted nothing more than to have Jerden near her— somehow she had an idea that his solid warmth would banish the chill that now permeated her being. Odd that she hadn't felt that way when he'd actually *been* there.

Perhaps it was Jerden's reassurance that she had nothing to fear from him that made the difference. *And, stupid me, I insisted that he leave.* Jerden would be more than a match for Nate. He could get rid of Nate for her. Then she realized what the difference was between the two men. When Nate was there, she felt the need for Jerden's... protection. But she certainly didn't want Nate when Jerden was around.

Oh, God, why does it have to be one or the other? Can't they both just leave me be?

Unlatching the gate, she led Yusuf out of the arena, intending to head straight for the barn. Zatlen would have the next horse ready for her, which meant that she wouldn't be alone with Nate. She also considered yelling for Reutal and Drania. Reutal's comments always irritated Nate. No, she didn't need Jerden. She could handle this situation. She'd managed it before. She could do it again.

Unfortunately, Nate was a little too quick for her and now stood between her and the barn. "I might be your closest neighbor soon." His eyes raked up and down her body, intensifying the numbing cold in her heart. "I've got an offer in for the land behind your farm. Between the two of us we could have quite a spread."

"What makes you think I'd go into business with you? I'm perfectly happy with what I've got here."

"I'm not looking for a purely *business* partnership, Sara." He took a step closer. "I think we could be very happy together. I'd like the opportunity to prove it to you."

At that moment, he went from being simply annoying to downright frightening. He'd never been quite that close or quite so blatant, and her experience with Jerden had her feeling more vulnerable than usual. Sara's knees began to wobble, and Yusuf chose that particular moment to give her a nudge from behind, sending her staggering toward Nate. He caught her in his arms. "You see? Even that horse thinks we should be together."

A scream bubbled up from her lungs but caught in her throat as Nate bent his head toward her. As his breath touched her face, her vision darkened and a buzzing sound filled her ears. In another moment, his lips covered hers, his tongue demanding entry. She struggled in his grasp, somehow finding the strength to push him away. Or attempted to. Sara was a strong woman, but Nate was taller and significantly stronger. His hand gripped the back of her head, holding her while he ravaged her mouth with his kiss. Growing weaker by the second, she heard the roar of distant thunder as her consciousness slipped away.

Chapter 9

JERDEN MAY HAVE LEFT SARA'S HOUSE AS SHE'D ASKED, but he had no intention of staying away for long. Something about her kept drawing him back, and it wasn't just curiosity about her lack of scent. He rode back toward her barn, wishing he'd never left. Naturally long-sighted, when he saw the man he'd assumed was Nate standing in front of Sara, his irritation level skyrocketed. When she wound up in his arms, Jerden was about to vow never to set foot on Sara's property ever again until he realized she wasn't a willing participant. Was *this* why she'd been so afraid when he'd gotten too close to her himself? As if he understood the need for speed, Danuban surged forward across the open field. Jerden had sense enough to back off when a woman fought against him, but apparently this idiot didn't know any better. Jerden was about to enlighten him in a way he wouldn't soon forget.

The stallion slid to a halt, and Jerden leaped to the ground. Snatching Sara into his arms, he gave her assailant a shove that sent him sprawling and fought the urge to sink his fangs into the man's throat. Cria advanced slowly, her growl indicating that she would've liked to do the same.

"What the hell are you doing?" Jerden snarled.

"I just kissed her and she... fainted."

Jerden could barely contain his anger enough to

speak. "And that's *all* you did to her?" Sara was ghostly pale beneath her tan as he smoothed her hair back from her damp forehead. Even unconscious, she was beautiful. Just once, he would have liked to have held her when she was awake.

"I've never touched her before this. I had no idea she would react that way."

"Well, now you know," Jerden said bluntly. "I suggest you leave her alone."

Recovering quickly, Nate got to his feet with a mocking smile. "So, you *are* staking a claim on her. That's funny, I wouldn't think a *decent* woman would want anything to do with a fucking man-whore like you."

Reutal came running up the path from the main barn, his flippers slapping the bare dirt. "What's going on?" he demanded, his eyes darting back and forth between the two men as though he didn't know which of them he wanted to deck first.

"This idiot kissed her," Jerden said with a nod toward his adversary.

"What does it take to get it through your thick skull, Nate?" Reutal snapped. "She doesn't *like* you."

"She could have slapped the shit out of me if she didn't like me," Nate countered. "She didn't have to faint."

"No one *chooses* to faint," Reutal scolded. "You must've scared her to death. It's all your fault."

Jerden had heard enough. "I'm taking her inside."

Reutal nodded. "Yes. Best to get her out of the sun."

As he strode toward the house holding Sara snuggly against his chest, he heard Nate say, "Doesn't that barbarian *ever* wear pants?"

Reutal barked a laugh. "Hey, if you had a dick like that, would *you* ever wear pants?"

Jerden never heard Nate's reply. He knew he should've stopped in the kitchen for some cold water to bring her around, but she felt so damn good in his arms, he hoped she'd be out for at least an hour. Heading straight for the bedroom, he put her on the bed and lay down beside her. With her head resting against his chest, he pressed a kiss to her temple, wishing he could hold her like this every night. A moment later he realized he was purring.

Sleep on, Sara. I'll keep you safe.

Kissing her again, he paused to lick the side of her face. The taste of fear still lingered on her skin, but, as before, her underlying scent fascinated him. He longed to free her of the bonds that trapped her desire and held it prisoner. Wanted to feel her hands on his body, caressing him as he caressed her. Hearing her soft sighs and moans of pleasure would be like music to his ears. Wooing her would be slow and uncertain, but the end results would be glorious; he was certain of it. Unfortunately, thus far, they seemed to get along better when one of them was unconscious.

Jerden wasn't surprised that he felt this need, this *compulsion* to bring Sara back from the solitary hell where she kept her passions locked down with no hope of escape. After all, bringing women pleasure had been his whole life up until a few months ago. It was what he did—his calling—but there was more to it than that. He wanted to rescue her, be her knight in shining armor, her hero. He wanted her to be a lover, and not Nate's lover or anyone else's. He wanted her to be *his* lover.

She wasn't alone in feeling unloved. Jerden had been

admired for his body, his looks, his sexual prowess, and his skill. If he'd ever been truly loved, he wasn't aware of it. Women wanted the pleasure he could give them, but he'd never been loved for himself. Sara felt no desire for him, but friends had become lovers before this. Had he ever had a woman who was truly a friend? He wasn't sure. Sex always got in the way.

Sighing, he realized that the best way to keep her from getting nervous was to put on a pair of pants. The loincloth he'd worn on his first visit to her farm probably wasn't enough. On Rhylos, he'd never worn anything. If he was out on the street, his nudity was good advertising, aside from the fact that clothing was optional everywhere on that world. Even so, he was pretty sure he had a pair of cutoff jeans somewhere. He vaguely remembered having worn them when he arrived on Terra Minor aboard his friend Dax's starship, the *Valorcry*. The ship's droid, Kots, had given them to him. Craving the feel of the sun on his back, he'd drawn the line at wearing a shirt, and he saw no need to start wearing one now. All he had to cover were his genitals. He smiled to himself, thinking that Drania might object when she couldn't see his ass anymore.

He liked Drania, but her needs weren't the issue. Sara was the only one he needed to consider right now. Becoming a part of her life was his goal. Being her lover would be the reward.

She raised roses and horses. He knew next to nothing about either of those things. But he would learn. He had lots of money and nothing to spend it on. He would ask her advice. Seek her out for her knowledge. She wouldn't turn him away if he asked her which roses to plant or what horses to buy. She thought Danuban was fancy. He would find out what sort of horses to import—some that would knock her socks off and make her want to hang around his place. He'd build a stable and fences. He'd buy a computer and a speeder. He'd get out more. He'd do the research and the work. She was his nearest neighbor. Hell, he'd borrow eggs or flour from her if he had to.

He'd become more sociable. He'd have a party. Invite her and all the neighbors to a cookout by the lake. Maybe Dax and Tarq could come. Even Onca, if he could be persuaded to take time off from the brothel. Bonnie and Lynx and their children would surely join the party. He'd even invite the milkmaid, Salan, who seemed to have the hots for him. He wouldn't oblige her—couldn't, in fact—but it wouldn't kill him to be more… neighborly. He might even invite Nate.

Somehow, some way, he and Sara would become buddies. Later, when she trusted him, he could take it to the next level.

If he was lucky, his dick might even be back to normal by then.

Soft laughter awakened her. Feeling heat and vibration, Sara opened her eyes to find Jerden gazing down at her with eyes that smiled. "I thought it would be best to let you wake up on your own, rather than throwing cold water in your face."

"Thanks, I appreciate that." His warmth and purring soothed her for a moment—until she remembered why she'd fainted to begin with. "Where's Nate?"

"Don't know and don't particularly care." Chuckling

softly, he added, "He left pretty quickly. I think I scared him a little."

"I certainly hope so. He scared the shit out of me." She paused, running a hand through her cropped curls. "He's always rubbed me the wrong way, but he's never gotten that close before. I... couldn't take it."

Jerden gave her a squeeze, drawing attention to the fact that he had his arms around her. She made a conscious decision not to draw away from him, focusing on how it felt, rather than any past memories it might dredge up. She had to admit that his nearness felt... good. Funny how Jerden naked bothered her less than Nate fully clothed. *Perhaps it's because Jerden only* mentioned *kissing me and never actually tried it.* Bonnie had also said he couldn't function sexually anymore, which meant he was relatively safe. Odd that she'd hadn't made that connection before.

She'd been wishing for Jerden from the moment she spotted Nate. Had he heard her thoughts and come galloping to her rescue? Or had he simply happened upon the scene when he returned from his ride? Either way, she was very glad he hadn't stayed home.

"Looks like you could use a bodyguard. I'd be happy to volunteer."

She could hear the smile in his tone and knew he was teasing her, but he was probably fishing for an apology, too. And she owed him one. "Guess I shouldn't have told you to get lost. Sorry about that."

He gave her another hug. "Believe me, I understand completely. There was a time when I never wanted to see another person again myself. But I'm getting over it."

Sara wasn't nearly as optimistic, but at least she wasn't feeling quite so terrified when Jerden got close to her. She wasn't so sure about anyone else. Maybe Jerden was the only one. "I'm glad to hear it. Bonnie and Lynx have been very worried about you."

"I know. And I'm going to thank them and everyone else for their concern. I'm going to throw a big party for all my friends and neighbors."

Sara couldn't completely suppress her shudder. "Nate, too?"

"Actually, I think it might be a good idea—you know, face the enemy head on? You just stick close to me and he won't bother you."

She tried not to think about what sticking close to him might entail. "I take it that means I'm invited?"

He nodded. "You, Drania—and her boyfriend if she likes—Reutal, and Zatlen."

Sara hated to decline, but she also didn't like the idea of leaving her horses unattended. "I'm not sure all of us should go."

"If you're worried about the horses, your stable hands can come in shifts. But I want *you* there the whole time."

She quirked an eyebrow at him. "What are we now? Joined at the hip?"

"Not exactly." He grinned wickedly. "I need a hostess."

"Ah. I see. I'll be there so the single women attending won't feel threatened by your, um, maleness?"

His burst of laughter thrilled her to her toes. *What is it about him?*

"Don't worry. I've decided I need to start wearing at least *some* clothes. I keep forgetting I'm not on Rhylos anymore."

An image of Jerden wearing boots and breeches flashed through her mind, making her gasp. *Whoa...* "That's probably a good idea, and I'm sure Drania's boyfriend would appreciate it. I doubt if he could compete with you."

"Why, Sara! Does that mean *you* think I have a really hot ass too?"

Sara eyed him askance. "I don't think that's what I said."

"But it was implied. I think you like me better than you'll admit." He dropped a kiss on her forehead and then got up so quickly she didn't have time to react. She heard him rattling ice cubes in the kitchen and moments later, he returned with a glass of iced tea. "Here. Drink this. It'll make you feel better."

Sara swung her legs over the side of the bed and sat up, a little surprised that her head didn't swim. "Thanks." She downed half the tea without stopping for breath, feeling the icy refreshment coursing through her limbs.

He held out a hand. Without thinking, she placed her hand in his, and he pulled her to her feet. "There's something else I'd like to discuss with you—maybe over dinner sometime."

Dinner? "Oh, and what's that?"

"I've been thinking of importing some horses. Maybe some like yours or something different. I don't know a damn thing about them, but I'm sure you could advise me."

She gave him a blank stare. "You mean you want to start up a breeding farm?"

He nodded. "Yeah. I really like what you've done with

your place. I'm not sure about raising feed and such, but I wouldn't mind having some horses."

"Well... you could buy hay and feed from me or Bonnie and Lynx. As for what kind of horses you should get, I'm not—" She stopped abruptly as she pictured something else. *Jerden on a Friesian. Holy shit...* "I know just the breed you need. I'd raise them myself, but I can't afford any more horses for a while yet." She gave him a sly grin. "I hear you're rolling in dough."

"Burning a hole in my pocket." He glanced down at his groin. "At least, it would be if I had any pockets to put it in. Speaking of which, if I'm going to be out and about more, I probably ought to get something to wear."

Sara let her gaze follow his and smiled wistfully. "I doubt if I'll recognize you with pants on."

"I'll be sure to introduce myself or—better yet—you could go with me to pick them out."

"I suppose I could," she said, chewing on a fingernail. "I was planning to go into town this afternoon—it's market day." She drew in a fortifying breath. "Would you like to come along?"

"Absolutely." Chuckling, he steered her toward the door with a hand pressed against the small of her back. "In the meantime, let's get you back on a horse where you belong."

Letting him guide her without question, she was halfway to the barn before she realized what he'd done. Or rather, what she'd *let* him do. *He's telling me what to do and pushing me around—sort of. And it didn't make me mad. How weird...*

Perhaps it was simply because he was Zetithian. She wasn't sure, but whatever it was, those brief moments of closeness had felt… nice. Certainly nothing like the way she'd felt with Nate, and *especially* not the way she'd felt when that boy had forced himself on her.

Go ahead and use the correct word, Sara. He hadn't merely tried to kiss her, he'd *raped* her. Every time a man got close, the panic, the total loss of control, overwhelmed her again.

That trauma had occurred such a long time ago. *Why am I still affected by it? Why can't I let it go?*

She had no answers to those questions. But for the first time since that assault, she could almost see a ray of hope. Faint, perhaps, but hope, nonetheless.

After lunch, Sara and Jerden set out for Nimbaza. She half expected him to insist on driving, but he simply climbed in the passenger side just as Cria jumped into the back. Sara chuckled to herself, thinking that Nate would *never* have relinquished the driver's seat.

Jerden gave her a curious look. "Should we leave Cria at home?"

"I didn't think that was an option." There were some things you simply didn't argue about with a leopard. "Actually, the reason I'm laughing is because I'm surprised you're letting me drive."

"Why not? Don't you know how?" His teasing grin took her by surprise, as much for its seductive glint as its genial nature. Most guys took piloting a speeder very seriously.

"Oh, you know how men are. They never seem to think a woman is capable of anything."

Jerden snorted a laugh. "On Zetith, that kind of

attitude could get a man blackballed from touching a woman for the rest of his life."

"Wow. Really?"

"Really. Our society isn't like that of humans. You'd probably call us all beta males as opposed to alpha, but what we really are is a woman's equal. Each sex is equally deserving of respect, and no one has the right to impose their will on anyone else."

Sara reflected on thousands of years of human history. If any social group had ever been based on total equality of the sexes, she'd never heard of it. Matriarchal or patriarchal, perhaps, but never entirely equal. "Sounds nice."

As his smile faded, Sara could almost see the memories flowing through his mind. "It was. At least, what I remember of it. My father practically worshipped my mother, and she adored him. There was never any question of one being stronger than the other. My father was more powerful physically, perhaps, but he never used that strength against her—only in support of her."

Tears welled up in Sara's eyes. "That's the way it should be." If only it *had* been, her life would have been so different. Starting the engine, she raised the windshield and slid her finger up the control panel for maximum acceleration. She left the canopy open, allowing the rushing wind to dry her tears—or perhaps explain them.

Jerden left it at that, and Sara made no further comments, preferring to keep her thoughts to herself. She wondered if letting her pilot the speeder was his way of allowing her to remain in control of the situation. True, the vehicle belonged to her, but his actions made her feel as though he truly did consider her to be his equal and saw no need to establish dominance—something she found both refreshing and reassuring.

As they approached the dairy, she gave a nod toward the house. "Look who it is." Salan stood in front of the rustic farmhouse on the hillside above them, smiling and waving, her long blonde tresses wafting in the breeze. "Guess we ought to stop and say hello, huh?"

Jerden grimaced. "If you say so."

"I know she's been a bit of a pest, but she *is* a neighbor of ours. If you're gonna break her heart, you should at least be nice about it."

He blew out a breath. "I'll try. But I could sure use some help discouraging her. Do you think maybe you and I could *pretend* to be interested in each other? Just for show?"

Since Sara had already given this idea some thought she didn't automatically refuse. "I scratch your back and you'll scratch mine?"

"Something like that."

He'd already come to her rescue once. She owed him one. "I'll see what I can do."

There was no mistaking Salan's delight as they drew nearer. "Hi, Jerden!" she called out as Sara brought the speeder to a halt. "I heard you've been sick. It's good to see you up and about. You look fabulous."

"Thanks." Jerden gave Salan a perfunctory smile, then shot a beseeching look at Sara.

"Um, we were just going into town to do a little shopping," Sara said. Unfortunately, she had no idea what she ought to say or do next, and wound up stating the obvious. "Jerden needs some clothes."

That sounded pretty stupid.

It also gave Salan the perfect opening. With a coy smile, she leaned forward, crossing her arms to rest them on the side of the speeder—a posture that put her ample bosom right in front of Jerden's face. Her luminous eyes roamed over his bare torso, registering a hint of disappointment when they drifted down to the loincloth. "I'm not so sure about that." Her gaze flicked back to Jerden's face. "Like I said, you look fabulous."

It's now or never… "Of course he does," Sara conceded. "But you know how it is. I'd rather be the only one who gets to see him undressed."

Salan recoiled as though she'd been slapped. "What? You mean you two are *dating* now?"

To Sara's relief, Jerden spoke up. "Absolutely. Sara is the most fascinating woman I've ever met." With a sidelong glance that was as wicked as his tone, he reached over and ran his hand up the full length of her thigh. "And by far the sexiest."

Sara sat gaping at him for a long moment. He obviously expected her to say something similar about him, but his hand on her leg had scattered her wits completely. Even after he brought her back to her senses with a gentle squeeze, the best she could do was to echo Drania's opinions. "He's such a… a hunk, and he's got a terrific ass." *There. That oughta do it…*

Salan's lower lip quivered as though she were about to cry. "Oh. Oh, I *see*… But when did all this happen? I thought you and Nate Wolmack were an item."

Sara snorted a laugh. "You must've heard that from Nate."

Frowning, Salan brushed an errant tendril back from her face. "Well, yeah…"

"There isn't a particle of truth in it," Sara said firmly. "Unless it's in his own mind. I've *never* been interested in Nate."

Salan's eyes darted toward Jerden and then back to Sara. She shook her head slowly. "He's really gonna be pissed."

"Not much he can do about it now," Sara said. At least she hoped he couldn't. After their last encounter, she wouldn't put anything past him.

"Besides, I'm pretty sure he already knows," Jerden added. "Or at least suspects it. You're the first person we've actually told."

A grimace marred Salan's lovely face. "My, how ironic."

Even though Sara knew exactly what she meant, she also knew that playing dumb was sometimes the best tactic — and certainly the kindest. "How so?"

"Nothing. Never mind." She sighed. "I won't keep you any longer. Have fun shopping." With a halfhearted wave, Salan turned and headed back to the house, her shoulders slumped and her head hanging low.

Jerden's fervent *Thank the gods* as they resumed their journey had Sara giggling like a schoolgirl. "She didn't look a bit happy, did she? Maybe she and Nate will get together and commiserate. With any luck, they might actually *stay* together."

"I wouldn't bet on it." Jerden gave her thigh another squeeze. "That wasn't so hard, was it?"

Sara might've agreed if her heartbeat had been a little steadier. "Speak for yourself. I'm surprised she believed any of it."

"Most people will believe anything they see. All we have to do is act the part."

"I suppose so." Keeping her eyes on the road ahead, she added, "You might have to give me some pointers, though. I'm not very good at that sort of thing."

"I'll keep that in mind."

They left the rolling hills of the dairy farm to fly by Bonnie's carefully tended fields, then on past Nate's land. Beyond noting that his pastures needed mowing and the fence looked a little worse for wear, Sara dismissed him entirely and certainly had no intention of stopping by to ask if he had any new foals.

The road stretched on over the northern spur of the mountains where the rocky terrain defied any attempts at cultivation. Nothing but iron grass, gorse, and juluva grew there. A wild, harsh-looking country, it was inhabited mostly by carrion birds and the hardy goatlike tempets. At least, that was all Sara had ever seen whenever she'd passed through that region.

She glanced at the rear viewscreen and caught sight of Cria's yellow eyes staring back at her. "Do you suppose Cria came from these mountains?"

"She may have," Jerden replied with a shrug. "I don't really know. She just showed up one day."

"Leopards are pretty rare around here. In fact, she's the only one I've ever seen—and she doesn't look like the indigenous variety, either. Maybe she wandered off the way Danuban did."

"Could be. I seem to be quite adept at collecting strays."

Cria stretched forward to nuzzle Jerden's shoulder as though she knew he was talking about her. Reaching up, he scratched behind her ear. If Sara had ever felt weak or unprotected, she certainly shouldn't feel that way now. Not with *two* big cats to escort her.

Jerden still made her nervous, though. She didn't see him as a threat—at least not as much as she had before—but she was a long way from feeling completely comfortable with him. She reminded herself that he was there to help and protect her. He wouldn't hurt her.

At least, not intentionally.

Chapter 10

MARKET DAY WAS IN FULL SWING WHEN SARA AND Jerden arrived in Nimbaza's main square. With stalls selling everything from enock eggs to fine fabrics and speeder parts, Sara was sure they could find something for Jerden to wear. Unfortunately, she had trouble picturing him in anything but his loincloth. Still, it was the rare hunk who didn't look like a million credits in a pair of low-slung jeans, whether he wore a shirt or not.

Considering Jerden's reputation, Sara probably should've expected the odd stares directed at him. Furtive glances, scuttling footsteps, muttering, and quickly averted eyes when they were caught looking seemed to be the norm. She couldn't understand the reason until she overheard two Davordian women say something about a crazy wildcat. Clearly, these two women weren't deterred by the rumors of Jerden's madness, for they gazed at him with unabashed admiration while others gave him a wide berth—though the fact that Cria followed him like a shadow might have had something to do with it.

Leopard or not, Sara was starting to get annoyed. She was about to yell *"Boo!"* at a couple of gawkers when Lynx called out to them from their booth. "Hey, Jerden! It's good to see you looking so well."

Lynx didn't seem to notice anything strange about Sara and Jerden being there together. Bonnie, however, eyed them with entirely too much interest.

"I'm feeling better than I have in a long time," Jerden replied. "And I have this lovely lady to thank for it."

Sara gasped in surprise as he took her hand and pressed it to his lips. She hadn't expected him to continue the ruse unless Nate or Salan were present. Making Bonnie think they were lovers was dangerous. Knowing her, she'd probably start planning a wedding.

Bonnie's eyes might have been as round as saucers, but Jerden's actions certainly had the desired effect on the Davordians. As if on cue, the two women wilted, letting out dejected sighs.

Unfortunately, the Twilanan woman in a nearby booth also overheard him and perked up considerably. "Ah, ha! I thought so!" Hilbransk said with a knowing smile. "If you should find yourself in need of a wedding dress, I have just the thing for you, Sara!" She held up one of the flowing robes favored by her kind, scaled down to human size.

Sara had never worn anything quite so colorful before, but then, she'd never worn white satin, either— nor had anyone ever suggested there might be wedding bells in her future. She stood gaping at Hilbransk for a long moment, then darted a desperate glance at Jerden before stammering her reply. "I—we—that is, neither of us have said anything about getting married. Besides, I can't see myself ever wearing anything that… fancy."

Hilbransk frowned, tapping her tusk contemplatively. "Hold on. I have something else you might like." Delving into the rack at the rear of her shop, she pulled out a plain white sheath with a plunging neckline. The high-collared sleeveless overdress that went with it was made from a filmy fabric dyed in hazy swirls of blue and green, accented with sparkling stars. The back was long enough to form a train.

Sara didn't care for Twilanan fashions as a rule, but this was beautiful. "How come you've never shown me anything like that before?"

Hilbransk laughed, her ornate earrings jingling in merry accompaniment. "You were never in love before, Sara."

Sara's breath caught in her throat. As far as she was concerned, she wasn't in love now. She was about to tell Hilbransk she needed her head examined when Jerden gave her a nudge.

"Uh, maybe so," she admitted. "But I'm still not sure I need a dress like that—at least not right now." She stole a glance at Jerden, who shot her a conspiratorial wink.

"Why don't you try it on?" he suggested.

Her mouth fell open. "I... I guess I could." Sara couldn't remember the last time she'd worn a dress. In fact, she wasn't sure she ever had. Then she made the mistake of looking over at Bonnie, who was grinning like the cat that got the cream.

I will never *live this down...*

The next thing Sara knew, she was standing in the tiny dressing room at the back of Hilbransk's booth, staring at her astonished reflection. If Jerden hadn't spoken, she might have stood there in a dumbfounded trance for days.

"Let's have a look, Sara."

She didn't want him to see her like this. Although the dress fit her perfectly, she felt overexposed, vulnerable. What was it he'd told Salan? That she was fascinating and sexy? She scowled at her reflection. *If he only knew*.

Drawing in a fortifying breath, she pushed back the

curtain. Jerden's eyes swept her from head to toe, set-ting off a fluttering sensation in the pit of her stomach.

"You look like a queen."

Heat flooded her cheeks. "I certainly don't feel like one." Unwilling to meet his gaze, she glanced down at the dress, plucking at the flowing fabric with nervous fingers. "This isn't exactly my style."

"I disagree." Moving closer, he raised her face to his with a finger beneath her chin. "You're a very beautiful woman, Sara—whether you'll admit it or not." Lowering his head, he leaned closer to whisper in her ear. "I think you should buy it."

His breath on her cheek made her chest tighten, and she backed away, clearing her throat with an effort. "I—I don't have any use for a dress like this."

"You never know," he said with an enigmatic smile. "You might need it someday."

Without another word, he turned and walked out of the shop.

Jerden had been warned that he'd acquired a rather dark reputation since his arrival on Terra Minor, and the wary behavior of the townspeople proved it. Unlike his near-celebrity status on Rhylos, he now appeared to have become something of a social pariah.

Time to alter that perception.

Favoring the Twilanan with his most winning smile, he drew a deep-throated chuckle from her as he paid for the dress. Then he headed over to Bonnie and Lynx's booth to wait for Sara, thankful that there were at least two friendly, familiar faces in the crowd.

"You and Sara appear to have reached an understanding," Lynx said as he approached. "When I asked her about selling you that horse, I wasn't sure she'd ever speak to you again."

"Me, either," said Bonnie. "Looks like you've won her over."

"Maybe," Jerden conceded. "Then again, I may have ticked her off just now."

Sara had already changed back into her own clothes and was leaving the shop when the Twilanan woman handed her a bag containing the dress. Scowling, Sara draped the bag over her arm and stalked over to where Jerden stood. "You already *paid* for this?"

"Yes, I did," Jerden replied. Lifting his brow ever so slightly, he met her stormy gaze with one of bland innocence, hoping she'd take the hint.

She glared at him for a moment before comprehension finally struck. "Oh. Well, then… thank you." Her expression lightened briefly before settling back into a frown.

"It's so nice to see you here in town, Jerden," Bonnie said. "I was beginning to think you'd never leave your place again."

Jerden shrugged. "I just needed a little time alone to get back to normal."

"We're here to buy him some clothes," Sara said abruptly. "I really didn't need any," she added in an undertone.

"Well, then, we won't keep you," Lynx said with a wink. "Unless, of course, you need some eggs."

Jerden waited while Sara bought a few items from Bonnie, then they set off in search of a men's clothing shop.

They hadn't gone far when Sara blew out an exasperated breath. "I swear to God, the next person who stares at you like you've got horns and a tail is getting a piece of my mind."

A sidelong glance revealed two Drells shuffling sideways to avoid crossing his path. Generally speaking, Drells didn't step aside for anyone, unless they happened to be shouting obscenities. Drells couldn't stand being sworn at.

"I used to get plenty of looks whenever I walked the streets of Damenk, but the people of Nimbaza apparently see me in a different light."

"Well, if you ask me, it's downright rude," Sara declared. "Maybe you should growl at them."

Jerden chuckled. "Please, Sara. I'm doing my best *not* to act like a beast. Trust me, I've heard the stories—and the names. Savage, barbarian, heathen, wildcat... Bonnie and Lynx have been at great pains to bring it to my attention—probably hoping it would shake me up enough to reform."

"Okay, then, *I'll* do it," she said crossly. "Or maybe we should sic Cria on them."

Jerden glanced down at the leopard, walking silently by his side. "She's much too peace-loving for that. Then again, she might be part of the problem."

"I doubt it," said Sara. "Everyone is looking at *you*, not her."

"Still, I'd rather not provoke an incident." One horrific episode on a crowded street per lifetime was quite enough.

"Suit yourself." Pausing as they reached the corner, she studied the next row of shops. "Maybe we should've asked Lynx where he gets his clothes. I have no idea where to look."

"Don't worry, we'll find something. Who knows? We might even stumble across some classy jewelry for you to wear with that dress."

Sara snorted a laugh. "You are *such* a spendthrift."

"Tightwad," he shot back.

They were both laughing when Jerden glanced up, his gaze meeting that of a woman standing in a doorway across the square—a Davordian woman with wild blue eyes and long dark hair. The impact from that brief eye contact nearly knocked him off his feet. Suddenly, the air in his lungs was too cold and thick to breathe. Then he blinked and she was gone.

Sara tugged at his hand, her brow furrowed with concern. "Are you okay?"

"Yeah," he whispered. "I thought I saw... never mind. It was nothing."

Her lips thinned and her eyes narrowed. "Don't lie to me. What did you see?"

Jerden sucked in a painful breath. "Sorry. I'm not used to talking about this. I get... flashbacks of Audrey's murder sometimes. For a long time afterward, every woman I saw reminded me of either Audrey or her killer." A shudder he couldn't suppress shook his entire body. "The woman I saw just now didn't look like Audrey."

Sara didn't pretend to misunderstand him. "But they caught her, didn't they? She'd be in jail or a mental institution on Rhylos, right?"

Nodding slowly, Jerden continued to stare at the doorway, half expecting the woman to rematerialize out of thin air. "I suppose so. Surely they'd notify me if she escaped or was released."

"And even if she did escape, the odds of her setting foot on this world are astronomical. You know how tough the restrictions are."

Sara's brisk tone cleared his mind better than anything else could. "You're right. I must've imagined her." He grimaced as it hit him that this explanation probably sounded even worse. "Not much better, is it? Either I'm insane or I'm being stalked."

"You're not insane and you're not being stalked. You just saw a woman who reminded you of someone. What did she look like?"

"A Davordian with long dark hair and crazy eyes."

Sara nodded. "There are lots of Davordians living around here. It's not surprising that you should see one who resembles Audrey's killer. You may even see that same woman again sometime."

"I certainly hope not," he declared. "That's the main reason I've been living out in the middle of nowhere and never set foot in town." He raked a hand through his hair, wishing he could rip the memory from his mind. "Damn. I thought I was over that." He studied Sara's clear green eyes—eyes that were steady, sober, and sane. "You were the first woman I'd met since then who didn't remind me of either of them. I looked at your face and only saw you."

For an instant, she seemed stunned but recovered quickly. "You were already improving by then." Her voice was firm, though her eyes wavered, glancing downward. "Don't attach any more meaning to it than that."

"And don't *you* discount your role in my return to

sanity." He cupped her face in his hands, focusing his gaze on hers. "You saved me, Sara. Whether you choose to believe it or not, you *saved* me."

Jerden closed his eyes, leaving only the warmth of her skin against his palms and her scent to identify her. His vision could betray him, but those other senses never had. "Being with you makes me feel almost normal again. You have no idea how much that means to me."

"I might." Her voice sounded choked with emotion. Opening his eyes, he saw tears glistening on her lashes.

The bustling crowd recalled him to their surroundings, dispelling the brief interlude of intimacy. Even so, he vowed never to forget the way she looked at that moment—her understanding smile, the way she tilted her head to lean into his hand, the tears swimming in her eyes.

Brushing away her tears, she attempted a smile. "We'd better get going before somebody fusses at us for loitering."

"Right." Turning, he curled his arm around her waist, noting her lack of protest. "You're getting better at this acting-like-a-couple thing, aren't you?"

"I'm trying—although I wasn't expecting to have to pretend in front of *everybody*. You nearly provoked a quarrel when you bought me that dress."

"Sorry. I probably should've warned you, but I wanted it to be a surprise."

"Oh, you surprised me, all right." She shifted the bags to her other hand. "Guess I should put my arm around you, shouldn't I?"

"Yeah—and you should let me carry those bags."

She handed the bags over without protest, then looped

an arm around him to rest her hand on his hip. Jerden drew her closely to his side, steering her away from where he'd seen that strange woman. He wasn't afraid for himself—the threat to his species from the Nedwut bounty hunters had long since been eliminated—but he couldn't shake the niggling fear that being with him might put Sara in danger. After all, Audrey had been killed while walking beside him on a crowded street...

As his eyes swept the market square, he spotted numerous Zetithian children playing with the offspring of a dozen other species. That fact alone should have reassured him, but he suspected it would be years before crowds ceased to have a disquieting effect, if indeed the memory ever left him completely. In the meantime, he would take no chances. Any crazy Davordian taking potshots at Sara would have to get past him first.

Regardless of Sara's intention to behave as normally as possible finding a shop, helping Jerden pick out clothes, telling him how great he looked in them—a sense of foreboding remained. She doubted that the woman Jerden had seen was actually Audrey's killer. However, the fact that she still haunted him was a little unnerving. Recalling her own lingering fears helped her to place it in the proper context, but she was astonished at how much Jerden's peace of mind concerned her now. That stricken look on his face was one she never wanted to see again.

The afternoon was warm and sunny, and he wore a pair of khaki shorts out of the first store they visited. She'd encouraged him to look at Terran apparel, preferring to avoid the exotic garb offered by the Twilanans and the heavier robes worn by those species that couldn't tolerate the sun. He'd also bought a couple of T-shirts, but in her eyes, they were all wrong for him. Actually, everything he put on seemed out of place—except for the jeans he tried on at the next shop.

He pulled back the fitting room curtain. "What do you think?"

Snug in all the right places, they even made Sara consider grabbing his ass. She could hardly wait to see Drania's reaction. "*Totally* hot."

"Really?" He twisted sideways to get a better look at himself in the mirror.

"Trust me. Women will swoon."

"If I wanted *that* to happen, I wouldn't be buying clothes."

"Can't be helped," she said with a slow wag of her head. "Once everyone realizes you aren't really a hissing, spitting wildcat, women will be panting after you just like they did on Rhylos—and even Cria won't be able to scare them away."

The leopard gave Sara a sly look, as though agreeing with her assessment.

Unzipping the jeans, Jerden skimmed them off. "Does that bother you?"

"Why would it bother me? I mean, we're not *really* dating." She paused, frowning. "Are we?"

He didn't reply immediately, taking a moment to pull on a pair of Paemayan lounging pants. "No, we aren't *really* dating. What about these?"

"Too baggy," she said after a moment's scrutiny. "They make you look like a harem slave."

"According to Lynx, harem slaves don't wear *anything*," Jerden pointed out. "I could wear them around the house."

Sara shrugged. "Suit yourself. They do look comfortable."

His eyes swept over her. "You'd look nice in the female version. Maybe I'll get you a pair for your birthday."

He'd already bought her a dress she'd probably never wear, whether she looked like a queen in it or not. "Don't bother. Besides, my birthday isn't for a couple of months yet." She grimaced. "I'll be thirty-four. Getting plumb old."

Jerden snickered. "I'm thirty-nine, but, trust me, I am *not* getting old."

"Yes, but you Zetithians live longer than humans. Thirty-nine is more like twenty-nine for you, isn't it?"

He nodded. "So, how does it feel to be dating—er, *pretending* to date—a younger man?"

Given the circumstances, his age was irrelevant. "Okay, I guess."

Rolling his eyes, he shot her a sardonic smile. "Think you could curb your enthusiasm?"

"Sorry. If you want enthusiasm, you should talk to my mother. She'd be positively ecstatic to see us together."

"Even though I'm not human?"

Sara's mother had given up on her daughter finding a man so long ago, she would see him as the answer to a prayer, whether he was human or not. "Trust me, she wouldn't care if you were a Norludian."

"What about you? Got a problem hanging around with a Zetithian?"

"Not if you don't mind hanging around with a Terran."

"I think I can do that." Quirking an eyebrow, he stripped off the lounging pants. "So, are we friends now?"

Since Sara had already seen him naked more often than not, she couldn't help chuckling as she glanced at his groin. "I certainly hope so."

━━∕∿∿∖━━

After dropping Jerden off at his place, Sara drove home, wondering what the hell she'd gotten herself into. Although she'd done fairly well in public, the return trip had been characterized by an awkward silence. Jerden didn't seem to be the problem. He was congenial and considerate, but his attempts at small talk had sent her anxiety level skyrocketing. On top of that, she'd never been more confused in her life. Were they a couple in private as well as in public? Could she expect frequent visits from him or would they simply go out on the occasional date to allay suspicion? There *had* to be an easier way to get Nate out of her life. However, short of having him deported, Sara couldn't come up with one.

Later that evening—unable to even *think* about trying to sleep—she lay on the couch with her computer in hand, scrolling through the list of building contractors in the area. She'd gotten a good deal from the company she'd hired to build her barns, but if Jerden's pockets were as deep as she suspected, he could build a real showplace if he wanted to. Sara could help him with that. Most women had ideas for their dream house. Sara's ideas were for a dream *barn*.

Searching for available Friesians was even more fun. With gracefully arched necks and curly manes and tails, Friesians were as big and black and powerful as Jerden himself. Most of the photos she found were three dimensional and could be rotated in any direction. She was drooling over a particularly fine stallion when she heard a tap at the back door.

She glanced at the clock. It was late—long past her usual bedtime and way too late for visitors. "Oh, let me guess," she muttered. "That dratted stallion is gone again."

But it wasn't Zatlen at the door this time. Nor was it Jerden. It was Nate.

And her door wasn't locked. Living out in the boonies as she did with her stable hands nearby, she'd never felt the need. Obviously, she'd been wrong. Suddenly, having Jerden as her bodyguard—or a live-in boyfriend—didn't seem like such a ridiculous idea. At least she'd had sense enough to flip on the light and not open the door before peering out the window to see who was standing on her porch. Engaging the lock, she shouted, "What do you want?"

"I wanted to make sure you were okay. I'm sorry if I scared you this morning."

"You could have just called me."

"I wanted to apologize in person."

"Took you long enough to do it," she muttered.

"What?"

She raised her voice a notch. "I said, you picked one hell of a time to come knocking on my door. I'm fine. Apology accepted. Just don't ever try to kiss me again."

"Why not?" He tried the knob. "Sara, please let me in. I won't hurt you."

That's what they all say. "Go home, Nate. I'm okay, but I'm in no mood to talk to you right now."

She'd have given a lot to have Jerden standing behind her, snarling. The mere thought of him gave her courage, but this time she wouldn't need Jerden. Surely Nate would respect the fact that her door was locked—wouldn't he?

She reminded herself that Nate didn't know anything about her past and couldn't have known how she would react when he kissed her. He was probably feeling bewildered and repentant.

Unfortunately, he didn't sound that way. He sounded bitter and angry. "You don't trust me, do you?"

"Nate, I don't trust anyone who comes to my house this late at night. You should have called me."

"You wouldn't have answered when you saw who it was."

He had a point. "Yeah, well, I'm not unlocking my door, either. Go home. We can talk some other time."

"You let that alien bastard in your house." His voice was sharp, accusing.

She chose to ignore the slur, even though it made her long to slap him. "I didn't *let* him in. I *carried* him in. There's a difference."

"Yes, and then he carried *you* in." Even in the dim light Sara could see the anger etched in his face. "That's been bugging the hell out of me ever since. Did you and that damned man-whore kiss and make up?"

She considered telling him where she'd been that afternoon and with whom, but she had an idea it would provoke him even further—especially without Jerden there to back up her story. "It doesn't matter *what* we did. What matters is that it's none of your business. Look, I suppose I should be flattered that you're interested in me in a romantic manner—at least, I think that's what you've been trying to tell me—but I'm *not* interested. I'm not going to explain it any further. Please, just accept it and go home."

He shook his head. "Not good enough, Sara. I won't give up that easily."

"Dammit, Nate, you scared the shit out of me! Nothing you can say or do will change that." She sighed wearily. "Just go home. It's been a very busy day, and I'm exhausted."

To her surprise, he actually nodded. "Okay. I'll leave, but we could be really good together, Sara. Promise me you'll give it some thought."

She'd give it some thought all right. All of the two seconds it would take to shout *Oh, hell no!* "Good *night*, Nate."

"Good night, then." As he turned and stepped off the porch, Sara caught sight of his clenched jaw and tight fists and wondered if he'd actually considered forcing his way in. The sick feeling in the pit of her stomach warned her that he very well might. Hurrying to the front door, she locked it, then waited until she heard the whine of his speeder before she went back to the couch. She picked up the computer, intending to continue her research, but thought it might be best to look into security systems instead. Then she realized that except at night, she wasn't even *in* her house most of the time. A security system would be useless.

Still shaking, she sank down onto the couch wishing she knew what to do. Jerden hadn't been wrong when he'd suggested that she'd come to Terra Minor to escape. She'd heard there were very few unmarried

Terran men living there—most had immigrated with their wives. Of course, that was before the Zetithians arrived. Human men were still scarce, but human *females* were everywhere. Why couldn't Nate have taken a fancy to one of them? Perhaps he would. She should suggest that Jerden invite all the unmarried Terran ladies in the region to his cookout. Maybe Nate would fall in love with one of them and leave Sara alone.

Jerden might find someone else, too. Then she wouldn't have to pretend to be something she wasn't just to keep Salan and the others from bothering him. The funny thing was, that thought didn't make her feel any better at all. She felt hollow and empty, like all the joy had been sucked out of her soul.

It was a feeling she knew quite well. She had only just begun to feel happy again in the time she'd been on Terra Minor. Her exhausted brain didn't know what to make of any of it.

"Guess it's time I went to bed." Then she remembered she hadn't changed the sheets. "Doesn't matter. If there are fleas, there are fleas. Not gonna worry about it now."

But there weren't any fleas. Only the lingering scent of the man who'd shared her bed for the past two nights, the man she'd spent a perplexing afternoon with and whose presence now haunted her dreams.

Jerden.

Chapter 11

AS SHE MIGHT HAVE EXPECTED, SARA RECEIVED A CALL from Bonnie bright and early the next morning. "Considering your *performance* yesterday, I thought you might want to come over for a little woman-to-woman talk."

Pulling the wool over Salan's eyes had been relatively easy. Bonnie had obviously seen right through it. "What gave me away?"

"Several things," Bonnie replied. "But I was particularly taken by your reaction to Hilbransk insinuating that you were in love with Jerden. You looked like you'd just swallowed an enock. Then there was the fact that Jerden actually bought you that dress."

"I never wear dresses," Sara said lamely.

"Believe me, I know. Want to talk about it?"

Sara blew out a breath. "Not really, but I guess I should. I'll be there in about an hour."

After saddling Akira, Sara mounted up and headed toward Bonnie's farm, still trying to figure out how her simple life had suddenly become so complicated.

Then it got even *more* complicated. She arrived at Bonnie's house only to find Danuban grazing in the yard and Cria sitting on the porch like a guardian sphinx.

Jerden was there ahead of her.

Her first thought was to turn tail for home, but Karsyn was already waving at her from the window. Moments later, the tiny blonde came flying out of the house. "Hi, Sara! Can I have a ride?"

"Sure, Karsyn." Sara positioned Akira close to the porch and Karsyn climbed up in front of the saddle like a little monkey.

"Jerden's here too! Did you see his big cat?"

"Um, yeah. She's kinda hard to miss."

Karsyn continued on, apparently immune to sarcasm. "I like her. Her name's Cria. Did you know that?"

"Yes," Sara said with a chuckle. "We've met."

"Really? You've petted her and everything?"

"You bet."

"She didn't bite you, did she?" Not waiting for a reply, Karsyn bounced up and down. "Can this horse go faster?"

"Sure can, but he won't unless I ask him to, so just sit still."

Karsyn spun around, scowling. "I want to go *fast*."

"And I want to talk to your mother."

"Jerden's talking to her now. Did you know he's going to have a party? We get to eat hamburgers and swim in the lake!"

"Sounds wonderful." She wondered if he'd mentioned the "hostess" thing, and also whether or not Bonnie had told him she'd figured out their little secret.

"Oh, it will be. Jerden was very sad for a while, but he's happier now. I like him. Do *you* like him?"

Sara wasn't sure how to answer that, but for the child's benefit, she figured she shouldn't complicate things too much. "Yes. I like him. We're… friends."

"Good. Now, make this horse *go*!"

Looping an arm around Karsyn's waist, Sara put

Akira into a slow, collected canter down the path that led
to the main road. Karsyn let out a squeal that would've
sent a lesser horse galloping for the hills, but Akira took
it in stride. "Want to do something fancy?"

"Ooh, yes!"

A couple of flying lead changes had Karsyn squealing again. "It feels like he's skipping!"

"Sort of. He goes sideways, too. Watch."
Transitioning to the trot, Akira performed a half pass
across the front yard to where Danuban was grazing.

"That's really cool!"

Sara pointed at the stallion. "If you think that's cool,
you should see what my new horse can do." *If I ever get
to ride him, that is.*

"You mean Jerden's horse?"

Sara bit back a retort. She couldn't very well fault
Karsyn for thinking that. The fact that it was becoming
truer with each passing day didn't help. "Actually, he's
my horse, and he can do all kinds of neat tricks."

If I can figure out how to get him to do them.

Sara had been boning up on her classical dressage
ever since she'd purchased Danuban, but the "airs
above the ground" were movements she'd never attempted. Akira could do a decent levade, but that was
about the size of it. Leaps like the courbette and capriole were beyond her expertise. Jerden, on the other
hand, could probably do it—bareback and naked—and
make it look easy.

"What else can this horse do?"

"Well, he can trot in place," Sara replied. "It's called
the piaffe."

"Show me!"

Akira responded promptly to Sara's cue, even with Karsyn wiggling around on him.

"Very bouncy!"

Sara laughed. "He's got nothing on you when it comes to bouncing, Karsyn. You're the champ." She glanced up just as Bonnie and Jerden came out onto the porch. Even knowing he was there didn't fully prepare her for the sight of him—though he *was* wearing his loincloth. Apparently he was saving his new clothes for when he went to town. Still, the loincloth suited him, making him look like some kind of primitive warrior. A tingle ran up her spine.

"Look at us, Jerden!" Karsyn yelled. "We're doing the—" She twisted around to face Sara again. "What's it called?"

"The piaffe. If you do it moving forward, it's called the passage. Like this." Akira stepped out, his springy passage giving Sara the same thrill it always did. "He can go backwards, too." While Karsyn dissolved into giggles, Sara backed Akira across the yard, coming to a halt by the porch.

"Mom! You gotta try this!" She clambered off the horse and into Bonnie's arms. "It's so much fun!"

"I'm sure it is," Bonnie said. "Maybe one of these days I'll take lessons."

"Maybe I should too," Jerden said.

Sara nearly swallowed her tongue. "I don't know if you *need* lessons, Jerden. You already ride better than I do."

"Not really," he said. "I don't know how to do any of that stuff."

"In your case, I think it's more a matter of not

knowing these movements are possible. I'll bet all you'd have to do is *think* about what you want a horse to do, and your body would automatically know how to cue it."

Bonnie elbowed Jerden in the ribs and giggled. "Sort of like how you are with women."

Sara frowned. "Huh?"

"Never mind," Bonnie said. "You'll get it someday."

"I can give you lessons if you like," Sara went on. "I'd like to see what Danuban can do, and it doesn't look like I'm ever going to get to ride him myself." As soon as the words were out of her mouth, she wished them unspoken. "Sorry, Jerden. That didn't sound very nice."

"It's true, though," he acknowledged. "I'm sorry to keep hogging him, but right now, aside from my feet, he's my only means of transportation."

"We've got to get you a speeder," Bonnie said firmly. "Believe me, I know what it's like to live out here without one. My feet had blisters on top of blisters back when I had to walk to the market in Nimbaza every week. Lynx can help you find one, and if it isn't running, he can fix it."

Karsyn nodded vigorously, her silvery blonde curls swaying with the movement. "Yeah. Daddy can fix *anything*."

"Anything with moving parts and an engine, that is," Bonnie amended. She smiled fondly. "He's good at a lot of things."

Sara was pretty sure she wasn't only referring to his ability to keep the farm machinery running, but that was a tangent she chose to ignore. "Until you get a speeder, I can take you into town anytime you need a ride."

Jerden grinned, displaying his fangs. "And until I get my own horse, I can ride yours?"

"Well, yeah," Sara said lamely. *So much for the occasional date to keep everyone guessing.* "We might even get you into a horse show. It'd be great advertising for the farm. Ulla's ready for training level. I bet you and Danuban could mop up the competition in first level, maybe even the second if you're a quick study."

"What about the stuff you were just doing?"

"Fourth level," Sara said with a flick of her brow. "I know Danuban can do all of that—and more. It's a matter of you learning how to ride it. Dressage is *nothing* like hopping on a horse and galloping off into the sunset. It's very precise and difficult. But if you can compete at that level… well, that would be… awesome."

~~~

The sparkle in Sara's eyes went straight to Jerden's heart. If riding well enough to win was what would make her think he was awesome, he was willing to give it a shot—aside from the fact that taking lessons from Sara would allow him to spend as much time at her place as he liked. He could come over for a lesson every day. "Guess I ought to get a pair of boots."

"You'll need more than that," Ulla said as she came out onto the porch. "Boots, breeches, spurs… Really *cool* stuff."

"She's been bitten by the horse bug, Bonnie," Sara said with a knowing smile. "You'll never have any credits to spare again."

Bonnie rolled her eyes. "Don't I know it! Lynx is already building a stable for the ponies when they arrive.

Feeding them won't be a problem, but all the stuff a rider needs... well, you *know* what I'm talking about."

Jerden caught himself before laughing out loud. The way he'd been riding, he didn't need *anything*. But that was about to change. He would miss the freedom, though. Maybe he could strip down and ride naked through the mountains sometime when Sara wasn't watching. Or maybe he would do it when she *was* watching. Jerden wasn't ignorant when it came to the things women liked, and he knew very well that the sight of a naked hunk riding a horse like Danuban was enough to make even the toughest woman melt.

Except the one who aroused feelings in him he'd never felt before. Sara was more than a passing fancy. He *liked* her—even when she was telling him to get lost. And if he ever caught Nate sniffing around her again, well... he probably wouldn't be quite as forgiving as he'd been the last time. Unfortunately, he wasn't sure she liked *him* very much, though he suspected her dislike didn't involve him specifically, but men in general. He had a feeling he was going to recover his sexual ability long before he caught the first whiff of her desire.

If he ever did. Someone had gotten to her, had destroyed any of the warmer feelings for the opposite sex that she might once have had. He wanted to take her in his arms and kiss away those fears. Unfortunately, if her reaction to Nate's kiss was anything to go by, he had a long way to go before he could ever hope to get that close to her—at least, not in private.

Sara nodded at Ulla. "Speaking of horses, would you and Karsyn mind looking after Akira while I talk to your mother?"

Ulla didn't bother to hide her enthusiasm. "I'd *love* to."

As Sara dismounted and handed the reins to Ulla, Bonnie gave her daughter an indulgent smile. "I'm sure you would."

"I want to ride by myself," Karsyn said.

"You aren't quite ready for that," Sara replied. "You can sit on him, but let Ulla lead him. Okay?"

Karsyn stuck out her lower lip in protest, but she nodded. "I want Jerden to put me on him."

Bless her heart, she gave him the best excuse for sticking around he could think of. He held out his arms and caught Karsyn as she leaped toward him. "I'll keep an eye on them."

"Thanks." Bonnie sounded grateful, but Sara's expression never changed.

"Where are the other kids?" Sara asked.

"Out working with Lynx," Bonnie replied. "Probably hindering more than helping. My two horse-crazy girls weren't about to leave the house when they heard you'd be riding over here." She glanced at Jerden. "And especially after *you* showed up on a black stallion."

Jerden had visited Bonnie more out of curiosity than anything, and though he would've preferred to tell Bonnie the truth about his relationship with Sara, she'd seemed so pleased to see them together, he hated to disappoint her. On the other hand, the fact that she'd been no harder to convince than Salan made him slightly suspicious. Bonnie was a lot smarter than the dairymaid, and she and Sara were good friends. Sara would probably tell her everything—including whether or not she was having second thoughts about their arrangement.

She'd been very quiet during the trip home from

Nimbaza, and Jerden hadn't dared to break that silence to suggest that their temporary liaison might eventually become permanent. She probably assumed that once Nate stopped bothering her—perhaps even marrying someone else—she would have no further need of him. Jerden would do whatever it took to eliminate that possibility. A few days ago, she hadn't liked him any more than she liked Nate. But that was changing. She'd at least agreed to be friends.

He'd used the excuse of inviting the Dackelovs to his party to get a better idea of how successful their performance had been, intending to stop in to see Sara on the way home to report what he'd discovered.

This was even better. Sara probably wouldn't stay long, and he had no intention of leaving before she did. He would make the most of the opportunity to ride home with her. He smiled to himself. Sara was either going to get really sick of him hanging around or get used to him. And once she got used to him, she might even decide she liked him. If he was *really* lucky, she might even fall in love with him.

Even so, he'd love to be a fly on the wall to hear what she had to say to Bonnie.

As he carried Karsyn down the porch steps and set her in Akira's saddle, he realized that Lynx had something that he'd only just discovered he wanted. A wife. Children. A home. To have children of his own who weren't being raised on distant worlds by women he'd only spent an hour or so with had a very strong appeal. He wanted to be with *one* woman; to get to know her, inside and out, delighting in the fact that she would probably still surprise him on occasion.

Children were even more surprising. Over tea and cookies, Ulla had actually admitted to cleaning his house while he'd been off running through the mountains. The strange thing was that he hadn't even noticed the difference.

"I want to ride *that* horse," Karsyn said, pointing at Danuban. "With Jerden."

Ulla rolled her eyes. "Might as well give it up and take her for a ride, Jerden. She'll never give you any peace until you do."

Chuckling, he gave Ulla a leg up on Akira and tossed her the reins. After adjusting the stirrups for her, he called for the stallion. Danuban stopped grazing and trotted up to him. Grasping the mane, he swung up onto the black's broad back.

"I wish I could mount a horse like that," Ulla said wistfully.

"You'll be able to when you're taller. And when you get those ponies, you won't have any trouble." Urging the stud closer to Akira, he took Karsyn by the waist and sat her in front of him. "Come on, girls," he said with a grin. "Let's go for a ride."

<hr />

"Jerden told me he had to rescue you from Nate yesterday," Bonnie said as she led the way into her sunny kitchen. "He didn't use those exact words, but that was the gist of it. I let him think I believed that crap about you two being lovers—which would've been damn sudden, considering what I already know about both of you. I'm guessing the only thing you actually got together on was concocting this scheme to keep Nate from ever bothering you again."

Sara nodded. "Jerden also wanted to discourage Salan. *She* seemed to believe it." With a rueful smile, she added, "Wasn't very convincing, was I?"

"Not at all." Bonnie gestured toward the table. "Have a seat. I'll make you a cup of tea." She filled her tea-kettle with water and set it on the stove. "Jerden was certainly talkative this morning. I don't know what you did to him, but he seems so much better now. More like he was before."

Sara still didn't think she'd had anything to do with his recovery, but she let it pass without argument, thankful for a slightly different topic. "So you knew him before he went to Rhylos?"

Bonnie nodded. "Not well, though I did meet him several years ago. A gorgeous hunk like Jerden is hard to forget. Big, handsome, charismatic… he had the most seductive smile I've ever seen. A real ladies' man. No one was surprised when he made a fortune on Rhylos. I'd be willing to bet there wasn't a woman in the entire galaxy who would've turned him down." The "except you" was left unsaid, but Sara could almost hear it reverberating off the walls. "So, you want to tell me what Nate did to make you faint?"

"He's always been annoying," Sara said bluntly. "But this time, he scared me."

Taking a mug down from the cabinet, Bonnie set it on the counter and dropped a tea bag in it. "Got a little too pushy?"

"Something like that."

"Still don't see why you'd pass out." She leveled a shrewd eye at Sara. "There's something you're not telling me."

Sara's chest tightened. Closing her eyes for a moment, she willed the pain to subside. "I've never told anyone, and I don't intend to now. Let's just say what happened was enough to make me believe that men can't be trusted."

Bonnie nodded. She may have looked like a delicate little blonde angel, but Sara knew she'd been through a lot. There was steel in her, and a fair amount of wisdom, too—most of which she'd learned the hard way. "I felt like that myself once. Swore off men entirely." A fond smile lifted the corners of her lips. "Then Lynx showed up." Her clear blue eyes gazed steadily into Sara's. "It makes a difference when you find the right one."

"Well, Nate certainly isn't the right one," Sara said briskly. "I think we've proven that much."

"But Jerden *might* be? I mean, you do seem to trust him a little."

"I don't know. I feel differently toward him, but love? I'm not sure I'm even capable of it. He asked me why I came here to live all alone, and I told him it was because I liked it that way. I don't think he believed me."

"There's more to it?"

"Of course there is. But that's not the point. The point is…" She stopped there, shaking her head. "Oh, hell. I don't know *what* the point is. I honestly don't. I'm not even sure what I'm *doing* here."

The kettle whistled, and Bonnie poured the boiling water into the mug and then set it in front of Sara before fixing a cup for herself. She nodded toward a plate of chocolate chip cookies. "Have some. They'll settle your brain better than anything." Chuckling, she pulled up another chair and sat down. "They sure got Jerden talking."

Grateful for a temporary reprieve, Sara picked up a

cookie and took a bite, savoring it slowly. *Might as well just come out and ask her…* "Did he tell you he wanted me to be the hostess for this party he's planning?"

"Oh, yeah." Bonnie hesitated. "He likes you, Sara. Do yourself a great big favor and don't ignore that—or push him away. He *needs* someone—probably more than you do. If you're only friends, I think he could live with that. But if a Zetithian man really loves you…" She paused, unable to suppress a smile. "Well, it just doesn't get any better than that."

Sara wasn't blind. She'd seen how much Bonnie and Lynx loved one another—and their children. Perhaps that was why both she and Jerden had come there—in the hope that the pervasive aura of peace and contentment would somehow rub off on them. Unfortunately, Sara had yet to convince herself that a man was something she actually wanted. All the things she'd said to Jerden were true. She knew some of it from personal experience, and some from observation. Happy unions between men and women were rare, and more often than not, they seemed to dissolve in annoyance, mutual dislike, and sometimes out-and-out hatred. She'd convinced herself she was better off without all that.

But the pesky little notion that there might be more to it nagged at her. *What if…* "No. He only wants me to be his hostess so all the single women will feel more comfortable. Of course, that was before we started pretending to be a couple. Not sure *what* it means now."

Bonnie arched a skeptical brow. "Did *he* say that was why he wanted you to do it, or did you?"

Sara honestly couldn't remember. "I don't know. It sounds like something I would have said."

"Uh-huh. Do yourself a favor, Sara, and don't sell yourself short. You have a lot to offer a man."

"Yeah. Good land and beautiful horses." She was pretty sure that was what Nate wanted from her. It wouldn't surprise her if Jerden wanted the same thing.

Bonnie scowled in response to Sara's comment, but went on as though she hadn't heard it. "And the woman who would pass up Jerden... well, I'm not sure one exists. At least, none that are single—and I'd bet plenty of married women would ditch their husbands for him."

"I thought sex was the Zetithian male's claim to fame. If he can't do it anymore..."

"Don't you worry about that. If Lynx can recover, so can Jerden. And when he does..." A wry smile curled her lips. "Look out."

Chapter 12

BONNIE'S COOKIES WERE BETTER THAN A DOSE OF TRUTH serum. In short order, Sara had related the events of the previous day, plus the details of Nate's late night visit.

"Whether he wants your land and horses—or you—doesn't matter anymore," Bonnie said. "Nate already sees Jerden as a rival, and I'm not sure he'll believe your ruse any more than I did. Chances are, he'll get even more persistent. Whether you're pretending or not, Jerden is some pretty serious competition. I mean, I know which one *I'd* choose."

Oddly enough, Sara would have chosen Jerden too, but for an entirely different reason. Not only was he currently incapable of sexual relations—something Sara saw as a definite plus—he also had an excellent rapport with Danuban. And if Jerden needed the scent of a woman's desire in order to recover his sexual abilities, well, he certainly wasn't going to get it from Sara. Though she found some comfort in that, she doubted he would see it in quite the same light.

The back door flew open and Karsyn came racing into the kitchen. "Oh, Sara, we had *so* much fun!" Sighing, she further expressed herself with a reasonably well executed pirouette. "I simply *adore* horses."

Bonnie shook her head, covering a smile as Karsyn danced her way into the next room. "She can be so... *theatrical* sometimes. Don't know where she gets it."

While Bonnie enjoyed a good chuckle, Sara glanced toward the door, taking Karsyn's arrival as her cue. "I guess I'd better collect Akira from Ulla and head on home."

Bonnie nodded. "She'd probably stay out there with him all day if you let her, but I'm sure you've got things to do." Sara did her best to ignore Bonnie's pointed look. No way was she going to go galloping after Jerden like some lovesick idiot. He was probably already halfway home by now.

"Yeah, gotta fix lunch for the gang." She got up from the table. "Thanks for the cookies, and for listening."

"Maybe someday you'll tell me the rest of the story."

Sara shrugged. "I doubt it. Even if I did, it wouldn't change anything."

"You might be surprised. Just remember, I'm always here to lend an ear if you need one."

"I'll keep that in mind."

Since she hadn't come back in the house with Karsyn, Sara expected to see Ulla sitting on the porch holding Akira's reins, or perhaps walking him around in the yard. No such luck. Jerden was waiting with both horses, Ulla apparently having gone off to do something else. Cria was curled up on the porch but rose to her feet as Sara came out the door.

Still mounted on Danuban, Jerden tossed her the reins. "I thought maybe we could ride back together."

Using the porch steps as a mounting block, Sara swung up into the saddle, wondering when she was ever going to stop having chest pain every time she looked at Jerden. She focused her eyes on Akira's ears and waited for it to pass. About the only advantage to riding home with him was that he'd be there if Nate were to come trotting up on one of his scrubby little horses and tried to put the moves on her again.

"Might as well," she replied. Then she remembered all the research she'd done the previous evening before Nate had interrupted her. With horse-hunting and barn-building as topics, she shouldn't have to worry about the conversation getting too personal. "I went online last night and found some nice-looking Friesians for sale. They're pretty pricey, though. Want to take a look?"

"Sure. I'd also like to see more of the things this horse has been trained to do." He ruffled Danuban's mane and gave him a pat as they started off. "You kinda got my curiosity going with everything you were telling the girls."

"Most people think it's pretty cool when they see those movements performed. Not many know how to ride them, though, including myself. About the best I can do is to show you some pictures and videos."

"Sounds good. I'm sure you'll be busy the rest of the afternoon. How about if I come over later tonight, maybe after dinner?"

After dinner? She was about to refuse when she realized that Jerden's presence was the perfect insurance against another visit from Nate. They wouldn't have to do any pretending, either. They'd simply be two friends getting together to talk about horses.

She was still coming to grips with the mind-boggling idea that she could actually be friends with a man. But were they more than friends already? The memory of him lying in bed with her the previous morning came rushing back. He'd been purring and had even given her a couple of hugs and kisses.

Then there was the excursion to Nimbaza—the way he'd touched her, walked arm in arm with her, and told her she looked like a queen when she tried on that dress. Of course, it had all been for show...

Holy shit.

They'd been alone in that dressing room. No one else could've heard him, which meant it hadn't been part of the performance. He must've truly meant it.

And after he'd seen that Davordian woman, he'd shared something with her that he claimed not to have shared with anyone else. No one was around to hear that, either.

Maybe we really are friends.

Noting her stunned expression, Jerden waited patiently while Sara wrestled with her reply. He knew he'd backed her into a corner of sorts, and was on the brink of withdrawing the suggestion when she finally spoke.

"Sounds good."

"Great! I'll be there around seven, then." Not too early, not too late.

She nodded her assent, but that touch of reserve was still there. She'd seemed much better the day before—at least, until the ride home. She'd been as quiet then as she was now...

Deciding it was best not to push her any further, he said nothing more, allowing her to ride on in silence. The day was clear and warm, and they let the horses walk most of the way. Cria followed close behind, and Jerden did his best to keep quiet and enjoy the scenery.

They followed the main road, which ran past Bonnie's farm and the dairy, then skirted Sara's property for a time before taking a turn to the west to avoid the mountains. Beyond that point, the road to Jerden's place dwindled to little more than a path, becoming almost nonexistent where his land began and hers ended. Understanding his need for solitude, Lynx had suggested the lake property as the most remote place available. Now that Jerden had spent more time with Sara, the remote aspect seemed less important, and he was able appreciate it more for its beauty.

They were passing by the gently rolling acres of the dairy farm owned by Salan's father when Sara finally broke the silence. "Karsyn seemed to have had a good time riding. You should have seen her dancing through the kitchen."

Jerden chuckled warmly. "She's something else, isn't she?"

"Uh-huh. She's really looking forward to your party. Said she gets to eat hamburgers and swim in the lake."

Jerden was thankful that Sara had managed to come up with what she apparently considered to be a neutral topic—unless she was intending to back out on him. "You're still planning to be there, aren't you?"

Her slight hesitation told him he'd been correct. "I suppose so, but do I *really* have to be your hostess?"

"No, but I *could* use your help." Jerden had yet to have a woman turn down an appeal like that. Knowing Sara, she'd probably be the first, so he backed it up with a little extra incentive. Rubbing his chin in a contemplative manner, he threw in the clincher. "Remember, the more time we spend to together, the less you'll have to deal with Nate."

Sara blew out a pent-up breath. "I sure wish you'd come home with me last night."

Jerden would've dropped his teeth if they hadn't been firmly attached to his jaw. "Why, Sara, I had no idea…"

"It's not what you think. Nate came over to apologize."

"Judging from the way you're gritting your teeth, I'd have to say you didn't appreciate his visit."

"Or his timing. I was up pretty late. I doubt if any of the gang even heard him."

"You didn't let him in, did you?"

"Hell, no! I locked the door and told the stupid shithead to go away."

Jerden couldn't contain his laughter. "You're starting to make a habit of that."

She all but snarled at him. "I didn't lock *you* out."

"No, I had the good sense to leave when you told me to." Figuring he had very little to lose at this point, he tossed out another lure. "I guess I *could've* stayed with you last night. I mean, if I'd been there, he would've felt pretty stupid."

Sara never missed a beat, skipping right past the suggestion that he would've spent the night if she'd asked him to. "Yeah, well, you weren't, so it's a moot point. Obviously he didn't get the memo that you're supposed to be my new boyfriend."

"I take it you didn't tell him."

"To be honest, I thought it would make matters worse. He was already saying some not-so-nice things about you."

"He didn't threaten *you*, did he?"

"No, but he scared the hell out of me, especially after what happened yesterday. I was about to call the Trackers on him—and I would have if he hadn't left when he did."

Jerden had been angry enough when Nate had forced his attentions on her, but his blood was really boiling now. Trying to kiss her was one thing, harassing her when she was alone late at night was something else. "Obviously I should've beaten the shit out of him when I had the chance. He didn't try to break in, did he?"

"Sort of. I'd already locked the door, but he did jiggle the knob. He was pretty angry. To tell you the truth, I thought he might try to force his way in." She shivered. "I still don't understand what's gotten into him lately. I mean, has he gone crazy or what?"

Jerden hated to admit it, but he suspected it was more due to his own presence in the neighborhood than any insanity on Nate's part. "Males of every species have a tendency to be territorial. Nate probably sees me as an intruder on what he considers to be his turf."

Sara nodded. "Bonnie said something similar, but I still don't know why he'd think that. I've never encouraged him. *Ever*." She paused, clenching her teeth. "I'm usually not up that late, but I was in the living room and the lights were on. The door was unlocked—hell, it's *always* unlocked! I can't help wondering what he would've done if I'd been asleep. He could've just opened the door and come right on in. I guess Reutal would've heard me if I'd screamed."

Jerden had heard enough. "That does it," he growled. "I'm not leaving you alone again."

"Don't be silly. You can't be with me all the time."

"I could if we were married," Jerden said bluntly. "I'd never leave your side."

This proposal was too blatant for even Sara to ignore. However, the only indication that she grasped his meaning was a tiny little choke, from which she recovered quickly. "Nonsense. Even married people aren't together *all* the time. They'd drive each other crazy."

He summoned up his best lady-killer smile and aimed it right at her. "Prove it."

"What?"

"Marry me and try to drive me crazy."

She glanced at him with a derisive arch to her brow. "That doesn't sound too hard. You're halfway there already—maybe even closer than that, come to think of it."

Jerden wasn't sure where the idea had come from—a moment before, he'd have counted himself lucky to be able to hold her hand—but like most of his better notions, this one had come to him straight out of the blue. "Trust me, I'm not insane—and I've been there, so I know what I'm talking about. If you'll just take a minute to consider the idea without whatever it is about men that you can't stand getting in the way, you'll see that it's the perfect solution to your problem."

"Which problem? How to drive you crazy?"

"No, how to keep Nate from harassing you anymore—and you can do that by marrying me." Jerden took full advantage of her speechless state and continued to blast away her resistance. "You can think of it as a marriage of convenience if you like. If your complaint about men is that you have to have sex with them, you won't have to worry because my dick doesn't work, and with your scent stuck in neutral, it never will. You'll get a full-time bodyguard and Bonnie won't try to fix you up with every new guy that comes along."

Her eyes narrowed in suspicion. "What's in it for you?"

"I won't have every Zetithian-hungry girl in the quadrant chasing after my hot little ass, and you and I won't have to fight over who gets to keep this horse." He grinned. "And I'd have the perfect excuse to mop up the floor with Nate if he ever bothers you again."

She stared at him for the space of about ten heartbeats and then let out a shaky laugh. "You really *are* crazy, aren't you?"

At least she's laughing. Jerden had never been quite so blunt with a woman before and couldn't have predicted how well it would work. Sara was different, though. There was a good chance it had been the right tactic. "Outrageous perhaps, but not crazy."

"Sounds like a match made in heaven."

It wasn't a definite yes, and her dry tone held a dash of sarcasm. *Wait for it…*

She frowned, biting her lower lip in a manner that was both innocent and sensuous. Jerden held his breath. "No sex?"

"Not unless you want it, and believe me, I'll be able to tell if you do."

She nodded slowly, staring straight ahead. "You're right about that being part of the problem. There are other things, though. Things that still hurt." Her voice dropped to a whisper. "Things I don't even like to think about."

"I won't hurt you, Sara. I've told you that before. And if I ever do, whether it's intentional or not, you can slap the shit out of me. In fact, I insist on it."

She turned to face him then, only the barest hint of a smile indicating that she'd heard him. In another instant, it was gone. "Don't lie to me."

"I'm not lying. I'm perfectly serious."

"I know. I mean *ever*."

So, trust is *the issue*. "I won't lie." *Starting right now*... "But I do have two requests. Physical contact is not only natural for Zetithians, it's essential to our well-being. I need to be able to touch you, hold you, even kiss you. Yesterday, when I picked you up and carried you into the house, I realized that, along with something else." Pausing for a deep breath, he took the plunge. "I've never loved anyone and no one has ever loved me. I want to experience that before I die. Don't refuse to let it happen between us."

She chewed her lip thoughtfully, then shook her head. "That doesn't sound like a marriage of convenience."

"Actually, it's the most convenient marriage of all. If and when we do fall in love—or even *make* love—we'll already be married."

"But what if only *one* of us falls in love? That would be worse than never loving each other at all."

Jerden knew he was the only one who would suffer in that event. But if he told her now, she'd never believe him. "That's the chance we have to take."

She nodded. "True. We could be making a terrible mistake, though."

"It doesn't have to be permanent, Sara. If it becomes unbearable, we can end it." He nudged Danuban and the stallion obligingly stepped sideways, moving close enough to Sara that their knees touched. Reaching out, he placed his hand over hers, surprised at how cold it felt. "But I don't think that's how this will turn out. Promise me you'll at least think about it."

Sara snorted a laugh. "How could I *not* think about it? It's not like I get proposed to every day of the week."

He couldn't help smiling at her jest, although, in his opinion, it ought to have been the truth. "Is that what it'll take? Proposing to you every day? If so, I think I can handle that."

She shot him an exasperated look. "No need for that. I do appreciate the offer, and I have to admit, I thought pretending to be interested in each other was a good idea—at least until I talked to Bonnie this morning. She didn't believe a word of it."

"I wondered about that. She never admitted it, but I had my suspicions."

"She said she wanted to hear my side of the story before she said anything to you, especially since *I* was the one who was acting so out of character." She shook her head. "I don't know about getting married, though. Seems kinda drastic."

"It might take something drastic to eliminate both of our problems, especially yours. I doubt if Salan would be as persistent as Nate, but if you like, we could just keep on saying we were dating."

"Which means we'd actually have to go on a date." She paused chewing on the thumb of her riding glove. "Somewhere public…"

Jerden chuckled as he thought of all the women who'd begged to go out to dinner with him, and here Sara was acting as though it was some kind of penance. "You don't have to make it sound like such a *chore*."

This time she actually seemed amused when she laughed. "It's not a chore. I'm just trying to decide what sort of date it should be. I…" She broke off there, her expression one of confusion mixed with a trace of embarrassment. She drew in a deep breath as though about to make a confession—and a painful one, at that. "I've never been on a date, Jerden—except one that I'd prefer to forget—and it was a *very* long time ago. I wouldn't know what to do—how to act… where to go… or anything."

"How about we go to dinner at Tarq and Lucy's restaurant? That's public enough, and they're bound to see it for what it is and spread the word."

"As long as Nate gets wind of it, we'll have accomplished our goal."

Jerden had an idea that his friend Tarq would be so glad to see him out with a woman, he'd probably alert the media. "I don't believe that'll be a problem."

She gave him a rueful smile. "You're right about that. Don't know what I was thinking, especially since everybody seems to know everything about everybody around here. It's more of an accomplishment to keep something quiet."

"True. And the more I'm seen out in public behaving like a rational person, the better. I'd like to put those 'insane wildcat' rumors to rest once and for all."

"Okay then," she said with a decisive nod. "I'll do it."

Jerden rolled his eyes. "Thank the gods above." He'd never had to work so hard to get a woman to agree to a date in his life.

First time for everything…

———————

Sara hadn't been kidding about not knowing what to do on a date. Should they hold hands? Gaze longingly into each other's eyes? Sit in a dark corner and kiss every time they thought no one was looking? The whole idea was as foreign to her as ballet dancing or flying a starship. She'd have to rely on him to take the lead.

She almost laughed out loud. Allowing a man to take the lead? The last time she'd done that had turned out to be the worst mistake she'd ever made. She doubted this date would turn out to be anything like that one, but as always, the fear that it might haunted her.

But this is Jerden. She had to remind herself of that. He wasn't like the others. She was slowly realizing that he was a man she could actually trust—trust not to hurt her, belittle her, or try to dominate her…

She glanced at Danuban. Walking placidly alongside Akira, he displayed no trace of the wild, vicious stallion that the spaceport officials had described to her. *If only you'd been a good boy and waited for me, none of this would've happened.* Yet it had. She could see the chain of events clearly now. The stallion's escape, Nate's renewed insistence that she breed her mares to his stallion, Jerden's entry into her life astride that missing horse, and the horse somehow determined to remain with Jerden, inadvertently bringing them together.

Or had it been intentional? A matchmaking stallion? *Highly unlikely.* He only appeared that way in retrospect. Thinking of him as anything other than an animal and therefore completely lacking in the devious nature required for such a plan was ridiculous. Only people and other so-called intelligent life forms were capable of that level of manipulation, which was yet another reason why Sara preferred horses over people. They were nothing if not honest.

These thoughts had been rattling around in her head for some time when she finally realized that Jerden was watching her, an amused half smile on his lips. "Planning on sharing any of those thoughts? They look mighty deep."

Sara shook her head. "Not that deep." A ragged sigh escaped her. "Still want to come over after dinner?"

"Sure." His gaze swept the entire length of her body, triggering a tingling warmth as if he'd actually touched her. "Unless you want me there sooner."

His inflection made it sound like a challenge—and a suggestive one at that. *Did* she want him sooner, or did she want him at all? Might be best to ease into it when they wouldn't be alone together. She wasn't sure she was ready for that. "Why don't you have dinner with me and the gang? If nothing else, you'd get the chance to sample more of my cooking. And if you don't like it, you can still back out of that… *other* offer."

"Trying to get rid of me already?" he said with a mocking smile. "I doubt if your cooking ability would change my mind. Besides, I'm not such a bad cook myself. I could take over if you like."

"It *would* be nice to have a break now and then." She frowned, recalling the kitchen disasters that had occurred when Drania volunteered—though they were nothing compared with Reutal's fiascoes. Zatlen had never even made the attempt. "The others can't cook at all."

"I think you have them spoiled. They'd figure it out if they got hungry enough."

"Maybe. I like cooking for them, though. They… appreciate it."

"What, you mean there are people who *don't* appreciate having someone to cook for them?" He paused as the possibilities sank in. "Unless it was really terrible."

She tried not to let it show, but the hurt came through anyway. "There are some people who don't appreciate *anything* you do for them." She glanced at her watch. "Speaking of which, we'd better get a move on or lunch is going to be late."

Leaving Jerden to make whatever he wanted of that, she urged Akira into a canter, focusing her eyes on the road ahead to avoid his questioning gaze. That wound was an old one, but it was still too deep, too raw to discuss with Jerden or anyone else. At least, not yet.

Jerden didn't ask Sara to explain her comment, merely promising to see her at dinner when they parted ways at the turnoff to her farm. Thankful for this reprieve, she rode into the stable yard alone and dismounted, still trying to figure out how she would feel once the news that she and Jerden were an item became common knowledge. Salan wasn't the type to nurse a broken heart in silence, which meant that Nate had surely heard about it by now. Sara had a feeling the previous night's visit from him wouldn't be the last.

Sara didn't share Jerden's optimism that her sentiments might change, even though her feelings toward him were already different than they'd been for any other man. Like his proposal, Jerden's revelation had taken her by surprise. The idea that such a man had never been loved or been in love was ludicrous, though it did make sense in some ways. A man in love wouldn't sell his body to any woman with a thousand credits to spare, just as a man who'd never been loved wouldn't see any point in saving himself for the one woman who did.

These thoughts were still in her mind as led Akira into the barn just as Reutal came dancing down the aisle.

"You look awfully happy," she remarked.

"Oh, I am," he said with a big, lopsided grin. "Happier than I've been in ages!" He sighed with what she could only assume was ecstatic bliss. "So tell me, Sara. When's the big cat moving in?"

Chapter 13

JERDEN'S ONLY MISGIVINGS WERE THAT WHILE A relationship with him might save Sara from being hassled by Nate, it could put her in danger in other ways. Seeing that Davordian woman in Nimbaza had served as a reminder that jealousy wasn't exclusive to Rhylos. Even though nothing of the sort had ever happened on Terra Minor, a repeat of what happened to Audrey wasn't beyond the realm of possibility. He reminded himself that the type of insanity Audrey's murderer suffered from wasn't common, and the fact that he was no longer available to any woman willing to pay for his services made the risk negligible. Since being designated as the Zetithian homeworld, more single women had immigrated to Terra Minor than ever before, but the odds that any of them were crazy enough to kill a Zetithian man's mate were slim—the screening process was very strict. So strict, in fact, that if Jerden hadn't been a Zetithian, the authorities might not have allowed *him* to remain on the planet.

There were exceptions to every rule—case in point, Bonnie's first husband, who'd been a criminal with forged identity documents—but fortunately, those were rare. And even though she clearly wanted a Zetithian husband rather badly, Jerden didn't see Salan as a potential murderess.

He looked down at Cria walking alongside the stallion. "What about you? Do *you* think there's any danger?"

Cria replied with a sidelong glance that clearly said *Not with me around*.

"You're probably right about that. I forgot to mention that I came with a built-in bodyguard myself. I'll have to remember to tell her tonight."

Tonight.

They had a lot to talk about and it might be quite late before he headed for home. After his wild, nocturnal rides through the mountains, crossing the fields from Sara's house after dark posed no problems. However, if she were to insist that he stay the night, he wouldn't say no.

He hadn't been joking when he'd said he'd never leave her side. Parting with her for the few hours until dinner had taken a tremendous amount of resolve, and right now, the need to turn the horse around and gallop back to her was so strong he could barely withstand it. He hoped she wouldn't mind if he got there a little early, because he intended to arrive before she'd even *started* fixing dinner.

The reason was simple.

I've asked Sara to be my mate, and I'm not with her.

Zetithians didn't need a ceremony; the bond between mates was physical as well as mental and incredibly strong. Sara might not have accepted him yet, but she *had* acknowledged the advantages. Given the way she seemed to feel about men, the fact that she'd agreed to dinner that night and a date at some unspecified time in the future was nothing short of miraculous. He knew exactly what he was doing and welcomed the consequences. Unfortunately, it might take a while before Sara felt the same way.

She wasn't heartless. There was plenty of love in her; she simply spread it around in other areas—horses, dogs, cats, roses, Bonnie's children. He even suspected she was fond of Reutal, though in a completely asexual manner. *Something* had happened to her—whether one single, horrific episode or many—and that something had shut off her desire for men entirely. He could understand how it might happen—a series of events compelling her to form a pattern of behavior that was reinforced until it became self-perpetuating. His task would be to break that pattern and establish a new one.

He knew what he was up against. Incidents of rape, abuse—both physical and mental—domination, and cruelty were scattered throughout human history. So much so that a fear of men had become ingrained in the women and very little was required to bring it to the surface. As a member of a species whose females were among the most independent and difficult to entice in the galaxy, a Zetithian man simply couldn't afford to do any of those things if he ever expected to find a mate. And because the scent of a woman's desire was necessary for a Zetithian man to get an erection, rape was impossible.

It didn't take a specialist in mental disorders to figure out that Sara was probably a rape victim, but she'd mentioned that there were other things she didn't even like to think about.

Jerden knew he wasn't perfect. He had flaws—arrogance being chief among them—and had been known to do some pretty stupid things in his time. He'd learned the hard way not to take a woman's affection for granted or to assume that his sexual ability could solve any problems that might arise between them.

She'd asked him not to lie to her. No problems there—deceit was something Zetithians weren't particularly good at anyway. She wanted her efforts to be appreciated. That was easy enough. The trick would be in doing it so subtly that it didn't seem rehearsed. She probably wouldn't like him to flirt openly with other women, either—yet another thing he didn't want to do anymore. He wanted to spend time with *her*, discovering as much as he could about who she was, but it worked both ways. He'd have to be more forthcoming about himself. He'd promised not to hurt her, and he wouldn't—not with words or actions. Most women liked receiving gifts as well as compliments—the more thoughtful, the better—and he'd detected a hint of relief when he'd offered to help her with the cooking.

It might take months—years, even—but he would figure out the ways in which she wanted to be loved, and in so doing, he might even discover the key to his own heart.

—⁂—

Sara wasn't able to answer Reutal's question regarding Jerden's plans immediately, partly because she'd been slightly stunned by it, and partly because she just plain didn't know the answer. "Moving in?" she echoed. "What makes you think he's moving in?"

He turned his bulbous eyes on her and blinked. "What makes you think he's not?"

Sara threw up her hands in surrender. "Okay. I give up. What have you heard?"

"Salan called while you were gone, wanting to know if it was really true that you and the cat were sleeping together."

"Holy *shit…*"

"I told her you'd already slept with him twice."

"You *didn't*."

"Oh, but I did. I also told her that he probably won't ever leave you here alone again—especially after that idiot Nate was out here pounding on your door last night."

"You heard that?"

"I have excellent hearing, although the fact that he was shouting helped. I believe I heard every bit of that conversation—his side of it, anyway—and some of yours." Which was odd considering he hadn't been anywhere in sight. Though relatively small, Norludian ears obviously worked better than hers did. She'd have to remember that.

"Oh, really? Mind telling me why you chose not to intervene?"

"You seemed to be doing fine without me—at least you didn't faint this time—which is something I might've already told you about if you hadn't gone tearing out of the barn this morning *without fixing breakfast*."

"Sorry about that," Sara said meekly.

"Ha! You think you're sorry *now*. Wait'll you see what a mess we left in the kitchen! But as I was about to say, what *really* pissed me off was him calling the cat an alien bastard and a man-whore." Pursing his lips, he shook his head angrily. "Not nice."

Sara chuckled. "But it's okay if you refer to him as 'the cat'?"

Reutal flapped his hand dismissively. "Term of endearment."

Endearment? That sounded promising. "So, you

don't *mind* that I'm going to—Wait a minute. Just what *is* it you think I'm going to do with him, anyway?"

He threw up his hands, his eyes agog with disbelief. "What any woman does with a hot hunk like that. Sleep with him. Go out on the town with him. Hell, *marry* him—that is, if you have any sense at all."

"And you're okay with all that?" Sara had an idea that similar news involving Nate wouldn't have met with any enthusiasm whatsoever.

"Absolutely! I like him—and you should've *seen* him riding to your rescue yesterday! Came galloping into the yard, swept you up in his arms, knocked Nate on his ass and told him to leave you the fuck alone, then carried you into the house." He gave his lips a lascivious lick. "*Totally* hot, heroic stuff. Made my tongue hard just watching it—Drania even had an orgasm."

Not wanting to hear any further details, Sara passed over these revelations with a slight gulp. "Told Nate to leave me the fuck alone, did he? Somehow I doubt that's how he would've phrased it."

Reutal blew out an exasperated breath. "Maybe those weren't his exact words, but it's what he *should* have said. My only complaint was that he didn't hit the son-ofabitch hard enough to draw blood. Aside from that, he was fuckin' awesome." Grinning from ear to tiny ear, he added fervently, "Good choice, Sara."

She arched an eyebrow. "I'm *so* glad you approve."

"Not that it was difficult," he went on, blithely ignoring her sarcasm. "Choosing between Nate and Jerden is a no-brainer. Just ask Drania."

"I don't believe that's necessary. She's made that very plain." She smiled as another thought occurred to her. "Drania's boyfriend will be pleased that I've, um, eliminated that source of temptation."

Reutal shivered with delight. "Maybe, but having the cat around will certainly liven things up—especially when you start fucking him."

Sara nearly swallowed her tongue. Somehow she didn't think that would happen anytime soon and couldn't see how it would make any appreciable changes in Reutal's life. "H-how so?"

"I'll be able to see it in your eyes." His own bulbous orbs gleamed with a carnal light. "We Norludians just like the idea that those around us are doing it, whether we're getting any or not." He smiled and patted her arm in a confiding manner. "We're very sexual, you know."

Sara snorted. "I hadn't noticed."

"You wouldn't," Reutal said bluntly, "because you're not a very sexual being. I've noticed that about you. Watch." He touched her hand with a sucker-tipped finger. Sara felt a subtle pull on her skin, but not much else. "If I were to do that with any other human female who was about to get all lovey-dovey with Jerden, my tongue would get so hard I wouldn't be able to talk." He shrugged and released the suction. "But, as you can see, it has no effect on me." He let out a deep, regretful sigh. "So sad." He paused as a wicked grin stole across his fishlike lips. "But the cat's gonna change that. You wait and see if he doesn't."

Sara stared at him blankly. How in the world should she respond to that? Thankfully, she didn't have to.

Reutal rubbed his hands together with greedy anticipation. "So, now that we've got that settled, what's for lunch?"

Sara shook her head. "I have absolutely no idea."

With Sara's culinary imagination temporarily on hiatus, lunch wound up being leftover *onpulyo* soup and grilled cheese. Although the food might have been a bit boring, the conversation was not. Zatlen voiced his approval of the new liaison, Reutal snickered constantly—when he wasn't making sexual remarks—and Drania giggled so much Sara was amazed she didn't choke on her sandwich.

As she heated the soup, Sara recalled that she'd gotten the recipe for that traditional Davordian dish from Salan. Would Salan be a more frequent visitor if Jerden became a permanent resident? Or had she shared her last recipe? The two women had never been particularly close, but Sara hated to lose the dairymaid's friendship, and she certainly didn't want to make any enemies. When Jerden proposed, avoiding the advances of Salan and Nate had been the primary objective—which, now that she'd considered it more carefully, wasn't much of a reason at all.

The funny thing was, she already missed him. Now that the gang was gathered around the lunch table, she felt his absence more acutely than she would if she'd suddenly lost an arm. In only a few days, he'd become a member of her little "family." Reutal liked him, Drania thought he was a hunk, and though Zatlen's reaction had been a bit more reserved, he'd voiced no objections. How had Jerden done it?

Must be a Zetithian thing, Sara decided as she took a sip of her soup. Either you really liked them or you wanted to hunt them down and exterminate them the way Rutger Grekkor had evidently done. She couldn't imagine anyone feeling that much hatred toward an entire race, but then, she wasn't an insanely jealous man with money to burn. Actually, the more she thought about it, the more it became clear that as things now stood, the Terran mate of a Zetithian man was in far greater danger than her husband. Audrey's death was proof of that.

Viewed in that light, even *dating* a Zetithian could be potentially deadly. The longer she sat there, the more restless Sara became—a restlessness that she suspected could only be relieved by one thing. Fortunately, he was coming over for dinner.

Sara spent the rest of the day working with the young horses and doing her best to put the morning's events out of her mind. However, by late afternoon, her anxiety level had reached the point that her icy hands could barely hold the reins and her gaze had darted toward the southern horizon so often her neck ached. None of the horses were going well for her, either. When she finally spotted Jerden and Danuban trotting down the hill with Cria bounding alongside them and felt herself relax, she realized why she'd been having so much trouble—particularly with Yusuf, whom she'd regrettably chosen to ride last. Horses didn't like tense, nervous riders and her rush of relief was so intense even Yusuf heaved a sigh.

Coming to a halt, Sara didn't bother trying to be subtle and turned toward them, her eyes drinking in the vision of man, horse, and cat. Poetry in motion, animal magnetism, nature at its finest… It didn't matter that she'd seen this sight before—the effect was even stronger now, making her scalp tighten as a thrill swept down her neck and shoulders. Captivating, entrancing, awe-inspiring, and just plain… *"Beautiful."*

Yusuf stood perfectly still and alert, a brief flick of his right ear the only evidence that he'd even heard her whisper—or felt her subsequent shiver. Like her, his attention was fixed on the approaching horse and rider.

Rather than slackening his pace, Jerden urged the stallion to pick up speed as they neared the arena. Sara's breath caught in her throat as Jerden rocked forward, his hands fisted in the thick mane as Danuban gathered himself to soar over the fence in a perfect arc. Landing as lightly as the leopard beside them, they made a quick turn and trotted over to where she sat motionless in the saddle. The man certainly knew how to make an entrance.

Jerden grinned, displaying his fangs. "Did you miss me?"

Sara had felt her jaw drop, so she knew she was gaping at him like an idiot. "I, uh, yes, I believe I did." She took a deep breath and glanced at the fence. "Didn't know he was that good a jumper. Granted, that rail is a little less than a meter high, but—"

Any further comment she might have made was cut off as Jerden vaulted from the stallion's back and proceeded to pull her off her horse and into his arms. "I missed you too, Sara."

She had less than an instant to realize his intent before he lowered his head. Their lips touched lightly at first—only a tentative nibble on her lower lip—then, as if sensing her lack of resistance, he deepened the kiss, covering her lips with his mouth. How he kept from biting her with those sharp fangs, Sara never knew. She only knew she wasn't afraid, and though her knees weakened, they didn't fail her.

Not that she needed them. His muscles were hard beneath her touch as she slid an arm up to encircle his neck, yet he was so gentle; holding her in a firm, but yielding grasp. Cupping the back of her head with one hand, he curled the other around her lower back, pulling her so close she could feel his heart beating against her breast.

He was purring. Soothing vibrations emanated from his throat while his tongue swept over her lips like that of a mother cat grooming her young. Her free hand crept around his waist, returning his embrace before slipping downward to encounter the back flap of his loincloth, making her wish he hadn't opted to dress for dinner. Thankfully, that was all he wore, giving her the opportunity to feel the play of muscles beneath the smooth skin of his back.

He was amazingly strong. She could feel the latent strength in the effortless manner in which he held her. Even if her legs were to suddenly give way, she would have remained standing. Knowing that he wouldn't let her fall allowed her to feel safe for the first time in more years than she cared to count—totally, completely, and utterly safe... Craving more of the comfort he provided, she leaned into his warmth, returning his kiss, even parting her lips when his tongue sought entry.

There had once been a young girl named Sara who'd dreamed of a moment like this. Long ago, that girl had felt the stirrings of passion, of desire, and the need to be loved. Life's misfortunes had caused those feelings to be shunted aside—deprived of all that might have nourished and brought them fully into flower. Their growth had been stunted, but the fact that she could allow Jerden to come this close proved they hadn't been destroyed completely. That girl was still there, buried somewhere deep within the woman she'd become, and she still retained the roots of those emotions. All she had to do was find them.

Chapter 14

JERDEN HADN'T HELD A WOMAN IN HIS ARMS AND kissed her like that in months. Yet even after such a long layoff, the effect on him was surprising. He would never have guessed she could feel that good or make him want her any more than he already did. Unfortunately, her neutral scent made him want to break down and cry. He could give her such joy if only she would allow it.

One kiss, Jerden. It's only one kiss—and the first real one, at that. Be patient.

It was difficult to be patient when his heart ached and his blood sang—everywhere, that is, except his cock. This time, he was sure the problem wasn't on his side of the equation. She was the one holding back. He was giving it his all.

While purring drove most women wild, Sara seemed immune to its effects. At least she wasn't fighting him— was even kissing him back. Sort of. Then it occurred to him that the last man to kiss her had been Nate, and she'd passed out from fear. This was a *definite* improvement.

Telling her she could trust him with her life—and her heart—wasn't enough. Kissing her wasn't enough. He had to convince her by doing. She hadn't lost her desire overnight and it wouldn't be restored overnight. That Jerden wanted it to return before the next heartbeat was irrelevant. He had to give her time.

Still, her scent was uniquely hers, be it neutral or

drenched with passion. Inhaling deeply, he let it fill his head and seep into his blood. His hands trembled with the need to tear her clothes from her body and caress every inch of her skin.

Unlike so many others he'd fucked, this one woman had him falling hard and fast for her. The one who'd saved him, whether she knew it or not—whether she'd done it intentionally or not. Salan would've given her right arm for the chance to rescue a Zetithian man and earn his undying gratitude. Sara had taken him in with no more emotion than was required to take in a stray puppy—perhaps even less. Most people *liked* puppies. Sara had apparently put men in the same category as rats raiding the feed bin.

It occurred to him then that he'd done just that. He'd come into her life, taken her horse, her hospitality, her food. Even rescuing her from Nate was something Zatlen or Reutal could've done. It was high time he gave something back. Something only *he* could give her…

The answer to that was obvious. *Joy, unlike any you have ever known.* How many times had he said that to a woman? Hundreds? And strictly speaking, it had always been true. Even women who had been with Onca or Tarq before had rated his performance as superior. Not that he could hold a candle to either of them now.

Still, he *had* been told he was the best kisser…

"Mmm, Sara," he murmured against her lips. "You taste delicious."

She drew back slightly. "Thought I was—what was it you said—neutral?"

"Your desire would taste better," he conceded. "But every woman has her own unique flavor and scent. I like yours very much."

"You certainly taste better than Nate—though that isn't saying a whole lot. He's a smoker."

"Filthy habit," Jerden agreed.

"Yes, it is. I can hardly stand the smell. Makes me want to throw up."

Jerden chuckled. "Sure it doesn't make you pass out?"

"Not usually."

"Speaking of passing out, did you notice anything just now?"

"You mean did I notice that I'm still conscious?"

"Yeah. I was half expecting to have to carry you into the house again." *Good sign, though.* "Care to explain that?"

She straightened up as he released her. "Well, you *did* warn me to expect it."

"That's all it takes? A warning?"

Sara touched her lips—lips that appeared more succulent than ever for having already been kissed. "I dunno. Haven't been kissed much."

"And now you've been kissed by the best." Jerden stifled the urge to do it again. *Better not push my luck.*

"Cocky bastard." Her smile took the sting out of her words.

"Hey, when it's true…"

To his surprise, she didn't argue, but her smile changed to a frown in an instant. "Apparently Salan called here, wanting to know if it was true we were sleeping together. Reutal, of course, told her we were, which means Nate will probably be the next to know." She glanced up, her troubled green eyes meeting his. "I don't mind telling you, I'm scared to death he'll come back."

"Guess we'd better have that date soon, then."

"Yeah, I guess we should." Drawing in a ragged breath, she continued. "I handled it the last time, and Reutal and Zatlen are right out there in the stables if I need them, but…" Her sentence trailed off as her eyes swept over him.

He hoped his grin wasn't too smug. "Why, Sara. Are you actually asking me to stick around?"

"Much as I hate to admit it, yes." She paused, chewing thoughtfully on her lower lip.

Jerden stared at her mouth. If she kept that up, she was going to get kissed again. He was surprised he wasn't drooling. With any other woman, his dick would not only have been hard as a rock, it would have been dripping all over the place. It was strange feeling the way he did without that response. Neater, perhaps, and certainly more discreet, but at the same time… disappointing.

Cria gave him a nudge just below his knee. He glanced down at her huge yellow eyes—eyes that advised patience.

He gave her a wink. *Message received.*

"You'll probably think this is funny," Sara went on, "but when Nate was here, I imagined you standing behind me, snarling at him. It… helped."

"Glad to hear it, but it's still good that you were able to deal with him on your own. Shows progress."

Sara didn't argue. "I guess so." She glanced at the horse she'd been riding and then back to a spot somewhere near the center of his chest. "You're early. As you can see, I haven't even started dinner yet. The gang wanted *hunela* tonight, and it takes *forever* to make."

"I thought I might help you with that."

"You mean you really can cook?"

He grinned. "Kissing isn't the only thing I'm good at, Sara. Does that surprise you?"

"Well, yeah," she admitted. "Kind of."

"I was on a refugee starship for twenty-five years. Our rescuer taught us all sorts of things. Languages, customs, history—you name it."

"Including how to kiss?" Her mischievous smile and twinkling eyes did peculiar things to Jerden's heart.

"I learned that on my own."

"Ah. I see."

She was learning, too—very quickly. Still, it was possible that she didn't even realize her coy expression was quite so teasing, beckoning, even seductive. But it was.

"Want me to do it again?"

Sara shrugged. "That's up to you."

"No, it isn't. It's *entirely* up to you."

"I didn't ask you to kiss me the last time." She frowned and began devouring her lip again. "Did I?"

Jerden didn't think he could take much more. If she didn't stop biting her lip, he was going to pounce on her and rip her clothes off with his teeth—whether his dick was hard or not. "Not in so many words, but you *did* say you missed me."

"And that's all it takes?" She sounded every bit as puzzled as she appeared.

"Sometimes."

She looked up at him with a grimace. "Look, I told you—or if I haven't, I should have—I'm not any good at this stuff. If you want something from me, you're gonna have to come right out and say it."

Had a man *ever* been given an opening like that?

And not taken advantage of it? "I probably shouldn't. I wouldn't want to scare you."

This time, her upper lip was the target for her teeth. "Oh. Well, maybe we should put these horses up and forget about it for now."

Jerden blew out a pent-up breath. "Okay, I'll say it. I want at least one more kiss."

He barely had time to register her nod before yanking her back into his arms and kissing her the way he wanted. Slowly, deeply, with all the sexual heat he could pack into it. She not only didn't resist, he could've sworn he heard her moan.

"Whoo hoo!" Reutal hooted as he hopped over the fence. "It's about fuckin' time! Hold on a second."

Scurrying over, he attached his fingertips to Sara's bare forearm. His eyes narrowed in concentration. "Not yet," he said as he released her. "But close. Very, very close."

"What are you talking about?" Jerden demanded.

"Never mind," Reutal said, giving him a pat on the back. "Keep going. You're doing a great job."

Jerden didn't think he could pick up right where he'd left off, particularly since Sara was now giggling uncontrollably. At least she wasn't mortified or taking a swing at anybody. More than that, he couldn't have said.

"Aw, c'mon, Jerden! Kiss her some more!" Jerden spotted Drania peering at them through the fence rails, her long pink ears wiggling like crazy. Zatlen stood next to her with a broad grin, looking far more masculine than usual. Apparently his male side appreciated watching a good seduction as much as the next fellow.

If it could be called a seduction. From Jerden's

perspective, it was beginning to seem more like a Rhylosian circus. He reminded himself that every circus he'd ever seen on Rhylos had included sexual acts, but that was beside the point.

"I'll just take these horses to the barn," Reutal said, gathering up the reins of Sara's mount. "Then you two can get started again."

Catching Danuban by the halter, he headed toward the gate where he handed the stallion off to Zatlen. Drania followed them down the path to the stable, her ears still quivering with excitement as she stole the occasional backward glance. Pausing at the doorway, she gave Jerden a firm thumbs up and then disappeared inside the barn.

Sara wiped the tears from her eyes. She couldn't remember the last time she'd laughed that hard. Perhaps she never had. One glance at Jerden almost set her off again.

"Oh, my," she gasped. "You should see the look on your face—somewhere between stunned and I don't know what."

Jerden grinned. "Stunned is right What was that bit with Reutal all about?"

"Something about my essence," she replied. "He can tell when the mares are in season, so I guess he figures he can do the same thing with me."

He appeared to consider this for a moment, and then shook his head. "I carry around a much more reliable indicator. And right now, it says you're not."

Sara didn't have to think very hard to know just exactly what he meant by that, somehow managing to keep her gaze from drifting toward his groin. "He's always spot-on with the mares. Maybe his senses are more acute than yours."

"I doubt it," Jerden said. "But if he says you're close, I guess I should take that as encouragement."

Since Sara wasn't convinced she *wanted* to be in season, she didn't know if Reutal's assessment was encouraging or not. What she *did* know was that this had been the strangest damn day of her life. "Whatever. Let's go fix dinner and see what happens."

———

The first thing Sara thought as she entered her kitchen was that it wasn't big enough for Jerden. Out in the open he'd seemed much less daunting. Now that they were alone together in a relatively small room, her anxiety returned. She wasn't afraid of him, but his size was—

No, it wasn't just his size, it was his entire persona. He was simply too much *man* for her tiny cottage.

She'd never felt crowded with any of the gang in there, which wasn't surprising, since she was taller than all three of them. Not only was Jerden taller than she was, but the sheer bulk of all those muscles made him seem much larger. She would have been more comfortable with him had they been in a palatial home with vaulted ceilings and arched doorways—one that had fewer places in which to be cornered.

The previous morning she'd been dropping things in his presence and had even ordered him out of her house. Now she understood why. She'd been cornered before—though in a much smaller space.

But not by him. She had to keep telling herself that. Nonetheless, her chest tightened and her hands started shaking. Again. "Um, why don't you have a seat in the living room? I'll fix dinner."

"I've got a better idea," he said, pulling a chair out from the table. "Why don't *you* have a seat and *I'll* fix dinner."

Her first impulse was to carry that chair out to the porch. Unfortunately, Cria chose that moment to stretch out between the table and the stove, effectively cutting off her escape route. Her huge yawn revealed fangs even longer and sharper than Jerden's. Suddenly, the room seemed to shrink by half. Sara ran a hand through her hair, her eyes darting back and forth in near panic as she tried to decide whether or not she could leap over the leopard's sprawling figure without losing a leg in the process.

Jerden didn't miss the gesture or her change of mood. "What's wrong? Afraid I'll mess up the kitchen?"

"No, it's not that. I feel... weird."

He stared at her for a long moment. "You're going to order me out of here again," he said flatly. "Aren't you?" He turned away from her quickly, but not before she saw the pain in his eyes.

"I'm *trying* to relax, Jerden. Believe me, I'm trying. But I can't help how I feel."

He took a deep breath and blew it out slowly as though trying to control his temper or some other emotion. "I thought we'd gotten past this. Look, I can understand you being nervous, but *please*, just stay here and talk to me—about anything. I only want to be with you and hold you if you'll let me. You make me feel... whole again." He paused, frowning. "In fact, I'm not sure I've ever felt whole—or grounded. Not for a very long time. I've been... adrift."

His gaze met hers; the glow from his vertical pupils was more apparent in the dim indoor light. He looked so alien with his upswept brows and pointed ears, and yet his expression was so intensely human.

"You left your homeworld by choice. Mine was blown to bits along with all of my family. I haven't had a real home since." His eyes swept the room. "Nothing like this. It's no wonder I wound up in a brothel on Rhylos. And then Audrey was murdered because of what I am. I'm sorry if it sounds selfish, but I *need* you, Sara. Most of all, I need you to understand."

She could've sworn there were tears in his eyes—or were those her own tears clouding her vision? Nodding, she sank down in the chair he'd offered, her gaze locked on his. "Go ahead. I'm listening."

He blinked, and yes, there really were tears. She could see them glistening at the corners of his eyes. "Our enemies had been very thorough. There was no way off the planet. We could see the asteroid heading straight for our world, and there wasn't a damned thing we could do to stop it.

"Then a ship landed, and my parents made sure I got on it. I was five years old and the only child they had left. I was screaming my head off when they handed me over. I didn't understand why they couldn't come with me. There wasn't room for them—I realized that later, but at the time…"

He paused, shaking his head. "Then the ship lifted off and left orbit just before the asteroid hit. Some of us were only babies, but the rest of us were watching the viewscreen and saw it happen." His voice dropped to a whisper. "Our entire planet was gone in a matter of seconds. I'll never forget the screams of those children until my dying day."

He brushed away the tears. "Later on, we were told that Rutger Grekkor, the husband of our rescuer, was responsible for the war against our kind. Amelyana had taken a Zetithian lover, and Grekkor, a very rich, powerful, and insanely jealous man, had retaliated by attempting to kill all of us. She stole one of his ships and did what she could to save as many children as possible.

"We spent the next twenty-five years in space, waiting until she deemed it safe to land. It wasn't until Grekkor was killed and the bounty was no longer being paid on any survivors that we came to Terra Minor. Grekkor's assets were then divided among the remaining Zetithians. We went from penniless to rich almost overnight.

"Some of us settled here. My friends Tarq and Onca and I decided to pool our funds and open a brothel on Rhylos. We'd been trapped on that ship for so long... I guess we were all a little nuts. Anyway, we made a fortune, but then Audrey was killed—and you know what that did to me. I came here to live and try to forget and maybe get back to normal." He sighed. "I'm not quite there yet—if I even know what *normal* is. Anyway, that's my story. When you're ready to tell yours, I'll be here to listen."

Sara sat gazing at him, trying to imagine the depths of his pain. The darkness in her own past was *nothing* compared to what had happened to him. Nothing, and yet she still couldn't find the words to tell him about it. She had *never* been able to speak of it—to anyone.

As if he read her thoughts, he went on, "And don't be thinking that what happened to you seems trifling compared to my history. Nothing hurt me. Not directly. I suffered no injuries—emotional trauma, yes, but nothing physical. I believe it was different for you, and therefore even more devastating—more critical to your life and who you are. When you do decide to tell me, don't make light of it, Sara, and don't compare your pain to mine or anyone else's. Believe me, it won't do any good. All that matters is how it affected *you*."

The only time Sara had initiated physical contact with a man was when Jerden had been lying unconscious in her bed. If she was ever going to do it with a *conscious* man, the time was now. Getting to her feet, she held out her arms.

And he walked right into them.

The impact of his body against hers was even more intimate than when he'd kissed her. She'd never clung to anyone like that before, and he returned her embrace with a fervor that shocked her to the core. Tears slid down her cheeks and onto his chest as she cried for those he'd lost, those he'd loved, but most of all, for him; one of the few left behind to remember the horror—who had to go on living, trying to be normal, trying to stay sane.

Sara had no idea what to say to him. What words could possibly make a difference? "I won't tell you to go. I'll… get used to you being here. I need you too."

She felt the tension leave him as he pressed his lips to her cheek. Apparently she'd said the right thing.

"Then I'm staying." He released her slowly, reluctantly, his tentative smile steadily gaining strength. "And I *will* be fixing dinner."

"We'll do it together."

Chapter 15

THIS IS JERDEN, SARA REMINDED HERSELF AS SHE pulled the ingredients for *hunela* out of the stasis unit. *Jerden*. Not Nate, and certainly not that asshole she'd once made the mistake of going to the movies with. She closed her eyes and tried to imagine herself in a spacious kitchen, acres in size, with plenty of room to retreat if necessary. Taking a deep breath, she willed her hands to be steady as she selected the chicken breasts, vegetables, and cheese. A sidelong glance revealed Jerden perusing her spice rack, looking like the answer to every woman's dream. Tall, tanned, and muscular, with black hair that hung to his waist, he was still wearing that same loincloth. Strangely enough, she would've preferred that he'd left it at home. True, it covered all the more erotic parts of him, but it also disrupted the natural flow of his skin and the perfect symmetry of his body—similar to a beautiful horse wearing a saddle.

Not that clothes didn't do that to everyone—and there were plenty of people who should never be seen undressed, no matter what species they happened to be. Jerden, however, fell into a different category of beings—one that made any covering or adornment completely unnecessary.

Of course, she would never tell him so. Any comments to that effect would surely be misconstrued as provocative, suggestive, and that was a thought she didn't want him to have. Not yet, anyway. Perhaps not ever.

Sara found it difficult to believe that a man like Jerden would want to marry a woman who might never want him sexually. It seemed to go against everything she'd ever heard about Zetithians. Granted, Zetithian *women* showed little interest in sex, which might explain why the men were seduction personified, but at least they had the *potential* to be enticed.

It occurred to her then that she was probably more like the women of Zetith than those of her own world. Human females had desires and they acted on them. Sara felt no desire and wouldn't have known how to attract a man if her life depended on it.

Wear something low cut and show lots of cleavage. Someone had told her that once. Sure. That was a great enticement, but for it to work, a woman had to have something to reveal. Sara's figure wasn't the slightest bit voluptuous, being more like that of a lanky teenage boy than a female in her thirties.

Why am I even thinking about this? He's already here. He even asked me to marry him. The thought made her shudder—or was it a quiver? He didn't need to be seduced or attracted to her, did he? All she really had to do was avoid pushing him away and quit acting like she was afraid of him.

She hadn't been afraid at all when he held her in his arms. *How very peculiar...*

"I like to put *lycaque* root in *hunela*," he said as he selected various jars of herbs. "Makes it more authentic. Do you have any?"

Sara was relieved to have this neutral topic to divert

her thoughts. "No, but there are plenty of Twilanans living around here. It'd probably be easy to enough to find."

"Maybe next time, then."

Obviously this lack of culinary perfection wasn't something he was going to lose sleep over—or berate her for not having. Considering the number of herbs and spices that were available throughout the galaxy, Sara considered her stock to be fairly decent, if not comprehensive. She'd have to add another room onto the house if she wanted them all—*and* take out a loan to pay for them. *Not* a high priority.

Then again, Jerden apparently had money to burn. She'd be a rich woman if she married him, and if she wanted to add a room, she could. It might have been better if she hadn't known he had money—and would make her seem less mercenary, which was probably what everyone would think of her now.

Assuming that Jerden would prefer to do something manly and exciting, like chopping vegetables, she handed him a knife. "I'll make the sauce."

He winked at her. "Minus the *lycaque* root."

"Yeah." She got out milk, butter, eggs, and flour. Scooping some butter into a saucepan, she set it over low heat to melt.

"I'm glad you've got a real stove," he said as he peeled the onions. "All I've got is one of those flash ovens, and it doesn't do a damn thing for me. At the time I moved in, I didn't really care. But now I do. Funny how that works, isn't it?"

"Uh-huh."

He was making small talk and winking at her. Not

long ago, he wouldn't have bothered to do either one—
had acted like the wildcat he was rumored to be. Now,
he only *looked* like one, though less so than when he'd
been naked all the time. The loincloth made him seem
a bit more civilized. Even so, he could have taken it off
and she wouldn't have minded. After all, Reutal never
wore clothing. Zatlen preferred boots, jeans, and a T-
shirt. Drania wore coveralls and no shirt. It was purely a
matter of personal comfort…

He nodded toward the iron skillet sitting on the stove.
"I like that kind of skillet, too. Food just tastes better
when it's cooked that way."

"I've always thought so." *He's talking about cooking
utensils and I'm thinking about whether or not he should
wear clothes. What's wrong with this picture?*

After pouring some olive oil into the skillet, she
turned on the burner and switched on the deep fryer.
She was about to suggest he lose the loincloth when she
glanced at his bare chest. Sautéing vegetables without
the benefit of clothing might not be the best plan—not
to mention deep-frying the chicken. "I've got an apron
around here somewhere—not sure it'll *fit* you, but…"

His brow went up in surprise and then dropped to a
frown. "Should I have worn a shirt?"

"No, that wasn't what I meant. You can wear whatever you like—or nothing at all, if you prefer. I just
don't want you to get splattered with hot oil." There.
She'd said it. The ball was in his court now.

A slow smile spread across his lips. "Why, Sara, how
sweet of you to be so concerned for my safety."

His words might not have acknowledged everything
she'd said, but his expression and inflection certainly

did. Arching an eyebrow, he eyed her speculatively, waiting for her to speak.

She shrugged, feeling somewhat helpless. "Well, why *wouldn't* I be concerned? You're my… boyfriend. Sort of."

"Yes, I am," he said. "Sort of." Setting the knife down, he took a step closer. "And since you don't care whether I wear this thing or not…" He hooked a thumb in the open side near the waistband. "I'll take it off." His smile intensified, allowing his fangs to peek past his lips. "Later."

Sara's face suddenly felt hot and tingly and she swallowed hard—actually, it was more of a gulp. "W-whatever you like."

Sara could've sworn he winked at her again. Returning to his task, he transferred the onions to the skillet along with a handful of *chuelas* and then began slicing the zucchini. "On the way over here, I was thinking about what Nate did last night."

His voice had lost its seductive note so abruptly, Sara questioned whether it had ever been there at all. "And?" Dumping some flour into the melted butter, she whipped it vigorously.

"I don't think I should leave you here alone anymore—especially at night—out of concern for your… *safety*."

So, he was going to stay all night and take off the loincloth. *Great. Now you've done it, Sara. Made him think you're going to fall into his arms and make mad, passionate love with him. All night. Every night. Maybe even until death do us part. Oh, my God…* Hell, he'd been sobbing in her arms just a few minutes before. Was he pretending all of it? Could she really trust anyone whose moods changed so quickly? God knows, hers did too. She inhaled sharply. "If you think that's best."

"I do." His sidelong glance glowed with anticipation. "I think we should sleep together, too. I never told you how much I liked waking up next to you, Sara. I should've told you at the time, but I wasn't sure how you'd take it." He turned his catlike eyes on her, holding her gaze effortlessly, completely. "When I woke up and found you in bed beside me, I picked up a scent that surprised me. I couldn't leave you then. I wanted to stay with you and find out why your dreams were so… haunted. Then I started purring and your despair seemed to lift a little. After a bit, I got up and almost went home. But I couldn't make myself leave, so I crawled back in with you." He paused to sprinkle a pinch of *yishush* on the onions. Within seconds, the aroma of the pungent spice filled the air. "I *liked* being there with you, Sara. Did you like waking up next to me?"

Knowing it wouldn't do a bit of good to deny it, she told him the truth. "I was a little afraid. I liked the warmth and the purring, but…"

"That's okay," he said quickly. "I understand."

"No, you probably don't," she said ruefully. "I don't even understand it myself." Adding milk to the pan, she continued whisking the mixture, thinking that maybe if she stirred it hard enough, the answer might come to her.

It didn't, of course. Thankfully, Jerden didn't pursue the subject any further.

She set the pan back on the stove and cracked the eggs with more force than necessary. That didn't help, either. *Careful, Sara. You'll break the yolks.*

Jerden was probably thinking the same thing, but he kept quiet. Tossing the zucchini into the skillet, he then cut the chicken into paper-thin slices. Sara caught herself watching him and shifted her focus back to the bowl full of eggs. She stared at it, unable to remember how to separate the yolks from the whites.

Gravy ladle. Getting the ladle out of the drawer, she used it to fish out the yolks and add them to the sauce. More whisking. For once, she didn't mind the monotony, as it gave her something to do with her hands. If she'd simply sat and let him do it all, she'd have gone mad.

Jerden made quick work of the chicken, crushed a few cloves of garlic, and added them to the vegetables before giving them a stir. She watched out of the corner of her eye as he seasoned the meat, adding a dash or two of the various spices he'd selected before dipping it in the egg whites. After dredging it in flour, he rolled it into perfect little scrolls. His actions were smooth and practiced, his lack of hesitation demonstrating that knew what he was doing.

"So, you learned to cook on the refugee ship?"

"Yeah, we had to take turns." He dropped the chicken scrolls one by one into the fryer. "And trust me, if the meals you prepared weren't any good, you *heard* about it."

"Kind of like cooking for my gang," she said with a chuckle. "They're pretty vocal, as you may have noticed."

"You like them a lot, don't you?"

She nodded. "They're my family." Which was perfectly true. She cared as much about Reutal, Zatlen, and Drania as she did her real family, perhaps even more.

"Reutal certainly acts like a brother out to protect

his sister. He gave Nate quite a tongue-lashing after he kissed you. I'm surprised he didn't take a swing at him."

Sara laughed. "He doesn't like Nate any more than I do. Probably dying for the excuse."

Noting that the sauce had finally thickened, she added salt and pepper and then set it aside. She slipped past Jerden and stooped to pull a baking dish out of the lower cabinet, doing her best not to stare at his powerful thighs. She set the dish on the cutting board and Jerden tipped the contents of the skillet into it.

He lifted the basket from the fryer, briefly inspecting the chicken scrolls before tossing them in with the vegetables. Sara poured on the sauce and Jerden smoothed it out with a spatula. "Got any *surlea* cheese to go on top?"

Sara snorted a laugh. "In your dreams, rich boy. Do you have any idea how expensive that stuff is?"

He shook his head. "Not really, but I do know it's worth it, whatever it costs."

"The best I can do for now is Asiago." She handed him a bowl of the grated cheese. "I've never tasted *surlea*, though from what I understand, it's pretty similar. I'm not even sure you can buy it in Nimbaza."

"Guess I got kinda spoiled on Rhylos. They had *everything*."

She switched off the fryer. "Terra Minor is coming up in the galaxy, but it's still basically a frontier planet. There are lots of things you can't get here."

Asiago wasn't exactly cheap, either. Jerden didn't seem to care, adding a liberal amount to the top of the *hunela*. Her gasp of dismay only made him grin. "You know something, Sara?"

"What?" *Aside from the fact that you're going to eat me out of house and home.*

"I think you and I need to discuss the advantages of being my wife."

Jerden put the *hunela* in the oven while he waited for the idea to sink in. Being married to him would have perks Sara obviously hadn't considered yet.

"Such as?"

"Among other things, as the wife of a Zetithian, your property taxes will be significantly reduced. As the wife of a *rich* Zetithian, you can afford to buy pretty much any kind of cheese you like. Granted, I'm not making money hand over fist anymore, but I've invested wisely and have a steady income from the interest. What I don't spend is automatically reinvested."

"So I'd be an idiot *not* to marry you?"

He shook his head. "That's not what I'm saying. I just want you to know that getting Nate off your back isn't necessarily the only perk."

"Everyone will think I'm marrying you for your money."

"I doubt it. Of course, there are disadvantages, as well. You got a taste of it while we were in Nimbaza. People here think I'm some kind of crazy hermit, but I've been called lots of other nasty little names—man-whore, prostitute, gigolo. Does that bother you?"

Quickly averting her eyes, she picked up a dishcloth and wiped off the cutting board. "It's a little late to be asking me that, don't you think?"

"Not really. You haven't committed to anything but dinner and a date so far. You can still back out if you want, but if you don't, this is something we'll both have to live with."

"Yeah, well, you know what they say about reformed rakes making good husbands." She frowned. "I mean, I *guess* you're reformed. Sort of." She paused, cocking her head to finally meet his gaze. "If you could, would you go back to that kind of life?"

"No. Not unless I was starving—and maybe not even then. Sure, we earned plenty of credits, but it certainly wasn't worth risking Audrey's life or anyone else's." He took a deep breath. "Let's just say I've learned from my mistakes."

She nodded and went back to her cleaning.

Jerden carried the dirty pots and pans over to the sink to wash, keeping an eye on Sara as he went. Her expression was thoughtful, but thankfully she didn't look like she was about to jump out of her skin anymore. Her shoulder had brushed his thigh ever so slightly when she'd bent down to retrieve that baking dish. He doubted she even noticed the brief contact. If she had, she surely would've acknowledged it with a gasp or at least begged his pardon.

Having related his history to her, he'd expected her to tell him something more about herself. No, make that *hoped*, rather than expected. He was beginning to understand how anxious his friends had felt when he was so fucked up. They'd wanted him to improve instantly, not take months or years to heal. He hadn't recovered overnight—it only seemed that way, the pain building up until he finally reached the breaking point. *His* breaking point. Where Sara's was and how long it would take her to get there, he couldn't begin to guess. What he *could* guess was that her pain was long-standing and deeply embedded in her personality. He certainly had his work cut out for him.

Still, he hadn't been the star hunk of the Zetithian Palace for nothing. If anyone could do it, he could.

Knowing that the *hunela* would take at least another hour to bake, he helped her with the cleaning up as quickly and efficiently as he knew how, wanting to spend most of that time doing something more pleasant. The last thing he did was to shoo Cria out of the way and set the table, frowning as he remembered they were a chair short. He'd have to bring one over from his place—that is, if he ever went home again. His pets must've known that because they'd *all* followed him this time.

"While we're waiting on dinner, why don't we take a look at some of those Friesians you were telling me about?"

Her eyes lit up. Someday Jerden hoped to see that same expression when he suggested they do something entirely different. *Someday*.

"They're the most gorgeous horses you'll ever see in your life. Absolutely breathtaking. Hold on while I get my computer." She darted down the hallway toward the living room.

Jerden bit back a smile as she snatched her computer off the coffee table and started back toward the kitchen, stopping short when she realized he'd followed her.

"Why don't we sit out here?" he suggested. "It's a lot more comfortable."

Her frown was fleeting, but not so quick he didn't see it before it was replaced with a blank look. "Oh… all right… I guess."

Apparently only the kitchen was safe. He could hardly *wait* to see her reluctance to shower with him. If he was ever going to smell her desire, she had to relax. *Guess I should bring a bottle of wine along with that chair.* Then he remembered he didn't even *have* a bottle of wine.

Sara's cats were sitting on the far end of the sofa, one curled up on the headrest beneath the front window and the other sprawled on the seat cushion. Jerden took a seat in the middle. "Chill out, Sara. I don't bite." Which, strictly speaking, wasn't true. "Not much, anyway."

She didn't seem reassured, glancing down the hall just as Cria came through the doorway. With a huge, jaw-popping yawn, the big cat stretched out across the threshold. The tabby registered Cria's presence with a slow blink. The chubby little black cat didn't even look up.

"And Cria won't bite you, either." He patted the seat beside him. "Just come on over here and show me those horses."

She hesitated a moment and then crossed the room to perch on the edge of the couch. It wasn't quite as cozy as he'd imagined, but it was a start. Not saying a word, she activated the receiver and projected the page.

"I can't see it very well," he said. "Can you scoot back a little?"

Sara heaved a sigh. Pivoting on her hip, she landed right beside him. "Better?"

"Much." He studied the image before him. The horse looked a lot like Danuban, but was taller, with a heavier build and a long, curly mane and tail and feathery hair growing on the back of its lower legs. "This is the stallion?"

She nodded. "Yeah. There are a couple more, but this is the best one." She switched to the video and the stallion began to move. "Awesome, isn't he?"

"Yes, he is." Whereas Danuban moved with dancing steps, this horse had thicker legs and larger hooves. "Graceful, yet powerful."

"They have a natural high-stepping action and are a little higher-headed than the Andalusians."

Jerden could see that. There was an arch to the neck, which was longer in proportion to its body than an Andalusian's. Even so, the stallion's mane was so long it covered his shoulder completely—thick, black, and curly. "He's got hair like mine."

"That's exactly what I thought." Her nervousness seemed to diminish as her enthusiasm grew. "I mean, you and Danuban make an incredible pair, but *this* horse… well…" She stopped there, her gaze fixed on the stallion.

"You think I look that good on a horse? Really? I'd never have guessed."

For a second, he thought she was going to smack him, but she apparently thought better of it, directing a reproving look at him instead. "Oh, come on, Jerden. You *know* you do. I mean, *really*. Weren't you paying *any* attention to Drania when you came riding into the barn? She practically swooned."

As Jerden recalled, he hadn't been looking at Drania. "Maybe. But what about you, Sara? I didn't notice you doing any swooning."

"Things like that don't make me swoon," she said stiffly.

"But what—no, wait. I remember now. *Nate* makes you swoon."

This time she really did smack him. "It wasn't like that, and you know it!"

"Okay, I deserved that," he conceded with a chuckle. "But tell me, if I'd come riding up on a Friesian, what would you have done?"

She was silent for a moment, chewing her lip pensively. "I probably would have fainted dead away."

"Then I guess I'd better buy that horse." He reached up and tapped the image, sending it back to the information page. In a few minutes, the transaction was complete.

She stared at him, openmouthed. "Do you have any idea how much money you just spent?"

"I certainly do. The same price as one of your swoons." He gave her his best lip-curling grin. "And when that horse gets here, you'd damn well better swoon."

Chapter 16

FAINTING PROBABLY WOULDN'T BE A PROBLEM, SINCE Sara already had an odd flutter in her chest. Her knees would give out next. Jerden had just purchased one of the most expensive, incredibly beautiful Friesian stallions in existence—and he'd done it purely on her recommendation.

She still couldn't quite wrap her head around it. "Are you prone to making impulse buys? If so, it's a wonder you've got any money at all."

He shrugged. "My land wasn't cheap, but you've already seen my house and my entire wardrobe. I'm not what you'd call a conspicuous consumer."

She certainly couldn't argue with that. Then again, he hadn't been particularly frugal with the cheese. She cleared her throat. "Want to buy some mares?"

"Later. Right now, I want you to kiss me and tell me how wonderful I am for buying that horse for you."

Eyeing him with suspicion, she eased back against the armrest. "Shouldn't I save that for when he arrives? I wouldn't want to waste a perfectly good swoon. Besides, you didn't buy him for *me*."

Jerden quirked an eyebrow as he gave her a slow, deliberate nod. "Oh, yes, I did. Don't you get it? I bought that horse to please *you*, Sara, not myself—just like I did when I bought you that dress. It's the sort of thing men do for the women they love."

Her eyes widened. "You aren't in love with me."

"Did you know the word love is a verb as well as a noun? To love someone requires an action." He traced the contour of her cheek with a fingertip, his half smile making him appear more approachable than ever before. "Most people would tell you that what I did for a living had nothing to do with love. But I believe it did. I gave pleasure to women and I gave life to children. There's nothing wrong with that. I've never forced myself on anyone. Never needed to, nor did I ever take advantage of a woman in a vulnerable state. They all had plenty of time to back out—a full year for most of them. I may never have been in love, but that doesn't mean I don't know what's required. Right now, I'm here because we need each other. I'll stay because we *want* each other."

Sara stared at him with disbelief for some time before she finally spoke. "So, what you're saying is that after we've been together for a while, we'll get so used to *being* together, we'll want to *stay* together?"

"Something like that—at least, that's how I see it." His smile broadened, projecting a warmth that was almost palpable. "I know you haven't had much experience with love of the heart—and neither have I—but physical love is something I know a great deal about. You could be my wife *and* my lover. Think of me as forbidden fruit, and you'll want me even more."

Sara had never had such a strange conversation in her life. She had no idea what to make of it. "You're still sure you want to do this?"

"More than ever—if for no other reason than to see the look on your face when you taste *surlea* cheese for the first time." His subsequent grin would've fascinated a far less susceptible woman than Sara. "I want to watch you discover the advantages of being in love. Most of all, I want to see your eyes the first time I give you joy—and all the times thereafter."

If it was a line, it was a damn good one. If it wasn't, he was offering her something she'd never been a part of—scarcely even knew existed. "Don't tempt me with something I can't have, Jerden. I'm not sure I can take it."

His smile was so full of understanding, it nearly broke her heart. "You've already endured more pain than you should have. It's even in your dreams. Let me help you find happiness."

She frowned at him. "I'm happy."

"Are you really? I don't see it—and even more than that, I don't detect it in your scent—at least, not the kind of happiness I can give you. But I'll do my best to put it there."

Her lips formed a grim line as an unwelcome thought occurred to her. "Is this your penance for what happened to Audrey? You'll atone for her death by making me happy?"

"You can think that if you like, because I do feel some guilt. However, I'm beginning to see the utter futility of focusing on the 'what-ifs' in life. If I'd never gone to Rhylos, she needn't have died—that sort of thing. If you look at it that way, it's her own fault she was murdered—after all, she volunteered for the job. But, of course, it *wasn't* her fault; she didn't bring it on herself, and no one can control the actions of others.

"There are so many things that should never have happened—like the destruction of my homeworld. I should still be living in the forests of Zetith, rather than the plains of Terra Minor. You and I should never have met. And yet we're here, together. And right now, I'm unable to give joy to the one woman I most want to give it to, mainly because she doesn't think she wants it or thinks she doesn't deserve it."

He reached for her hand. It was a testament to her growing trust that she didn't jerk it away. When he pressed his lips to her fingers, warmth swirled up her arm, coursing its way toward her heart.

"Kiss me, Sara. That's the only thanks I'll ever ask for giving you anything your heart desires. It's true that money can't buy love, nor can it buy genuine gratitude, but it can give you the freedom to choose. Necessity drives most people's lives. Having those needs met frees you to explore life and live it to the fullest."

He pressed her hand to his chest. "Do you have any idea how many women would envy you this simple touch? And yet, it isn't something you think you want. But perhaps you do. You just don't realize it."

All he wanted was a kiss? It seemed such a small, insignificant thing. Then it struck her that he wasn't talking about trading sexual favors for expensive horses. He was giving her something he knew she wanted, and the only thing he asked for in return was for her to be near enough to kiss him.

In placing her hand on his chest, he'd already pulled her closer to him. The realization that she wasn't frightened anymore surprised her. When had *that* happened? While he was looking at the Friesian? When he'd bought him? She wasn't his prisoner, whether Cria lay across the doorway or not. Not feeling trapped might seem like a trifling matter to anyone else, but it was the most amazing thing that had happened to Sara in years. *He's holding my hand to his chest, asking for a kiss, and I'm not afraid*.

He was so unlike any man she'd ever met and diametrically opposed to any that had ever touched her. He'd kissed *her* before. What would it be like to kiss *him*—to take the lead and know that she wouldn't be ridiculed or scorned? To know that he truly wanted her kiss, welcomed it, and even craved it?

Still, he shouldn't have to pay quite so much for them. "You don't have to trade horses for kisses, Jerden."

"I'm not. I'm only attempting to show you how much one of your kisses is worth to me." He paused, smiling at her in a way that made her heart race and her arms long to hold him. "Oh, I might eventually make you swoon when I come riding up on that new horse, but I'd much rather have a kiss. Right here, right now."

After so many years of believing herself to be the kind of woman no man wanted for herself alone, she realized that Jerden didn't *need* her for anything else. Danuban was his whether she liked it or not. She couldn't keep them apart, nor could she deny that their bond was something rare and special. Nothing else she owned could begin to match what he already possessed. Jerden was a rich man. He could buy anything he wanted. Yet all he wanted was a kiss—from *her*…

A kiss. So simple. So easily bestowed. Most people tossed them out like candy on Halloween—and with even less thought. She could do this. It wasn't *that* hard. She leaned toward him, her hand sliding out of his grasp to his shoulder. He was right about one thing—the number of women in the galaxy who would have given anything to be in her place was shocking. And yet, she was the only one with him now.

His aura surrounded her, his scent and his presence drew her to him like a magnet. In another heartbeat, her lips were touching his and a soft, sensuous thrill stole inward from the point of contact. Feelings long dead sprang to life, and her heart reached out to his, entwining, holding, caressing. She had no choice but to deepen the kiss, to let her arms cling to him for support, and let him support her in turn.

She melted into him as he lifted her onto his lap, his dusky curls whisper-soft against her skin. Bowing his head, he returned her kiss, his hand on her back sending ripples of pleasure cascading down her spine. As her fingers laced through his hair, he eased her down onto the couch, her shoulder touching the cushion just as her cat scooted out of the way with a squeak of protest. Jerden's legs stretched out beside hers and his arms cradled her upper body. She was nearly pinned beneath him but she didn't feel the slightest bit restrained. She wasn't being held down; she was being *held*. There was a difference.

His hair was a curtain, shielding her from anything that might distract her from him, keeping her thoughts focused on him and him alone. He embraced her with his entire body, his leg drawing up to cover hers in a manner that should have felt confining but didn't. He was purring. She could feel the vibration deep in her chest. Soothing, stimulating…

Let it happen, Sara. Don't fight it.

The back door slammed. "Hey, Sara!" Reutal yelled. "That *hunela* smells fuckin' orgasmic! Isn't it ready yet? We're starving!"

Jerden's purr became a chuckle. "And here I thought I liked that guy."

"Oh, and just so you know, I brought an extra chair from my room," Reutal added. "That way you and the cat can sit next to each other."

Sara put a hand on Jerden's chest and gave him a gentle push. "Better let me up before he comes in here to check up on my... essence."

"I dunno. I think I'd like a report, myself," Jerden said, but he let her up anyway.

Swinging her feet over the side of the couch, she stood, frowning down at him. "So, your own *indicator* isn't telling you anything?" Somehow, she thought it should have.

"Not really," he admitted. "But you've got to remember, it hasn't been working so well lately."

"There's nothing wrong with your nose, is there?"

He shook his head. "No. Your scent seems slightly different. Then again, it could be the *hunela*."

If *hunela* gave him an erection and she didn't, they definitely had a problem. On the other hand, if her essence made Reutal's tongue swell up, well, she'd just as soon not hear about it.

―――

Jerden didn't know if it was the company or the kisses on the couch that were responsible, but he hadn't enjoyed a meal as much in a very long time. It wasn't because the *hunela* was the best he'd ever tasted, either—which it was, even without the *lycaque* root—but because of the change in Sara. She was like a new person—or perhaps a different version of the old one. All those bits and pieces he'd only caught glimpses of before were now given free rein. The odd thing was, no one else remarked upon the transformation.

That's because this is how she behaves when I'm not here.

Although momentarily stunned by that realization, he knew it was true. She laughed along with the others, she smiled, she frowned, and she clearly enjoyed the food. It was similar to the moment their eyes had met while she'd been making pancakes the previous morning, only it went on throughout the entire meal. It occurred to him that he was probably the only adult male humanoid who had ever seen this side of her—the warm, laughing, fun side that she kept locked down tight.

Did she notice the way she'd modified her behavior? Was she deliberately trying to act more normally, or was it automatic? He studied her as unobtrusively as he could and came to the conclusion that this was a natural occurrence. Her laughter didn't seem the slightest bit forced, nor did her smiles seem less than genuine.

Her scent *had* altered subtly. Before it had been a mixture of roses and Sara—the roses coming to the forefront because her own scent was so neutral—but now her own aroma dominated. Now if his dick would just work, everything would be fine. True, she didn't smell of desire, but of a natural ease and rapport. Relaxed. Not stressed, and certainly not filled with despair.

But how will she smell when she's asleep?

Only one way to find out. He smiled to himself as he thought about the coming night. Sara soft and warm in his arms, his body wrapped around hers—and, yes, he fully intended to lose the loincloth. Even if she wore a gown, he'd do his best to get skin to skin with her—couldn't wait to feel her lying against him. He'd heard somewhere that male pheromones were transmitted via touch, and he intended to touch her as much as he possibly could. No hardship there; his whole body yearned for the contact. Night couldn't come soon enough. He might even feign fatigue—there was bound to have been something in the day that could explain why he was tired and wanted to go to bed so early—anything to shorten the wait.

Yet another thing I've never had to do—make up stories to entice a woman into my bed. But how to go about it?

If only the weather had turned cold and she needed to snuggle up with him for warmth, or there was something to make her sleepy, or—

Reutal yawned and stretched his arms above his head. "Well, I guess we'd better get back out to the barns and let you two lovebirds get back at it."

"Back at it?" Sara echoed. "What makes you think…?"

Drania rolled her eyes. "Oh, come on, Sara. You're frickin' *smiling* at him—even stealing peeks at him when you think no one is looking. Did you really think we wouldn't notice?"

So, they *did* see the shift in her demeanor. He hadn't been imagining it.

Sara seemed put out by the question—or perhaps embarrassed was the better word. Her face grew flushed and her expression was flustered.

Reutal stretched his fingers toward her. "Can I just have one touch?"

"Oh, please, don't," Zatlen begged. "That tongue thing you do almost makes me sick."

Jerden expected Sara to shudder, but she did the unthinkable and offered her hand to the Norludian. "Sure, Reutal. Have at it."

She was laughing when she said it, but Jerden felt only tension. *What if she can affect Reutal, but not me? Definitely* not *something I want to hear…*

Unfortunately, it was already too late. Reutal had sucked a fingertip onto the back of Sara's hand. Within moments, he began snickering like a schoolboy, his eyes alight with mischief. "Oh, boy, someone's gonna get lucky tonight." He released his hold on her skin with a perceptible pop. "C'mon, gang. We've got to get out of here *now*."

Sara's eyes were almost as round as the Norludian's. Clearly this wasn't what she'd expected him to say. Jerden felt like he'd been punched in the gut. If she was that close to sexual arousal, his cock should have been hard enough to drive nails—and it wasn't. Then again, Reutal wasn't having any difficulty speaking. So, how did he know?

Reutal got up from the table and gave Jerden a nudge. "Not drowning in lust, but *definitely* receptive. Keep at it."

Jerden had serious doubts about getting lucky that night, particularly since Sara looked like she'd just been kicked by an enock. She sat there without saying a word as her stable hands filed out of the kitchen and was still staring in their direction when the back door closed behind them with a decisive click.

Or perhaps it only seemed so loud against a backdrop of complete silence.

Jerden had never been one to experience performance

anxiety, but he was beginning to understand why many men did. The whole *what if my dick doesn't work* horror was enough to make any man's cock deflate.

He almost laughed out loud. *A Zetithian with performance anxiety? Too funny.*

Particularly in Jerden's case. He'd been voted the best fuck on Rhylos three years straight. Still, with that kind of reputation to live up to, it was perfectly understandable for a guy to be a little nervous around a woman like Sara. This wasn't recreational sex by any means, and there was a helluva lot more than a thousand credits riding on the outcome.

Sara stood so quickly her chair fell over. Blushing crimson, she righted it and then snatched up the leftover *hunela*. "Guess no one felt like sticking around to help with the cleanup."

Jerden didn't bother to argue about their motives. "Doesn't matter. I'll help you."

Her beaming smile took him by surprise. "Thanks. I appreciate that."

Though he'd already suspected it, the way to Sara's heart clearly wasn't with trinkets or even horses. She wanted action and she wanted help. He could do that—even *wanted* to do it.

She rummaged around in the cabinet and found a container for the leftovers. "Your *hunela* was delicious," she said as she scraped the dish. "That's the most raving I've heard from the gang in quite a while."

"Oh, come on, Sara," Jerden protested. "They rave about your pancakes every morning."

"True. Maybe they think I'll make them eat scrambled eggs if they don't rave."

"Would you?"

"I might," she admitted. "Like I said, I'm a little sick of pancakes."

Jerden stacked up the dirty dishes and put them in the sink. The next thing he would buy for Sara would be one of the new compact waterless dishwashers. She couldn't say no to a gift like that—unless she particularly enjoyed washing dishes the old-fashioned way. Some people did.

He filled the sink with water and added the soap. He'd washed several plates before he realized that Sara found this activity somewhat amusing.

"Now that I've had time to think about it, the local *wildcat* looks pretty tame," she said with a chuckle. "Downright domesticated, in fact."

He grinned back at her. "I guess it isn't every day you see a guy with fangs and pointed ears washing dishes."

"Actually, it's the loincloth that tips the scales. If you were wearing anything else, it wouldn't seem so odd." She went on with her task. Snapping on the lid, she put the food into the stasis unit.

It was now or never. Unbuckling the belt that held it in place, Jerden dropped the loincloth to the floor and kicked it aside. "Better?"

She gave a tiny gulp as her eyes swept down his nude body. "I was thinking more along the lines of *adding* clothes, not subtracting them."

"Hey, I said I'd take it off later, didn't I?"

"Yes, you did." She continued on as though naked men washed her dishes on a regular basis—which, if Reutal ever took on the chore, was perfectly true. The gulp and its accompanying stare might never have happened. "How come you never wear your new clothes?"

Jerden shrugged. "They aren't as comfortable. I'll wear them when I'm in town, but the rest of the time…" Around the house, he preferred to dispense with clothing altogether—as he had just done. At the moment, however, Sara's feelings on the subject were more important than his.

"You'd rather be naked?"

He nodded. "Yeah. If you don't mind."

"No, I don't mind." Her voice sounded a shade too strained for the level of nonchalance she was attempting to convey.

"You *do* mind," he said bluntly. "Don't you?"

After clearing her throat, her voice sounded normal but her expression displayed even more anxiety. "No, really. Whatever you want to wear—or not—is fine with me." She handed him the empty pan to wash. "Unfortunately, mine isn't the only opinion you need to consider."

Jerden didn't figure anyone else on the farm would care one way or the other, but things could get embarrassing if her scent ever got stronger. There was a time when his cock could reach its full size in two seconds flat. He had a feeling that if it ever got started again, it would be hard all the time.

No, not if. *When*.

"I'll wear something during the day, but when we're alone together at night…" He left the last word hanging while he washed and rinsed the pan and put it in the rack to dry. Her long silence made him turn to look at her.

Her eyes—far bolder than he'd ever dreamed they could be—roamed from the tips of his ears all the way to his bare feet.

"You'll be naked." Despite the breathless note in her voice, her expression underwent a subtle change, appearing more certain, as though she'd arrived at a difficult decision. "Good. I enjoy looking at you. You're like Danuban that way—so perfect, I can't help but stare."

Jerden knew how hard it was for her to admit that. The breath he was holding came out as a soft purr. "You can do a lot more than look, Sara. And I hope you will. Every chance you get."

She nodded absently as her gaze continued to caress his body the way he imagined her hands would do. "You enjoy being touched, don't you?"

"There's only one thing I'd love more."

"And that would be?"

"Touching *you*."

It never occurred to Sara that a man could feel that way—about her or any other woman. If a man wanted to get his hands on a woman, it was to get her to reciprocate—or at least cooperate—not that he relished the act itself. However, Jerden's slow, deliberate blink and tiny grin of pleasurable anticipation were quite convincing.

She wasn't sure she *wanted* to be touched. Somehow, it seemed safer for her to put her hands on *him*, rather than have to endure being groped—which was the only context she could put it in. In the past, Sara had never been caressed; she'd been grabbed and manhandled. The experience had been painful, rather than pleasant, and the memory carried with it a frisson of fear.

"Please don't hurt me." The whispered words were

out before she could stop them, making her feel weak, small, and ashamed.

"Sara. I've already promised not to hurt you. Don't you remember?"

Jerden's deep, gentle voice served as a reminder that he was unlike any man she'd ever known. She nodded slowly. "Yes, I remember. It's just…"

Unbelievably, he smiled. "Force of habit?"

So, he does understand. "I've been in that mind-set for so long…" She paused, attempting for a lighter tone. "You know what they say about teaching new tricks to old dogs."

"I do, and it's patently untrue." His smile transformed into a mischievous grin. "You just have to start slowly, be very patient, and use *lots* of repetition." He reached into the sink and picked up a handful of silverware. "My hands are kinda busy right now. Why don't you take advantage of the situation?"

He was standing there in her kitchen like a prize stallion, and, unlike the time he'd been unconscious in her bed, she now had his permission. She was dying to get her hands in his hair again. Ulla had said that Lynx loved it when Bonnie combed his hair. She didn't have a comb handy, but she *could* use her fingers…

Her breath caught in her throat as she moved in behind him. This close, she could feel his body heat, its warmth drawing her to him like a moth to a flame.

Permission. She had it now. He not only wanted her touch, he seemed to crave it. Arching his back as she smoothed her palms over his shoulders, he purred his approval, widening his stance and pushing against her hands like a cat seeking a caress. She smiled to herself as she remembered he *was* a cat. A wild, savagely sweet pussycat. She glanced at Cria sitting by the doorway. Even *she* was tame when she should have been a dangerously wild animal. With a slow blink similar to Jerden's, the big cat let out a purr and stretched out on her side.

Jerden seemed able to tame anything, from a leopard to a woman who'd sworn she'd never let a man get near enough to hurt her again. Still, she had a hard time imagining what it would be like to stand before Jerden as naked and vulnerable as he was right now. What an amazing display of trust…

"You feel so good," she whispered. Closing her eyes, she leaned closer. She'd already kissed him, now she buried her face in his hair, feeling the soft silkiness of it along with the vibrations emanating from his throat. Her arms encircled his waist, allowing her fingers to skim over his chest and downward, feeling the crisp curls that trailed across his stomach. She breathed in his scent, letting it fill her head, and was astonished at the effect it had on her—relaxing, yet stimulating.

Gliding over his waist, she felt the ridge of his oblique muscles and the hollow dip of his flanks. That fine ass Drania had referred to fit snugly into the space where her thighs met her torso. Again, he moved into the contact, the barely perceptible rotation of his hips sending a rush of heat coursing through her, taking her breath away. Her nipples tingled. Her hips curled under and an ache began between her thighs, growing steadily stronger until she let out a groan that could have been due to agony, ecstasy, or both.

An ear pressed against his back allowed her to hear the deep intake of his next breath—a breath he held as though savoring a scent so rare and delightful, he refused to exhale. Moments later, a sigh escaped him, accompanied by a low moan. Purring louder than ever, his hand covered hers and pulled it forward and down until it rested on something much harder and hotter than the rest of his body.

"Way to go, Sara."

Chapter 17

WHEN IT FINALLY HIT HIM, JERDEN KNEW HE'D NEVER smelled anything sweeter in his life—far sweeter than roses, candy, or any other woman's scent. It was Sara's desire, flooding his body, filling him with the most powerful urge to mate he could possibly imagine. That he retained enough control to keep from turning around and plunging into her was nothing short of a miracle. The knowledge that he might never inhale anything so heavenly again kept him still, hardly daring to trust his luck.

He'd heard that when he found the one destined to be his mate, he would know it beyond a shadow of a doubt. If he hadn't already decided that Sara was the one, he would certainly realize it now. His cock was unbelievably hard, the starlike points of the coronal ridge already dripping with orgasmic secretions.

Her soft gasp of surprise was quickly followed by the touch of her exploring fingers as they skimmed the upper surface of his cock from root to crown. Jerden held his breath until she discovered the slick fluid.

"Taste it, Sara." With his throat so tight and his purr so strong, it was a wonder the words even made it past his lips. "You won't believe what it can do to you."

One taste. Surely she'd go back for more. Every woman he'd ever been with had done it. The moment her hand left his skin, he tamped down his own sense of loss and turned around. Her lips parted as she raised her hand to her mouth, and he held his breath again—watching, waiting, hoping the sight of his gleaming cock didn't terrify her.

She hesitated, and he was about to chastise himself for being too forward when she touched her fingertip to her tongue. Sara was the one woman he'd ever truly wanted; if it didn't work for her, he'd probably lose his mind—and this time, he'd lose it for good.

Her astonished eyes met his in the split second before she doubled over, her face brushing his swollen cock-head, leaving a glistening streak on her cheek. Without a second thought, he gathered her up in his arms and cradled her against his chest, kissing the top of her head, her temple, and any part of her his lips could reach. Her arms twined around his neck as she raised her face to his, and when she pulled him down for a kiss of her own, Jerden knew he was lost forever—if he hadn't been already.

The taste of her tingled as their tongues met and mated in a dance he never thought he'd enjoy again. Again, her boldness surprised him, though it shouldn't have. She was independent, confident, and strong in all other aspects of her life. This was the kind of lover she would've always been if fate hadn't dictated otherwise. He despised the men who'd hurt her, but the fact that in so doing, they'd left her for him to discover was a stroke of luck he'd never thought to deserve.

Perhaps he *didn't* deserve her. Perhaps he'd ruined every chance he'd had at happiness by selling himself. But at that moment, the past didn't matter. He felt as though his destiny was and always had been to make a lover out of Sara and to give her joy. His only hope was that in becoming his lover, she would also *love* him.

———

"Unbelievable."

A much cockier man would have said *I told you so*, but all Jerden said was, "More?"

As he was already halfway to her bedroom, Sara deemed this question unnecessary. However, his expectant expression when he stopped made her realize that he truly was waiting for her reply.

"Yes, please."

He gave her a squeeze. "I was hoping you'd say that."

"You *knew* I was going to say that."

"Not really." He continued on down the hall. "Wouldn't be the first time you surprised me."

He'd certainly surprised *her*. One taste had triggered the orgasm of a lifetime. Inexperienced or not, she had a feeling that other men had to work a lot harder at it. "I'm beginning to understand how you Zetithian boys managed to get into so much trouble."

He barked a laugh. "I used to give out those free samples all the time. Never had a single woman who didn't book an appointment afterward." He shook his head and sighed with regret. "After our world was blown to bits by one jealous man, you'd think we would've figured out that it might be best to keep the whole joy juice thing quiet. But no, we had to advertise. I wonder if any of those women ever enjoyed sex with a human male again—or any other species, for that matter. We're simply the best fuckers in the galaxy. No ifs, ands, or buts."

His grin took all the boasting out of this declaration, but Sara giggled anyway. "And *so* modest."

"Aw, I don't have to be modest with you, do I? I'm doing my damndest to impress you. You're a lot like a Zetithian woman that way. I have to try harder." Entering her room, he lay her down on the bed and then climbed in beside her.

"Sorry."

"Don't be. You are *definitely* worth the effort. Do you have any idea how incredible you smell right now?"

"Well... no, I don't." If she'd had to guess, she'd have said she smelled of saddle soap and horses, but there was no accounting for taste.

"Trust me, you smell good enough to wake up a dick that's been on hiatus for months. No small feat, that."

Sara considered *his* accomplishment to be even more significant. At the moment, she was in the throes of emotions she'd forgotten existed. And he was the reason. "So... what are you planning to do with that dick?"

"Anything you want," he replied promptly. "I like it all."

She glanced down at his groin. "Uh, yeah. Right. I'm not precisely a virgin, but that looks like it would hurt."

"What do you mean, not *precisely* a virgin?"

"I mean I've had sex before. Once. But it was a very long time ago." *And it hurt like hell.*

"And it was so bad that you swore off men?"

Put that way, it sounded a little silly, though she knew there was more to it than physical pain. "Something like that."

"Fuckin' amateur," he said with a scornful laugh. "I'm a *professional*. You will *not* have any cause to complain."

For all that her one experience with sex was the most frightening episode of her life, Sara laughed right along with him. "He wasn't any good at it. Didn't even try to be." She bit her lip, trying desperately not to utter the next words, but they refused to remain unsaid. "He did it on a bet. All my life, I'd been teased for being tall, skinny, and homely. More than one classmate led me on, just to see how much I would do for a little male attention—and, stupid me, I let them do it. This guy's buddies bet him fifty credits he wouldn't ask me out and do the deed." She shuddered as she recalled that feeling of complete mortification. "I wasn't exactly willing, either."

Jerden's pupils dilated to the point that fire seemed to blaze from his eyes. If this was what he looked like when he was angry, Sara made a mental note to never get him riled. "He *raped* you? I hope the stupid fuckwad rots in jail."

"He might, if he were ever arrested. I never told anyone about it."

"Ever?"

Sara shook her head. "You're the first." She paused, frowning. "If I'd gotten pregnant, I suppose I would've had to explain it, but I didn't, so I just kept my mouth shut. It was too… humiliating."

Jerden pulled her into his arms. The fire in his eyes had banked down to a slow burn, but she could tell he was still angry. "Thanks for sharing that with me. It explains a lot."

It didn't explain why she'd let it affect her so strongly, though. Now that she'd told Jerden, the burden seemed lighter, blowing away like bitter smoke in a lively breeze until the pain disappeared. Completely. *How extraordinary*. "Thank *you* for listening. It… helps."

"And for the record, the hottest hunk in the galaxy—at least, according to the *Damenk Tribune*—thinks you're beautiful. Not homely, not skinny, and certainly not someone he'd only fuck on a bet. You're perfect, Sara. Just the way you are. Remember that."

"I'm not perfect," she protested. "*You* might be, but I'm not. No way."

He halved the distance between them, which wasn't a whole lot to start with. "Are we going to argue, or are we going to make mad, passionate love to one another?"

"I don't really care for arguments."

"Choice made." The remaining space between them evaporated as Jerden covered her body with his. Licking her cheek, he kissed his way to her lips, which parted seemingly of their own accord when his tongue sought entry. She had only a moment to wonder whether licking a woman's cheek prior to kissing her was a Zetithian custom before her core contracted with another mind-blowing orgasm.

Tricky fellow. Apparently his "joy juice" didn't have to be all that fresh in order to set off internal fireworks. He knew so much more than she did, he'd have her under his spell in no time—and she wasn't sure she liked the idea. Having him under *her* spell seemed much safer. Unfortunately, she didn't have the first clue as to how to get him there.

Her eyes fluttered shut as Jerden kissed her again with lips so warm and sensuous, they ought to have been illegal. Nate's kiss had been *nothing* like this, which wasn't surprising. After all, this was a man who women paid a thousand credits a session for. Sara was not only getting his services for free, all she had to do was say the word and she'd have access to his entire fortune.

And she'd also be getting *him*—every luscious bit of him. The rumor mill might have likened him to a feral cat, but he was more of an intoxicant. Sara wasn't even *attempting* to resist him anymore. Instead, she let her hands roam over his skin, delighting in every contour and marveling at his strength. She remembered what he'd said about what to do if he ever hurt her. He'd told her to slap the shit out of him—or words to that effect. Although he hadn't done it yet, she still had the most peculiar urge to bite him…

That would be wrong, especially when he was making her feel as though she were floating. She might have felt like an angel but her thoughts were increasingly wicked. To be allowed the opportunity to explore, without that urgency and fear. Was that what he liked? He'd said he liked it all, but did he have a preference?

A whispered voice in the back of her mind told her she had all the time in the world to discover those things—even her own likes and dislikes. Strange that she should consider *anything* about the sexual act to be enjoyable. Disturbing memories surged back, only to have Jerden kiss them away. He was a far stronger presence than any memory could ever be.

Threading her fingers through his hair, she explored its silky texture, the shape of his head, and the curved point of his ears. On this last place, he responded first with a moan and then with a chuckle.

Leaving a trail of kisses across his cheek, she repositioned his head with gentle tugs on his hair until her lips followed the curvature to the tip of his ear. His soft sighs encouraged her to be more adventurous. If kisses could do that to him, what would her tongue do?

Tracing the outer shell with her tongue made him purr. Sucking on the point made him scream with laughter. Simply knowing this filled her with a sense of power, whereas before, she'd felt completely at his or any other man's mercy. Now he was at hers.

Pushing against his shoulder, she rolled him onto his back. She focused on his neck and chest, doing her best to ignore the stiff cock waiting for her below, which was difficult. The damn thing drew her eyes like a beacon. Powerful muscles corded his neck, and though he seemed to enjoy being touched there, his penis was calling to her.

Forcing herself to be strong, Sara let her lips and fingers move on to his chest. His flat nipples hardened at her touch, and while Jerden groaned and arched his back to press them against her lips, she couldn't help noticing that his cock wasn't just calling to her anymore. It was *waving* at her.

She ought to have known that with a dick that was more like a stallion's than a man's, he might also have the ability to control its direction. As she suckled one nipple and teased the other with feathery touches of her fingertips, his phallus pulsed, sending rivulets of glistening moisture pouring from the serrated points of the coronal ridge to cascade down the shaft. His cock appeared as strong as the rest of him—long, thick, and laced with prominent veins. The blunt head was so engorged, it might have been made of polished granite.

Simply letting her eyes follow the droplets of fluid to

where they puddled in his groin made her ache. She'd bred enough horses to know what was happening to her. Her labia were filling with hot blood, the same as his penis was. Soon, that huge cock would penetrate her delicate membranes and the forceful plunging would begin. This thought made her quiver with anticipation, rather than fear or revulsion. She'd seen many a mare back into the stallion, taking his full length inside her, groaning with each deep thrust. One mare had been so anxious, she'd taken not only the stallion's penis inside her, but Sara's entire arm as she helped to guide him in. Pinned between the two horses, Sara had no choice but to go along for the ride, leaving Reutal rolling on the stable floor with laughter.

But no one was laughing now, and for the first time ever, Sara wanted to strip off her clothes and be as naked as Jerden. She wanted that cock inside her too, filling her to capacity. If simply tasting that fluid was enough to bring on a climax, what would happen when she received a continuous supply of it?

Suddenly, she simply couldn't take the suspense anymore and she grasped his rock hard cock and licked the purplish head. "Oh, my *God*. You even *taste* good."

Jerden grinned. "And I adore being sucked, so you can help yourself anytime you like."

The only downside to this offer was how sore Sara would be from the violent contractions of muscles she'd seldom used until now. Those involuntary exercises would strengthen her in ways she'd never imagined.

Preparing me to give birth to triplets. Yet another factor she hadn't considered. Rumor had it that Zetithian semen acted like a fertility drug, causing multiple ovulations and thus, multiple births, even in humans. Sara wouldn't be the first and certainly not the last to face this eventuality. That she hadn't heard of the human wife of a Zetithian man dying in childbirth was some consolation. Still, she didn't particularly care for the idea of being the first.

She also questioned the wisdom of sucking a cock that caused such a spectacular reaction. "You're sure I won't inadvertently bite you when the juice gets to me?"

"Hasn't happened yet." His cheerful tone didn't sound like that of a man who'd ever had his dick bitten. "Love it when someone bites my ass, though. If you ever feel the urge, you go right ahead and sink your teeth into me." His wicked grin was accompanied by a wink. "Makes my dick hard."

Sara burst out laughing. "If it gets any harder, it'll explode."

"Oh, it'll do that in a little while whether you bite me or not."

Her teeth tugged her lower lip. "Yeah. I guess it will."

"Don't look so disappointed, Sara," he chided. "It's not a once a day occurrence. My turnaround time is negligible." His lips curled enticingly and his purring roughened as he traced the curve of her cheek with a fingertip. "Later on, we can do something a bit more… creative, but right now, I want you underneath me—naked and on your back—while I drive you absolutely wild."

"Creative?" Her mouth was so dry, the word nearly stuck in her throat.

"Sara," he said gently. "This is supposed to be fun—not educational or competitive, and certainly not a chore." He aimed her face toward his with a finger beneath her chin. "Just *fun*. Your brain might not under-stand, but your body does—finally. I can smell it. If you doubt it, just *try* to put a thumbprint in my dick."

"I already did," she said drily. "Couldn't do it."

"Then if you don't trust yourself, trust me to know what you want. Believe me, I'll know."

Cocking her head, she quirked an eyebrow at him. "Naked, underneath you, and driven wild?"

He inhaled deeply. "I believe you found that idea… irresistible."

She blew out a long breath, nodding. "Yeah. *Completely* irresistible."

"Then let's get rid of those clothes."

Sara had already changed out of her riding clothes, or she would've had boots to contend with. As it was, she was out of her shirt, jeans, and panties in record time— one of the rare times in her life when she didn't regret not needing to wear a bra—though she did feel a mo-ment of concern that her flat-chested body wouldn't be to Jerden's liking. However, when she caught the glint of lust in his eyes and the lascivious manner in which he licked his lips, she stopped worrying.

With a satisfied purr, he rolled her onto her back, trailing kisses from her neck to her chest. Her breasts may have been small, but the nipples were no less sensi-tive. As he suckled first one and then the other, she cap-tured his head in her hands, spearing her fingers through his dark curls, praying he would never stop. Her back arched just as his had when she'd done the same thing to him. She understood the reason for it now—the hunger, the urgency, the flaming need…

Despite her protests, he moved onward, his lips

traveling ever lower on her abdomen, teasing her navel before moving on to the rise of her mons.

"Gotta have a quick taste first," he whispered as he parted her thighs. His head dipped down and his tongue darted into her slit with precision. His hot breath and even hotter tongue set her on fire, intensifying an ache that was already almost unbearable.

His purr added a vibration to his sigh. "Ahh… the Divine Essence of Sara Shield." He sucked a breath in through his fangs and then went back for more. His rough tongue found her clitoris and teased it mercilessly— licking, sucking, devouring—until a piercing sensation heralded her climax.

"Jerden!" she cried. "*Oh—*" Her next words were lost in the throes of a pleasure so intense, so exquisite, she could only gasp and moan, unable to form an intelligible word or even a coherent thought.

With a low growl, he crawled up over her, hooking his arms under her legs as he went. Rearing up on his knees, he lifted her legs and thrust his hips forward. His hot, wet cock pressed against her labia—pushing, probing, teasing—until she finally understood why those mares had backed into the stallion, impaling themselves on his phallus. Jerden was a big man—a shorter woman couldn't have done it—but Sara wrapped her long legs around his hips, crossed her ankles, and pulled him in.

His huge cock filled her so completely, there was some left over. Even so, she wanted all of him. He began to pump into her, exhaling with a hiss on the outstroke. "You wouldn't believe how good that feels—how good *you* feel. Oh, *Sara…*"

His pleasure couldn't possibly be any greater than

hers. The coronal fringe raked her inner walls with each stroke, and the blunt head bumped against a highly sensitive spot deep inside her, steadily escalating the pleasure until tears stung her eyes. Determined to give as good as she got, she squeezed him with her vaginal muscles, impeding his progress and prolonging each thrust.

His breath grew short, his pelvic thrusts more sweeping. No, it wasn't his pelvis that was moving, it was his cock, rotating in circles deep within her tight passage. A moment later an orgasm seized her—similar to the ones she'd already had from tasting his coronal secretions, but different because he was inside her.

Her grip on his cock strengthened, and with a guttural cry, Jerden fell forward onto his hands, his face suspended directly above her own. His glowing pupils shone forth from the black iris like molten gold. "Bite me. Hard."

His shoulder was closest, and she sank her teeth into it, not hard enough to draw blood, but enough that he felt it.

The sound he made was indescribable—like a snarl on top of a purr on top of a groan—as his head snapped back and his cock drove forward. Sara saw stars as he plunged in more deeply than ever. His ejaculation was so strong she felt each spurt of his semen. She would've screamed if she hadn't felt something else, something truly extraordinary, almost as though the scalloped edge of his cockhead was moving, even though he was holding perfectly still.

Seconds later, a ball of heat formed in the small of her back, throbbing for a long moment before bursting forth in a flood that washed through her in great, crashing waves all the way to the outer limits of her being.

In the deepening twilight, she could only see the glow from his pupils but her vision seemed distorted—as though his eyes were two pebbles tossed into a quiet pool, sending concentric waves spreading out over the surface. The heat ebbed, leaving behind warmth so soothing and peaceful, it nearly broke her heart.

Jerden sank down onto his forearms, his lips seeking hers as though he would draw sustenance from them. "Okay. So you drove *me* wild. Nothing wrong with that… maybe next time I'll do the same for you."

But he already had.

Chapter 18

SARA SMILED AT HIM. "DIDN'T I SCREAM LOUD ENOUGH for you?"

"Well, yeah, you did… It's just that…" Jerden wasn't sure what the difference was. She'd responded as well as he could've hoped—perhaps even better. It was his own response that left him stunned. He'd intended to dazzle her with his technique, but his professionalism had deserted him at the most inopportune moment—and he wasn't even sure when that moment was.

I lost control.

He was as bad as her damned rapist. Never intending to pound into her that hard, he was surprised she wasn't sobbing. He'd wanted to take it slow, building on each new pinnacle until she was ready for more. She might've had sex once before, but with so many years in between, it might as well have been her first time.

"You're sure you're okay?" he asked.

"I'm fine, but I'm not so sure about you. What's the matter? Did I do something wrong?"

"I didn't hurt you?"

She shook her head. "No. I feel *great*. Better than I've felt in my whole life. That part at the end was incredible."

"That's the effect of Zetithian *snard*. It'll make a woman feel great even if she's got a knife in her chest."

"Somehow I doubt that. Nice feeling, though." She frowned. "Wait a minute. What the hell is *snard*?"

"It's the Zetithian word for semen. It sounds a little silly in the context of other languages—too much like other words for things that aren't so nice—but then, it's the only word we ever had for it. English and Stantongue have a hundred slang terms for semen, but for most species, semen is just sperm, a little prostatic fluid, and some hormones. Ours packs more of a punch."

"I'll say it does. I feel like I could sleep for a week."

"That feeling is called *laetralance* in Zetithian— there's no other word for that, either. We had daybeds for our clients at the Palace, so they could recover before they had to go back out on the street."

"Glad I'm in my own bed, then. The thought of having to get up and go anywhere right now is—well, let's just say I'd rather stay put."

"So you aren't mad at me? You'll still consider my proposal?"

Her peal of laughter delayed her reply long enough that Jerden *really* felt nervous—though her laughter felt pretty nice from the standpoint of his cock.

"Are you out of your Zetithian mind? You convince me beyond a shadow of a doubt, and now *you're* not sure?"

She had a point. "I guess it does seem a little stupid."

"*Very* stupid." Her expression sobered in an instant. "Oh. Oh, I *see*…"

"See what?"

"Why you asked me that. You don't need me anymore, do you?"

He gaped at her. "What are you talking about?"

"Now that you know your dick works, you don't need me. You can do it with anybody."

Although her reasoning was sound, obviously he hadn't made himself clear. "Sara. I thought you understood. You're *already* my mate, whether you agree to marry me or not. I won't be *able* to do it with anybody else now."

"Wait a minute. Don't I have to *agree* to be your mate?"

He shook his head. "You would if you were Zetithian. The mating between two Zetithians involves a commitment plus the physiological attraction. The fact that you're human is what makes the difference."

A frown clouded her face. "That's what happened with Audrey, isn't it?"

"No. My connection to Audrey was strictly physical. I've mated with you because it's what I *want*—body, mind, and soul."

She still seemed uncertain, her head tipped to one side, her expression puzzled. If Salan had been there, his lack of response to her would've proven it. He realized then that their mating *was* similar to what had happened with Audrey. He must've been *physically* mated to Sara for some time, otherwise he would've responded to Salan, or even Drania. The only reason he hadn't known it was because Sara's neutral scent had never given him an erection.

No, that wasn't true. Deep down, he'd known she was the one for him—probably from the first moment he'd seen her and inhaled her scent. He just wasn't sure *she* knew it. From now on, he would make a point of reminding her every chance he got.

"You mean I don't even have to accept your proposal and marry you?"

"There was no such thing as a marriage ceremony

on Zetith—no need for it. The unions between men and women were established purely by mutual consent. But that doesn't mean we can't have a wedding."

She nodded. "To be legally binding on this world, we'd need the ceremony. Not sure Nate and Salan would be deterred by anything less—well, Salan would be, but not him. At least, I don't think so…" Her voice grew ever softer, her expression pensive.

Jerden held his breath, waiting for her to speak.

"I suppose we could turn your party into a wedding— the only thing we'd have to do differently is to make sure the regional magistrate is there. Two weeks from Saturday, you said?"

Jerden would've preferred two minutes, but he also wanted his friends to attend—and her family, if possible. "We could put it off longer if you like. I assume you'd want your family to be there." She hadn't accepted his proposal yet, but discussing plans for a wedding seemed… promising.

She rolled her eyes. "Absolutely. My parents would *never* believe it otherwise."

"Cat and Jack Tshevnoe would want to be here too— along with Leo and Tisana, of course. Have you ever met them?"

"Are you kidding? *Everyone* knows Captain Jack. Market day just isn't the same unless she makes a stop in Nimbaza. She carries the most amazing cargo on that ship of hers. Very clever trader, too." She shook her head, chuckling. "Her husband was the first Zetithian I ever met. Scared the shit out of me the first time I saw him—what with those fangs and that scar on his cheek—but he's always been very nice to me. She's quite a character herself. Best I can tell, she's the champion of Zetithian procreation."

"Giving birth to three litters *is* pretty impressive. She thinks Tarq deserves a medal for spreading his *snard* over half the galaxy."

"I'm surprised she hasn't gotten him one by now. She's the most resourceful woman I've ever met."

"I'm sure she's working on it. You know, her ship is really fast—depending on where they are right now, she could probably pick up your family and still make it here in two weeks."

Jack would undoubtedly jump for joy when she heard the news. Lynx's impotence had had her bugged for months. Jerden's was less of a problem, since he'd fathered hundreds of children through his work at the Palace. Still, in Jack's eyes, an unmated adult Zetithian male was an abomination.

"Maybe." She hesitated, nibbling a fingernail. "Then again, we might have to put this off another month or so. It's starting to sound a whole lot more complicated than a cookout."

"Not really. I mean, you've already got a dress. We'll have a simple ceremony and then party the rest of the day."

"I can see us now," she said with a chuckle. "Me in a dress and you in your loincloth. We'll look like Beauty and the Beast."

Jerden shrugged. "Works for me. I can be quite beastly when I want to be."

"So I've noticed," she said slyly. "Remind me never to piss you off."

"As if you ever could." He meant it, too—at least,

from his current perspective, which was looking down into her eyes while his cock was still firmly lodged inside her. Despite an ejaculation that he'd felt clear to his toes, his erection hadn't faded one iota. An experimental side to side movement proved it—and so did her response.

Sara's eyes rolled back in her head and a blissful smile touched her lips. "Something tells me that getting mad at you would be just as impossible."

"I certainly hope so." Lowering his head, he gave her a kiss that contained all of his heart and most of his soul. "And if you ever do, I'll just kiss you until you're not mad anymore."

Her eyes misted as her lashes lowered. "Shouldn't take more than a couple of kisses." She drew in a deep breath, holding it for a moment before letting it out with a sigh. "Now that we've discussed all these plans, I guess there's only one thing left for me to say."

Jerden's skin tingled with anticipation as she ran a fingertip down the center of his chest, then reached up to trace the line of his jaw. He leaned into her touch, purring.

"Yes, Jerden," she whispered. "The answer is yes."

Relief, exhilaration, and pure joy washed through him as he leaned down to capture her lips with a deep, lingering kiss. "I promise you'll never regret it." He made another careful move, this time an in and out stroke as he rotated his shaft. Seeing her capture her bottom lip with her teeth halted him. "Doesn't hurt, does it?"

Releasing her lip, she shook her head. "Feels fabulous. Don't stop."

Jerden let his hips and back glide in a leisurely

undulation that he knew he could keep up for hours. "Don't worry. I won't."

"I think the *snard* effect must've worn off. I'm not having the constant—" Her breath went in with a hiss as another climax gripped her. "Well, I guess I am."

"That's actually the cock syrup effect. If I keep going long enough, you'll get to where it won't trigger orgasms anymore." He smiled. "Then I can fuck you into oblivion without any chemical interference."

"You like doing that?"

"Oh, yeah." He altered the angle slightly and was rewarded with a soft moan. "I want to see the joy in your eyes when I make you come all on my own. I missed it last time." It was difficult to see a woman's eyes with his face buried in her pussy—much easier when his dick did the work. "Of course, the *snard* effect is pretty awesome to watch, too."

He leaned closer, nuzzling her neck. No other woman's fragrance had ever intoxicated him the way Sara's did. He felt warm, languid, unhurried. He had control now, but he was drowning in her scent.

He simply allowed it to flow through him and guide his movements, exploring her inner surfaces with his cock, finding the places that made her sigh and moan, searching for the ones that made her cry out with pleasure.

The rising moon cast shadows on the planes and curves of her face. Jerden had never seen anything more beautiful. His own night vision was excellent—he could've seen her even in total darkness—but the moon added a romantic, ethereal touch to the scene that no other form of illumination could provide.

Unlike his clients, she didn't demand fireworks at every turn, seeming content to let him rock her gently while he savored every moment, loving her with a depth of feeling he'd never known before.

And he *did* love her. There was no point in denying it now. Just as her scent washed through him, so did the power of love. "I love you, Sara." The words were out before he even realized he'd spoken.

Her eyes sparkled with unshed tears. "I never thought I'd hear that—from anyone."

"You're hearing it from me now, and I'll tell you every day until you believe it." *Until you tell me you love me*. It wouldn't stop there, of course—he'd still tell her every day, and if words weren't enough, he'd prove it with actions. He never wanted her to doubt it, not even for an instant.

"I suppose I should tell you I love you now, shouldn't I?"

"You'll tell me when you're ready. Not before."

She nodded slowly, but anything else she might have said was swallowed up by another orgasm. Her body contracted around him, squeezing even more fluid from his cock, prolonging the effect.

"See what I mean?" he said with a chuckle. "They tend to hit at the most inopportune times."

"Whoa, momma, that was a good one!" Sara gasped. "Seems like they're getting stronger, rather than going away."

"Like I said, it takes a while. And we've got all night long."

"No sleep?"

"Later. It's not as late as you think—though we can

stop if you like." Quitting now was the last thing Jerden wanted to do, but he figured he should at least make the offer.

"No, keep going. I like the way you look—the way your hair sparkles in the moonlight. Love your eyes, too."

He grinned wickedly. "What else do you love about me?"

"Well… let's see now… I love your sense of humor, the way you look on a horse, you make a great *hunela*, and—I never thought I'd say this—but if anyone on the planet has a more awesome dick, he probably walks on four hooves."

Jerden shouted with laughter. "Meaning I'm hung like a horse?"

"Oh, *yeah*…"

The tender moment had passed, but Jerden had come out of it better than he'd hoped. There would be others. Right now, he focused on doing what he did best, but had actually only done once before: giving joy to the woman he loved.

Easing his hips forward, he penetrated her fully, feeling his nuts brush against the roundness of her luscious bottom—muscular, and yet soft, with skin that rivaled silk. She was such an interesting mix of traits. Strong, but yielding, firm, yet kind. How did a man explain why he loved a woman? What was it that drew him to her? Jerden didn't know, but if a woman had ever gazed up at him with more adoration, he'd already forgotten her. Sara loved him. She just couldn't say it yet.

Raining kisses on her upturned face, he felt her body give in to the pressure, relaxing enough to allow the freedom of movement he needed. Dancing, circling, vibrating, his cock fell back into old patterns and then found new ones. She gripped him with one orgasm and then another until they ceased altogether. Concentrating his efforts on her sweet spot, he raked it with his cockhead, feeling his way as he watched her face. Her eyes were closed, her lips parted, a light sheen of sweat highlighting her skin.

"Look at me, Sara."

Any moment now, he would see what he'd worked so hard for. Tears sparkled on her lashes and trailed into her hair from the corners of her eyes. Her breath came in short panting gasps.

"Don't close your eyes. *Please*." If she closed her eyes, he'd live to love her another day, but this was the ultimate fulfillment for him. The absolute knowing that he'd given her something no one else could match.

Her brows arched and a soft *oh* escaped her lips. Tingles raced over his skin as her body contracted around him and his cock erupted at last, pouring his seed into her.

And then it happened. Fringed by glittering lashes, her eyes grew round with wonder, the pupils constricting for the briefest moment before dilating until the iris was nothing more than a faint green rim encircling the darker pupil. For an instant, he seemed to catch a glimpse of her soul.

Joy.

Her joy was his reward and the source of his own contentment. He would die rather than leave her now. She was his mate. For now, and for all time.

To have lived as long as she had without knowing such ecstasy was even possible had Sara questioning whether she'd ever truly been alive before. Her entire being was infused with an inner peace so profound that her past might never have been, her future as yet unseen. Only the present moment existed.

Already, the moon seemed brighter, as though a filter had been removed from her perception of the world. The wind had died. The song of night birds and insects drifted in through the open window along with the scent of roses. She could hear Danuban quietly grazing just beyond the rose beds. She knew precisely where he was—each sound, each scent as sharp and clear as writing on a wall.

She lay on her back, relaxed and sated, gazing up into the glowing eyes of a man whose existence she'd been unaware of only a few months ago. How could she have known that something like this awaited her, just beyond the hill at the foot of the mountains on the shore of a crystal lake? She'd had no warning, no premonition. Nothing could have prepared her for this moment. She was afraid to speak or even move for fear of breaking the spell.

A loud purr interrupted the quiet sounds of the night. Cria yawned and stretched beside the bed. Sara didn't have to look to know she was there. Her presence was as much a part of Jerden as one of his limbs. Still, she was thankful to know that even this disturbance didn't alter the way she felt. Perhaps words wouldn't ruin it after all.

"Can you feel that?" she whispered.

He didn't even have to ask what she meant. "All the way to my heart."

She gazed up at him, still unable to believe he was real. She'd known there were decent men in the

universe—she'd even met a few of them—but to believe that one such as he could ever be hers and she his?
Never. Not in her wildest and most hopeful dreams.

"Do you remember what you said about us *being*
together would make us want to *stay* together?"

"Or words to that effect, yes."

"You were right. I've been alone most of my life—
had convinced myself that I *preferred* to be alone—and
yet now I can't imagine ever letting you go. Do I love
you, or am I already addicted to you?"

She thought he winced. "A little of both, I hope,"
he said.

"I'm sorry. Shouldn't I have asked that?"

"I'd like to think you loved me. But Zetithians *are*
addicting, and the longer you're with me, the stronger
the bond will become. You won't go into physical withdrawal if we're ever apart, but you *will* crave me, just as
I can barely stand to be away from you."

"You say that like it's already happened."

He nodded. "Didn't you wonder why I came back
so early today? It was all I could do to ride home and
leave you here." He smiled, his fangs gleaming in the
moonlight. "You're stuck with me now, Sara. I hope
you don't mind."

"No, I don't mind." She smiled back at him. "In
fact, there's nothing I'd like better than to spend eter-
nity with you."

"Sounds like love to me." His kiss was whisper soft,
his breath warm on her cheek. "I can't ask for more
than that."

His careful withdrawal reminded her that they were
still joined. When had that become something that felt

so right she was bereft without it? She only missed him
for a moment, however, for he pulled the sheet up over
them both as he lay down at her side. The contact was
every bit as sweet when he gathered her up in his arms.
Once again, she was amazed that someone so strong
could be so gentle. Safe and warm in his embrace, she
drifted off, noting yet another difference between him
and other men. He didn't snore in his sleep; he purred.

———

Jerden purred softly as Sara's breathing deepened and
her body relaxed, waiting patiently until the glow of
laetralance faded and was replaced by the scattered
emotions of ordinary dreams.

Ordinary dreams. Not terrifying nightmares or sinis-
ter illusions, merely untroubled images that carried with
them no hint of fear or despair. He sensed nothing but
joy, contentment, and peace emanating from her.

Only then did he allow himself to sleep.

Chapter 19

REUTAL LET OUT A TRIUMPHANT WHOOP FOLLOWING the announcement of Sara and Jerden's engagement, and then snickered all the way through breakfast, eliciting the occasional glare from Zatlen and an almost continuous blush from Drania. Finally, Sara couldn't stand it any longer and held out her hand. "Okay, Reutal. Check my essence. You *know* you want to."

"Oh, no need for that," Reutal said with a flap of his fingers. "I can see the bulge in the cat's loincloth."

Which, thankfully, Jerden was wearing—ostensibly to keep from nailing her while she made the pancakes. Or so he'd said. Sara had thought that one round of early morning nookie and a hand job in the shower would make that boner go away, but so far, it hadn't. He'd even asked for her help in getting it tucked into the loincloth—though she suspected that had been simply a ruse to get her to touch him again.

Not that she minded. She was having a tough time keeping her hands off him as it was. No further encouragement was necessary.

Sara had never been intimate with anyone and hadn't wanted to be—at least, not in a very long time. But that was changing. Already she looked forward to spending another night with him—a night without troubling dreams to disturb her rest, a night with Jerden there to soothe away even her worst nightmare. She'd always enjoyed having a purring cat lying on her bed, but a purring man was infinitely better. His solid warmth was like a shield against anything that might harm her, and though the rainy season was over for another year, she knew that stormy nights would never be as frighteningly lonely again.

She could admit that now, if to no one but herself. She had put on a brave front in coming to Terra Minor alone, but there had been times when the strangeness and isolation made the long, dark nights almost unbearable. She'd improved with time, but the feeling of disquiet never truly went away—almost as though she sensed her past following her, even across the expanse of space between Earth and her new home.

Having Bonnie as a neighbor had helped enormously. A fellow human wasn't easy to find on this world, but Bonnie's pioneering spirit was an inspiration. Bonnie had begun raising vegetables and enocks with a man as her partner, but had been deserted, only to hire Lynx and find love and happiness in his arms. The same thing seemed to be happening to Sara. She was having a hard time believing it was real, though.

She gazed at Jerden, his large presence far more comforting now than it had been only a few days before. Being able to not only tolerate his presence with her in the shower, but to enjoy it was proof of how far she'd come. He'd been grateful for the care she had taken of him when he was ill, but she'd really done very little. What Jerden had done for her couldn't be measured and could certainly never be repaid.

Even now, he took Reutal's remarks in stride. "Obviously I need a better loincloth—or maybe I should just give up and wear some of those pants I bought the other day. They aren't as comfortable, though." With a wink at Sara, he added, "Or anywhere near as practical."

Sara shot him a quelling glance, which would've been far more effective without the accompanying chuckle. "Speaking of which, Jerden and I are going into Nimbaza for dinner this evening, and we might do a little shopping while we're there. Do any of you need anything?"

Zatlen snorted. "A Norludian muzzle?"

"We can look," Jerden replied, silencing Reutal's sputter of outrage with a reassuring grin. "But I doubt we'll find one."

Drania dissolved into helpless giggles. "Probably sold out."

"Don't worry, Reutal," Sara said. "No one is going to muzzle you here." Norludians had often been persecuted on other worlds, and Sara wasn't about to have Terra Minor become one of them. Besides, she liked Reutal. Aside from being very useful, he made her laugh.

And so did Jerden. Sara could see herself getting used to that.

—⁂—

Sara and Jerden were still tidying up the kitchen when Reutal came flying through the back door.

"The stallion's sick," he gasped. "Acting really weird. Stumbling around, drooling. He walked right into the fence and didn't even seem to notice it. Then he went nuts when Zatlen touched his nose."

"Holy shit." The dishcloth she held fell from Sara's nerveless fingers. Following a moment of near panic, her logical mind regained control. "Sounds like something neurological—maybe a type of poisoning."

"Poisoning?" Jerden echoed. "You mean it was intentional?"

"Probably not." Sara dried her hands on the seat of her pants. "Horses get into plenty of trouble without help from anyone. Better call Lowinski."

Sara ran into the living room and flipped on the comlink. With fumbling fingers, she put in a call to the regional veterinarian, who, fortunately, was at the dairy down the road.

"I'm only a few minutes away, Sara," he said. "Just try to keep him from injuring himself until I get there."

Sara pulled on her boots and ran out to the barn. Jerden and the others were already there and had somehow gotten Danuban into his paddock. "Oh, God. He looks awful!"

Caked with sweat and filthy from head to tail, the stallion looked like a ghost of his former self. His eyes were hazy and unfocused and his normally fluid and effortless movements were now uncoordinated and weak. The tremors in his hindquarters suggested that he wouldn't be on his feet much longer. Sara felt like throwing up.

The whine of a speeder heralded the vet's arrival. Flying right into the barn, the speeder came to a halt by Danuban's stall door and the little Rutaran man hopped out of the cockpit. Loping through the stall and into the paddock using his long arms to propel himself forward, he gave Sara a brief greeting and then whipped a scanner out of the pocket of his coveralls. "Let's see what we have here."

"Zatlen and I found him out in the yard," Reutal said. "He was fine last night, but this morning…"

"He looks like crap," Zatlen finished for him.

Sara held her breath while the vet ran the scan. Danuban seemed to be worsening right before her eyes. Drania rested her head against Sara's hip, sobbing. Even the dogs were whining.

"Ah, hah!" Lowinski said triumphantly as he checked the reading on the scanner. "Got just the thing." Without another word, he scurried back to his speeder and delved into the medication box in the rear compartment.

Moments later, he returned with an injector and a small vial of purple fluid. Loading the vial into the chamber, he then pressed it to the underside of Danuban's sweaty neck. With a quick hiss, the dose was delivered into the stallion's thick jugular vein.

"I've given him the antidote for juluva weed ingestion," Lowinski said. "He should improve shortly."

Sara gaped at him with disbelief. "Juluva weed? How the hell would he have gotten any of that? Even if he found it growing, there's plenty of good grazing around here. I can't imagine why he would've touched it."

"Well… he *does* run loose," Zatlen said. "No telling where he might have picked it up."

"Juluva weed?" Jerden looked slightly bewildered. "Never heard of it."

"It's a great natural insect repellent," Sara replied. "But it's toxic to horses—I made a point of eradicating it from my pastures and hay fields before I imported any horses. I still find a sprig of it now and then, but it's never caused any problems."

Lowinski nodded. "Fortunately, it takes quite a lot to poison a horse."

"It could be growing on my place," Jerden suggested. "He's spent a lot of time over there."

Sara was unconvinced. "Maybe. But you've been living here for several days now. Danuban wouldn't leave you to go back there just to nibble on some juluva."

Lowinski tried to hide a smile, but Sara saw it anyway. "He and Jerden have some sort of bond," she explained. "He kept running away from my farm to go back to him."

Jerden apparently had a different idea about the vet's surreptitious grin. "Sara and I are engaged to be married."

The doctor, who had simply nodded at Sara's explanation, said, "Ah, yes... I *see*..." in response to Jerden's comment.

"What's that got to do with anything?" Sara demanded. "My stallion is dying and you're—"

"Now, Sara," Lowinski said firmly. "He is *not* going to die. Thanks to Zatlen and Reutal, we got to him soon enough. He will recover."

"I sure hope you're right. Juluva weed," she muttered with disgust. "It smells *horrible*. I never *have* understood why horses eat it."

Not for the first time, Sara wished the local vet was a Mordrial, rather than a Rutaran. Scanners could only tell you so much, but some Mordrials could actually communicate with animals telepathically—a decided advantage in a case like this. On the other hand, the Rutaran's strength and agility were useful when dealing with some of the more difficult patients.

The vet scratched his thatch of fuzzy hair. "Some horses develop a taste for it—it essentially becomes an addiction—and since the effect is cumulative, it doesn't kill them right away. According to my scan, he's been eating it for some time."

Sara frowned. "He's only been on the planet for a couple of months. I guess when he got loose, he started eating whatever he could find and decided he liked it. I've seen it growing in the northern mountains."

Lowinski shook his head. "Oh, no. He's been exposed to it for much longer than that. The toxin leaves traces in growing tissues, and it's present in some of the older parts of his hooves. There's a section of new growth that contains quite a bit of it, followed by a period of reduced exposure, then an older band where the concentration is even higher."

Sara was dumbfounded. "How in the world could *that* happen? He came from Earth. Juluva weed doesn't even grow there."

Lowinski shrugged with an apelike gesture and a flick of his ears. "I can't be sure, but based on my findings and what you've told me, I believe this was deliberate. He's been fed significant amounts of the weed, then none—during which time he seems to have recovered almost completely—and now that he's getting it again, the symptoms have redeveloped."

"Don't forget how he went crazy and got loose at the spaceport," Drania said. "If he'd been fed that stuff during the flight…"

"And if he found none at first, he got better, but now it's coming back." Sara nodded at Jerden. "Maybe it *is* growing on your place, and he found it, and now it's finally getting to him."

"We'd better keep him confined while we check out

my land," Jerden said. "The trouble is, it might also be growing in the mountains there. We could never eliminate all of it."

"Looks like his free-ranging days are over," Sara said. "If we can't keep him in his paddock, I may have to put up a force field." She paused, wincing. "Which will cost a small fortune."

Jerden grinned for the first time since the stallion's distress was discovered. "I can probably help you with that."

"Oh, yeah. Right." In the midst of all the drama, she hadn't stopped to consider the size of Jerden's bank account. "Guess we can afford at least one force field, can't we?"

"Absolutely. You'll have to show me what that weed looks like, so I can search for it on my place."

Her lips formed a moue of distaste. "It's a small plant with tall spikes of orange flowers and gray leaves. Pretty easy to spot when it's blooming, but it won't flower again until the start of the rainy season."

"Gray leaves? Sort of ragged-looking?"

"Yeah," Sara replied. "The flowers are actually quite pretty. Too bad it's so toxic."

Jerden nodded. "I think I know the plant you mean. There's a lot of it growing on the far side of the lake. I don't think there's any around the house, but Danuban could have found it quite easily."

"Well, that explains his recent ingestion, but not the original exposure," Lowinski said. "Any idea who might want to harm this horse?"

"Yes, I do," Sara said grimly. "But I have absolutely no way of proving it."

Now that Danuban was addicted to juluva, he would

keep poisoning himself if left free to roam—which would no longer be an issue. After that, if he were to ever get sick again, Sara knew exactly who she would blame. A confrontation would serve no purpose, but if she were to toss the particulars of the stallion's illness into the local rumor mill, it might serve as a warning that she was well aware of what was going on—and why.

Later that afternoon, Sara glanced up from her post by Danuban's paddock just as Jerden flew her speeder into the stable yard.

With Cria at his heels, he strode over to Sara and handed her a wilted clump of juluva weed. "I probably pulled up a hundred of these plants, and there's a lot more of it growing in the mountains. No wonder he got sick." He smiled ruefully. "Sorry about that."

"It isn't your fault. Besides, how could you have known?" She nodded toward the stallion. "And he *does* seem to be improving."

Zatlen stuck his head out of a nearby stall. "Which, having checked on him at least fifty times today, she would know." With a weary sigh, he shot Jerden a beseeching look. "Would you *please* do me and the horse a favor and take her out to dinner? She's driving us nuts."

"What?" She gaped at Zatlen. "I know we were intending to go into Nimbaza today, but you expect me to leave *now*?"

Taking her hand, Jerden steered her toward the house. "Lowinski said he'd recover. Staring at the poor horse won't make him get well any faster."

"I know that," she said. "But what if he has a relapse?"

"I'll let you know if he does," Zatlen said. "And I can call the vet just as easily as you can. Go. *Please.*"

"Oh, all right," Sara finally agreed. "But call me the minute he starts acting weird."

"Don't worry, I will," Zatlen promised.

"Come on, then," Jerden said. "Let's go get cleaned up. This is our first date, remember?"

"Yeah, right." After subjecting the stallion to another moment's careful scrutiny, she reluctantly allowed Jerden to lead her away from the paddock.

Zatlen heaved a sigh. "Thank *God.*"

<center>~~~</center>

How Sara could've had lunch in Lucy and Tarq's restaurant as many times as she had without noticing what a looker Lucy had married was a mystery. Jerden had opened her eyes to a lot of things, male beauty being one of them.

Tarq was a handsome square-jawed, blue-eyed blond with broad, muscular shoulders and thick, heavily muscled thighs. Sara could appreciate that now, even though she still preferred Jerden's taller frame with his bronzed skin, black mane, and smoldering eyes.

Lucy, on the other hand, was a slightly plump, dark-haired woman with a sweet smile, big brown eyes, and a scattering of freckles on her nose. Sara suspected that the two of them standing side by side was probably similar to the way she must look next to Jerden.

Gorgeous hunks and plain women.

"Great food, isn't it?" Jerden asked.

Sara nodded as she took another bite of her chicken. "Almost as good as your *hunela.*"

"Don't let Tarq hear you say that," he warned. "He was always the better cook. He's got this knack of being able to identify the ingredients in any dish just by tasting it and can duplicate almost any recipe."

"Handy talent for a restaurateur to have—or would you call him a chef?"

Lucy paused as she passed by their table. "Actually, he prefers to be called a cook. Says it sounds less pretentious."

"And Tarq was never that." Noting Sara's frown, Jerden went on to explain. "He's always been the quiet, shy one. Never thought he was good for anything but sex." He winked at Lucy. "She proved him wrong."

Lucy grinned. "Yes, but he's good at that too."

"I'm sure he is," Sara said. "And he *is* a darn good cook. This fried chicken is delicious."

"That reminds me," Jerden began. "I'd like for the two of you to cater our wedding reception—or cookout or whatever we're calling it—that is, if you wouldn't mind having to work at a wedding where you're both invited guests."

Lucy gasped. "You're getting married? Are you kidding me? Of course we'll do it! As soon as Tarq hears the news, he'll start working on the menu. Consider it our wedding present to you."

"Well, that was easy," Sara remarked. But not too surprising—aside from being a partner in the Zetithian Palace, Tarq had been one of Jerden's closest friends for nearly his entire life.

"Not at all." Lucy nodded at Jerden. "These guys made so much money on Rhylos, they probably never need to work again for the rest of their lives. Cooking is what Tarq does for fun."

Sara could certainly relate to that. Even with all the money in the world at her disposal, she'd probably still be raising and training horses. "There's a lot to be said for enjoying your work."

Jerden cleared his throat audibly. "Amen to that."

Sara had just aimed a questioning glance at him when it hit her what he *used* to do for a living. "You're retired, remember?"

He shook his head. "Not really. It's more of a hobby now—only I'm limiting myself to just the one woman."

Lucy let out a peal of laughter and headed back to the kitchen. Chuckling, Sara shot a reproving glance at Jerden as she reached for her wineglass. In that brief moment, her eyes slid past him just as a man and a woman hurried by the window that looked out onto the street. She couldn't see the woman's face, but that one fleeting glimpse was enough for her to recognize the man. "Holy shit."

"What?"

She nodded toward the window. "Nate. I sure hope he's not coming in here for dinner." She shook her head as Jerden started to turn around. "Don't bother; he's already gone. Looked like he had a woman with him too."

"Salan?"

"No. I only saw them for a second—they might not have even been together." She paused, searching her memory for more details. "I don't know for sure…"

"Well, if he *has* found himself a girlfriend, so much the better."

Sara chuckled. "If that's the case, there's no need for me to marry you, is there?"

"Oh, yes, there is," Jerden said. "You're not getting rid of me that easily."

She took a sip of her wine. "Glad to hear it. You'd have a tough time getting rid of me now." She gave him a wink. "I think I'm hooked."

He winked back at her. "So am I."

———

The next day, Jerden rode over to help Lynx build a new fence, leaving Sara anxious for his return. She was listening for approaching hoofbeats as she finished rubbing down her last mount of the day when she heard the whine of a speeder coming down the road. A few moments later, it came to a halt out in the yard. Fearing the worst, she stabled the horse and went out to meet her visitor.

Jerden hadn't been serious when he'd promised never to leave her side—and she hadn't expected it, either—but one glimpse of Nate's angry scowl as he strode toward the barn made her wish otherwise. Suppressing a groan, she gave herself a mental boot up the ass and pasted on a smile she didn't feel in the slightest. "Hey, Nate. What's up?"

"I heard you and *Jerden* were engaged." His emphasis on the name made it sound like a curse.

"Didn't take long for *that* news to get around," Sara said with a dry chuckle. "Who'd you hear it from? Salan?"

He ignored her question, his lips forming a thin line as a muscle twitched in his cheek. She could almost hear his teeth grinding. "So it's true then. I don't get it, Sara. I thought you were smarter than that. I can't believe you'd take that alien freak over me—especially since I have it on good authority he won't be fathering any children."

So, the gloves are off now... Sara shrugged, trying to seem nonchalant when her courage was already beginning to crumble. *Come on, Sara. Be strong... and if he comes any closer, slug him.* "I'm not marrying him to have his children. I'm marrying him because I *want* to marry him." A few days before, she couldn't have said that, but now the words rolled off her tongue with surprising ease.

He snorted in disgust. "Yeah, right."

"Why is that so hard to believe? He's a kind, wonderful man." She attempted another smile, but as always whenever Nate was around, she found it difficult. "You should be congratulating me—not calling my fiancé a freak. Which he is *not*, by the way. Nor is he a barbarian or a wildcat or anything of that nature. Best I can tell, he's more civilized than you are."

"He isn't human, Sara. I can love you better than him."

By that she assumed he meant that his dick was in proper working order. *If he only knew...* "You're entitled to your opinion, but so am I. The fact that he isn't human doesn't matter to me. We get along great. He's an absolute whiz with horses—and any other animal you'd care to name. And—oh, what the hell, I might as well say it—he's stinkin' rich. Why *wouldn't* I want to marry him?"

Nate's skin took on a darker flush. "Is *that* how you justify it? Because he's rich and good with animals? I can't believe you'd marry a man for stupid shit like that."

"You're missing the point, Nate. That stuff is just icing on the cake. I *love* him." *Now I just have to tell* him *that*. "Besides, you don't know me well enough to even begin to guess my motives for marrying anyone. If you'd stop and think for a second, you'd realize you don't know me at all."

"That's not my fault," he countered. "I've been trying to get to know you better ever since you moved into the district. Just when I thought we might be getting somewhere, that damned Zetithian got in the way."

Sara forced out a chuckle, hoping to mask her growing irritation. "Actually, I think it was more Danuban's fault than Jerden's. If he hadn't run off, Jerden and I might never have met."

Nate's eyes widened like he'd been sucker punched, leading Sara to suspect this idea hadn't occurred to him. Despite seeming momentarily stunned, he recovered quickly. "I still think you're making a mistake—"

Sara cut him off with a wave of her hand. "No, I'm not. I'm sure there are all kinds of good, sensible reasons to choose you, but there are more for marrying him." *For one thing, he doesn't scare the bejesus out of me.*

"Be that as it may, I still think you'll regret it. He's not the right man for you."

And you are? Sara laughed grimly. "Possibly. But if he isn't the right man, he's the next best thing."

"So, I finish second, then." His words didn't quite match his demeanor, which was *not* that of a man conceding defeat. Clearly the mere announcement of her engagement to Jerden hadn't been enough to deter him—though just *why* it wasn't was difficult to understand. It wasn't as though he'd sworn his undying love for *her*, either.

No matter how true it might be, Sara knew that a

flat-out *You're not even in the running* would be needlessly cruel. Nevertheless, something had to be said.
Heart pounding, she took a deep breath and pictured
Jerden standing beside her—feet planted, arms crossed,
and fangs bared as he snarled at his rival. The mere
thought sent a flood of courage coursing through her
bloodstream. Lifting her chin, she looked him right in
the eyes. "Yes, I guess you do."

"Yeah, well, I'll believe it when I see it," he said.

"We'll be sure to invite you to the wedding."

He seemed about to say more, but his grimace of disgust heralded Reutal's approach even before she heard
the determined slap of the Norludian's footsteps behind
her. Picturing his fierce glare and pugnacious posture
had Sara bowing her head as she bit back a smile, not
daring to risk another glance at Nate. Her subsequent
peal of laughter was bound to piss him off even more.

"See you later, Sara." Turning on his heel, Nate
stomped over to his speeder and climbed in it, firing up
the engine.

"*Please* tell me we've seen the last of that son of a
bitch," Reutal muttered as he appeared at her side.

Sara stared off into the distance, watching as the dust
settled in the speeder's wake. "You know," she said
slowly. "I believe we may have."

"Good." Reutal didn't even bother *trying* to sound
diplomatic. "I never *could* stand that asshole."

Chapter 20

"KISS ME, JERDEN."

He leaned closer—so close he could feel her breath on his lips. "What did you say?"

"I said, kiss me." Her sigh trailed off as his fingertips grazed her nipple. "I love your kisses. They make me feel... I don't know... different somehow."

Darkness had fallen and Jerden was back in Sara's bed. *His* bed, now. He was never going back to his house again—not unless she was with him.

The plans were all made and a date had been set for the wedding. Dax would bring Onca from Rhylos, and Jack would pick up Sara's family from Earth. Tarq and Lucy were coming from Nimbaza, and Bonnie and Lynx were bringing all the kids. The other neighbors were invited, including Salan and Nate—following the old adage to keep your friends close and your enemies closer.

Not that they were truly enemies—quite harmless, really—and certainly not an impediment to the marriage. Sara had told Jerden about Nate's visit that afternoon, and although he wished he'd been there to rip Nate a new one, Jerden was very proud of the way she'd stood up for herself. Hopefully, they'd finally heard the last from him. Jerden still retained an uneasy feeling about the woman he'd seen in the square, but Sara was probably right. The odds against her being Audrey's killer were astronomical.

The touch of Sara's hand drew his attention back to the present. He had no business thinking about Audrey or her murderer or anyone else at the moment. Not when Sara was there with him, her scent luring him to her, her soft skin begging for his caress. Her kisses made him feel different too. He'd never felt quite like this with any other woman. If nothing else, that should've told him she was the one.

Not that he'd ever doubted it. As his lips touched hers and the kiss deepened, her lips parted with a welcome so warm it sent the heat of her passion rushing to his groin. He was astonished at how easily she'd become accustomed to his body. Even now, her hands drifted down to the cock that had been craving her touch the whole day through. A purr escaped him as her fingertips traced the rim of the head—teasing, stroking—until her hand was slick with his syrupy fluid.

"Do you have any idea what that does to me?" he asked.

"I think so. You make more noise when I do that—but perhaps you'd like something different."

"Doesn't matter what you do, Sara. As long as you're the one doing it."

He could hear her smile in her reply. "But you adore being sucked. You said so."

"Yes, I did. And I do. But that's up to you."

"I'll try it, then."

Without another word, she slid down beside him, leaving a path of kisses from his chest to his groin. "As I recall, you taste pretty good."

"So do you."

"Ah, but not right now. It's *my* turn."

In the next instant, she opened her mouth and took

him in, displaying no hesitation whatsoever and certainly no aversion. He could see her in the darkness, her luminous skin calling to him, her eyes heavy-lidded with desire, and the curve of her lips on the crown of his cock. *I'm lying flat on my back and Sara is sucking my dick.* It didn't get any better than that.

Well, perhaps it could, but at the moment, it was perfect. Her tongue delved between the fleshy points of the coronal ridge, sending fresh spurts of orgasmic fluid into her mouth. She savored him slowly, and though her body occasionally contracted in climax, she didn't let it stop her for an instant.

Shifting from his cock to his balls, she sucked them as easily as his cock. "I do believe you adore sucking me as much as I adore being sucked," he said.

When she let go of his nuts, he wished he'd kept his mouth shut. "I absolutely love it. Actually, I haven't done anything yet that I didn't enjoy. Incredible, isn't it?"

Jerden snickered. "Yeah, well, remember who you're with, sweetheart."

She slapped him on the thigh. "Don't get cocky, now."

"Hey, if it'll make you smack my butt, I'll make a point of being cocky—though I'd much rather you bit me."

She rose up and sat back on her heels, eyeing him with suspicion. "You told me to slap the shit out of you if you ever hurt me. D'you mean to say you actually *like* it?"

Catching his lower lip in his fangs, he nodded. "Kinda kinky, huh?"

"Just a bit." She gave her lips a tantalizing lick. "Roll over."

He did as she asked, but he made sure his dick was

still in reach. Spreading his legs wide, he aimed it toward the foot of the bed, hoping she'd take the bait.

His balls clenched as she climbed over him to settle
between his legs, resting her arms on the back of his
thighs. Jerden bit back a chuckle that turned into a groan
as she nibbled his buns. She backed off for a second, and
he held his breath waiting for her to strike.

"Ohh… *yeah*."

She'd chosen the perfect spot, the lowest part of the
muscle, just above where his legs met his butt. The
pain shot through him like a lightning bolt and his cock
pulsed, forcing even more syrup onto the sheets. He'd
never been able to understand why it had that effect; he
only knew that it did.

A stinging slap sent another flood of heat to his
groin. His cock already felt like it was going to explode, but knowing he could keep pumping out *snard*
all night made him urge her on. Growling, he shook
his ass at her.

"More."

When she hit him again, it occurred to him that
there was an assortment of long, slender dressage
whips out in the tack room. *There might even be one
in the house…*

Quivering with excitement, he rose up on his elbows
and shot a scorching glance over his shoulder. "If your
hand hurts, you could always use something else."

She gulped, her voice a hoarse whisper. "You mean
a whip?"

He nodded slowly. "I'll even run out to the barn and
get one for you."

Her eyes widened and her jaw dropped, but what

was most astonishing was that she appeared to have an orgasm—triggered by what he'd said, rather than by any of his orgasmic body fluids.

"I—I've got one in the closet. It's the one I use in competition—show equipment never goes *near* the barn. It's the only way to keep it clean."

"I promise not to get it dirty," he said with a wink.

She pointed at the closet. "Top shelf. In a box with the other show stuff."

Jerden got up on his hands and knees and turned around. Purring, he crawled toward her, pausing to plant a heated kiss on her lips before climbing off the bed. His dick was dripping like a faucet, the fluid running down his thigh as he quickly found the right box and opened it. The long, tasseled whip was inside, along with assorted cuff links, tie pins, and white leather gloves.

The whip itself was exciting enough, but his breath went out with a hiss when he discovered the spurs.

As she'd always worn spurs while riding, he'd never given them a second thought. But now, the idea of fucking her while she spurred him on almost made him lose it right there in front of the closet. Their long neck and rounded tip would apply more pressure than anything, but he liked that too.

He held up the spurs. "These are incredibly sexy."

"You astonish me," she said drily. "I've been riding horses all my life, never dreaming that whips and spurs could be so hot."

Actually, it was more the thought of *Sara* using them on him than anything inherently sexy about the items themselves. He tossed her the whip. "*You're* what makes them so exciting."

—◆◆◆—

Sara caught the whip on the fly and watched as Jerden came toward her with a smirk that was far sexier than whips or spurs could ever be.

The spurs dangled from his finger. "Lie back and I'll put these on you real quick."

If he'd asked her to put them on *him*, she might've balked, but since it was she who would be wearing them, Sara did as he asked. Picking up her foot, he placed the loop of the strap in her instep and buckled the spur around her ankle. Once he had her properly outfitted, he stood back, surveying his handiwork. The fire in his eyes cast a glow over the rest of his tightly coiled body, highlighting his drooling cock, which twitched like a cat's lashing tail. Sara had a sneaking suspicion that the "wildcat" was about to pounce.

She waved the whip. "Ah, ah, ah," she warned. "No rough stuff—at least, not *yet*." With a wink, she crooked a finger at him.

He was on her in seconds—purring, growling, snarling—his cock penetrating her with unerring accuracy. It wasn't until her second orgasm that she remembered she was supposed to be using the whip and spurs. So far, she hadn't needed to, because, within moments, his back arched and his semen blasted into her.

"Now," he groaned. "Do it *now*."

Sara could barely raise her legs, but somehow summoned up the strength to bounce both spurs off his ass.

The results were instantaneous. With a feral growl, his pupils dilated until they were completely round and so bright it was a wonder they didn't set fire to everything touched by his gaze. His hair swung forward as he bucked into her like a wild bull, the long tendrils sweeping over her skin in thrilling waves, leaving behind a trail of heightened sensitivity.

The peaceful *laetralance* that should have followed his ejaculation never materialized. Instead, Sara's vision blurred as though a veil had been draped over her eyes, becoming crystalline as the veil shattered into a million glittering fragments. Incredible pulses of intense pleasure accompanied every plunge, each one surpassed by the next as though the effects were cumulative.

Unable to take much more, Sara raised the whip, thinking if she smacked him with it, he'd stop. Why she thought that, she didn't know, but she tried it anyway.

Wrong move, Sara.

Jerden hissed like an angry cat and climaxed again, his *snard* setting off a chain reaction that culminated in a cataclysmic internal explosion that seemed to lift her right off the bed.

Okay, so it was the right move after all…

Granted, Sara's experience with orgasms wasn't extensive, but this went so far beyond orgasmic as to be something else entirely. She wondered if there was a Zetithian word for it—something along the lines of nirvana, only better…

Her mind drifted through space, afloat on a surging wave of joy. Jerden still moved inside her, but it felt different now—peaceful and serene rather than ecstatic. It seemed odd that he didn't stop, not when the whole of her being was wrapped around him so snugly. Surely he'd had enough…

Then she realized that her being wasn't the only

thing wrapped around him. Her legs had crossed over his back, catching the neck of one spur in the strap of the other, allowing her heel—and also the spur—to bump him in the butt with each thrust of his hips. She straightened her knee, releasing the spur, and her legs slithered to the bed.

Jerden collapsed on her with a heavy sigh. "Oh, Sara, that was *so* amazing."

"It was accidental," she said with a chuckle. "My spurs got locked together."

"Doesn't matter," he murmured. "Still good." He rolled off her, sprawling across the sheets. "You should always wear spurs to bed."

"No way I could take *that* every night," she declared. "I'm surprised I can still think."

Sara heard him yawn. "You might have trouble getting me out of bed in the morning too." He yawned again. "I feel like I could sleep for a month."

"Don't worry. I can get you out of bed. Remember, I've got a whip—or, barring that, an omelet for breakfast."

"With bacon and cheese?" He sounded slightly more alert.

"Sure."

He combed an errant strand of hair from his face. "Better make it a big one. Probably best not to use the whip, though. You *know* what it does to me."

"I certainly do." She shifted slightly, noting a drag of her heel on the sheets. "Think you could take off my spurs?"

"Yeah. Give me a minute."

But in much less than a minute, he was fast asleep. Sara sat up, unbuckled the spurs, and tossed them on the floor. Pulling the blanket up over Jerden, she snuggled in beside him. Within moments, she'd followed his lead, falling into a deep, satisfying slumber.

———

A week later, Sara leaned over the paddock fence, watching Danuban as he grazed. The setting sun added golden highlights to the stallion's coat, but even Jerden could see that he'd lost weight.

"He looks much better," she said after a few moments of careful scrutiny. "But I doubt he'll ever be capable of performing the capriole again." She frowned. "Not that he needs to, but damn, he was spectacular. I never showed you the video, did I?"

Jerden shook his head. "No, you didn't." With a suggestive lift of his brow, he added, "We've been too... *busy.*"

Sara nodded. "Amen to that."

Jerden had spent several days scouring his land for juluva weed, and by the time he was sure he'd dug up all of it, it had found its way into his dreams. Even so, he considered it well worth the effort. He was taking no chances that the stallion would ever ingest any of the toxic plant again, but by the time he returned home in the evenings, he and Sara were too exhausted to do anything but have dinner with the crew and then head straight to bed.

They hadn't fallen asleep immediately, of course. Each night with Sara held new surprises, whether Jerden had fucked a thousand different women or not. The whip and spurs event would remain forever etched in his memory, but there were others that were every bit as memorable.

Sara had gone from a woman with seemingly no

desire to one who wanted him constantly—at least, that was what her scent told him. She was making up for lost time, and he was more than willing to accommodate her. Drawing in a breath, he could sense her need for him as her scent was carried to him on the wind. The astonishing thing was that he had already noted differences in her scent and was sorting and cataloging them according to what happened next. Of course, just when he thought he had her pegged, she stunned him again.

She had gone into this relationship out of necessity, but she would stay because she loved him. It was in her eyes, as well as in her unique aroma. Her lips were the only part of her holding back. She hadn't spoken the words. Yet.

Their wedding day was drawing near, and as it approached, Jerden felt certain it was the right move. He loved Sara with all his heart and wanted to spend the rest of his life with her. That was a given, but he also looked forward to seeing his old friends. He hadn't seen Onca in months. How he would laugh. "The hottest hunk in the galaxy has finally been caught," he would say.

Onca had vowed that he would never fall into that trap himself. He was happy being the sole Zetithian in the Palace, though after Audrey's death, he'd limited himself only to those species whose scent aroused him naturally. That was where they'd gone wrong, he said. They'd catered to too many whims, fucked too many women they should never have fucked. Strange that a rascal like Onca would have such scruples.

Still, he was probably correct—yet another strike against them in the book of right and wrong. Had they ignored Audrey's suggestion, she might still be alive.

Don't start that again.

Jerden knew he should heed that warning, lest he risk returning to the depths of depression—a place he never cared to visit again. He would much rather focus on the future—the new places he and Sara could go together. They would travel to the moon and stars, whether they ever left *this* place again or not.

"It's very sweet of you to pull up all those weeds," she said. "I'm sure Danuban would thank you if he could." She looked up at him and smiled as though she understood his concern. "You miss riding him, don't you?"

A few short weeks ago, that would've been the problem. True, he liked to ride the stallion, but he'd ridden some of Sara's other horses in the interim, and though the bond between them wasn't nearly as strong, the lines of communication were quite clear. Odd that he should instinctively know how to get a horse to do exactly what he wanted them to when he'd never even *seen* a horse before Danuban arrived at his home. Sara's skill as a trainer had come about through hard work and dedication, and she admitted to being rather envious. Jerden couldn't blame her for that. His own ability was more akin to falling off a log.

"Yes, but that isn't what I was thinking about." And neither was she—that is, if her body wasn't lying to him. Somehow he doubted that it *could* lie to him. Perhaps at one time it might have, but no longer.

She probably didn't even think she looked enticing at the moment. There was a smudge on her cheek where a horse had kissed her, and her short curls were wind-tossed and unruly. She wore no jewelry, no adornment— only a plain white shirt and buff breeches with her tall black boots. Still, she could have been decked out in emeralds that matched her eyes and a gown worthy of a fairy princess and he couldn't have wanted her more.

Letting his gaze roam over her face, he drank in a vision he never wanted to forget. "I was thinking about *you*."

Her cheeks blushed, reminding him of her roses. Even now, after a day's work, their scent still lingered on her skin, reminding him of how she had smelled when she'd stepped out of the shower the night before. The air had been filled with the heady aromas of Sara and rose-scented soap, rising from her damp, flushed skin. He'd wrapped her in a towel and carried her to the bed, making love to her until her eyes grew hazy, then drifting closed as she sank into slumber.

Draping an arm around her shoulders, he pulled her close. "I want to make love to you in the rose garden sometime." He smiled. Purring was automatic now. He couldn't imagine holding her like that and *not* purring. "I can see you now, lying on your back in the grass, the moon shining down on your face, the roses blooming all around us, and the scent of your desire filling my head."

She leaned against his shoulder. "Sounds lovely."

———

Sara had never thought of her rose garden as anything but a place of peace and beauty — a meditative spot in which to linger when her mind was troubled. Having sex there had never occurred to her, and the underlying current of disquiet regarding Danuban's illness now drew her to Jerden, rather than her roses. He had become her new source of solace, and if it weren't for worrying about the stallion, she would have been at total peace with the world.

Security in the barn had never been an issue before. But now, she thought of installing a surveillance system—something she could never have afforded until Jerden came along. She'd like to have proof of her suspicions, but she suspected that the actual poisoning attempt had taken place several months previously. With the stallion running loose, free access to the addictive plant would mean his eventual death, which meant that his escape from the spaceport might also have been deliberate. A confined horse would require a more direct approach. She shuddered at the thought of the stealth required for such an act.

The person she needed was Tisana, the Mordrial/human witch who could actually understand the thoughts of animals. True, the evidence probably wouldn't stand up in a court of law, but Sara would know her suspicions were correct—that is, if there was any direct evidence, which she was beginning to doubt. If what she suspected was true, there had to be minions involved—something Danuban wouldn't know anything about. The prime instigator would have been nowhere near the horse, thus protecting himself from suspicion.

However, there was only one person Sara could think of who didn't want Danuban around, for *any* reason. Would marrying Jerden eliminate the threat or not? She wasn't sure. The motive was murky—there didn't seem to be a valid reason for anything so drastic. Still, it was the best lead she had.

"What are *you* thinking about?" Jerden asked. "Somehow I don't think it was sex in the rose garden."

"No, it wasn't. Sorry." Looping an arm around his waist, she gave him a squeeze. "I'm still worried about Danuban. What Lowinski said about him being deliberately poisoned has me bugged."

"You said you knew who might be responsible. I'll take a stab at it and say it's Nate, but I'm not sure why."

"Me, either." She frowned. "He was against my getting that horse from the moment I mentioned it to him. I know he wanted me to use his stallion, but I don't understand why it should matter that much to him. Stud fees are a source of income, but not *that* much—after all, I only have four Andalusian mares—and a scheme like this hardly seems worth the trouble."

There was something she wasn't seeing here—a significant part of the puzzle that eluded her. She had every intention of letting Nate know she suspected him, short of coming right out and making an accusation. It would take careful wording, but it could be done.

"Still want to invite him to the wedding?"

Sara snorted a laugh. "Yes, if for no other reason than to prove to him that we are, indeed, married and that I'm not available anymore. I don't know where he ever got the idea that I might be interested in him in the first place." She paused, giving her head a rueful shake. "Maybe he's just cocky enough to think that *any* woman would want him."

Jerden chuckled. "But you aren't just 'any woman,' are you?"

"No, not when it took the hottest hunk in the galaxy to make me see the light." She gazed up at him. He was so solid, so strong, so kind, so handsome. Was *this* the right time?

She swallowed hard, thinking this was perhaps the most difficult task she'd ever faced. And yet, as her eyes met his, the words came easily. "And to make me fall in love with him."

His smile displayed nothing but genuine pleasure and affection—nothing cocky about it at all. "I was beginning to think you'd never say that." A kiss followed, unsurpassed in its sweetness.

Tears stung her eyes, filling her lids before coursing down her cheeks. "I love you, Jerden. I never thought I'd say it, but I do." She ought to have known from the first moment she laid eyes on him. She hadn't, of course. Something that stunningly beautiful could never belong to her—not unless it walked on four legs. Danuban was similar in that respect—the epitome of his breed, one that took your breath whether you fancied horses or not. She'd stopped looking at men that way years ago.

And yet, here she was with Jerden—in love and about to be married. The impossibility of it rocked her soul. Touching his face, she threaded her fingers in his hair, proving to herself once again that he was real. How many times would she have to do that before she believed it?

The full moon was already peeking above the eastern horizon, and, as it traded places with the sun, the shadows deepened and the light from his eyes grew brighter. Even in darkness, Jerden was beautiful. Not merely handsome or attractive, but beautiful—with a beauty that went far beyond his appearance, reaching to the depths of his soul. Her hand slid through his hair to cup his neck, pulling him down again. This time, she kissed him. *I love you*, her mind whispered. *So very, very much...*

His lips slanted over hers, setting her heart racing as heat rushed to her core. She couldn't get enough of him. Never, ever. Her arms couldn't hold him tightly enough; her lips couldn't kiss him deeply enough. She could never show him how she felt.

Jerden took the lead, gathering her in his arms and turning toward the house. She never broke the kiss, still savoring his flavor. The heat of his body surrounded her and kept her warm, kept her safe, and drove her mad with desire... He did all of those things simply by being who he was. Her one and only love.

His purr vibrated her chest. She could imagine nothing more stimulating or more soothing. Nothing. His skin was hot beneath her touch, rivaling the fire he ignited deep down inside her. She lost track of where they were until the fragrance told her. She smiled against his lips.

The rose garden.

He was wasting no time making his fantasy a reality. How many more did he have tucked away in his brain? Fantasies weren't something Sara had ever indulged in. She would have to leave it to him to be creative.

The ground was still warm from the sun as he laid her down upon the grassy verge. A shadow crossed in front of the moon as Cria took up sentinel duty. One of the dogs—the little Yorkie, perhaps—scampered over to investigate but didn't stay long after Cria hissed at him.

Jerden took his time, slowly pulling off Sara's boots, unbuckling her belt, and letting his hands glide up beneath her shirt and then down to push off her breeches. The night air was still warm, but his hands were even hotter on her bare skin. Undressing him was much easier. He seldom wore his new clothes, preferring the loincloth. She didn't mind. It suited him, and all she had to do was unfasten his belt, and it fell right off. The perfect apparel for a man like Jerden.

He crawled up over her and kissed her again, each kiss increasing the tension, driving her closer to the point of seizing him. Reaching out, he grasped the nearest blossom, pulling the petals off in his hand. He held them above her, letting them fall on her skin like raindrops.

She inhaled the fragrance. "The Don Juan. Good choice."

Smiling, he picked a flower from the only other bush within reach—the McCartney. A deep, vivid pink in daylight, by night it appeared silvery, but there was no mistaking the intoxicating scent.

"I think this is my favorite." He held it to his nose. "It smells like love."

Sara had heard that particular variety described as seductive. She'd planted both it and the Don Juan near her bedroom window, never realizing the significance. Now she understood.

Jerden showered her with more petals, then plucked another blossom by the stem, dropping it on the ground next to her ear. She turned, sniffing the heady aroma. "It *does* smell like love." *Like him*. Not the same scent, perhaps, but it evoked the same feeling.

"So do you." His lips brushed her neck, and then moved lower, scattering kisses among the petals as he went. Nudging her knees apart, he licked her clitoris, sending shock waves resonating throughout her body. "You *taste* like love, too." With a low growl, he went back down on her, devouring her with his lips and tongue, not stopping until she rewarded his efforts with a climactic cry.

In the throes of her orgasm, she suddenly knew what she wanted. A fantasy of her very own… "Come here and let me suck you."

Like a panther stalking its prey, he came closer, pressing the head of his dripping penis against her lips. She opened her mouth and he slid inside, fucking her mouth gently, thoroughly. It was good—nothing that triggered orgasms of that magnitude could be considered bad—but it wasn't quite what she wanted.

She pushed him aside. "Turn around."

He knelt over her, his knees positioned above her shoulders, straddling her head. His nuts dangled just above her eyes, and she arched her neck to capture them, sucking one into her mouth. "*Mmm*…"

Jerden was purring like crazy and groaning with each swipe of her tongue. She was in no position to bite his ass, or even smack it, but she could grab it. Digging in with her fingertips, she squeezed him hard as she switched to the other testicle. Holding on with one hand, she used the other on his cock. Grasping it firmly, she slid her hand from head to root, spreading his slick sauce down the shaft. She loved making him come—and since he could continue indefinitely, she could make him ejaculate as often as she liked. Pumping her fist up and down his dick, she kept on until his cock erupted, spraying a line of *snard* that ran from her breasts all the way down to her pussy, landing on her exposed clit.

The explosive climax that followed was muffled by having his scrotum against her mouth, but even so, it drew her body into a writhing ball of ecstasy, forcing her to release him. Jerden's cry was unhindered, sounding like a lion's roar as it echoed across the fields.

His cock never lost its erection, and once she recovered, she pulled it toward her lips, sucking it into
her mouth while his balls brushed her face. His *snard*
still bathed her slit, and she pressed her thighs together,
savoring the orgasmic creaminess. Placing her hands
on his hips, she encouraged him to move up and down,
fucking her mouth until he came again. His cum tasted
like candy as he obligingly gave her more of it to savor
and swallow.

Her body was already on fire when the *snard* effect
hit her, sending more heat pulsing outward from her
core. She could barely move, but she could talk.

"Fuck me, Jerden. Hard."

—∿∿—

She didn't have to ask him twice. The gentle, romantic
lovemaking he'd begun could wait. He was hers to com-
mand, and if she wanted a good, hard fuck, he would
not deny her. Time had no meaning when they were
together anyway. He could give her anything she asked
for and still be able to indulge in any whim of his own,
whether it be showering her with rose petals or fucking
her senseless.

The moon rose higher in the sky, casting a glow on
her face as he placed her feet up on his shoulders. Sliding
into her slick passage, he groaned as he swept her inner
walls with his cock, leaving no surface untouched. Her
soft moans drove him onward, making his cock pulse
and forcing out more of his own lubricating fluids. If she
wanted it hard, she would need the extra juice.

The sharp scent of her lust filled his head along with
the pleasing fragrance of her love, enhanced by the

smell of the earth, the grass, and the bruised petals of her roses. He slammed into her hard and deep, delighting in the sounds she made and the expressions on her face. Her eyes had drifted shut, but she was missing so much.

"Open your eyes, Sara."

The wind picked up, tossing the roses about as clouds scudded across the moon, momentarily dimming the light. Once they'd passed, he glanced down to see his semen glistening between her breasts. Letting go of her legs, he fell forward onto his hands and licked it off. With a loud purr, he kissed her, his cum-slick tongue delving deeply into her mouth. As he backed off to watch, another orgasm burst into flower behind her eyes.

"My God, that's beautiful," he whispered.

Her fingers toyed with his long curls as she traced a line from the point of his ear to the center of his chest. Her gentle touch sent waves of anticipation spiraling toward his groin. He wasn't done yet. Not by a long shot.

Rocking into her slow and deep, he reveled in the way her body hugged his cock, squeezing it, milking out every drop of cream. When he came again, he waited only long enough to see her eyes react before pulling out and rolling her over. Lifting her hips with both hands, he dove into her from behind. The moonlight shone down on her back, illuminating her tumbled curls and her firm, shapely bottom, his brown hands in stark contrast to the white glow of her skin. Separating her cheeks, he ran a fingertip down the cleft of her buttocks.

Her shuddering gasp told him all he needed to know.

"Hold on." His withdrawal made her groan in protest until he pressed the blunt head against her anus, bringing himself to climax with a few quick strokes of his hand. As his *snard* spewed into her, he felt her body contract and then relax completely. Moving carefully, he teased the tight ring of muscle until it, too, relaxed and allowed him entry.

"Fuck me, Sara."

In seconds, she was up on her hands and knees, her head thrown back, creating a hollow dip along her spine. With a guttural snarl, she backed into him until he was balls deep in her ass.

"*Ohhh…*"

He didn't have to see her face to know how good it felt to her; her eager backward thrusts were proof enough. "I can't believe it," she gasped. "I never—" The rest of her words were cut off by an orgasm that squeezed him so hard he saw stars where there weren't any and wrenched a yell from her that made him grin.

As she banged into him again, Jerden shifted his knees apart and settled his weight for maximum stability, fully intending to hold that position until she wore herself out. *She* was the limiting factor here, not him. The view of her gorgeous, moonlit bottom coupled with her scent would keep him hard until morning or until she passed out, whichever came first.

Her moans became increasingly higher in pitch until she was practically screaming with each thrust. Still, he waited, forcing his eyes to remain open, knowing what was about to happen.

With one final push, she let out a cry that would've curdled his blood if he hadn't known the reason for it. In the next instant, she lay sprawled in the grass, sobbing helplessly. In another instant, he was beside her, cradling her in his arms while she wept.

"You could have *warned* me," she wailed.

"Ah, but that would've spoiled the surprise." He chuckled wickedly. "Good?"

"You have no idea," she whispered. "*None*."

"I probably don't."

But he did. Not from firsthand experience, perhaps, but he'd seen it with many of his clients. Still, he liked to think that her pleasure was greater than theirs had been. Perhaps it was. The only thing he knew for certain was that his own enjoyment was quadrupled. He'd never had anything more at stake than a woman's enthusiastic response to his technique—the testament that she'd gotten her money's worth. Love made a huge difference in the way he felt. He could only hope it did the same for Sara.

Chapter 21

THERE WAS A LOT TO BE SAID FOR LIVING IN A CLIMATE that consisted of a rainy season and a dry one. An outdoor event could be planned without fear that rain would spoil it. Even so, Sara was pleased to awaken on the morning of her wedding day to a cloudless sky and the promise of a hot afternoon.

Bonnie had volunteered to help with the preparations. Lucy and Tarq would be providing the main course, and the rest was a pitch-in. Salan and her parents were bringing cheese and ice cream, which was all Bonnie's kids cared about, aside from the chance to swim in Jerden's lake. Sara was surprised when Nate accepted the invitation, but she wasn't about to let his presence ruin the day for anyone else. Perhaps he and Salan could commiserate.

Bonnie's friend Zuannis, a Twilanan native and the best baker in the region, was providing the wedding cake, and fortunately, didn't charge an arm and a leg for it. Sara reminded herself that Jerden's fortune made her continued attempts at economy superfluous, but it was a hard habit to break.

Sara's parents, Bob and Linda Shield, had arrived two days before, and her brothers, who were unable to attend, both sent their love. Neither of her parents had ever met a Zetithian before, but having traveled from Earth on Jack's ship, which was filled with two families of them, her mother—a tall, slender woman from whom Sara had also inherited her coloring—was in complete accord with Sara's decision to marry one.

"I've always considered your father to be a handsome man," she confided to her daughter. "But he can't hold a candle to these Zetithians." She paused, tapping her chin with a contemplative finger. "They seem to age well, too—and so have their wives."

Cat and Jack might have been in their fifties, but they certainly didn't look it, and neither did Leo and Tisana, who were roughly the same age. Being Zetithian, Sara wasn't surprised that Cat and Leo didn't show their age—Leo's hair was as golden as Cat's was black, and both were still tall and handsome, despite the scars acquired during twenty years of slavery—but why Jack and Tisana didn't was a mystery.

Jack's tall, athletic build hadn't sagged anywhere. Her only wrinkles were the laugh lines around her eyes and mouth, and her hair was still dark brown without a hint of gray. Tisana was bewitchingly lovely with dark hair and green eyes and a body that hadn't suffered a bit from giving birth to two sets of triplets. Now that she thought about it, Sara realized that Bonnie didn't look like a mother of seven who was pushing forty, either.

Being the outgoing sort who rarely guarded her tongue, Jack showed no reluctance to enlighten anyone who cared to listen. "Vladen says it's from carrying Zetithian children. It's pretty technical, but apparently mothers pick up billions of stem cells from their babies, which help them live longer than men in general. Getting stem cells from the children of a race with a longer lifespan and remarkable regeneration capabilities is sort of like finding the fountain of youth, whether the mother is Zetithian or not." She gave Sara a hearty pat on the back. "I've carried three litters so far. Best I can tell, I'm gonna live forever."

Sara couldn't imagine a better fate than living a long, healthy life with Jerden. And to think, she'd actually resisted Bonnie's efforts to introduce them.

Things happen for a reason.

It was the kind of cosmic karma thing best not dwelt on for very long, because otherwise simple, random events would take on too much significance. If, for example, at this point in time, she were to turn left instead of right, how would that affect the rest of her life?

Sara's reverie was interrupted when Jack eyed her with sudden suspicion. "You aren't doing anything to *keep* from having children, are you?"

Sara's eyes widened. "Well... no. I'm not."

"Good," Jack said with a firm nod. "Glad to hear it. Jerden's already sired a bajillion kids, but a few more couldn't hurt."

Actually, Sara had an idea that delivering triplets would hurt a great deal. The fact that Jack had done it three times said a lot for her dedication. Then again, Cat was probably every bit as irresistible as Jerden was.

"And don't worry," Jack went on as if she guessed Sara's thoughts. "Having triplets isn't as bad as it sounds, and there seems to be a built-in form of birth control so that litters don't arrive too closely together. Tried like hell to get around that, myself, but no dice. Still haven't figured out why that is, but it's probably for the best."

Sara tended to agree. Jack had already given birth

to nine children, ranging in age from eight to sixteen—something Sara couldn't imagine doing herself.

"She'd have had *ten* litters by now if she could," Tisana said drily. "With nineteen of us aboard, the ship is already pretty crowded."

Jack waved a dismissive hand. "The *Jolly Roger* is plenty big, and there's lots of room to expand if we put living quarters in the cargo hold." She ran a hand through her short locks, shaking her head. "And to think I used to fly around in the damn thing all by myself. Shocking waste of space." She winked at Sara. "Nothing to stop you out here, though. With two houses and all this land between you, you and Jerden could have *dozens* of babies."

Linda gave a little gasp and Sara felt the blood drain from her face. "Dozens?"

Tisana chuckled. "Don't pay any attention to her, Sara. Like she said, Jerden already has children scattered all across the galaxy. One litter will be plenty."

Once again, Jack fixed her penetrating gaze on Sara. "All those other children don't bother you, do they?"

Sara had already given this some thought and knew exactly how she felt about it. "No. That all happened before Jerden and I ever met. I mean, everyone has a past." *Some better than others.*

"Good girl." Jack nodded her approval. "Now that that's all settled, let's quit fiddling around and get this show on the road."

Sara and Jerden might've had two houses, but since the number of bedrooms was limited, they had set up

several tents for their guests. As a result, the area around
the lake looked like a family campground. Sara gave up
her room to her parents, and she and Jerden moved to
his house for the duration of the festivities. Though her
own home was comfortable and peaceful, the lakeshore
setting and rustic furnishings appealed to Sara.

With so many children visiting, Jerden's pets got
plenty of extra attention. Cria was especially content,
purring serenely while the younger kids brushed and
petted her. The rest of his menagerie seemed pleased to
be back home, the wide verandah being far more con-
ducive to lounging than the small stoop that constituted
Sara's back porch.

My back porch… She sighed, recalling the night that
Danuban had deposited a senseless Jerden on that very
spot. Yet another turning point in her life, as well as his.

*What if Danuban hadn't brought him there? What if
I hadn't taken him in?* The thought of how close she'd
come to never meeting him at all chilled her to the
marrow—yet another possibility it was probably best
not to dwell upon.

Jerden must've noticed her pensive mood, despite
the flurry of activity as they set up tables under the
large canopy they'd erected near the lake. "Having
second thoughts?"

She smiled, shaking her head. "Not at all. Just thinking about everything that had to occur before we wound
up here together."

"Scary, isn't it?" Obviously, he understood.

"You bet it is." She glanced toward the road where
a large hovercraft was approaching. "Looks like we've
got more company coming."

"That'll be Dax, Ava, and Onca—and three more kids." He raised a hand in greeting and then lowered it to shield his eyes from the sun. "Looks like they've brought Waroun, too. He's Dax's partner and navigator." With a wink, he added, "Don't worry, you'll like him. He's Norludian."

Though she'd never considered the matter before, Sara *did* like Norludians, possibly because she envied them the ability to carry on sexually oriented conversations without batting an eyelash—something she'd never been able to do herself. "I don't think I've ever been around two of them at the same time, which should be interesting. Reutal will be pleased."

"Jack won't be. She can't stand them, but they'll keep us laughing, you can count on that."

Sara certainly couldn't argue with that. "When you're right, you're right. C'mon, let's go say hello."

Jerden took her outstretched hand and kissed it before tucking it into the crook of his arm.

They waited while Dax brought the *Juleta* to a halt and shut down the engine. Onca was the first to climb down the ladder. "Hey, hot stuff! I hear you got your mojo back."

Jerden hugged his old friend. "You could say that. I prefer to say I fell in love."

Onca laughed, his green eyes twinkling with mischief as he shook his thick auburn mane back over his shoulder. Having known Onca nearly all his life, it was a gesture Jerden remembered well. He hadn't realized how much he'd missed him until that moment. "I always knew someone would catch you eventually. I just hope it doesn't happen to me."

Onca had been one of the few babies rescued from the demise of Zetith, and thus had no memory of his family or his homeworld. His only home had been aboard the ship, his fellow refugees his only relatives. Jerden could understand his attitude toward settling down; never having had real a family, Onca had no idea what he was missing.

"You got something against being happy?" Jerden teased.

"Nope. Just not ready to tie myself to one woman. Not sure I ever will be."

"With that attitude, it's probably just as well," Dax said as he climbed down the ladder. He took up a position at the bottom while his pregnant wife, Ava, came down after him. "But then, I once felt the same way myself."

Actually, Dax's problem stemmed more from not finding a woman whose scent aroused him than not wanting to be tied down, but until recently, Jerden had never appreciated how much the love factor must've added to the equation. Dax had been a thirty-three-year-old virgin when he met Ava and had fallen hard for the lovely human/Aquerei woman.

Their three daughters were herded toward the ladder by Waroun, the Norludian navigator. "Hurry up, you little catfish! Jerden's waiting!" Squealing with laughter, the tiny girls clambered down the rungs and ran to Jerden. He knelt down as they approached, receiving multiple hugs and kisses from each of them.

Why they remembered him with any kind of affection surprised him a little. He couldn't imagine why a bunch of three-year-olds would care anything about the man he'd been when he'd traveled to Terra Minor aboard Dax's ship. Then again, having still been in shock from Audrey's death, he didn't remember much about that voyage.

What he *did* remember was how beautiful the children were. Unlike the offspring of unions with other species, these girls didn't appear to be pure Zetithian. They all had the larger, more rounded eyes that Ava had inherited from her Aquerei father, and, like their mother, could breathe underwater. And if the way they greeted Jerden was any indication, they didn't share the stand-offish attitude toward men that characterized purebred Zetithian females. Aside from that, they resembled their father, with the same catlike fangs, pointed ears, and long, curly hair—though not as tightly curled as Dax's, which grew in such tight spirals it was often mistaken for dreadlocks.

Though Dax still wore a single earring and a tattoo flamed up over one side of his face and neck, he clearly no longer lived up to the renegade bad boy persona he'd done his best to cultivate. He was a family man to the core—a goal to which Jerden now aspired. He couldn't wait to have lots of kids with Sara's flaming locks and dazzling green eyes.

The girls ran off to join the other children as Waroun scampered down the ladder. "I hear you've got a Norludian working for you, Sara. Bet he's getting high on your essence!"

"I doubt that," Sara said drily. "It isn't as though he's got his fingers on me all the time."

Waroun smacked his lips. "Not like he hasn't tried, I'll bet." He waggled his fingers at Sara. "I'm surprised I can't feel it in the air. You've got a hot one there, you know."

"Yeah, I know," Sara said, grinning.

"He can go all day and all night—or so I've been

told. There are a lot of ladies who were *very* upset when he retired."

"I didn't exactly *retire*," Jerden said. "It was more like a permanent sick leave."

Waroun waved a dismissive hand. "Makes no difference. They're still pining for you."

"As long as none of them come looking for me, we're okay," Jerden said. A frisson of warning tightened his scalp as he remembered the woman he'd seen on the square in Nimbaza. In a purely instinctive move, he put his arm around Sara, pulling her close. "None of them have been asking questions, have they?"

"Don't worry. We're not telling anyone where you are," Onca said quickly. "Though I can't promise word won't get out. You know how people talk."

Jerden figured he had nothing to lose by tossing the idea out for discussion. "Haven't heard anything about the woman who killed Audrey, have you?"

"Chantal Benzowitz?" Onca shook his head. "As far as I know, she's still locked up somewhere."

Sara gaped at him. "As far as you *know*? They'd tell you if she wasn't, wouldn't they?"

"Let's hope so," Onca said with a shudder. "That woman was nuts."

Chantal... Jerden had somehow managed to block the name from his memory—if indeed, he'd ever known what it was. He couldn't even recall testifying at her trial, though he must have. Then again, he hadn't been the only witness. She'd killed Audrey right out in the middle of a busy street, making it an easy case to prove. Unfortunately, it was also a relatively easy crime to commit—and one for which there was no protection.

Cat and Jack came over to greet the new arrivals, along with Leo and Tisana. As usual, Jack jumped right into the conversation.

"They should've thrown away the key when they locked her up," she said briskly. "She's a menace to society. I'm so glad you came here to live, Jerden. This is the safest planet in the galaxy, but you never know. There might be others out there like her." She rounded on Onca. "Which reminds me... when are you gonna give up that Rhylos gig and settle down?"

Onca laughed. "Not anytime soon. I'm having too much fun."

Jerden could've sworn Jack growled. With fists planted against her hips, she leveled a stern glare at Onca. "It only took one woman making the wrong man jealous to get your planet blown to smithereens, bucko. I'd think you guys would've learned a lesson from that."

"I'm simply providing a public service." Onca was still smiling, but it was clear that he wished Jack would mind her own business. "The price keeps the numbers down and the casual clients away."

Apparently considering these arguments to be rather flimsy, Jack continued with her lecture. "Tarq was providing a *free* public service—which I thought was a great idea until he got the shit beat out of him on Talus Five. Then that Chantal woman killed your fluffer, and as crazy as she was, she could just as easily have killed Jerden while she was at it. You're playing with fire."

Jerden felt Sara stiffen beside him and immediately wished he'd kept his worries to himself. Giving her a reassuring squeeze, he took her hand and pressed it to his lips. Though she smiled bravely, he could still see the fear in her eyes.

"I'll quit when I'm ready to quit," Onca said with a flick of his brow—yet another gesture Jerden knew quite well. "And I'm not ready yet."

"Better give it up, Jack," Jerden said. "He can be very stubborn when he chooses."

Unfortunately, Onca wasn't the only one with a stubborn streak. Scowling, Jack threw up her hands. "It's your life, Onca, but don't say I didn't warn you when some jealous asshole tries to mop up the floor with you—or comes hunting for your scalp."

"I won't," Onca said. "I'll retire eventually—but not right now."

Jerden knew precisely how he felt. He'd enjoyed his job every bit as much as Onca did and would probably still be working at the Palace if circumstances hadn't made it impossible for him to continue. The money was extremely good, and if there was a better job than giving women joy, he'd yet to hear of it.

"Okay, then," Jack said. "I've given you my two cents worth. Just be careful."

Jerden snorted. Jack might've pretended to wash her hands of the situation, but he doubted Onca had heard the last from her. Still, it *was* his life. Of course, before Audrey's murder, Jerden hadn't considered that his lifestyle might put anyone other than himself at risk. Now he had Sara to worry about. He hadn't been in love with Audrey, and her death had affected him more profoundly than he would've guessed. Sara's death would probably mean his own.

"We should *all* be careful," he said. "Even here on

Terra Minor." He glanced at Jack. "What about all the trading runs you make? Aren't you worried?"

"Not as much as I used to be when the damned Nedwut bounty hunters turned up everywhere we went. It's much better now, but I'm still prepared. Never go anywhere without Tex." She patted the pulse pistol in the holster at her side. "You just never know."

"Can we talk about something else?" Waroun asked. "This is giving me the creeps."

"Hey, you started it," Dax pointed out. "Should've kept your mouth shut."

To Jerden's surprise, Sara spoke up. "No. I'm glad he did. Zetithian history being what it is, I can't help but be concerned, and it's nice to know that my worries aren't completely unfounded." She gazed up at Jerden and his heart skipped more beats than he cared to admit when she smiled. Would her effect on him ever dissipate? He hoped not. "Don't worry, Jack. I'll do my best to keep him safe and whole."

Jack nodded her approval. "You do that. Let me tell you, it's quite a responsibility." She swept the surrounding countryside with assessing eyes. "Should be safe enough here, though—broad field of vision, clear field of fire…" She frowned. "I'll give you a pulse pistol if you don't have one. Anytime you're out and about with him, you need to carry it—*and* a comlink. We can't take any chances on anything happening to him." With a wink, she added, "After all, he *is* the hottest hunk in the galaxy."

Chapter 22

SARA WORE THE DRESS HE'D BOUGHT HER FROM THE Twilanan woman in the market square. Jerden had never seen anything more beautiful—unless it was Sara without the dress. A garland of yellow roses adorned her hair, and the flowers in the matching bouquet had been picked from her own garden. Her vows were spoken clearly and firmly, and the kiss she gave him was filled with love and passion.

After the ceremony, Jerden was surprised when Salan hugged Sara as though she were truly happy for her. Nate even shook his hand with the air of a man who'd been beaten in a fair fight—though the low growl from Cria might have had something to do with it. Was it really going to be that simple? He hoped so. The aura of contentment he felt with Sara beside him while they received the congratulations from their guests was unlike anything he'd ever experienced.

Gazing out over the lake that was now filled with laughing children, Jerden daydreamed of making love with Sara there. Some night when the moon was full and the water calm, he would swim with her, kissing her, letting her body glide up and down on his stiff cock until her eyes filled with joy. *Perhaps later tonight while everyone else is asleep...*

"What are you thinking about?"

He leaned closer, pressing a soft kiss above her brow. "Our wedding night, actually."

A seductive smile curved her lips. "But we're already mated. Tonight won't be any different. Will it?"

Inhaling her scent, he began to purr. "Perhaps."

Following a brief quiver that assured him she was as anxious for that moment as he, she nodded toward the lake. "I noticed you watching the kids. So that's how it's done? The older siblings look after the little ones?"

Jerden followed her gaze to where Bonnie's youngest children tended Lucy and Tarq's babies while their parents set out the noon meal. "It's about the only way to manage that many children, which might be why litters are seldom conceived less than four years apart. Usually five."

Sara chuckled. "Not sure I'd want five-year-olds looking after my babies, but they seem to be quite adept— even Karsyn. I'm amazed they have the patience."

"It's a bond almost as strong as that between parent and child. I remember—" A memory long-suppressed came rushing back with a vengeance and his voice cracked, forcing him to take a deep breath to steady himself. "My older brothers and sisters looked after me and my littermates—until they were killed in the explosion that demolished our home. My parents and I were outside at the time. Otherwise, we'd have been killed, too."

"Oh, Jerden…" Her eyes shimmered with tears. "You don't have to—"

"Talk about it? No, I don't, but I should. I've tried to forget what happened when I should be doing everything in my power to keep their memories alive. My mother Lislla, my father Etash, my beautiful sisters Dersa, Brielan, and Tulla. My brothers Katken and Wedfon. All gone." He paused, shaking his head as the grief threatened to overwhelm him. "I haven't spoken their names aloud in so many years. They deserve better."

The touch of Sara's hand on his arm soothed him and gave him strength—yet another thing a mate could do that a mere lover could not. "We can name our children after them."

Jerden took her hand and carried it to his lips. Tears slid down his cheeks as he closed his eyes. "Do you have any idea how much I love you?"

"I think so," she replied. "Almost as much as I love you."

Opening his eyes, he gazed at her face; her smile was as warm as the twinkle in her eyes. "You can think that if you like. I won't quibble." Lowering her hand, he laced their fingers together. He never wanted to let go of her strong, capable hand again as long as he lived. "Tell me, Sara. Are you happy?"

"Happier than you are."

"No way."

She grinned and glanced over at Salan and Nate, who stood near the refreshment table, deep in conversation. "Do you think *they'll* be happy together?"

Jerden chuckled. "I have absolutely no idea. But I hope so. It would certainly make life in these parts a bit less dramatic."

"Don't care much for drama, do you?"

"Not really. I'm ready for some peaceful, happy living—though I must admit I did enjoy snatching you out of Nate's arms and carrying you off."

"I'll try to faint more often," she said with a wry smile.

"Don't bother. Once was enough. I'd much rather you stay safe and healthy without any need for rescuing."

"The same goes for you. No more carrying your unconscious body into the house and watching you lie there for days on end, wondering if you'll ever wake up."

"Were you worried about me, Sara?" Though he kept his tone gentle and teasing, he really *did* want an honest answer. Had she been attracted to him then? If so, her scent hadn't betrayed her.

"Yes, I was. But at the time, I didn't realize why. Now I know." Her arm tightened around his waist. "I was only doing what Vladen told me to do, but I felt *something*, even then. I barely knew you and envied the bond you'd formed with my stallion, yet I was drawn to you in a way I didn't understand." She glanced up at him. "I tried so hard not to love you. Looking back, I realize I didn't stand a chance. You're the most inherently lovable man I've ever met. From the moment I saw you, I was yours."

Returning her hug, he kissed her again, his lips lingering over the softness of her skin while he drank in her intoxicating scent. "At the time, I didn't care if I ever inhaled the essence of desire again, which made being miffed that you *didn't* want me that much more peculiar. I should have given up and kissed you right then. Instead, I behaved like a churlish lout and slammed the door in your face."

"You *were* rather rude." Amusement colored her tone, taking the sting out of her words. "I half expected you to sic Cria on me, but she gave me this smug look instead."

Jerden glanced down at the huge cat sitting beside him. Except on rare occasions, violence was beneath her. Giving him a long, slow blink, she began licking her paw. "She can be quite queenly at times."

"It would be interesting to hear her side of it," Sara said. "Maybe we should ask Tisana to translate."

Jerden shook his head. "I prefer the mystery. If I knew *why* she sticks so close to me, her behavior wouldn't be nearly as intriguing."

"True," Sara conceded. "And she might not be able to explain it. After all, I can't explain why I feel love for you when I haven't felt it for any another man since, well... you know."

"No need to take that any further if you don't want to. Keeping my family's memory alive is quite different from suppressing the memories you'd prefer to forget."

She shrugged as though it truly didn't matter anymore. "I should probably mention it more. Then it might become so commonplace a memory that it will disappear among the mountains of trivial events in my life."

Jerden doubted it would ever become *that* mundane, but didn't argue with her logic. "Whatever helps."

"I'd rather *not* talk about it, though," she went on. "I'd much rather discuss what you've got planned for tonight."

"Ah, but that's a secret. For now. Shall we join the party?"

"Yes, but I've got to get out of this dress first. It's a bit much for a cookout." She cast him an appraising glance. "You probably ought to wear something different too."

Jerden couldn't argue. His high-collared white shirt and black slacks constituted the most clothing he'd worn in years, and he was as anxious to get out of it as she was. "Let's go change real quick." He had an idea it might take a little longer than that, but since everyone else was having a good time without them, he didn't think they'd be missed.

Escorting her back to the house, he led her into his bedroom—a room he'd never thought to share with any woman.

But then, Sara wasn't just any woman. She was his love, his mate, his salvation. Purring, he helped her out of the spangled robe with its long train and gazed at her. The white dress clung to her slim body in soft, gleaming folds, accentuating her curves—not voluptuous, perhaps, but nonetheless tantalizing, alluring, and infinitely sexy. A deep groan mixed with his purr as he let his eyes roam over her. "My beautiful Sara."

"Must be the dress," she said with a rueful smile.

"Oh, no," he assured her. "Let's have none of that. You're beautiful with or without it. In fact, I find you sadly overdressed at the moment."

"So are you. You look very handsome in that outfit, but I much prefer you in the loincloth—or better still, nothing at all."

"As you wish." He unfastened the buttons with slow deliberation, never letting his eyes wander from hers. Peeling off the shirt, he tossed it over a nearby chair, then eliminated the confining nuisance of his pants. Aiming his cock toward her, he gave it a quick pulse, forcing beads of moisture from the points of the corona. "Better?"

"Much. Undo me."

Turning around, she stepped out of her sandals and pointed at the tie on the halter top of the gown. Her back was bare, the waistline scooped low enough to reveal the spot where her back flared out to meet her bottom—the perfect place to begin...

Pressing his lips to the skin just above the white fabric, he blazed a path up her spine to the nape of her neck. Tugging at the knot with his fangs, he untied it, allowing the dress to fall to her feet with a whispering sigh. As he encircled her with his arms, he cupped her breasts in his hands, teasing the nipples to firm peaks as his cock pressed against the small of her back. His pounding heart sent the hot blood of passion racing to his groin, filling it to the point of pain—a pain only Sara could assuage. Dropping his head, he captured her earlobe in his fangs. "My lovely bride... mate with me now, and I will give you joy unlike any you have ever known."

He was certain he'd used that line before—it was, after all, the classic Zetithian opening for seduction—but even if he had, its meaning had changed. She was his mate, and it would be his life's work to give her all the pleasure and love within his power.

Turning in his embrace, she looped her arms around his neck, pulling his head down. Her mouth found his, her tongue slipping past his fangs to war with his own until the fire in his loins threatened to consume him. Her firm nipples brushed his chest as he reached down to cup her buttocks. Pulling her up against him, he spread her thighs with a nudge of his knee, letting out a hiss as he settled her down on his painfully engorged penis.

Her sex engulfed him with wet heat, and he swirled his stiff shaft inside her, delving deeply to caress the depths of her tight passage. Undulating his hips, he plunged into her, her soft moans of pleasure driving him onward until her head fell back, her heavy-lidded gaze holding him in thrall. Pressing his hands against the small of her back, he pulled her even more tightly against his groin. This time, he didn't simply move his dick, but ground his hips against her, loving the way her ass massaged his balls.

"D'you like that, Sara?"

"Mmm, yes… don't stop. Fuck me, just… like… *that*…" Her head snapped forward as her first orgasm detonated, her pussy squeezing him so hard he could barely move.

"Oh, Sara… you… *oh*…" Her tight muscles milked his cock, forcing more fluid from the head and sending it flowing down over his balls. He slid her side to side, and then bounced her against his nuts. On the third bounce, he lost control and his cock erupted, filling her with creamy wetness. He tried to stop then—had every intention of doing so—but she felt so damn good he simply couldn't do it.

He kept on—dragging her up and down on his cock, then back and forth over his balls while he watched her face, her eyes suffused with the joy he'd promised her. The sensation was incredible—ultimate pleasure, tumultuous joy, and endless sensuous fulfillment. He knew there was a party going on outside—guests to be entertained, a lake to swim in, and food to be enjoyed—but he couldn't imagine anything better than Sara wrapped around him like a hot, wet blanket of love. Wedding cake, no matter how tasty, couldn't begin to compare with his delicious Sara. Then he imagined licking icing from her fingers and came again.

Sliding a hand up her back, he pulled her face to his, capturing her lips and plunging his tongue into the recesses of her mouth. She was as addictive as candy, and he couldn't stop tasting her.

Her need seemed every bit as powerful as his own. Spearing her fingers through his hair, she forced his head back as she kissed down the side of his neck, nipping harder as she reached his shoulder while her strong legs gripped him like a vise.

His voice was deep and rasping as he begged her for more. "Bite me."

As she sank her teeth into him, his neck arched farther back and he came with a sharp exhale. This time, however, he felt more than semen leave his body. Somewhere in the center of his being, a tiny particle of his soul detached itself from the whole and hurtled toward a corresponding mote deep within his beloved Sara.

Cat was noted for being able to sense when a new litter of Zetithians was conceived, but Jerden didn't need his friend's confirming nod to know what had just taken place. He felt the truth of it with every fiber of his being. Sara—his lover, his wife, his *mate*—was now the mother of his children.

Their children. Babies whose births he would actually witness and whose lives he would be a part of—not merely names and numbers listed in the Zetithian Birth Registry. Hundreds had gone before this litter, but these would be the only offspring he could truly claim as his own.

His and Sara's.

Smiling, he lifted her off his cock but never allowed her out of his arms for an instant. Should he tell her, or would she already know?

Even though her feet were on the floor and she was clearly able to stand on her own, Jerden hated to release her. A spell had been cast, one he didn't want to see broken.

Sara nuzzled his neck, sending ripples of renewed desire rushing through him. "I believe you like being married."

"You think?" He hesitated, reluctant to say it aloud. Would she believe his Zetithian prescience, or would she tease him for being superstitious? He could wait and tell her of his vision after it was confirmed by other means, but that same intuition told him that now was the perfect time. "I also like being a father." *Present tense.* Would she notice?

She drew back, studying his face as though searching for a trace of deception. Then she nodded. "I felt that, too—didn't know what it meant at the time, but I'm pregnant, aren't I?"

Relief washed through him even stronger than the previous wave of desire. Against all odds, she believed him. "Yes, you are. Does that make you happy?"

"*Very* happy." The pleasing aroma of loving contentment that rose from her as she snuggled up against his chest made her reply unnecessary, but he was still glad to hear it. She raised her head. "Should we go out and make an announcement?"

"I have an idea someone else will do it for us. You know how Cat is about the pregnant mates of fellow Zetithians."

"Haven't heard that one," she said, clearly puzzled. "Are you saying he'll already *know*?"

"Oh, yeah. He'll know. You wait and see."

She heaved a sigh. "Guess we need to get back to the party."

Jerden watched as Sara donned a T-shirt and a pair

of shorts, then stood with his feet spread apart while she tucked his cock into his loincloth. "Seems a shame to cover that up, but I suppose we must consider our guests." Lifting the front flap, she buckled the belt. "That's better. More like the man I first met and fell in love with."

He grinned wickedly. "I wasn't sure who that ethereal beauty was that I just married, either, but it's coming back to me now."

She stooped to pick the dress up off the floor, examining it briefly before tossing it onto the chair with his shirt. "Not my style at all, is it?"

"I dunno," he said, shaking his head. "It looked damn good on you. Maybe you could wear it once in a while, just for fun."

"I'll do that." Arching her brow, she gave him a sly smile. "Whenever you've been ignoring me."

He loved that smile—the one that said she trusted him enough to tease. "Won't be any need for it, then. Might as well toss it in the corner and let the cats sleep on it."

Laughing, she took him by the hand. "C'mon, let's get going before anyone wonders what we've been doing in here."

Jerden was quite certain that everyone—all the adults, at least—knew precisely what they'd been up to. Jack was probably sitting on the porch with her pistol drawn, guarding the house so they wouldn't be disturbed.

As it happened, he was right—though Jack had a chicken wing, rather than a pulse pistol in her hand. "That Tarq makes better fried chicken than the Colonel," she declared. "I think he needs to start selling franchises."

As always, Cat sat beside her. If they'd ever been more than ten meters apart, Jerden hadn't seen it. Cat smiled at Sara before aiming a significant twitch of his brow at Jerden. Oh, yes, he knew.

Jerden aimed a questioning look at Cat. "Boys or girls?"

"Both," Cat replied. "One girl and two boys."

Jack's smile was smug. "You probably didn't know that part, did you?" Apparently noting Sara's derisive snort, she added, "He's never wrong."

"Oh, I don't doubt his word," Sara said. "I just find it hard to believe he knows so much when conception only took place a few minutes ago."

"It's a gift," Jack said proudly. "Just one more reason to love him."

Cat's voice was roughened by his purr. "I am pleased to be able to provide many reasons, my lovely master." Even without the purr, his meaning was quite clear.

"Master?" Sara echoed. "She's your *master*?"

Jack grinned. "Yep. I found him in the slave market on Orpheseus Prime and bought him for five measly credits. Best money I ever spent."

Cat nodded. "Though she set me free, she remains my master. We are bonded to one another, as well as married and mated."

Sara regarded Jack curiously. "I never noticed it before, but is that why your pupils have a reddish glow?"

Jack gazed at Cat with unabashed adoration as she caressed his cheek. "Yeah, we were bound together by a Zerkan ritual. Drives me absolutely nuts to be separated from him—and I can smell him a mile away."

Cat leaned into her hand, purring. "I would never

leave her whether we were bonded or not, but her ability to find me has been… useful."

Sara frowned at Cat. "And the same ritual turned your eyes blue?"

"No," Cat replied. "My eyes are blue because I was healed by a Zerkan *female*. The one who treated Jacinth was male."

"Well, that's about as clear as mud," Sara muttered.

"Never been healed by a Zerkan, then? Lucky you! They've got this nasty green spit…" Jack paused, shuddering. "It'll cure damn near anything, but it's so gross I thought the sonofabitch had poisoned me at first—and that was only the beginning of our little adventure."

Sara looked a little green herself but seemed enthusiastic. "Sounds exciting. I'd love to hear the story sometime."

Jack waved a dismissive hand. "Would take hours to tell it all, and I'm sure you've got *much* better things to do."

Her suggestive tone and knowing smile were evidently wasted on Sara, who still seemed oblivious to innuendo. "Maybe you could write a book about it."

Jack considered this for a moment, then shrugged. "Might do that someday—if I ever find the time." She nodded toward the lake where her children swam and splashed along with the other kids. "That bunch keeps me pretty busy these days. Might not get around to it until I'm old and gray."

Jerden couldn't help chuckling. If nothing else, Jack's memoirs—if, indeed, she ever wrote them—would certainly be colorful.

"Hey, you've already got the opening line," Sara said.

"I found him in the slave market on Orpheseus Prime…"
Sara grinned. "It'll probably sell millions."

Jack's eyes lit up. She was nothing if not an entrepreneur. "Really? I'll give it some thought."

Cat leaned over and kissed her, purring softly. "And if there are any episodes you have forgotten, I will help you *remember* them."

Jack winked at him. "I'm counting on it." She glanced at Sara. "Bet your story would make interesting reading, too."

"Maybe," Sara conceded. "But I can't write it now. Something tells me the best is yet to come."

Jack grinned. "Couldn't have said it better myself."

Chapter 23

SARA AND JERDEN LEFT THE HOUSE AND STROLLED OUT to the lake together. The kids were all splashing about in the water while the adults relaxed near the shore, lying on chaise lounges or blankets spread out on the ground. The sight of so many Zetithians together struck Sara in a way it hadn't before. She was a part of that community now—married to one of their kind and already carrying a litter of his children. True, they weren't blood relatives of Jerden's, but with so few of them left, the sense of kinship was very pronounced.

That feeling was new to Sara. She'd been part of a loving family, but with others, she had always been on the outside looking in, first as something of a misfit child, then a damaged teen, and later, a woman who shunned men like the plague. Her relationship with Jerden had changed her in so many ways she barely recognized herself. She now felt no reluctance to join the group, plopping down on a chaise to soak up the sun while Jerden pulled a chair up beside her, even laughing when she heard Onca's response to Salan's blatant sexual overtures.

"Oh, hell no," he exclaimed. "Not for a million credits."

Salan clearly didn't know what to make of that. "I don't understand. You're willing to do it for money on Rhylos. I would've thought…"

"Even *my* dick needs a break once in a while," he

said. "I fuck for a living, and right now I'm on *vacation*." Stretched out on a chaise lounge beneath the blazing sun, he *did* look relaxed, and if he smelled the scent of Salan's desire, it certainly didn't show.

Salan frowned. "But don't you enjoy your job? Jack told me you did."

"I do. And I'll be happy to ask Roncas to schedule a session with you just as soon as I get back to Rhylos." Onca paused, lowering his voice slightly. "You must understand, Salan, I've got to draw the line *somewhere*. Otherwise, I'd be fucking all the time and *never* get any peace."

Coming from any other man, this statement would've sounded unforgivably cocky if Sara hadn't already known it to be true. Even so, Lucy snickered. "Trust me, that will change if you ever get married, Onca. You guys have a way of making your mates insatiable, and if you're anything like Tarq, the scent of your pregnant mate will drive you wild. You'll be doing it all the time."

"Which is the very reason I'm staying single," Onca declared. "When I'm off duty, I'm off duty." He settled himself back on the chaise, closing his eyes as though doing so might block Salan from his mind. Sara wondered if he could shut off his sense of smell as easily.

Jerden leaned his head against Sara's. "He's obviously never been in love."

"I heard that," Onca said, opening one eye. "And you're right, though I'm not sure what love has to do with it. A scent is a scent is a scent, and it doesn't matter whose it is as long as it makes your dick hard."

"*Definitely* never been in love," Dax said with a glance at his wife. "Want to go for a swim?"

"Absolutely." Ava's hair began to wave back and forth as though tossed by the wind. Only there wasn't any wind, at least none that Sara could detect. "Don't forget your mask."

"Oh, I won't." Dax got to his feet, holding a curved piece of a crystalline substance. "Can't ever forget *that*." The two of them ran down to the shore and swam out into the deepest part of the lake, well away from the children.

Salan had that puzzled look on her face again, but it was Waroun who chose to enlighten her. "Ava can breathe underwater. Dax can too, as long as he's wearing that mask."

"So?"

Waroun waggled his fingers and licked his lips. "Underwater nookie."

"With a *Zetithian*." Salan let out a whimper. "Oh, *wow*…"

"Book an appointment, Salan," Onca said, not bothering to open his eyes. "I'll give you a discount."

She hesitated, chewing on a fingernail. "How long would I have to wait?"

"I dunno," Onca replied. "I think I'm booked up through 3020, but you'd have to ask Roncas to be sure."

Salan groaned. "That's two whole years."

"Gives you more time to save up your credits," Onca said. "Don't worry about the trip. Dax will take you there cheap."

Waroun nodded. "He sure will, but you know, if you'd just give me a try, I think you'd forget all about those cats."

Salan shook her head. "I've done that already.

Not with you, of course, but with someone else, um, *like* you."

"And you *still* want one of the cats?" Waroun tapped his lips with a fingertip. "Oh, Salan, you have been *so* misguided. He must've been a real dud."

"Maybe, but you've got to admit that Zetithians are better looking than Norludians. At least, they are to a human."

Waroun frowned. "Didn't think you *were* human, Salan. Got Davordian eyes, don't you?"

Salan nodded absently, her longing gaze still fixed on Onca, whose eyes remained closed. "I'm half human—and Davordians are more like humans than Norludians. So are Zetithians."

Sara could definitely relate. She wouldn't have taken Waroun over Onca, either. However, she could also understand Onca's position, though it did seem odd for an unattached man to turn down a woman like Salan. Jerden's refusal of her had been due to a rather unique set of circumstances. Normally, he probably would've been happy to be of service to her.

A strange sensation crept through her at the thought of Jerden consorting with Salan. Glancing sideways, she caught him smiling at her as though he'd heard her thoughts. Covering her hand with his own, he gave it a reassuring squeeze. No. He wouldn't be doing anything with Salan. Ever.

A slight nod and a flick of his eyes directed her attention to Nate, who sat alone at a table a little apart from the others, his fingers drumming on the tabletop as he hitched in his chair. He'd seemed fine during the ceremony and immediately afterward, but now he looked like a man who longed to be elsewhere. He fidgeted for several moments before finally voicing his irritation. "Got something against humans, Salan?"

Salan tore her eyes away from Onca with obvious reluctance. "No, but there aren't many of them around."

Nate's eyes widened. Sara thought he was about to say more, but he didn't. The muscles along his jaw bulged slightly as though he'd clenched his teeth. Apparently he was still having rejection issues.

In light of her suspicions, Sara didn't give a damn how he felt, but it gave her the perfect opening. "By the way, Nate. I've been meaning to ask you. Have you had any problems with juluva weed poisoning? Danuban's been chowing down on it here at Jerden's place and nearly died."

"Not that I'm aware of." Nate's voice was smooth, his blue eyes gazing directly at hers with no hint of guile. If she'd thought to trip him up during a vulnerable moment, she'd failed. "Sorry to hear that about your stallion, though. He's a fine animal. I'd hate for you to lose him."

"Me, too." She glanced at Jerden. "Which reminds me, we need to check out the creek that runs along the eastern border of our land. There was an awful lot of that weed growing here by the lake. Might be more of it in the creek bed."

Jerden nodded. "We can take a ride out there tomorrow."

"I'm surprised you didn't notice it growing here before he got sick, Sara." Nate didn't bother to add a smile, which might have taken some of the sting out of his words. "You must've been over here enough."

That's it, Nate. Let's make this seem like it's all my fault—or Jerden's.

Sara focused on keeping her reply civil, which was difficult when she was itching to hurl accusations at him. "Not really. I'd only been to the house once or twice. The juluva was growing on the far side of the lake."

Nate registered this with a slight lift of his brow. "Well, that explains it, then."

"Funny thing, though. Lowinski said he'd been exposed to juluva before." She paused for a moment, giving the idea time to sink in. "The scan showed traces of the toxin in the older sections of his hooves."

The muscles along Nate's jaw hardened. He might as well have confessed. "That *is* odd."

"Of course, we'll probably never know how that happened," Sara said smoothly. "But you still might want to check your pastures, just to be sure."

"I'll do that."

I'll just bet you will.

─ ⁓⁓⁓ ─

Jerden thought she'd handled that rather well, particularly when Nate didn't jump up and leave immediately. However, it wasn't long before he pleaded the need to get back home to tend his stock. After offering more congratulations—which actually seemed sincere—he left.

Nate hadn't been gone more than ten minutes when Jack strolled over and dropped a plain wooden box in Sara's lap. "Wedding present."

Sara's eyes widened. "I'm almost afraid to open this." She glanced up at Jack. "It won't bite me, will it?"

"Go on," Jack urged. "I didn't have any fancy wrapping paper, but it's something you need." She frowned slightly. "Couldn't find what I wanted when Cat and I went shopping yesterday, so we took a run back to the spaceport. After poking around in the cargo hold for a bit, I found just the thing."

Cat glanced at Jack with a smile that was as loving as it was tolerant. "I am not sure you will agree, Sara. But she means well."

Tisana winced. "Oh, Jack, you *didn't*. Not again." Her husband, Leo, patted her hand. Living aboard a starship with Jack had to be trying at times, though Jerden would've bet it was certainly never dull.

"Nice gift there, Jack," Onca remarked as Sara gingerly lifted the lid. "A pistol and a comlink?"

"A *universal* comlink and a *Nedwut* pulse pistol," Jack said. "And a holster. Sara is married to a Zetithian now." She leveled a steely-eyed glare at Sara. "Jerden needs protection. You must carry them always and maintain *constant* vigilance. Do you hear me, Sara? Constant. Vigilance."

Sara's jaw dropped, though she shouldn't have been surprised. Jack had already mentioned giving her a pistol, and if she hadn't expected the woman to follow through with the offer, she obviously didn't know Jack well enough.

"That comlink will work on any system on any planet," Jack said. "And that isn't one of your run of the mill pistols, either. It's a Nedwut pulse pistol. Even the stun setting is lethal to some species, and it's got a kill setting on it."

"A *kill* setting?" Sara echoed. "Isn't that a bit extreme?"

"Maybe," Jack admitted. "But if some crazy-ass Nedwut who hasn't gotten wind of Grekkor's death ever finds a way to land here and is looking to collect the bounty on Jerden, you'll be ready for him. Nothing sold on this world will stop a Nedwut." She paused, grumbling. "Piss-poor weaponry. Probably wouldn't even stun a Drell."

Lucy frowned, casting a nervous glance at Tarq before addressing Jack. "Maybe so, but that's pretty unlikely, don't you think? The regulations here are very tough. And no one is paying the bounty anymore."

"There's never been a regulation yet that someone didn't find a way to get around," Jack declared. "And, generally speaking, Nedwuts are fuckin' idiots anyway." Her lips formed a moue of distaste. "Greedy bastards." She nodded at Sara. "Carry that with you all the time. It needs to become a part of you." She patted her own holstered weapon. "No one is ever gonna get past me if they come after Cat. Ever." Without another moment's hesitation, she rounded on Lucy. "And where's *your* pistol, Miss Lucy? I distinctly remember giving you one."

"I didn't think I'd need to bring it to a *wedding*," Lucy protested.

"Don't worry," Tarq said. "I've got it. I *knew* she'd ask."

Once the collective laughter died down, Onca gave Jack a wink. "Gonna wear yours while you're swimming?"

"Absolutely," Jack replied. "They'll fire underwater." She paused, scowling. "Not as accurately as they should, though. I need to speak to the manufacturers about that. *Definitely* room for improvement." She nodded at Jerden. "Got a present for you, too."

Sara burst out laughing as Jack handed Jerden a small stone. "A rock? You're giving him a *rock*?"

"Darconian glowstone," Jack said. "Great for setting the mood."

Jerden nodded, tucking the stone beneath his belt just as one of Cat and Jack's oldest boys ran past, his inky curls plastered to his wet back.

"Hey, Larry!" Jack called out. "What's your hurry?"

Larry paused briefly, giving his mother a long-suffering look. "I gotta check the deep space coms."

"Yeah, right," Jack said with a wave. "Carry on."

Grinning, Larry jogged over to one of the tents and ducked under the flap.

"Looks like you've got those boys pretty well trained," Jerden remarked.

"No need with him," Jack said. "He fiddles with that com system constantly. Pulls it out of the damn ship and carries it with him everywhere. He's got it set up in the tent." Jack shook her head, but her proud smile was hard to miss. "I'm surprised he doesn't sleep with it."

"He hates to be out of touch with the rest of the galaxy," Cat explained.

"*I* think he's got a girlfriend on Derivia," Jack confided. "Those two are yakking back and forth all the time."

"Are you sure it's a girl?" Leo asked. "I've heard some of their conversations. They don't sound very lover-like."

"Well, I *thought* it was a girl." Jack raked a hand through her short locks and gave her head a scratch. "Hard to tell with Derivians. I'd just as soon he didn't take up with one of them anyway. Better to find a nice Terran girl."

"Someone like you?" A soft blue glow emanated from Cat's eyes.

Jack reached out, tracing the line of his cheek with a fingertip. "Aw, Kittycat, you always say the sweetest things."

—∿∿—

As afternoon gave way to evening, Sara's parents went back to her house to rest up for their departure the next morning. Sara's stable hands went back to the barn to feed the horses. The local guests also took their leave, though Salan elected to remain—presumably in the hope of changing Onca's mind. None of those camping out in the tents seemed inclined to call it a night, so Jerden built a fire near the shore and everyone gathered around it, enjoying their time together, until one by one, the children grew sleepy and disappeared behind the tent flaps.

"Great wedding," Onca remarked during a lull in the conversation. "Didn't think it would be this relaxing."

Sara could certainly relate to that. She took a sip of her wine, trying to recall when she'd ever felt so joyous or so at peace with herself and the world. She'd never dreamed she would ever marry, let alone be as happy as she was at that moment, lounging on a blanket near the fire with Jerden spooned up behind her. She could feel his erection pressing against her backside and wondered how he could be content to simply lie there and hold her when she knew he had to be uncomfortable.

"Glad you're having a good time." Jerden's purring was so soft she couldn't even hear it, but the vibrations resonated throughout her body, sending tendrils of warmth and love curling around her heart. "We'll have to do this again someday."

Sara doubted that would ever happen. Not like this. People changed, paths diverged, perhaps never to cross again. Closing her eyes, she savored the moment, knowing it was one she would attempt to recall quite often in later years, and she wanted to remember every detail. The crackling fire, the still night air, the solid ground beneath her, Cria curled up beside them, surrounded by Jerden's other assorted pets. And Jerden. Above everything else, Jerden.

Onca yawned, his catlike fangs gleaming in the firelight. "Sounds good to me."

Hearing a sigh, Sara turned her head in the direction of the sound.

Salan was lying on a blanket in the shadows beyond the fire, and though she didn't appear to be looking at Onca, the sigh had undoubtedly been hers. An arm was draped over her, much the way Jerden's arm surrounded Sara. Nate had left the party earlier. Sara couldn't imagine who it might be until he got up, motioning for Salan to follow. Sara stifled a gasp as Waroun took Salan's hand and led her into the darkness.

Whether Jerden noticed this startling event or not wasn't clear, but nonetheless, he seemed to take it as his cue. "Time to say good night, though. It's been a long day."

Jerden put his arm around her shoulders as they walked back to the house, and she caught herself thinking about that first night they'd spent together. As sick as he was, he'd been unaware of her presence. Tonight he would be more responsive, but that night had been special in its own way, for her life had undergone a significant change as a result. She could never have predicted this outcome; happily-ever-afters weren't for the woman she'd been back then. They were for the woman she had *become*.

Having reached the porch, Jerden's eyes glowed with golden fire as he swept her into his arms and carried her across the threshold. "I'd forgotten about this Earth custom. Something Lucy said a while ago reminded me."

Sara slid her arms around his neck and nibbled the tip of his ear. "Oh, and what was that?"

Laughter mixed with a purr delayed his reply. "She said I'd swept you off your feet."

"You've certainly done that—in more ways than this."

"Better get used to it, Sara. This won't be the last time." The living room was pitch-dark, but he stepped around the furniture as easily as he would have done in daylight and carried her into the bedroom. The sheets were still rumpled from their last tryst and, thankfully, there was less clothing to remove this time. He set her down and pulled her shirt off over her head.

"You like sweeping me off my feet?"

He nodded. "I like seeing you lying naked on my bed even more."

She slipped off her shorts. "As you wish." Sliding to the center of the bed, she held out her arms in invitation.

"Not yet. I just want to look at you for a minute."

"I'm surprised you can even see me, it's so dark."

"A Zetithian advantage, I believe. It's almost impossible to hide anything from one of us—day or night. Even in total darkness, I can see you perfectly." Sara shivered as his eyes swept over her body. "And you're beautiful, Sara. Absolutely beautiful."

Sara heard rather than saw him unbuckling his belt.

"This is so unfair. You can see me all the time, but I can't see you."

"Watch." A pinpoint of light appeared, growing steadily in intensity until she was able to discern a glowing orb resting in the palm of his hand. "You have Jack to thank for this one."

"The glowstone?"

He nodded. "Very expensive and highly sensitive to thought. You have only to direct your wish for more light to the stone, and it will illuminate." He tossed the stone onto the sheets, then let his loincloth slowly slip from his body and fall to the floor.

Softer than moonlight, the glow from the small stone caressed his skin, highlighting his broad chest and rippling muscles. His hard cock jutted from its nest of dusky curls, droplets of moisture already welling up from the serrations along the coronal ridge. He smiled, his fangs gleaming as he shook back his long dark hair like a stallion tossing his mane. Sara sucked in a breath.

"Turn around."

His hair hung past his waist in long spirals, accentuating the width of his shoulders and drawing her eyes downward to his muscular buttocks and thighs. Sara drank in the sight of him, longing to press a kiss into each of the dimples that peeked out from beneath the tips of the curls that curtained his lower back.

"Now, *that's* beautiful."

He turned his head, fixing his smoky gaze on her nude form. "I'm all yours, Sara."

"Then get in bed right this second or I'll have to smack those hot, succulent buns."

His purr roughened. "Promises, promises…"

Sara gave him a sultry smile. "Thought I'd forgotten you liked that, didn't you?"

"Oh, I hope *not*..." Climbing onto the bed, he stalked back and forth like a great beast unable to decide how best to attack his prey. Then, as though he'd made his decision, he crawled up over her and rose up on his knees, his cock a breath away from her lips. "Suck me."

Sara opened her mouth and took him in, making no protest as he threaded his fingers in her hair and began gliding his cock over her tongue. No shadow of past abuse remained to taint her enjoyment of him. He was hers to enjoy, and she would continue to discover endless ways to please and tease him.

Massaging his buttocks while he fucked her mouth, she gazed up at his blazing eyes and the blissful smile curling his lips. The view of him from that perspective was a treat too delightful to miss, yet her eyes continually squeezed shut as her body contracted in orgasm, each one following closely on the heels of another. Determined to witness his climax before the next blast of ecstasy took her, she opened her eyes wide, drew back a hand, and slapped him hard on the ass.

Instantly, his back arched and he came with a hiss, his *snard* flowing over her tongue like sweet, molten chocolate. Within seconds, heat pooled low in her back before exploding in a thousand different directions, infusing every particle of her being with joy.

Jerden barely took the time to savor his own pleasure before withdrawing from her mouth. Backing away, he buried his face in her pussy, licking her clitoris and sucking it into his mouth. The onslaught of delightful sensations forced a cry from her throat, and she fisted her hands in his hair, refusing to let him go. She was already screaming his name as he sucked her to yet another piercing climax, one that turned her body into a quivering mass of ecstasy and threatened to rip her soul into shreds.

—⁓—

Sara's scent had kept him aroused all evening, but even after coming harder than ever before, Jerden was still drowning in it. "I can't believe what you're doing to me, Sara. Your scent... it's different... more intense, more... I don't know what, but it's incredible."

"Remember what Lucy told Onca? That the scent of his pregnant mate would drive him wild?"

Jerden nodded, surprised he could even move his head. "That must be it. I've never been with a pregnant woman before. I had no idea. You've only been pregnant for a few hours and I already feel like a stag in rut."

"No complaints here."

He leaned down and kissed her, letting his tongue glide in and out of her mouth until his dick hurt so badly he couldn't stand it anymore. He rubbed the head against her wet entrance. She wrapped her legs around him, pulling him closer.

With one quick thrust, he sheathed himself in her warmth. The act of penetration had always felt fabulous, but this time, it felt as though his freezing body had suddenly been plunged into a steaming hot bath. The heat touched off a chain reaction, sending more blood rushing to his swollen cock, driving it in deeper, making it swim circles inside her, thrumming with each pulsing beat of his heart. "Ohhh…"

"Good?"

"Simply the best." That wasn't a line, either. He meant every word of it. She was the best, the only, the one. "I love you so much."

"I know the feeling. Love you dearly." She cupped his cheek in her palm, and he leaned into her touch as though drawing life from it. Perhaps he was. She *was* life; the mother of his children and the source of all joy. Control shattered, leaving him helpless to withstand the force that drew him into her. As his muscles contracted, sending jets of semen coursing through his cock and into her waiting body, life seemed to unfold within the depths of her eyes.

Scenes shifted and flickered as he watched—laughing children, dancing horses, sparkling sunshine, driving rain—it was all right there, shining forth from the eyes of the one he loved without limit. And through it all, Sara was there to share it with him—eternally beautiful, joyously loving, and forever by his side.

Chapter 24

A KNOCK AT THE FRONT DOOR STARTLED SARA AWAKE. She barely had time to throw on a robe when Jack stormed inside, her jaw set and her eyes aflame.

"I had Larry do some digging to see what he could find out about Chantal. I'm surprised no one tried to contact you, Jerden—or maybe they *did* try and couldn't find you. Either way, they could've at least told Onca." She snorted in disgust. "Fuckin' idiots! Anyway, the story is a little vague. It seems that Chantal and another female patient escaped together recently, but one of them died in the attempt. At least, they *think* she died. The guard was sure he shot one of them but they never found a body."

Sara's eyes met Jerden's. "So the woman you saw in the square *could* have been Chantal."

"What woman?" Jack demanded. "Are you saying she's here on Terra Minor?"

"I don't know," Jerden replied. "I saw a woman in the square when we were in town not long ago. I could've sworn it was Chantal, but then, that was part of the reason I was living out here all alone to begin with. I saw Chantal's or Audrey's face on every woman I saw." His smile was fleeting but sheepish. "I went kinda nuts after all that, you know."

"Not surprising," Jack said. "But you're in much better shape now. How long ago did you see her?"

"I don't know, three weeks, maybe four?" Jerden said. "It was before you all got here, and before the stallion got sick."

Jack nodded. "Recently, then. Seems Chantal went even more berserk than usual a few weeks ago and killed two of the staff, then escaped, which is why the guards were taking potshots at her. The other woman appears to have taken advantage of all the excitement and slipped out at the same time."

"Even so, she couldn't have gotten here that fast," Sara exclaimed. "Could she?"

Jack gave her a tight smile. "Not unless she had help."

Sara's jaw dropped at the thought of what this implied. Jerden looked completely bewildered. "But who would *do* that?"

"I dunno," Jack said. "You tell me."

Sara sifted through the details but was unable to imagine how helping Chantal land on Terra Minor would have been in Nate's best interest or anyone else's. Nate may have seen Jerden as a rival, but bringing Chantal into the picture would be more likely to get *Sara* killed than to eliminate any threat from Jerden. It wasn't as though Jerden *wanted* Chantal. Still, if Jerden thought Sara was in danger, he might've withdrawn his proposal.

No. An escaped murderess could be dealt with in other ways. Chantal would be recaptured, and Sara and Jerden would still be together. Nate couldn't possibly benefit.

"There's something here we're not seeing," Jerden said slowly. "That is, if there's anything to see. I can't believe anyone would help Chantal come here. There's simply no reason for it."

His words were an echo of Sara's own thoughts.

There had to be another explanation. "Maybe she paid off someone or arranged this in advance."

"But she was *insane*," Jerden insisted. "No one in their right mind would have—" He broke off there, barking out a laugh. "I see your point. No one in their right mind would've done *any* of this. She might have an accomplice who's even nuttier than she is."

Nate had his faults, but Sara didn't think insanity was one of them.

"I'll check with the guys in immigration," Jack said. "If there've been any Davordian immigrants recently, they'll know. Though she *could* be here illegally."

"Which is even scarier," Sara said. "She could be anywhere. No implant, no way to track her..."

"But *very* tough to do," Jack said. "I wouldn't even *attempt* to land here without authorization, and I've snuck onto lots of planets in my time." She sighed. "Nothing you can do but keep your eyes peeled and be careful. We'll be outta here after breakfast. Dax is leaving this morning too."

Sara would've felt much more at ease with all of their friends nearby, but without solid proof of any danger, there was no reason for them to stay.

She and Jerden dressed quickly and went out to say good-bye to their guests. Sara knew she probably wouldn't see her parents again in years, possibly never, and their farewells were even more tearful than when Sara had left Earth.

She'd only been gone from her own home for a few days, but it seemed strange to simply go back to life as usual. So much had happened in that short time. She and Jerden were married and expecting their first litter—thankfully, Bonnie would still be available for advice on caring for triplets—and Sara now had access to Jerden's fortune. Even so, she would go home and fix breakfast for the crew, feed the dogs and cats, water and prune her roses, and then head out to the barn, just as she had done every morning before she and Jerden ever met.

The only difference was, she would no longer be doing all of it alone.

———

Reutal's eyes danced with excitement as he took his seat at the breakfast table. "You gotta tell me all the details, Sara. I still can't believe it."

If he wanted details of her wedding night, he was in for a big disappointment. Sara wasn't sharing *that* with anyone. She handed him a plate of pancakes. "Believe what?"

"Salan and Waroun! They were awfully chummy at the wedding." Reutal pressed his fingertips together and then popped them apart with gusto before dousing his pancakes with syrup.

"Well, I did see them go off together last night," Sara said. She glanced at Jerden, who threw up his hands.

"Don't look at me. I don't know anything about it—though, come to think of it, she *was* still there this morning."

"Ah ha! So they *did* spend the night together. I knew it!" Reutal waggled his eyebrows. "Did you see her doing any kissy-face stuff with Waroun?"

Jerden frowned. "Not that I recall, but then, I wasn't paying much attention to them."

Sara's hands shook as she dished up Jerden's breakfast.

"After the bomb Jack dropped on us this morning, I'll admit, I wasn't giving them much thought, either."

"Bomb?" Zatlen echoed. "What bomb?"

"Apparently Chantal Benzowitz—the woman who killed Jerden's—" Sara stopped, unsure how to refer to her.

"Fluffer," Drania said. "We know all about that part. What about Chantal?"

Sara set Jerden's plate down in front of him, then recounted the details of Chantal's escape. "We doubt the woman Jerden saw was Chantal. It was probably just someone who looked like her."

Drania's long pink ears twitched. "That still has to make you a little antsy, though."

Actually, Sara was perilously close to being terrified, but she did her best to put those thoughts aside. "Jack said the Trackers promised to check up on all the recent immigrants, but if she's here illegally, they may never find her."

"We'll keep an eye out for anything suspicious," Zatlen said. He took a big bite of his pancakes and chewed blissfully, swallowing before he spoke again. "Davordian woman, right?"

Jerden nodded. "Long dark hair, rather pretty—or she would be if her eyes weren't so crazy-looking."

Zatlen kept his gaze focused on his food. "One of your clients, I take it."

Jerden hesitated for a moment. "Yes, she was."

Zatlen's comment was one that Sara had never even considered, and this was clearly something Jerden didn't care to admit. Of course she'd been a client. How else could she have developed such an obsession? Still, the thought of Jerden having sex with her was disturbing.

She gave herself a mental shake. Jerden's past was just that. His *past*. She couldn't hold it against him anymore than he could blame her for her previous experiences. Chantal was similar to the nutso girlfriends that lots of men told stories about—some of them as murderous as Chantal. The fact that she'd been a paying customer shouldn't matter.

"Too bad you only screened clients for physical, rather than mental illnesses," Zatlen said. "Might've saved a lot of grief for everyone involved."

"That wasn't a concern at the time," Jerden said. "Besides, I don't think they've invented that kind of scanner yet."

"Hindsight is always sharper than foresight." Drania reached out a long arm and patted Jerden's hand. "Nobody can blame you for what someone else did."

Jerden smiled his thanks and began eating his breakfast, though with slightly less enthusiasm than usual. Sara knew Audrey's murder still bothered him. He wasn't the kind of man who could simply shrug off her death as part of the price of doing business. Jerden had a kind heart and a conscience. Sara couldn't have loved a man with anything less.

—⁓—

Sara was saddling up for their ride when Jerden spotted her holster. "Better let me carry that."

"Are you kidding me? Look, I know we're only going for a ride on our own property, but you heard what Jack said. If I let anything happen to you, she'll— well, I'm not sure *what* she'll do to me, but I have no intention of ever finding out—aside from the fact that losing you would—" She broke off there, choking on words left unsaid.

Jerden pulled her into his arms. There were some things he didn't want her to have to worry about. His personal safety was one of them. "Jack's a little on the paranoid side—and she had good reason to be at one time. But there isn't a bounty on Zetithians anymore. No reason for anyone to kill any of us, let alone risk coming here to do it. I'm more concerned with *your* safety. The way I see it, you need protection far more than I do. If anyone is going to carry that pistol, it should be me."

"I'm beginning to wish she'd given us two of them." She pressed her forehead against his chest. "Maybe we should just stay home."

"No. We can't allow fear to disrupt our lives, Sara. Particularly when those fears are probably groundless."

She shuddered. "The whole thing still gives me the willies though, and Jack seemed very concerned."

"Yes, but remember, there've been no reports of Chantal attempting to slip through the immigration barriers. True, she could have landed illegally, but that's highly unlikely."

"What about that woman you saw in the square? Are you saying she was just a figment of your imagination?"

"Possibly, or you might have been right in that she only resembled Chantal."

She looked up at him with fear in her eyes. "I can't help thinking it really *was* Chantal. Bribes have worked before, and Bonnie's ex-husband is a perfect example of how the system can be manipulated. He faked his ID. Chantal could have done the same."

"Maybe, but I doubt she has the connections to pull off something like that."

Sara took a deep breath. "But what if she *did* have help? What then?"

"I think we're putting too much emphasis on things that *could* be rather than focusing on the facts. Chances are, she never made it off Rhylos."

Sara still seemed doubtful. "You know what that planet is like. She could have stowed away on a hundred different starships. We have no idea what her state of mind is now. She might have escaped, intending to kill you for betraying her."

"I didn't betray her, Sara."

"I know that and you know that, but does *she*? Look, Jack may be overly suspicious, but her vigilance kept Cat alive even when that bounty was still being paid. I'm not taking any chances."

"Neither am I." Jerden smiled and held out his hand. "I promise I'll buy you a fancy new pistol just as soon as I get the chance, but right now, your safety is of more concern than mine." When she didn't hand over the pistol, he gave her a wink. "Don't make me fight you for it."

That at least drew a smile from her. "Think you could take me?"

"Probably, but I'd rather not have to prove it."

"Okay, but I'm keeping the comlink." Shaking her head, she unbuckled the holster and handed it over. "You'd better be right about this. If anything happens to you, I'm dead meat anyway. Jack'll kill me."

"I doubt that. Remember, you're carrying three un-born Zetithians."

"Yeah, she'll let me live long enough to give birth to them, and *then* she'll kill me."

—⁓—

Sara hadn't been to the eastern border of her land since the oats had been planted. With the onset of the dry season, the harvest was about a month away and the stalks were already turning brown. They skirted the edge of the fields, Sara mounted on Yusuf and Jerden riding Danuban for the first time since his illness. Jerden had been reluctant to ride him, but Sara felt that the exercise would do him good. As always, Cria followed Jerden like a shadow.

The stallion seemed happy to be out of his paddock and probably would've unseated a lesser rider. Jerden rode out his high jinks without difficulty, and he soon settled down enough that Sara could ride alongside them.

"Not bad for a horse that was near death such a short time ago," she remarked.

"He doesn't feel any different to me, either. Seems as strong as ever."

"I hope you're right. You wouldn't believe how much money I have invested in him." Then she recalled the Friesian he'd bought. "Well, maybe you would, at that."

As they approached the dry creek bed, Sara let out a groan. "Son of a bitch! Should've known there'd be a ton of that weed growing back here." The juluva wasn't in bloom, but the grayish foliage was easy to spot. "I never thought to look for it here."

"Seeing as how your pastures are nowhere close, Danuban is the only one who could've gotten to it, so it probably wouldn't have been a problem."

"Not unless it seeded into my oat fields." She eyed the noxious plants with distaste. "I've never used an herbicide before—the regulations are incredibly tough—but this time I may have to."

She was staring at the weeds—actually considering setting fire to them once her grain was harvested—when Cria let out a snarl. Sara glanced up just as Danuban tossed his head and leaped sideways out from under Jerden. Her startled cry echoing across the field, Sara stared openmouthed as Jerden flew through the air to land heavily on the rocks below.

"Oh, my God! Jerden!" Cria and Danuban both bounded away from the creek's edge as Sara vaulted from the saddle and ran to the spot where Jerden had fallen. The ravine wasn't deep, but the sides were extremely steep and rocky. She was scrambling to find a way to reach him when she heard a woman's scream.

Whirling around, she spotted two people running toward her. She'd never seen the woman before in her life, but the man, she recognized.

Nate.

For an instant, Sara thought they were rushing to Jerden's aid, only realizing her error a moment later when she caught sight of the pistol in Nate's hand.

The woman was in the lead, but Nate caught her just short of the precipice. She fought him like a wild beast, kicking and snarling, even using her teeth. Sara didn't have to see her electric blue eyes to make a guess as to who she had to be.

"You fucking idiot!" the woman snarled as Nate wrestled her into submission. "You weren't supposed to kill *him*. You were supposed to kill *her*."

"You *shot* him?" Sara's heart seemed to stop, leaving her frozen in place, her attention divided between the drama playing out before her and the need to get to Jerden.

Nate laughed grimly. "Of course I shot him." Hooking his arm around the woman's neck, he tightened his hold and spoke right in her ear. "How else was I supposed to get my hands on Sara's money?"

Gasping in horror, Sara shifted her gaze from the struggling pair and directed it to where Jerden lay motionless on the rocky creek bed. *He can't be dead. He can't be.*

"You promised I could have him." The Davordian's flat, deadly tone reclaimed Sara's attention. Her face was white with anger and her eyes so steeped in hatred, Sara could almost feel their icy chill.

"And you were just crazy enough to fall for it." Nate grinned, ramming the pistol hard against her temple as though he enjoyed hurting her. "You were my scapegoat, Chantal."

The truth struck Sara like a blow. "You're *both* crazy. How could killing Jerden help you get *my* money?"

"Quite simple, my dear Sara. With him dead, you'd need comforting. And I'd be here to provide it."

Sara snorted a laugh. *No way in hell.* "That might have worked if I didn't know you were responsible for poisoning my stallion."

"You only *suspected* me, Sara. You couldn't prove I had anything to do with that. I covered my tracks much too well."

"But, Chantal… how?"

"I found out about her a while back and managed to

get a message to her that if she could escape, I'd help her come here for Jerden. She was easy enough to convince. After all, she *is* certifiably insane."

Chantal struggled in his grasp. "I'll kill you, you son of a bitch!"

"Not likely." He glanced at Sara. "You were my ticket out of debt, Sara—and you *know* what happens to people who go bankrupt on this world."

She *did* know. Deportation wasn't the worst of it. Depending on how deeply in debt he was, he would probably lose what little he had left. "Didn't realize you had money trouble, Nate. Not that it would have made any difference."

"You should have listened to me when I told you to save your money and use Kraken instead of importing your own stallion. With Danuban standing at stud, I knew you'd have no need of me, and I'd never have the opportunity to show you how charming and loving I can be— even toward a woman I don't find particularly attractive."

At one time, that comment would've hurt, but Jerden's love was like a shield. *If he's still alive.* Her heart slammed against her breastbone.

"It was *your* stubbornness that brought us to this point, Sara. I arranged to have Danuban poisoned, hoping he'd die en route. He didn't, obviously. Just went crazy enough to escape from the spaceport." He nodded toward the place where Jerden had fallen. "My plan still would've worked if you hadn't started consorting with that Zetithian bastard."

Chantal hissed like a spitting cat. "He is mine! You said I could have him!"

"Shut up, Chantal."

Sara blinked. She understood it now. "You were going to kill her, weren't you? Once Jerden was dead, you'd kill her and make it look like she'd committed suicide after missing me and hitting him instead."

"Very good, Sara." Nate's smile sent a chill of dread through Sara. She'd never liked him. Now she knew why. "Too bad it didn't work out quite the way I'd planned. Clearly, I should have killed her first. That way she wouldn't have started screeching the moment he hit the ground." He paused, pursing his lips as he tilted his head to one side. "Or I could've killed her a few moments ago when she started running. You would've seen me do it, and I would've been your hero for killing your husband's murderer."

Sara's body no longer seemed willing to obey her brain's instructions, her reactions made sluggish by the weight of dread pressing down upon her. Nevertheless, she forced out a laugh. "Too bad you aren't any good at thinking on your feet."

"Perhaps not." He sighed with evident regret. "You'd have been an *extremely* rich widow, Sara. Now you're nothing but a liability."

A movement behind him drew her eye. Cria stood poised, her huge yellow eyes fixed on Nate. She might not have understood the words, but she clearly understood the intent. Eyes narrowed, she advanced toward him.

"Are you intending to kill all of us?" She almost wished he would go ahead and get it over with. Death would relieve the misery of not knowing whether Jerden was alive or dead and eliminate the bleak prospect of having to go on without him.

"Much as it pains me, I may have to. Chantal can still

take the fall for a double murder and subsequent suicide. By the time anyone finds your bodies, I won't be anywhere around. Nothing will tie me to this event. Nothing."

"You won't gain anything by it," Sara said desperately. "No money, no land…"

"Ah, but I'll still have my life and my freedom."

Sara couldn't argue with that. No one would ever figure it out, either. *That's what I get for not telling anyone my suspicions—no one but Jerden.* The injustice of Nate going free at the expense of their lives gave her resolve the impetus it needed. Strength coursed through her and her spine stiffened. "I was willing to let you get away with what you'd done to Danuban. I can't let you get away with this."

"No? I don't see that you have any choice."

"Come on now. It doesn't have to be this way. We always have choices. You don't have to kill anyone." She almost added the word "else" but that would be admitting that Jerden was already dead, something she simply refused to believe.

Nonetheless, his mirthless laugh made Sara's skin crawl. "I suppose you'll marry me if I let you live?"

Sara felt the blood drain from her face. She couldn't marry Nate unless Jerden was dead. *Which he is* not. She set her jaw, glaring at him.

"I didn't think so," Nate said, correctly interpreting her reaction. "So, what now? I put down the gun and you'll just let me walk away? Is that it?"

"Possibly." Sara tried to keep her voice calm, her tone even. "We don't know whether you've actually committed murder yet or not. Jerden might not be dead."

If the weaponry on Terra Minor was as "piss-poor" as

Jack said it was, Jerden might have only been stunned, but Sara wasn't sure she dared believe it. He'd fallen hard on some very sharp rocks, but Zetithians were notoriously hard to kill. Chantal, however, was as good as dead. Even set on stun, a pulse pistol could kill if pressed against a person's head.

"You think not?" Nate's grin made him seem more evil than ever. "If he isn't, he will be, very shortly. Trust me, it will be my pleasure."

Chapter 25

As Jerden regained his senses, he heard the voices and quickly grasped the situation. *From now on, she carries the fuckin' gun.* However, this was not the time to kick himself for being macho. The pain in his left leg was like nothing he'd ever experienced, and one brief movement was enough to inform him it was broken. Raising his head slowly, he studied the rocky slope before him. He wasn't far from the edge, but it was very steep, and he could only see Sara.

For the moment, Jerden's only advantage was that if he couldn't see Nate, Nate couldn't see him, either. He would have to climb up to get a clear shot—or at least stand up—and do it without making a sound. *C'mon, Jerden. You're a cat, remember?* He wondered what had become of Cria. If Nate had already shot the leopard, he'd lost a valuable ally.

"You will not kill him!" Chantal's voice sounded every bit as shrill and frenzied as it had the day she killed Audrey. "If he dies, you will burn in the far reaches of hell!"

"Shut the fuck up, bitch!" Nate growled.

Jerden heard the sounds of a struggle, the pop of a pulse blast, and Cria's hiss. It was now or never. Ignoring the pain, he leaped onto his good leg just as Cria pounced.

Chantal fell, staring at Jerden with lifeless eyes as he

fired a narrow beam that caught Nate in the center of his chest. Cria's momentum pushed him over, the pistol flying from Nate's hand as the big cat landed on top of him, fangs and claws bared.

Sara screamed and staggered, nearly falling backward over the edge, but somehow managed to regain her footing before running to retrieve Nate's pistol. She had already found it and had it aimed at Nate when she glanced up and saw Jerden. Their eyes met and she let out a squeal.

"Jerden!" She ran back to the edge of the creek. "I thought you were dead!"

"Not yet." Jerden had never seen a more beautiful sight in his life as Sara reached out a hand to help him up. Eyes blazing, cheeks flushed, her hair like a flame— she was the living, breathing image of a heroine.

With her help, he made it up the slope and into her arms. Their lips met in a desperate, hungry kiss that couldn't even begin to convey what he felt. Relief, sadness, and yet ultimate joy that they were both still alive. Jerden vowed never to let a day pass without telling her—and showing her—exactly how much he loved her.

Cria sat on top of Nate's motionless body, licking her paw.

"I'm guessing you shot him," Sara said, frowning. "Was that pistol set to stun or kill?"

"Stun. But you know how it is with these Nedwut weapons."

Sara helped ease Jerden to the ground, then shooed Cria away from Nate. "He's still breathing."

Jerden was pleased he hadn't killed the man, but at the same time, he almost wished he had. "Chantal?"

"Dead," Sara replied. Her lip quivered slightly. "H-how much of that did you hear?"

"Enough to know he lured her here." Jerden shook his head in disbelief. "He did all this for *money*?"

She knelt down beside him. "Other people have done worse for less." Covering her mouth, she choked back a sob. "Terrible, horrific, *inhuman* things. Things you wouldn't believe."

He didn't have to think long to understand what she was referring to—and that was only what had happened to Sara, herself. Pulling her close, he held her, stroking her back until her sobs subsided.

She sat up, brushing away her tears. "Here I am, carrying on like a fool when you're the one who's hurt. How bad is it?"

"That's about the only thing I can feel right now," he replied, nodding toward his leg. "You know, I'm still not sure what happened. One minute I was sitting on the horse, the next, I was flying through the air."

"You *remember* that? I thought you'd been stunned."

Jerden smiled sheepishly. "No, much as I'd like to *think* it happened that way, I was conscious when I hit the ground. I actually fell off the horse."

"Really?" She glanced at Cria as the big cat sat down at Jerden's side, purring as she nudged his hand, seeking a caress. Danuban grazed nearby along with Yusuf. "I thought that was what happened until I saw Nate brandishing a pistol and heard Chantal screaming at him for killing you. Right before you fell, I heard Cria snarling, and Danuban went sideways. Nate claimed to have shot you. Obviously, he missed. Do you think Cria *knew* Nate was there and spooked the stallion on purpose?"

Cria yawned as though the conversation bored her. Jerden scratched her behind the ear. "She may have."

"Where's the Mordrial witch when you need her?" Sara muttered, getting to her feet. "Guess we'll have to wait until Tisana's back in town again so she can interpret for us. Should be an interesting story." She pulled the comlink out of her pocket and flipped it open. "Reutal's gonna have a field day with this one. He never *could* stand Nate."

Jerden's leg was lying at a very odd angle. He shifted it slightly, but no amount of repositioning eased the pain. All it did was make his head swim. "Might want to call Vladen while you're at it. My body can deal with the fracture, but if we don't straighten it out first, it'll heal crooked."

Nate groaned and began to stir.

Sara stomped her foot. "Nate Wolmack, if you so much as *think* about getting up, I'm gonna shoot you with your own damn pistol."

Jerden nodded. "Better listen to her. She's armed, and so am I."

"And I'm *really* pissed." Sara gritted her teeth. "So don't move, say a word, or even make a sound. Honest to God, Nate, I never liked you, but I never figured you for a murderer."

For a moment, Jerden thought Sara might be tempted to follow suit. Then he remembered that *he* had the pistol with the kill setting on it—which was probably just as well.

~~~

Sara made three calls. The first to Vladen, who seemed delighted to have a Zetithian patient he could actually treat for once and promised to arrive within the hour. The second was to the regional magistrate's office, and the third was to the comlink in the barn.

Reutal answered. "What's up, Sara?"

"Plenty. Can you fly my speeder back here to the creek? Jerden's hurt."

"Sure thing," Reutal replied. "Why do I get the idea that there's more to it than that?"

"There is. I'll explain later. Bring Zatlen with you." She flipped off the comlink. "I'll be giving up guard duty shortly, Nate. And guess who'll be taking over? Reutal, your biggest fan. He probably won't be as forgiving as I am. He might even stun you a couple of times just for the hell of it."

Nate raised his head and opened his mouth as if to speak.

"Don't," Sara warned. "I am *so* not in the mood to listen to *anything* you have to say."

She was torn between wanting to do something—*anything*—to ease Jerden's pain and her determination to keep Nate from moving a muscle. With her pistol aimed at Nate, she moved closer to Jerden. The best she could do was to place a hand on his shoulder, but he seemed to appreciate it nonetheless, giving her a brief smile. Cria remained close by, her vigilant gaze fixed on Nate.

"Hang on, Jerden," she whispered. "The Trackers and Vladen are on their way."

"Keep talking to me," Jerden said. "I'll conk out if you don't, and I need to speak to the Trackers when they arrive." He already sounded strange—his voice was growing faint and distant.

"Just tell me you love me."

"I do love you, Sara, and I'll keep telling you so—every half hour for the rest of my life."

Nate let out a snort. Sara felt an overwhelming urge to kick him but somehow managed to restrain herself. Cria, however, had no such scruples and spat at him.

Zatlen and Reutal arrived a few minutes later. Reutal climbed out of the speeder, his eyes even more protuberant than usual. "What the hell happened?"

"It's a long story," Sara said wearily. "And I'd rather not tell it twice. The Trackers will be here pretty soon. You'll hear it all then. In the meantime, would you *please* catch those horses before they eat any juluva weed? The creek bed is infested with it."

By the time the horses were rounded up, Sara heard a humming sound in the distance and glanced up at the sky. "Looks like your ride's here, Nate."

The Trackers landed in a hoverpod, the large, bug-like vehicle sprouting legs as it settled on the ground nearby. After Sara relinquished guard duty to one of the officers, she and Jerden gave their statements to a young Levitian with cropped blond hair and jaw ridges even sharper than Vladen's. Nate, for once, had the good sense to keep his mouth shut.

"There's just one problem," the tall Levitian said after scanning the dead woman's implant. "This isn't Chantal Benzowitz. Her name is Treanna Hwerthen."

Sara frowned. "But I distinctly heard him call her Chantal, and Jerden recognized her—didn't you?" She glanced down at Jerden, whose eyes were already heavy-lidded as he sagged against her.

"Definitely Chantal." His voice was a faint whisper.

"Jerden!" Kneeling beside him, she cradled his head in her arms as his eyes drifted shut. Even though she'd known he would lose consciousness eventually, it still frightened her. "Where the hell is Vladen?"

"He'll be here soon," the officer said. "We flew over his speeder on the way."

There was nothing to do now but wait for him to arrive. She sat down behind Jerden, resting his shoulders on her outstretched thighs, his head pillowed on her stomach. She traced the line of his brow with a fingertip and stroked the curve of a pointed ear. Zetithians were a strong, beautiful race, but so vulnerable while they healed themselves. She remembered Ulla telling her that she would get used to it eventually, but Sara wasn't so sure about that. Even knowing he would awaken completely healed, it was still tough to see him so helpless.

When the whine of a speeder heralded the doctor's arrival, Sara heaved a sigh of relief. Vladen greeted the young Levitian with a pat on the back. "My nephew," he explained to Sara as he stooped to examine Jerden's leg. "Hmph. Don't need a scanner to see what's wrong with him, now, do we?"

His hearty tone was undoubtedly meant to be encouraging, but Sara wasn't buying it. "Better scan him anyway," she said. "He landed on those rocks pretty hard."

"Don't worry, Sara. He can probably heal any other injuries without a bit of help from me, and I promise to give him a good going-over, but right now, setting the leg is far more critical." Vladen reached into one of his many pockets and pulled out the scanner, took a quick reading on the leg, then knelt by Jerden's foot and placed a leather loop around his ankle. "Good thing he's not wearing boots—or pants for that matter. Makes my job much easier. Wish all of my patients wore nothing but loincloths."

Sara was only grateful Jerden was unconscious. Vladen manipulated the bones back into place, pulled the leg straight, and sprayed it with a clear fluid, which hardened instantly.

"There you go, Sara," he said, getting to his feet. "Call me when he wakes up and I'll remove the cast. Shouldn't take more than a day or two."

"You're forgetting the full scan," Sara reminded him.

"Oh, right." Running the beam of the scanner over the length of Jerden's body, he glanced at the results. "Perfectly healthy, with the exception of the fracture and a few bruises. You, however, are pregnant with triplets." Vladen grinned. "But I'm guessing you already knew that."

"Yes, I did. But thanks for confirming it."

"My pleasure," Vladen said. "Well, must be off. I was on my way to deal with an inflamed appendix over at Bonnie's."

"Oh, no!" Sara exclaimed. "Whose appendix is it?"

"One of the younger ones. Karsyn, I believe." Vladen rubbed a hand along his bony jaw. "Might be nothing but a tummy ache, but she's been fussy for a while, which is unusual for a Zetithian child. Better have a look at her."

"She seemed fine yesterday," Sara said, frowning.

"Yes, I'm sure she was, Sara. But then, so was *he*—and the day before that, *you* weren't pregnant." With that parting shot, he waved good-bye to his nephew, climbed into his speeder, and took off.

He had a point. Things had a way of changing

drastically in the space of a heartbeat. How much time
had passed since Sara's world had turned upside down?
An hour, maybe two? Perhaps not even that long. Nate
had already been taken aboard the hoverpod. As Sara
watched, two of the Trackers carried Chantal's body
into the pod. The men returned a few minutes later, offering to fly Jerden back to the house.

Sara didn't want him on the same pod as Nate and
Chantal. It just seemed wrong. "No, but if you'll help us
get him into my speeder, Reutal and I can take it from
there. We've carried him into the house before, we can
do it again."

Once Jerden was settled in the back of the speeder,
the Trackers took off. Within moments, Sara couldn't
even hear the humming of the pod anymore, only the
wind whispering through the oat stalks. She nodded at
Zatlen, who stood nearby with the horses. "Go ahead
and take them back to the barn. Reutal and I will fly
back in the speeder."

Zatlen mounted Yusuf and cantered off, leading
Danuban. Sara watched until they disappeared over the
low rise of the oat field. "Why don't you fly the speeder,
Reutal? I'll ride in back with Jerden."

Reutal frowned. "Are you okay, Sara?"

She shook her head. "No. Not really." Glancing in the
direction Zatlen had taken with the horses, she almost
wished she'd gone with him. A gallop across the fields
would have helped to banish the terrors she'd faced that
morning. Cria leaped gracefully into the front seat of
the speeder, almost as though she knew Sara intended
to ride in the back with Jerden. "But I'll be better soon
enough—and so will Jerden."

Later that evening, Sara received a call from the regional magistrate. A Mordrial by the name of Suharken, his ability to read emotions enabled him to spot a liar quicker than anyone on the planet. Sara didn't have to be able to read minds to know he hadn't believed a word of Nate's statement. The look on his face was quite enough.

"We ran a DNA test on the deceased, comparing it with the police records on Rhylos. She's Chantal Benzowitz all right, but her identchip identifies her as Treanna Hwerthen—and her implant matches it." Suharken's swarthy skin and piercing black eyes made him a forbidding presence, but his smile was apologetic. "Our friend Nate obviously has connections with some pretty shady characters. Chantal landed here with a fake ID—a damn good one, by the way—and was married to him at the spaceport."

"Married?" Sara could hardly believe her ears. "After all that crap about him wanting to marry *me*?"

He nodded. "And as the spouse of a current resident, she was automatically granted permanent status."

Sara took a moment to put the pieces together. "Oh God, that was brilliant! Single men advertise offworld for wives all the time. Nate would've looked as though he'd been duped into bringing her here to find Jerden— and with her dead, she couldn't say otherwise. He'd be a widower and free to try again with me."

"Possibly." Suharken scratched the back of his neck, tugging at his collar as though it choked him. "For the record, at the time of her arrival, we had no reports of the escape of Chantal Benzowitz and therefore had no reason to question her identity. It wasn't as though she'd escaped from jail here, and Rhylos is a long way from Terra Minor."

He was either explaining or making excuses, Sara wasn't sure which, but she wasn't interested in that. She had other questions. "What I want to know is if Nate was broke, who paid her passage? Space travel isn't cheap and neither are fake identchips."

"He isn't saying," Suharken replied. He leaned back in his chair. "My guess is he borrowed the money from someone, promising a big payoff after he gained access to your fortune."

Sara's face grew hot with anger. "He would never have gotten a single credit out of me. I would *never* have married him. Ever."

The magistrate shrugged. "Maybe someone owed him a favor. You never know with those types. His record was clean, or he couldn't have immigrated here to begin with, but there's no way of knowing who his friends are. We can't screen everyone for everything."

Sara heaved a sigh. "I know that, and right now, I'm not sure I care. I'm just glad it's over."

She was letting him off the hook, and Suharken obviously knew it. He seemed relieved now, his smile almost genial. "I'm afraid the formalities will take a while, but it's nothing you need to worry about. We'll keep you posted."

Sara thanked him and terminated the link. She sat for a moment, only then realizing how exhausted she was. It had been a very long day. She got ready for bed and went into the bedroom, just as she had done the first night Jerden ever spent in her house. Cria lay beside him and several of the cats were curled up at the foot of the bed. As before, Cria relinquished her post when Sara approached.

She stroked the big cat's broad black head. "Thank you for saving his life, Cria. And don't look so modest. You saved him, and you know it."

Cria purred, nudging Sara's hand.

"And now it's up to me to *keep* him safe." Her other hand slid across her stomach where Jerden's children were growing. "I've got to keep them safe, too."

Cria blinked slowly, as though promising her assistance.

"Thanks. I'll need all the help I can get." Sara shut off the lights, pulled back the covers, and slid in beside Jerden. Unlike that first night, she didn't hesitate to draw close to him, resting her head on his chest. His heartbeat was slow, but steady. He would sleep a while longer yet.

And so would she.

Chapter 26

"HE'S GORGEOUS!" BONNIE EXCLAIMED AS SARA TROTTED out Ajax, Jerden's new Friesian stallion.

Sara nodded her agreement. "Too bad Jerden hasn't seen him yet."

Contrary to Vladen's prediction, broken bones did not heal in "a day or two" even when said bones belonged to a Zetithian. Jerden had already been out for three days and counting when the stallion arrived at the spaceport. Sara had barely gotten Ajax settled in his new home when Bonnie dropped by for a visit, along with Ulla, Trent, and Karsyn, whose "inflamed appendix" turned out to be nothing more than a stomachache from eating too much at the wedding.

Unable to drag the kids away from the horses, she and Bonnie returned to the house without them. "I'm surprised that a Zetithian child would even *have* an appendix," Sara said, taking a seat at the kitchen table.

"They don't, actually," Bonnie explained. "Vladen was just being melodramatic—probably so he could have an excuse to spread the news about Nate and—what's her name?"

"Chantal," Sara replied. "Isn't that a breach of etiquette or confidentiality or something?"

"On some worlds, perhaps," Bonnie replied. "But not around here. It's impossible to keep *anything* quiet."

"Which makes me wonder how in the world

Nate married Chantal without it becoming common knowledge overnight."

"You have a point," Bonnie conceded. "He must've paid somebody off."

"Yeah," Sara said with a snort. "But with what? One of his horses?"

"Maybe. I had no idea he was in such bad financial shape. He obviously managed to keep that quiet too."

Ulla and Karsyn came dashing in through the back door. "Can we see Jerden now?"

Bonnie laughed. "If anyone could wake a sick Zetithian, it would be those two."

Sara was anxious for him to recover but wasn't sure the timing was right. "Is that a good idea? I mean, can you wake them up too soon?"

"They get better anyway," Bonnie said. "Sometimes I think they just like having an excuse to sleep."

Assuming that Bonnie knew what she was talking about, Sara nodded and the two girls raced off. Moments later, Trent came inside, followed by Salan.

"She was afraid you wouldn't let her in," Trent said, nodding at Salan. "I told her you wouldn't mind. She says she's been trying to get up the nerve to talk to you for days and days."

Salan *did* seem distraught. Her long blonde hair had lost its shine and there were lines on her face Sara hadn't noticed before.

"It's all my fault," she wailed. "I told Nate about Chantal *weeks* ago. I'd heard the story from Bonnie. He was so upset about losing you to Jerden, I had to tell him I knew exactly how he felt, and I… Oh, *Sara*, I'm *so* sorry."

"No need to feel bad about it. You couldn't have known what he'd do." Sara took a deep breath. "But *please* tell me I'm not going to have trouble with you over Jerden."

"You won't. I promise." Salan smiled shyly. "Besides, I'll be going on an extended trip pretty soon."

Sara raised an eyebrow. "With Waroun?"

Salan nodded. "I can't explain it. He's, well, he's as ugly as any other Norludian, but at the same time, he's... different."

"I know the feeling," Bonnie said. "Just when you've given up and think you'll never find the one, you do—and when you least expect it."

"You do understand, don't you, Sara?" Salan pleaded.

"Of course I do!" Sara replied. "I never thought I'd ever fall in love with *any* man, let alone one that wasn't even human. But Jerden is the most *humane* being I've ever met. He's everything I could possibly want in a man, and I love him with all my heart." Sara registered Salan's wry smile with one of her own. "He's standing right behind me, isn't he?"

"Uh, yes, he is."

A moment later, Jerden's arms were around her, his lips pressed against her neck and his hair tickling her cheek. A surge of excitement rose to a peak, sending thrills cascading over her like a wave. "Nice to have you up and about again."

"It's good to *be* up," he said. "And I plan to stay that way."

"Guess I'd better call Vladen to take that cast off—I assume you're completely healed?"

"Never better," Jerden asserted. "How about you?"

"I've been a little lost without you."

"It's ridiculously easy to get hooked on them," Bonnie confided.

Sara glanced at Salan, who gave Jerden a hasty, "Glad you're better" and left as quickly as she'd arrived. Karsyn and Trent went out to play with the dogs, but Ulla took a seat at the table beside her mother. She was growing up so fast. *I guess it'll seem that way with our children, too.*

Sara waited until the door closed behind them before she told Jerden the news. "Guess what? Salan is going on vacation with Waroun!"

"That has *got* to be a first," Bonnie declared. "A Davordian woman giving up a Zetithian for a Norludian?" She chuckled, shaking her head. "No one will ever believe it."

"That's because it isn't true," Jerden said. "She couldn't give me up because she never had me to begin with."

As he kissed her cheek, Sara blushed clear to her toes. She could hardly wait to be alone with him again, but she had other news to report. "Someone else dropped by while you were laid up. After Jack heard what happened with Nate and Chantal, she turned the ship around and came right back."

"Oh, let me guess," Jerden said, chuckling. "She brought us another Nedwut pulse pistol, right?"

"Close. She brought us a rifle."

Jerden rolled his eyes. "Why am I not surprised?"

"She brought a scabbard for it, too," Sara went on. "She thought it would be easier to carry while on horseback—though I'm not sure she knows you never use a saddle. Guess I'll be the one who carries it.

Anyway, she said she'd bring us a security system the next time she visits."

"That's Jack for you," said Bonnie. "She is one dedicated woman."

"She sure is," Jerden said. "Without her help, we'd have all been hunted down like animals by now."

Sara grinned. "Guess I'd better give *her* a present— though I can't imagine what anyone could give Jack that she doesn't already have. Makes me glad I don't have to buy Christmas gifts for her."

"You're already carrying the best presents anyone could ever give her." Taking her hand, Jerden pulled her to her feet and into his arms. "And the best presents anyone could ever give *me*."

Sara gazed up at her husband, thanking God or fate or destiny for saving her for this one special man. Being the mother of his children would undoubtedly give her as much joy as being his wife, perhaps even more. "I'm glad you think so. But until they're born, I've got this fabulous Friesian stallion out in the barn. Want to see him?"

Jerden's lips curled as he began to purr. "I'd much rather see you swoon—which, as I recall, you promised to do when he arrived."

Sara faked her best swoon and was instantly scooped up into Jerden's arms.

"Excuse me, ladies," he said, nodding at Bonnie and Ulla. "Must go revive my wife now."

"I didn't *really* faint," Sara muttered against his chest.

"Of course you didn't." His purr became a growl as Jerden threaded his fingers through her hair, tilting her head back, his blazing eyes locked on hers. "But you *will*."

As their lips met, Bonnie pushed back her chair and got to her feet. "That's our cue, Ulla."

Sara waved good-bye to her friends, unable to take her eyes off Jerden. He was handsome, yes, but she'd seen handsome men before and had never been tempted by any of them—had never even *considered* loving them.

He'd been called so many names—savage, loner, wildcat, hunk. He was all of those and more, but in the best possible way—and he was hers, forever. Crushed in his embrace with his purr roaring in her ears, she barely heard the back door close behind Bonnie and Ulla.

Jerden nuzzled her neck. "Did you miss me, Sara?"

"More than you will *ever* know. Promise me you won't do that again for a long, long time."

"I'll do my best to stay safe and healthy." With only a trace of a limp, he carried her into the bedroom and laid her on the bed.

Jerden climbed in beside her, and, as always, Cria stationed herself at the door. The big cat gazed at her for a moment before blinking—slowly and deliberately. Sara didn't need Tisana to translate, for the leopard's meaning was quite clear.

We will keep him safe, you and I, and he will live to see his grandchildren's grandchildren. His race will be restored to its former glory and there will be peace, joy, and prosperity for all.

The words echoed through Sara's mind like the ringing of church bells. Blinking hard, she shook her head. Had she actually read the leopard's thoughts? Was that a prophecy or a wish? She stared at Cria, half hoping she would say more, but the huge cat simply curled up on the threshold, letting out a soft, purring sigh.

I'm imagining things. Nonetheless, Sara vowed to do her best to keep Jerden alive and well and give birth to as many of his children as fate saw fit to bestow upon her. There'd been times when she'd seen fate as needlessly cruel, but no more, for fate had saved her for Jerden. He was hers to love, cherish, and protect. She would do nothing less.

Otherwise, Jack would come after her with a very big stick.

And no way am I risking that...

———

Sara's scent filled Jerden's head like never before—her pregnancy the obvious cause. After all, she'd been his mate for some time. The babies were the only change.

Or were they? He recalled the vision in which his fields had been as green and well tended as Sara's. Looking back, he could see that his vision represented more than the mere state of his land. The tranquility he'd felt at that moment now filled his entire being. The threats were gone—whether Jack would ever admit it or not—he was sure of it. Already, he could sense joy and serenity infusing his life and the lives of his fellow Zetithians with peace.

His world had been destroyed, his race hunted to near extinction, but the future was filled with hope. He would be there to witness that future, and Sara would be with him—his life, his love, his partner, his mate. The danger had passed, and the healing process was now complete. The time had come for life to begin.

Again.

Acknowledgments

I'd like to extend my thanks to:

Ed Pegg Jr. for his suggestion regarding the effect of stem cells on the longevity of the human mates of Zetithian males.

My amazing critique partner, Sandy James, for her valuable input and support.

My beta reader, Mellanie Szereto, for being that extra set of keen eyes.

My agent, Melissa Jeglinski, for her editorial suggestions.

The people of Sourcebooks Casablanca for their hard work and dedication.

My family and friends for their love and support.

And most of all, my readers, for their unflagging enthusiasm throughout the Cat Star Chronicles series. I cherish each and every one of you.

Stud

by Cheryl Brooks

They're galaxies apart…

Even for a Zetithian, Tarq Zulveidione's sexual prowess is legendary. Believing it's all he's good for, Tarq sets out to perpetuate his threatened species by offering his services to women across the galaxy…

But one force can bring them together

Lucinda Force is the sensitive dark horse in a self-absorbed family, repeatedly told that no man will ever want such a plain woman. Lucy longs for romance, but is resigned to her loveless lot in life—until Tarq walks through the door of her father's restaurant on Talus Five…

Praise for The Cat Star Chronicles:

"You will laugh, fall in love with an alien or two, and be truly agog at the richness Ms. Brooks brings to her worlds." —The Long and the Short of It

"A phenomenal series that just gets better and better. It's sexy space travel at its finest." —Night Owl Romance

For more Cheryl Brooks books, visit:

www.sourcebooks.com

Virgin

by Cheryl Brooks

—∿∿—

He's never met anyone who made him purr…

Starship pilot Dax never encountered a woman he wanted badly enough. Until he met Ava Karon…

And he'll never give his body without giving his heart…

Dax is happy to take Ava back to her home planet, until he finds out she's returning to an old boyfriend…

As their journey together turns into a quest neither expected, Ava would give herself to Dax in a heartbeat. Except he doesn't know the first thing about seducing a woman…

—∿∿—

Hero

by Cheryl Brooks

He is the sexiest, most irksome man she's ever encountered…

Micayla is the last Zetithian female left in the universe. She doesn't know what's normal for her species, but she knows when she sees Trag that all she wants to do is bite him…

He has searched all over the galaxy for a woman like her…

Trag has sworn he'll never marry unless he can find a Zetithian female. But now that he's finally found Micayla, she may be more of a challenge than even he's able to take on…

Praise for the Cat Star Chronicles:

"Sexy and fascinating… leaves the reader eager for the next story featuring these captivating aliens." —*RT Book Reviews*

"The kind of delightfully hot read we've come to expect from Ms. Brooks." —*Star-Crossed Romance*

For more Cat Star Chronicles, visit:

www.sourcebooks.com

About the Author

A native of Louisville, Kentucky, Cheryl Brooks is a critical care nurse by night and a romance writer by day. A lifelong lover of horses and animals in general, she lives with her husband, two sons, two horses, four cats, and two dogs in rural Indiana. She enjoys cooking, gardening, and has played guitar since the age of ten. She is a member of the RWA and IRWA.

Wildcat is the ninth book in the Cat Star Chronicles series, preceded by: *Slave, Warrior, Rogue, Outcast, Fugitive, Hero, Virgin,* and *Stud.* Cheryl has also published several erotic novellas with Siren/Bookstrand, and has self-published two novels to date.

Cheryl loves to hear from readers! Visit her website (cherylbrooksonline.com) or email her at cheryl.brooks52@yahoo.com